A Falling Star is a novel in tapestry form, interwoven from the various threads of an exiled Cuban family, tied to the mystery of one daughter's disappearance during the ocean crossing. The surviving daughter, Daysy, is the inquisitive Penelope figure who weaves and unweaves the story of her family through old photos, newspaper articles, and constant questioning. Chantel Acevedo writes with insight and tenderness about the complex reality of unanchored lives both in Cuba and in the U.S., while at the same time involving us in a captivating tale of loss and redemption.
—JUDITH ORTIZ COFER, author of *Call Me María* and *An Island Like You*

A Falling Star is filled with the ghosts of lost children and siblings, lost cultures and minds. It's as if the characters are standing on a Florida shore looking toward Cuba, waiting for the remnants of their former lives to wash up along with the refugees who appear again and again. Chantel Acevedo has created a world so steeped in longing and lore that it's entirely possible missing children can fall star-like from the sky, or emerge fish-like from the ocean. This haunting novel delivers not only secrets and lies, pounding guilt and grief, but glorious redemption.
—MARIE MANILLA, author of *The Patron Saint of Ugly* and *Shrapnel*

The enduring love for a lost sister is the focus of this beautifully written novel set against the chaotic backdrop of the Mariel Boatlift. Daysy del Pozo is having a hard enough time dealing with adolescence when her beloved grandfather reveals an explosive family secret in the confusion of dementia. What really happened to the del Pozo family after a rescue at sea creates a gripping mystery, and the suspense builds to a dramatic climax and bittersweet denouement. The homesickness, fragmentation, and disorientation of the Miami exile community are vividly portrayed and deeply moving. This is a beautiful story about instincts that keep families together in even the most horrifying of circumstances.

—SANDRA RODRIGUEZ BARRON, author of *The Heiress of Water* and
Stay with Me

In one unforgettable scene in this fine novel, a woman travels far just to stand outside the prison that holds her lover. She wants to listen to the same singer he hears at nightfall—it's the only way to be close to someone she'll never see again. In evocative, careful prose, *A Falling Star* tells a simple tale of family loss, exile, of two worlds forced apart. But Chantel Acevedo does something more: she conjures the secret history of the Cuban-American soul.

—MOIRA CRONE, author of *The Not Yet* and *Dream State*

A FALLING STAR

© 2014 Chantel Acevedo

Editor: Robin Miura
Design: Lesley Landis Designs
Author Photograph by Orlando Acevedo ©2014
Cover Image by Elaine Palladino ©2011

*The mission of Carolina Wren Press is to seek out, nurture, and promote literary
work by new and underrepresented writers, including women and writers of color.*

This publication was made possible by Michael Bakwin's generous establishment
of the Doris Bakwin Award for Writing by a Woman, and the continued support
of Carolina Wren Press by the extended Bakwin family. We gratefully acknowledge
the ongoing support of general operations by the Durham Arts Council's United
Arts Fund and a special grant from the North Carolina Arts Council.

Library of Congress Cataloging-in-Publication Data

Acevedo, Chantel.
A falling star : a novel / by Chantel Acevedo.
pages cm
ISBN 978-0-932112-95-8 (alk. paper)
1. Immigrant families--Cuba. 2. Domestic fiction. I. Title.

PS3601.C47F35 2014
813'.6--dc23
2014001309

A FALLING STAR

A NOVEL

CHANTEL ACEVEDO

Carolina Wren Press

For Penelope
and
Mary-Blair,
who changed
everything

I spilt the dew —
But took the morn —
I chose this single star
From out the
　　wide night's numbers —

EMILY DICKINSON,
from "One Sister
Have I in Our House"

DAYSY DEL POZO

HIALEAH, FLORIDA 1990

The front door of Daysy del Pozo's house was a massive thing, gracing a small, modest ranch house, and made of iron bars. Behind the bars was a solid sheet of mustard-yellow plastic, dented to look like hammered gold. In the center was a lion on its hind legs, its claws extended and its mouth wide open. Daysy always put her fingers on one of the fangs when she came home from school as she imagined the door coming to life, the iron jaws snapping, and swallowing her fingers whole. The door was her mother's prized possession.

"Like the castles in Spain," Magda Elena said, though she had never been there.

"I don't like it, Mami," Daysy told her when she first saw the door.

"Be quiet, Daysy. Don't you see it's just the thing?" Magda Elena swept her arm to present a neighborhood of squat, pastel-colored homes, each with terracotta tiles, busted-up cars, birdbaths of *La Virgen*, twisty iron bars on the windows, and menacing, iron doors, the kind seen all over Hialeah, a city just north of Miami where the del Pozos lived, famous for its racetrack that now stood empty and decaying in the east side of town, the flock of flamingoes it once showcased still living and breathing, guarding the center island of the track. Hialeah was famous, too, for its Cuban population, for the street signs in Spanish, and for the flooding that happened after every rainfall when the canals swelled and took over the roads.

"Our house looks like a prison," Daysy muttered. She had turned fourteen at the end of May, and her birthday had marked a change in Daysy that Magda Elena had not yet recognized. Daysy hid the signs well. Sometimes, a huge sadness would well up in Daysy's chest for no reason, triggered by the whiteness of the sun, or by a sappy commercial on television. When she first discovered blood in her underwear the day after her fourteenth birthday, Daysy hid in the toolshed out in the backyard for hours, breaking up the hard, dirt floor with a stick. With some difficulty, she buried the stained clothing deep in the center of the shed. Two lizards scampered to the scene and marked the turned earth with their tiny feet, prompting Daysy to leave the shed at last and enter the house. She didn't tell her mother, and bought herself sanitary pads with her lunch money.

There were other things Daysy did not tell Magda Elena. For instance, when two thin, sweaty men came to install the iron door, one of the saw blades used to trim the iron leapt from the machine and flew into the house, just as Daysy was walking from the kitchen through the dining room. She felt the swish of a flying thing behind her, just at her neck, and heard the thud as the circular blade lodged itself in the china cabinet. The saw had wanted blood, and it sliced open the leg of one of the men before it took flight. The man bound his leg with his shirt and kept working. Daysy didn't tell either of her parents how close she'd come to death. The moment marked her in a way, as if the blade had nicked her, so that later, if she felt a cool draft on her neck, Daysy sensed a phantom pain there. She thought she'd keep that secret, along with her period, as a treasure in her pocket, a reminder of mortality, of growing up, of something to show for her life.

The del Pozos all stood in front of the house to look at the door, the sunset lighting the yellow plastic insets on fire, so that the lion was in a state of perpetual immolation, or at least until the sun finally went down. Magda Elena, Angel, and Daysy stood a little to the side, to avoid stepping in a dried puddle of the workman's blood. From outside, Daysy could hear her grandfather singing loudly in his bedroom, "Don't cry for me, Argentina," in wavering tones, the few English words he knew. If her grandfather had been in his right mind, Daysy imagined he would have hated the door, too.

"My brother, Eddy, would have loved to see this," Magda Elena said about the door, her voice a whisper. She mentioned her brother daily, the one who had died in Cuba, the uncle Daysy did not remember. It was as if his name clung to the inside of Magda Elena's mouth and had to be spit out every once in a while or she might choke on it. The more she described this Eddy, this man who liked hideous iron doors, the less Daysy thought she would have loved him.

Daysy was ten when a letter arrived to report Eddy's death in Havana. A massive heart attack had come upon him at dawn, as he was stirring sugar into his coffee. His wife Catalina's letter described the scene—she'd found him on the kitchen floor with the spilled coffee on his chest, the liquid still steaming and releasing a wispy vapor into the air. Magda Elena had stayed in bed for days after the letter arrived, her eyes dry, wide, and dull. Her hair turned brittle from lack of combing. When Daysy turned on the stereo in her room a week later, Magda Elena had come in like a lioness, alive again, brandishing a worn flip-flop with which she hit Daysy over the back and shoulders until she turned off the music.

"¡Atrevida!" Magda Elena had yelled. "How dare you play music when my Eddy is gone from this world?"

Daysy was stunned. Later, after the moment had settled in her mind, she imagined a brave retort. Something like, "All you had to do was ask, Mother." But the make-believe comeback didn't alleviate the pain in Daysy's jaw, the aching effort of keeping the tears away.

That evening, Daysy had sat in the recliner with her father and cried into his chest, soaking his undershirt that smelled like car exhaust. "Okay, okay," he said, scratching her back. "She didn't mean it. She's upset about many things, not just her brother. Your mami has lost more than most, and when someone dies, it's like she suffers every loss all over again. Understand?"

"What else has she lost?" Daysy asked then, and her father's face had gone very still.

"Nada," he had mouthed, unable to speak.

≈ ✳ ≈

The night Daysy's mother had come into her room brandishing her sandal over her head in grief and fury was a singular occasion. More familiar to Daysy was the routine of the day to day. Dinner, for example, seemed to follow the same script each evening. Silence was mandatory, except for Magda Elena's incessant demand, "Daysy, *come, come, traga, no hables*," to eat, eat, swallow, and not talk. From TV, Daysy knew that families came together for dinner to talk about school, work, and politics. Sometimes they fought at the table. Or resolved a family issue. There were mashed potatoes to be passed, and grace to be said. In the del Pozo home, dinner was only for Magda Elena and Daysy. Angel would eat early, as soon as he came home from the parking lot where he worked, slurping his steaming, thick, creamy soup in the kitchen, and then complaining about a burnt tongue all evening. "*Coño, me quemé la lengua*," he would repeat, louder and louder, until Magda Elena would bring him an ice cream sandwich. Abuelo would eat whatever was on hand—bags of chips, bites out of avocadoes, skin and all, chunks of Cuban bread—all day long.

Magda Elena and Daysy ate in silence, because dinnertime was for eating, not speaking. They could talk later. Magda Elena watched Daysy eat, making sure she swallowed every single grain of rice. If Daysy drank too much water, Magda Elena would say, "You're getting full on water. Eat. Eat!" and then push Daysy's glass to the center of the table, out of reach. At the end of the meal were the obligatory slice of guava and cream cheese ("It's very fattening, so eat up") and then the lecture about how a girl had to be curvy to get a boyfriend someday.

One night, between gulps of water, Daysy had said, "Mami, do you think I'm smart enough to go somewhere like Yale some day? Someplace like that?"

"Jail? Jail? What are you talking about? Eat."

Daysy laughed. "No, Yale. The university." She had seen a movie set in New Haven, on Yale's green, elm-filled campus, and had imagined an older version of herself there, wearing lab goggles like the character in the film and holding test tubes up to fluorescent lights.

"*Ah, sí, la universidad*," Magda Elena said. "And where is this 'Jale'?"

"Connecticut, Mami."

"Co-netty-koo? No way, *mi'jita*. Nice girls don't go away for college. That's only for Americans." Magda Elena dropped her voice to a conspiratorial whisper. "They don't love their children and want to be rid of them, that's the truth. Besides, there are plenty of good schools here."

"What if I want to become a scientist?" Daysy asked, testing her mother. The truth was that she'd given it some thought. In the comic books she read, the scientists were always elevated above mere mortals. They had the power to turn even the mousiest human into a god. Just one radioactive zap would do the trick, Daysy thought.

"You can't even wash yourself properly, and you want to go away?" Magda Elena said. "Who will make your bed? Who will cook your meals?"

"I'll be grown by then. I'll be—"

"Don't be so ambitious. It's not good for you," Magda Elena said, shimmying Daysy's plate so that the beans Daysy had so carefully compressed into a tight heap flattened out, filling the plate again. "You haven't eaten a thing," Magda Elena said, sighing.

During those meals, Daysy wished that Florida wasn't flat, and that it wasn't so long, so hard to get out of. She swore to herself that it was easier to leave Cuba than to leave this place. She wished her mother would let her go to sleepover parties, or to summer camp out of state. No, she had to be within Magda Elena's reach at all times, in her vise-like embrace. Sometimes Daysy imagined her mother transforming into a giant, rusty anchor that held the family in place. This anchor, her mother, was lodged at the bottom of a murky Hialeah canal. It would never let Daysy go.

"Don't be such an *arrepentida*," her mother said, when Daysy brought up Yale at dinner again the next night.

"What does that mean?" Daysy asked and rolled her eyes so far back in her head that her left eyelid twitched.

"It means you are ashamed of who you are. That you regret you were born to this family. That you…"

"Am not."

"*No, que va*," Magda Elena said. "Not a thing. But let me tell you something, *muchachita*. You leave Miami, and there will be lots to regret." Magda Elena cleared Daysy's dishes, though she hadn't finished her food. Daysy thought she was done getting told off, but her mother whipped around, pointed a dish at Daysy and declared, "You don't know what alone means. Alone. *Sola*. Your father and I had nobody in *este país. Nadie. Y ahora*, you want to throw away your family. *Arrepentida* is what you are."

≈ ✳ ≈

Some days, Daysy thought her mother was right. She felt she would trade her foreign birth certificate in a heartbeat, would delete from her family's history the story about crossing the ocean from Cuba to Miami on a stranger's yacht, and do away with the feeling of rocking waves in her dreams, a feeling she explained in great detail in her dream journal. In it, Daysy described the vivid images that came to her at night in colors more stunning than reality. The dreams had gotten more peculiar after her first period, and Daysy chalked it up to another downside of womanhood. They woke her at night with their brightness, as if someone had turned on a light in her room. Perhaps that was why her mother always looked so tired—the awful dreaming left no time for restful sleep.

Daysy dreamt often of hands, her own hands around her mother's damp neck in the dark. In the dream, panic rose inside her chest, and a feeling like falling, slipping down her mother's body accompanied the fear. The dream played itself out the same way each time—her limbs would go slack with exhaustion, she couldn't get hold of her mother, and she was afraid of dropping into the darkness. She even dreamt her mother's pulse under her fingertips, beating furiously.

She would wake in the morning feeling clammy, her chest hollow, the way one feels when she's forgotten something important. Once, she described the dream to her mother over breakfast. She told her of the blackness of that place, how it felt as if she had no eyes. She described, too, her mother's neck, her throat, and the desperation she felt in the wake of the memory, as if the moment had not resolved itself in the past, but rather, had only paused for a moment. Her mother choked on a piece of buttered bread, coughing, her eyes watering, as Daysy tried to finish the story.

"*No es nada*," Magda Elena said without meeting Daysy's eyes. "The bread went down an old road," she said in English after clearing her throat a few more times. Magda Elena busied herself removing dishes then, coughing softly every so often.

"About my dream," Daysy asked, looking at the curve of her mother's neck and wondering if the skin there still felt the same.

"*Mi'ja*," Magda Elena said, and took a breath so deep she seemed to grow taller. "I'm glad you told me. Dreams shared before noon can't come true. Leave it alone. It's those *muñequitos* you're always reading."

Daysy bent low over her cereal. "I don't think it has anything to do with comic books. It's, I don't know, different. I've even looked up some of the elements in a dream dictionary, but it still makes no sense, and even when I..."

"*Mi amor, ya.*" Magda Elena wiped her hands on her pants. "You're swimming so much, for what? To die on the shore," she said in English.

"That doesn't make sense."

"It does in Spanish," Magda Elena responded. "*Tanto nadar para morir en la orilla.*"

"I still don't get what it means."

"It means stop trying so hard, Daysy." Magda Elena closed her eyes then, and sighed with a long, drawn out, "*Ay.*" The hand on her hip came up to rub the back of her neck, and Daysy knew the conversation had ended.

Daysy also pasted pictures in her journal, and she would draw lines between the pictures and the descriptions of her dreams, trying to make connections between her waking life and the one she created at night. One such picture was a photograph Daysy had found of her father's parents, Gregorio and Nieve, standing in front of an old stove, Nieve's arms around his waist. Daysy knew that after Nieve died, Abuelo secured a visa to Spain, that he lived in Madrid for two years before getting to the States, and that when he arrived, he smelled like something dead. "It's too cold for baths in Europe this time of year," Magda Elena had said to Daysy at the airport, quite seriously. Daysy was only seven then, but she remembered her grandfather's earthy smell, and sometimes caught the scent of it still when she passed the closet in which he kept his old Sherpa coat, the one he had worn in Spain. Magda Elena said nothing about Nieve, and when Daysy asked about her, her mother wrinkled her nose and shook her head, as if she had taken a mouthful of very bitter medicine. Daysy drew a straight line from the pasted picture to a lopsided box she had drawn and shaded. Inside the box, she described a dream in which Nieve had given Daysy a pair of hoop earrings. Beside the box, Daysy wrote the question, "What did Nieve ever do to Mami?"

Daysy had found another picture, too. It was in black and white. There, in a small apartment in Cuba, Daysy posed with her parents. She guessed herself to be about three years old in the photo. She wore a lace dress cinched at the waist and tied with a pale ribbon. Her hair was cut short, and little curls sprang up around her ears and on her forehead. Where had the curls gone, she wondered when she looked at the photo and, sighing, touched her straight hair. In the picture she was sitting on her father's lap. Angel wore a short-sleeved shirt open at the chest, his white undershirt exposed, his strong muscles stretching the material. He smiled so broadly that his molars showed, and his hands rested on Daysy's little thighs. In the picture, his left eye was still good and whole, not the way it was now—the lid thick and heavy, nearly always closed over the eye that looked fine except for a jagged, black line underscoring his iris.

The injury had occurred at Mariel, though Daysy had never been told exactly how it happened. Sometimes, she thought she remembered what the boatlift out of Cuba had been like, though she wasn't always sure that the memories weren't lifted from textbook pictures. She'd been nearly four when they left, old enough that something of those days stuck with her, but too young to string it into a logical story. Daysy stared at the image of her father a long time and found that with both eyes intact, he was less formidable, more handsome.

Then there was Magda Elena. In the photograph, her face was set in a partial smile. In her arms was a baby, its head covered in tufts of fair hair, only an eye and a nose peeking out over the patchwork blanket surrounding it. Daysy noticed her mother's long fingernails, and how the dark, painted nails stood out against the white fuzz of the baby's blanket. She tried to remember that moment, and sometimes, she thought she did, catching fragments of it in her head, of her mother pushing a curl behind Daysy's ear, of a rotating fan in the corner. But the rest was blank. The memory came to her at odd moments, as all her memories of Cuba did, like when she was brushing her teeth, or rinsing a bowl of rice before cooking it. They were like waves, coming, going, pulling her under, then, letting her breathe again.

"A cousin," Magda Elena explained when Daysy asked about the baby in the photograph. Magda Elena swore she couldn't remember the baby's name. "*Ay, m'ija.* That's not your real cousin. Just one of the neighbor's girls," she explained when Daysy pressed her for more information. "Everyone's family in Cuba," Magda Elena said, slashing the air with her hands the way a conductor signals the last notes of a song. Daysy, who knew when to stop asking questions, pocketed the picture. She had no dream to link it to, but was sure one would come to her eventually one night, quiet and unassuming like the dew.

Daysy had found the photographs in her mother's dresser, on one of her rummaging excursions. She had taken to searching for nothing in particular, opening closets and peering into the back of them, her hands flitting over oddly shaped items in the dark. She crawled into attic spaces and jimmied open closed boxes with hairpins. Daysy found a tarnished Aztec sun medallion fit for a chain, her parents' marriage certificate, a drawer full of plastic saints, airmail letters from Cuba, a lone fork with a G initialed into the handle, a bag of shells, an old parking ticket, a packet of postcards from New York City, fur-lined gloves, and the photograph of her family and the strange baby. The find had thrilled her, had made her feel as if the world were shifting suddenly, the way it does when one closes one eye, then the other, back and forth. It was like this, too, when she found her birth certificate, and when she discovered her father's wedding ring, the one he'd outgrown. Each time she'd unearthed something it was like finding a dollar bill—unexpected and gratifying. And each time she'd bring the found item to her mother, in the hopes that the story attached to the thing, the ring, the photograph, would be told. Daysy didn't know what she expected of her mother, but what she usually got wasn't it.

"Your father's," Magda Elena said when Daysy asked about the ring.

"Why doesn't he wear it?"

"Fat fingers."

"Where did you buy it?"

"A store. Enough questions. Eat your *pudín de pan*." The conversa-tions usually went in that vein. Daysy hoped to learn about how much the ring had cost, what she'd meant by inscribing his ring with her middle name, whether it hurt her that he no longer wore it. But Magda Elena was reticent in general, and when it came to telling sto-ries about Cuba, ones that weren't made-up tales meant to scare her into eating more, or staying away from the telephone during light-ning storms, or keeping off sandbanks in the ocean, Magda Elena was nearly mute.

≈ ✴ ≈

Daysy's fourteenth summer was long and strange, beginning on the day she discovered a bunch of bananas tied up by ribbons of every color, lying on the tiles of the front porch like a gift. She'd brought them into the house. Upon eyeing the bundle, Magda Elena screamed "*Solavaya!*" a word Daysy didn't know, though it seemed the kind of thing one would say to cancel a spell. Disappearing in the kitchen for a moment, Magda Elena emerged with a broom held high over her head. Daysy flinched as her mother ran toward her with the broom, and she felt the stiff bristles come down hard on her arms, knocking the bananas out of her hands. Magda Elena used the broom to shoo the bananas out the door, down the driveway, and into the gutter, where they bobbed up and down in the murky water. Daysy held her breath as she watched the last of the bright ribbons soak up water and sink.

Later that afternoon, they found a dozen broken eggs smeared on the fender of Magda Elena's car. She gave the eggs the same treatment as the bananas. Then Magda Elena burned the broom inside an alu-minum garbage can. The broom crackled and sent up golden sparks as it burned. Every once in a while, a bit of burning straw caught flight just over the garbage can and hovered for a moment in the atmosphere. Then it would fall back down, sizzling into ash as it went. Daysy stood by her mother the whole time, repeating "*solavaya*" with her.

At dinner that night, Magda Elena said, "It's revenge, of course. That María Luísa, *la muy hija de puta*. I accidentally got her fired yesterday." She said it as matter-of-factly as if she'd been commenting on the summer heat, but Daysy noticed how her mother's hands shook as she dipped a ladle into the beans.

According to Magda Elena, what happened was that she'd asked, at her sewing station, "Where in the hell is María Luísa?" when she ran out of pockets to sew onto pants. It was María Luísa's job to pass them on to Magda Elena, and Magda Elena's job to sew the pockets and get the rest of the piece off to the next worker, and so on. The foreman got up from his recliner in the corner, where he had been reading the paper and drinking his fourth *cafecito* of the day to search for the unfortunate María Luísa. He found her in the women's bathroom, smoking a joint and eating a giant Cuban sandwich, and he fired her on the spot.

"That'll do it," Angel said.

"I don't believe in *Santería*," said Daysy.

Magda Elena coughed a little, turning her head to the side. Her hands had stopped shaking, though every so often, Daysy heard her mother saying "*solavaya*" underneath her breath. "Me either," Magda Elena said once she'd sat down. "But I respect it."

Two weeks after that incident, Abuelo started acting strangely, yelling, removing all of his clothes to work in the backyard, eating only guava paste at every meal. In time, the doctors diagnosed him with dementia, because they couldn't say Alzheimer's for sure until he was dead and a chunk of his brain was under their microscopes. Magda Elena blamed it on the curse brought on by the bananas and the eggs, and Daysy shuddered at how badly she had wanted those

ribbons, ribbons she now dreamed about in strange patterns and per-
mutations. She dreamt ribbons wrapped around her throat, ribbons
leached of their colors, ribbons braided into her hair.

Abuelo's deterioration happened with such rapidity it caught the
family by surprise. Daysy had been the first to see him disrobing in
the yard. She'd covered her eyes as fast as she could, but she'd seen a
shadowy thing between his bare thighs anyway. She'd had a hard time
looking her grandfather in the eye for a few days.

Some time after that, they'd lost power to the house, and a techni-
cian from Florida Power and Light had come by, clambering up the
pole in the backyard, his tools clinking on his tool belt. With a yelp,
the man slipped and dropped to the ground. Daysy watched him fall
from her seat at the patio table where she'd been sketching. Later,
she'd remember the slowness of his fall. It seemed to her a kind of
dance, almost. She'd expected the thud, but the crack of bones surprised her. Electric lines dangled like jungle snakes after him, spitting
light just out of reach of him on the grass. Daysy had gone screaming
into the house, afraid to go near the moaning man. It was Abuelo
who comforted him as they waited for the ambulance, helping the
man with the broken leg sit up and lean against an old, gnarled
lemon tree that Abuelo had grafted a naval orange limb onto.

Other strange occurrences followed. On the Fourth of July, Daysy
had found three dead kittens in the metal shed in the backyard. Her
grandfather had shut the door, which was always left open. He had
been yelling all day about shadows that creep into dark places and
play foul tricks on people. The door stayed closed for days, and when
Daysy opened it, she found the three small bodies, curled together in
a pile of sawdust. At first, she thought they were sleeping in the sti-
fling heat. The shed was like an oven in the summer. She lifted one
and found that it did not drape over her hands in that way of kittens,
but rather, was a hard thing, the skin and fur no longer pliable, but
stuck to the bones and matted. Daysy shivered so hard her teeth rat-

tled. She dropped the kitten, and the dull sound it made when it hit the ground reminded her of the man falling off the electric pole. She thought of Abuelo, too, getting sicker and stranger by the day, and Daysy imagined that all of these terrible things were connected in some way, perhaps, to the curse of the bananas and eggs. Daysy cried over the dead kittens for a long while. A lanky, full-grown cat stalked the doorway to the shed. It meowed at Daysy, but the sound was deep, like a growl, and Daysy guessed this was the grieving mother. The cat locked eyes with Daysy for a moment, then crouched low, its ears flattened on its skull. Leaping at Daysy clumsily, the cat struck a shelf and knocked down some PVC pipes Abuelo had put there. The plastic tubes tumbled onto the kittens and rolled off them. Stepping out into the sunlight, Daysy made room for the cat, which sniffed the bodies for a long time, passing her tongue over their heads. Later, Abuelo would dig a grave by the fence for the kittens, humming a slow tune as he turned over the earth.

Abuelo was always singing, or drumming his fingers against whatever hard surface he had at hand. His rhythms were the soundtrack of Daysy's life. Long ago, her grandfather had been the set director at the Teátro Tacón in Havana, Cuba. Though his hands were calloused from sanding and lifting, his voice raspy from the years of swallowed sawdust, Abuelo could sing along with the operas. He enjoyed wispy kisses from the prima ballerinas backstage every night. Or so Daysy imagined. The stories he told of those times were long and colorful, and were the only clearly defined images left to him, it seemed. He told Daysy how he taught himself to play the flute, how from behind the curtains, he watched over the heads of the actors onstage to observe the orchestra below, miming their movements. If only he hadn't been so dark skinned, his hair coiled so tightly against his head, he might have had one of the seats in the pit, playing his flute for the best productions on the island. He named his son Angel after the cherubs encased in the theater's tapestry and arranged it so that his son might marry his girlfriend, Magda Elena, on the theater's grand marble staircase. Abuelo still remembered the theater, could describe it in such glorious detail that each shining brass tack of each red velvet seat was accounted for in his head.

Out of all the stories Magda Elena told, Daysy's favorite had to do with her grandfather and his gift for music. As the story went, Magda Elena was not yet married, and she'd gathered enough courage to visit Angel's house on her own. Gregorio had opened the door and sung "*¿Quien es ella?*" operatically. Magda Elena smiled, wondered if she was being courted by a man with madness in his gene pool, and allowed herself to be led in by Gregorio. He'd sat her down then and sung a few more bars from the Spanish opera, *Laura y Don Gonzalo.* Sometimes, when she told the story, Abuelo would make his flute appear, as if by magic Daysy sometimes thought, and play a tune as Magda Elena spoke.

He'd smuggled the flute out of Cuba when he left in 1983. Those leaving the island for good were stripped of all belongings. The guard at the airport had pulled the flute out of Abuelo's pocket and attempted to throw it onto a large pile of confiscated photo albums behind him, when Abuelo took hold of the guard's wrist with one hand, seized the flute, and shoved the head joint underneath the guard's chin, as if the flute were a knife. "My wife is dead and I've got nothing to lose but this flute," he had said, and the guard, perhaps seeing something of his own father in Abuelo's eyes, had let him go. Abuelo had told the story often, and even now, when his memory was failing him, he spoke of the guard he had bullied into letting him keep his flute.

These days, telling that story served as a moment of clarity for Abuelo. Mostly, he was lost in his illness, imagining that his backyard in South Florida was the park he'd played in as a child in Cuba. Sometimes, he called Daysy "Eugenia," after the infant daughter he'd lost to dengue fever in 1935, before Angel was born. Once, in the shade of the lemon-orange grafted tree, Abuelo had crushed Daysy to his chest, crying, "*Mi Eugenia, mi tesorito,*" so loudly that Daysy could hear the air whooshing in and out of his lungs, her ear pressed so close to his body.

Days like that frightened Daysy. Even so, she enjoyed spending time with him in the backyard. That summer, while her parents went to work, Daysy stayed behind to watch Abuelo. In the fall, they'd have to hire a nurse to babysit the ailing man. For now, Daysy didn't mind staying in the house with her grandfather, especially on sunny days. After breakfast they'd go outside, and she'd help him pull up the dwarf banana trees that grew in clumps. Abuelo's movements were swift and strong as he killed the baby plants that seemed to sprout overnight, choking their tall, leafy mothers. His head bumped the low, flowery spike that was just forming into bananas. As they worked, she sometimes told him about the events of her life that she was afraid of sharing with her parents.

"You know that boy I told you about, Iggy Placetas?" she'd begin, tossing aside a small banana plant, then filling the dark hole where it had been with more dirt.

"*Sí, mi vida,*" he'd say, examining the banana tree's flower, picking at the smooth, purple surface of its pointed petals with a tough nail.

"He and I, well, we made out in the art closet. Do you know what 'made out' means, Abuelo?"

"*Sí, mi vida.*"

"I think I love him," she said. Abuelo nodded, and heaved against a stubborn plant. Daysy did not say that she didn't think Iggy Placetas loved her back, that he'd gone into the art closet with another girl later in the day, and that when the teacher pulled them out, Iggy's face was covered in pink lipstick. "I'm ready for a boyfriend," Daysy told her grandfather, "but Mami and Papi would kill me."

"*Sí, mi vida.*" Their conversations would go on into the afternoon this way, with Daysy telling her grandfather the things she could tell no one else, because he was a good listener, and because her secrets were often accompanied by his humming, which Daysy liked.

≈ ✶ ≈

It was mid-July when Daysy found Abuelo crouched behind the boxy air-conditioning unit, picking at the skeleton of a little lizard trapped in the fan, just shy of the blades. His eyelids were a little swollen as he stared at the tiny bones. Daysy tried to get him to stand, but he was immoveable. Sweat formed on his forehead, and his cheeks burned red. It was noon, and the sun overhead was making Daysy dizzy. Above the metal AC unit, the air was blurry in the heat.

"Abuelo, stand up!" Daysy shouted, but he sat there, sweating and staring, as if he couldn't hear her. Daysy ran inside, filled a glass with cold water, and brought it out to her grandfather.

"*Mira*, Abuelo. Take it. Drink, please." She pressed the cold glass to his lips, and he opened them slowly, looking into Daysy's eyes as he did so. He reminded her of the people who took Communion at church, the gold chalice brought so tenderly to their lips, their eyes often wide in anticipation of the moment. Daysy herself had only taken the wine once, her mother admonishing her that to drink from the cup, no matter that it was blessed, was to invite catching someone's cold.

"Where is my mother? She said she'd be here at noon," Abuelo said in Spanish.

Daysy closed her eyes and thought for a minute. She'd have to say the right thing to shake him out of his confusion. Mindlessly, she put her hands into her pockets, and her fingers brushed against the picture she'd found earlier in the summer, the one of her family in Cuba, which she hadn't yet put in her journal. She'd hung up the jeans without washing them, and the photograph had remained in the pocket.

Daysy held the picture up for her grandfather to see. It trembled in the heated air coming out of the A/C unit. "Abuelo, *mira*, this is Cuba. See the picture? That was a long time ago, remember?"

Abuelo took the photograph, his face softening. It looked to Daysy that the many years of his life were returning him to the present in all their precision, so that his expression was more like the one he'd worn before he became ill. "*Ay*," he said, "poor baby. She died so young."

"That's not Eugenia, Abuelo," Daysy said, her voice sounding exasperated even to her own ears. She was often able to check herself, control her patience around Abuelo, but the day was so hot, the rumbling of the air conditioner so loud, that Daysy felt on edge.

"*¡Claro que no es Eugenia!* You think I was born yesterday? I mean your sister, Belén."

"I don't have a sister, Abuelo. Please, let's go inside."

"Your ignorance is your parents' doing. When Nieve and I were told Belén had drowned on the way to Florida, that she fell into the ocean somewhere between Mariel and Key West, *ay, que sufrimiento!* It was too much for your poor grandmother, losing you both forever. They say people can die of sadness, and I think it's true."

"Abuelo, I don't have a sister. That's a cousin."

"*Pal carajo*," Abuelo said then, stood, and kicked the A/C unit so hard the motor stopped running for a moment, as if the machine had been shocked temporarily, before starting up again. "You shouldn't call people liars, Daysy. Not people my age," he said again. He thrust the picture back into Daysy's hand and stomped into the house.

≈ ⋆ ≈

It was not until the evening of the next day, during a torrent of rain and wind that loosened three terracotta tiles from the roof of the house, that Daysy thought of the baby Abuelo had recognized in the picture.

She'd been in the living room when Angel came in and turned on the television, sighing as he sat down. In another chair sat Abuelo, wittling away at a bit of mango wood. The shavings came down between his slippered feet. His face held a fixed expression on the little branch in his hands, and it was that look that reminded Daysy of Belén, and Abuelo's assertion that she had been his other grand-daughter. It was the same look he had given the photograph. Daysy watched his hands, so leathery and dark. On his good days, he'd call Daysy over onto his lap and scratch lazily at her back, and she would close her eyes and pretend that Abuelo was not losing his mind. Now, she suppressed the inclination to sit on his lap again, afraid Abuelo might return to the subject of a dead sister. Daysy had never given much thought to Abuelo's ramblings. He went on about ghosts one minute, the location of his long-dead mother the next. He called her Angel, by mistake, and once, Nieve. All of this had somehow become familiar and unsurprising. But when Abuelo told the story of Belén, Daysy felt unease. This story had come out of nowhere, had been so earnestly told, as if Abuelo were his old self again, and now, it troubled Daysy's imagination.

Daysy sat on the floor between her father and grandfather and soon felt her father's heavy hand on her head, rubbing her scalp as he watched the Spanish news come on. Images of rafts at sea, overloaded with sunburned, ragged humans, filled the screen.

"So many of them," Angel said. Daysy watched her father watching the television. It was as if someone had injected hot water into his veins and he couldn't keep still. Every muscle in his face tightened, and he began drumming his fingers on the top of her head, making a tap-tap noise deep in her ears that made Daysy nervous.

"You're going to catch a heart attack. Calm down." Daysy jerked her head away from her father's fingers.

"Of course I'm going to catch a heart attack! Look at this disaster of a country!" Angel meant Cuba, and pointed at the television as if he were pointing to the island itself, as if he were marking it with a fingerprint, smudging its edges. Daysy squinted her eyes at the televised horizon, imagining that perhaps there was a slice of land out there that her father, bad eye and all, had seen and scored with a fingernail. Abuelo's hand slipped, and he dug the tip of his pocketknife into his palm.

"*Pal carajo,*" he muttered, then began to suck at the blood.

"They've picked up hundreds," Angel said, "not counting the ones who drowned."

Again, Daysy thought of Abuelo's story. Outside, the wind whistled through the screen mesh of the sliding glass door. Daysy felt her breath quickening, and her nose, stuffy from a slight cold, whistled along with the wind, sound mimicking sound. What if it's true, she thought. After all, Daysy had no clear memory of her life in Cuba, nothing substantial at all to hold onto. She only remembered images here and there, like a quilt made of scraps.

"It's been thirty years," Angel said at the television, as if he were uttering a malediction that would travel through the electrical wires, speed underground and undersea, and kill Fidel in his sleep. "Thirty years!"

Then Daysy said a thing she didn't mean to and that she didn't really believe. It escaped her lips without permission, having erupted from that place in her that raged against her mother's imperatives, that vibrated with anger whenever they were asked to stand in size order, arms' distance at school, that threatened to explode whenever her mother stuck a piece of food into her mouth during dinner when she wasn't looking. Later, she would convince herself that she'd been trying to get the story of Belén out of her mind.

"Get over it."

The moment she said it, Daysy wished it back.

"*Coño,*" Angel cursed quietly. "*Coño.*" And in that word Angel had expressed the vast sadness he felt with such eloquence that Daysy felt her eyes sting.

"I'm so sorry, Papi. I didn't mean it."

"You meant it. You did." Angel turned off the television. The house felt abandoned without the noise, though the wind outside howled. Daysy could see that the blood was still raging in her father's veins. His cheeks were red, and his bad eye had twisted toward the ceiling, as if in imploration. "What if I asked you to say goodbye to your mother? Right now. Goodbye *para siempre*."

There were times in the past, when she was younger, that Daysy had imagined life without her mother, and the thought had constricted her chest, had coiled around her body like a python, and so she always shook off the idea as quickly as she could. When she thought about it now, about life without either one of them, Daysy found that the python had lost its strength, that the idea hurt, but not with the same urgency, the same sense of panic as before.

"I…I, *no sé*."

"*Ah, no sabes*. That's a luxury." Angel left the room, but Daysy stayed on the cool tile, her scalp burning, her throat tight. She hid her face in her arms, knew it was guilt that drove her to do it, and wiped her nose on her sleeve.

"Don't do that. It's disgusting," Magda Elena said from the entrance of the living room. She'd brought a cup of coffee for Abuelo, who finished licking the tiny wound on his hand, then sipped at the hot, sugary drink. Daysy, her face still hidden in her arms, heard her mother drop into the chair beside her. "Did I ever tell you about the time I got sick with *la fiebre del caballo*?"

"What's that?" Daysy muttered from underneath her arms.

"Like meningitis. *Y bueno*, I thought I was dying. And your Papi, so *galante*, picked me up and took me down two flights to where a doctor lived. He knocked on the door, and I remember this as clear as crystal, he told that doctor, 'Doctor, save my wife,' just like that. And you know what that *desgraciado* said? He said, 'You missed the meeting, *compañero*,' and *fuacatá*, he closed the door on us." Magda Elena brushed her hands against one another, as if the memory had left behind its dusty remnants. "I'll never forget it. Committee four, zone twenty-five. That was our neighborhood watch group, where those gossipy comunistas got together to talk about who bought a puny quarter pound of chicken on the black market, and who called Fidel a comemierda, writing names down in black ink. We skipped meetings all the time. Your father wanted to kill the man, but lucky for all of us, that doctor relented and opened the door. It's the law there, you know. They have to treat you *a las buenas o a las malas.* He cured me with an enormous shot to the spine."

Magda Elena turned the television back on, and the news was still replaying the scene at sea. They watched while the reporter interviewed one of the Coast Guard.

"That's why my back hurts when it rains," she said, as if there hadn't been a break in her story at all.

"It's a second Mariel," Angel said, reappearing in the living room, "but worse now. Look at them all." He seemed himself again. Daysy said nothing, and Magda Elena clucked her tongue.

"Who can blame them?" Magda Elena put in. "We all saw the wall going down in Berlin. Everyone knows the Soviets are in a panic," she said, raising the volume on the television. "And now, it's the Cubans *pasando hambre.* Hunger makes you do crazy things," Magda Elena said. Then she turned to Daysy and lightly smacked the top of her head, saying, "And you with your terrible appetite. Those poor *balseros* are risking their lives for what you throw away."

"Quiet," Angel said. Magda Elena gave up her seat for Angel, and he took it, and leaned forward, his elbows on his knees. "*Mira pa' eso.*"

There was silence among them as the news flashed images of the rafters. The footage was shaky, taken by tourists on the beach. The camera held steady on a young woman with a small, brown dog in her arms, its fur matted and its eyes bloodshot from so many days out in the sun while at sea.

Daysy's abdomen rumbled with cramps, and she winced. She
began to fiddle with a comic book she'd left on the floor earlier.
Batman looked out at her from between the Joker's legs in a neat
trick of perspective, his cowl wrapped around him in the fury of his
righteous anger. It seemed to Daysy a stupid thing, suddenly. What
could Batman do to help the people on television? The ones who
didn't make it? What did comic book heroes have to do with crossing
the ocean in the dark, without a gun or spear to keep the sharks away,
without a bed to sleep in, riding on crashing, devastating waves,
stomach cramping, no toilet, dark, dark depths beneath a thin raft,
babies drowning. Not even Batman, thought Daysy, would know
what to do out there.

She set the comic book down and looked at her parents. How
pained they looked, their eyes narrowed in concentration, their brows
wrinkled. The del Pozos' arrival in the United States had been so different from what they were now seeing on television. They had not
washed up on Miami Beach, as some were now doing. The Mariel
refugees had come in boats, fleets of them bought or rented by Cuban
exiles. They'd been processed on the football field of the Orange
Bowl, which was large enough to hold the thousands of Cubans
who'd arrived. Of her few memories of that time, Daysy recalled a
crush of bodies, long lines, touching her father's injured face with
her small fingers.

As they watched the television, Magda Elena, sitting now on
the arm of Angel's chair, held Daysy's hand, grinding her knuckles
together without noticing. When Daysy finally whispered, "Ow,
Mami. Let go," Magda Elena took hold of Angel's hand instead. They
continued to watch. The flickering light of the television began to
give Daysy a headache. Every so often, a flash of lightning would
brighten the dim room, startling Daysy.

The report on the *balseros* continued, irritating Daysy, who wanted
to ask about Belén. She felt a kind of electricity in her chest, like

when Iggy Placetas first put his thin hand on her shoulder in line for lunch. Daysy had wanted to press her cheek against it, the fluttering current traveling under her skin pushing her to do it, but she had held back. The urge to ask about Belén was just as insistent now. How easy would it be to say, casually, the way one talks about a lightning storm, "Hey, Abuelo said the craziest thing the other day." And yet, Daysy could not bring herself to do it.

She felt herself grow nervous, and so Daysy blurted out, "Hey, you know Marisel?" instead. No answer from her parents. "Marisel? My best friend? Well, she is going with Julio Alvarez."

"Going where, *mi'jita*?" Angel asked, his attention diverted from the news at last. Daysy smiled in response, happy that the thick silence was gone from the room.

"Going, Papi, *going*. You know. Boyfriend girlfriend going."

"I don't like that," Angel said, and wagged his thick finger at her. His hands were tinged blue, red, and purple from the ink he used to stamp parking passes all day. He left rainbow fingerprints on the bathroom walls at home.

"But Papi," Daysy said.

"No way, *mi'jita*," Magda Elena jumped in. "You can bet I never had a boyfriend at your age. But I did have a neighbor in Cuba who had a boyfriend when she was young. And you know how boys are. They promise and promise until they get what they want. Then, pum! No promises. This girl stayed out with her *noviecito* late one night. Two weeks later, a baby was on the way. And babies bring only heartache. Her son died before he knew how to walk. It's better not to have babies at all." Magda Elena looked away and began pushing back the cuticle of her thumbnail.

Daysy had not heard this one before. Usually, Magda Elena's stories seemed more fantastical, more grotesque. Daysy's mother claimed to have known all the poor, unfortunate souls in Cuba, the ones who had not listened to their parents. There was the boy at the zoo who didn't listen when his mother said, "Don't you know your head weighs more than the rest of your body?" as he hung his pendulous skull over the wall of the alligator exhibit. Then, *pum!* The kid fell over and was eaten. And there was the girl who watched television during a lightning storm. The storm blew up the set and shards of glass flew into her eyes and blinded her. Best of all was the girl who didn't tie up her long hair when riding a roller coaster. The hair was, of course, entangled in the ride's monstrous gears and her head came clean off. It was no wonder that Daysy had a sustained fear of amusement parks, of lightning, of heights, of dark places, of green food, of portraits of Jesus, of cats, of rocking chairs, of kissing a boy for too long. The list grew with each passing year, each place or thing attached through the strands of memory and imagination to a nameless child who gave up his life for the benefit of giving Daysy a lesson to learn. But Magda Elena had told this last story so quietly, without meeting Daysy's eyes at all. And the final bit, about it's being better not to have children at all, stung Daysy.

"So what was her name?" Daysy asked.

Magda Elena perked up then and Daysy thought that her mother, suddenly, sat so tall that it was as if she'd shaken off a heavy coat. "*Ay*, I forget. But who cares now? I'm the only one who remembers her."

There was silence for a moment, and Daysy knew that her mother was still constructing an argument in her head. Daysy understood her mother's methods. Magda Elena knew when to press on, when to back out of a discussion, and when to go in for the kill. Daysy recognized the way her mother lifted her chin when she was about to make a final pronouncement. She braced herself for the final thrust. "*Mira, niña*, names are important," Magda Elena began. "Let me say it in English so you understand. You name a person and you choose a path for her. And you are named after your *abuela*, Margarita. She was a good woman who died in church. Margarita was her name.

Margarita. Daysy. Same flower. Different language. You have a lot to live up to, *señorita. ¿Me oyes?*"

"Daisy is spelled with an *i*," Daysy mumbled, rolled her eyes.

"You think I didn't study English in school? Besides, in Cuba, it's spelled with a *y*."

"No, it isn't. You just made that up!"

"Fine. Your new name is Margarita," Magda Elena said, and rolled her *r*'s loud and long. Daysy cringed dramatically. "*Ay, ya,*" Magda Elena said at last, and swatted her hand, as if brushing away a gnat.

Daysy chanced a look at her father, who sat very still, his eyes back on the television. Magda Elena took his hand and rubbed his knuckles until his fingers loosened and intertwined themselves with hers.

"And let me tell you something else," Magda Elena began, pointing a long finger at Daysy, but Angel silenced her with a booming "*¡Ya, coño!*" that vibrated in the room. It was a shout so loud, and so unlike him, that the curse lingered in Daysy's head, far more frightening than any of Magda Elena's reprimands could be. He'd released Magda Elena's hand with a movement so swift it reminded Daysy of a whip, and Magda Elena's face registered the motion as if, indeed, she'd been struck by an invisible lash.

"*Mi vida,*" she said softly, trying to calm him, but Angel would not offer his hand again.

"We are watching something important, and you two are talking nonsense! How many cousins, aunts, uncles, friends, my own mother, *coño*, did we say goodbye to and haven't seen in ten years? *Cuéntame,* how many?" Angel said, but this time, he let her take his hand, and he rubbed his thumb roughly against hers, as if he were rubbing out a spot, pushing the loose skin up and down.

"Too many," Magda Elena whispered, then coughed a little. Angel's breathing slowed and his eyes shone. Daysy hated it when her father became agitated. He was usually so calm, as if he were fixed in some kind of meditation even as he spoke and worked, but when it came to

Cuban politics, he changed. The timbre of his voice would magnify, his hands would become more animated, and his eyes would take on a glossy sheen, his bad eye darting to the left, as if in anticipation of an enemy coming up to surprise him.

"He wasn't always this way," Magda Elena would sometimes whisper to Daysy in the middle of one of Angel's rants about political prisoners, communists, or Fidel Castro. "I was the hot-headed one about these things years ago."

Daysy once asked why they were so different, why her mother and father had switched roles, but Magda Elena became serious, and her face contorted as if she would cry. "Because I think that once you lose everything, there's no reason to fight anymore, while your father thinks that it is all the more reason to wage war. I refuse to fight about something I can't change," Magda Elena had said, and Daysy remembered that now as she watched her mother calming her father down. Angel looked as if he'd just been in a boxing match. His face was red and his left hand was in a fist. Magda Elena watched Angel the way a mother watches a misbehaving child, with both frustration and love.

Daysy left the living room then, gathered her pajamas, and started running a bath. Lightning filled the small bathroom, and with each burst of light, the name Belén came to Daysy's mind. Names are important, her mother had said. So, Daysy whispered it, rolled her tongue around the letters, and even wrote out the name on the foggy bathroom mirror. Belén del Pozo. The name conjured up a mud-splattered stone fount of ancient days, the soft-shoe shuffle of donkey hooves and sandals on dirt paths, the muted groaning of a woman in labor. "God, I'm stupid," Daysy said aloud, and erased the name with the heel of her hand. Thunder shook the glass doors surrounding the bathtub, and soon enough, Daysy heard Magda Elena's frantic knocking at the door.

"Get out of the tub," she was shouting. "I knew a girl in Cuba who was electrocuted while taking a bath during a thunderstorm…"

≈ ✳ ≈

Daysy remembered someone punching a hole through the edge of a turtle's shell and looping a leash through the little opening. She remembered crying as she watched the turtle open its mouth wide, in agony she imagined, and her cries filled the emptiness within the turtle's sharp mouth, the pointy beak. Daysy remembered a tiny red rocking chair in a foreign backyard, recalled rocking back and forth with such violence that she tumbled backward, and could still smell the bright orange iodine her mother put on her elbow scratches. She thought she could recall the feeling of her grandmother holding her so tightly that Angel pulled her away by force, and she dreamed of the buttons on her dress tearing in her grandmother's hands. "*No, no me la lleves,*" yelling over and over again. Watery vomit over the edge of a boat she remembered, too. And there, beneath the riotous color of all the other images, was a chubby little hand, perhaps her own, and a gold bracelet with a name on it she couldn't make out.

These were her thoughts as she changed into pajamas in the bathroom, her mother knocking on the door to hurry her the whole time. Daysy had been repeating the name Belén over and over again as she brushed her teeth, slipped off her jeans, combed her hair. It certainly was the kind of crazy name her mother seemed to like, but that was all the evidence Daysy could muster. Her days came and went without flourish, without surprise. But, scanning her memory now, Daysy recalled one afternoon hearing a sob from her parent's bedroom. Her mother never cried. Didn't seem to know how. When Daysy pushed open the door, she saw that the sound came from her father, his head buried in Magda Elena's lap, Magda Elena's hand drawing circles on his back. Daysy had been too scared to ask what had happened, and when Magda Elena lifted her head and saw Daysy, her eyes were so wild and frightened that Daysy shut the door softly and ran to her room.

The knocking continued on the door as Daysy remembered how every Christmas her mother placed a single figure under the tree, a tiny, parentless glass infant in a little glass manger. For years Daysy had asked about the rest of the set, and Magda Elena had always said, "They were left in Cuba," without further explanation, so Daysy stopped asking. And she realized now, as she sat on the toilet, the things she did not know mounting in her head, that she'd often seen her mother holding the crystal Jesus, stroking its diminutive head and touching its hard bump of a nose before setting it down, and even worse, that she'd never asked her mother why she did it.

Daysy emerged from the bathroom and received a kiss from her mother, who said, "Finally. I was afraid you'd slipped and given yourself a concussion!" She settled into her room for the night, sleeping fitfully, and when she awoke in the morning, the unsettled feeling she struggled with overnight remained, amplified by an odd silence in the house. Typically, mornings at the del Pozos' house were chaotic, with Angel slamming the front door against its iron frame on his way out so that the whole house rattled, and Abuelo singing one thing or another, or Magda Elena shouting at Daysy to wake up. But on this morning, the house was quiet save for the sour-sounding chimes of the grandfather clock in the dining room.

The silence caused a curious sensation in Daysy, similar to the way she often felt when she had the flu, or a bout of bronchitis, and was given medicine for it. Her mother, distrustful of doctors in general, often visited the pharmacy around the corner, owned by a man known to Daysy only as Márquez, who doled out medicine and advice without prescriptions. So it was that Magda Elena treated every one of Daysy's afflictions with thick, pink medicines, and put dropperfuls of prescription-strength appetite enhancers in Daysy's glasses of milk. The result of all this was that, when given the drugs, Daysy often felt as if the world had slowed down. Faucets dripped at impossibly slow rates. Her limbs moved through a thickened atmosphere. Voices turned single words into operatic notes. When the effects of the medication wore off, Daysy found that the universe returned to normal, and, to Magda Elena's satisfaction and eternal loyalty to Márquez, her cold symptoms would be much alleviated. Daysy had never described the reaction to her mother because she was convinced that the feeling of torpidness that came over her at such times was a symptom of something wrong, not with her body, but in her head. Now, the immense quiet in the house made Daysy feel leaden, though her heart thumped at a killing pace. There was nothing for it, Daysy decided at last, but to step out into the silence and ask, once and for all, about Belén.

Daysy opened her door to find her mother just outside it, her hand in the air, poised to knock. Magda Elena took a step back, her hand flying to her forehead, startled by the sudden opening of the door. She laughed a little, and rubbed her cheek. "*Qué susto,*" she said. Daysy had not moved at all. She felt heavy still, unable to react quickly.

"I was only coming to wake you. Would you like toast?"

"Not hungry," Daysy said, not sure now where to begin asking about Belén.

"*¿Qué pasa?* Not feeling well?" Magda Elena put a damp hand on Daysy's forehead. She'd been washing dishes, and Daysy caught the scent of lemon soap. She inhaled deeply, a sign Magda Elena took as the relief a feverish person feels when something cool touches her. "*¡Ay! ¡Fiebre!*" Magda Elena shouted, finally breaking the muteness of the house. As if in celebration of the return of sound, Abuelo began singing a song with a few well-placed *la, la, las* to fill in the spots where he'd forgotten the lyrics.

"No, Mami," Daysy said, and peeled her mother's hand away from her skin. She found that with the quiet gone an opportunity had been lost. Secrets might come out of hiding in a hushed place, but now, she thought, the mood for telling tales was ruined. "Come inside, please." Daysy tugged at her mother's arm and closed the door, dampening Abuelo's song a bit.

Magda Elena bent low to rub the carpet as she walked in, gathering fallen strands of Daysy's hair until a small, wooly ball lay in her hand. She was incapable of entering any room without trying to clean it in some way. "*Oye*, Daysy, you need to vacuum in here more often," Magda Elena announced, and Daysy winced at the volume of her mother's voice.

"Abuelo told me something," Daysy whispered.

"*¿Qué?*"

"Abuelo said you and Papi have kept a secret from me."

"*¿Cómo?* Speak up. Why are you whispering?" Magda Elena said, and began rubbing a smudge of dirt off the light switchplate with the heel of her hand.

"Why aren't you listening?" Daysy asked, and Magda Elena stopped mid-rub. She stared down at her hand for a moment, before looking at her daughter.

"I'm listening." She kneaded her hands for a moment. Magda Elena's eyes went to the switchplate again, her body turning toward it, as if the little bit of dirt was enticing her to wipe it out.

Daysy felt the heaviness coming on again. It made her dizzy, so she sat on the edge of her bed. "Abuelo said I had a sister. Her name was Belén, and that she died when we came to Florida." It seemed to Daysy, for a moment, that her mother's face was no longer one she recognized. The sensation came and went quickly.

Magda Elena began to cough, soft at first, then so violently she hunched over and Daysy began to pound on her mother's back.

"Mami! Are you okay? Deep breaths," Daysy said. Galaxies of spit and dust hovered around her mother's head, glittering in a shaft of morning light.

"*Sí, sí*," she choked out, and stood erect again. "That same old cough. I can't get rid of it," she said. Afterward, Magda Elena's mouth opened and closed, but she didn't make a sound.

"It's just in Abuelo's crazy head, right? Belén, she's not real?" Daysy asked.

It felt like a long time before Magda Elena answered. She polished the switchplate with her skin until it shone. Outside, Abuelo's singing was sonorous now, pealing through the house in long, vibrating notes. "No," Magda Elena answered at last without looking at Daysy and left the room, the door wide open behind her.

The flood of sound, not only of Abuelo, but of a lawnmower starting up outside, a car blasting salsa music a block away, and the deep barking of a neighbor's pit bull hurt Daysy's ears. The world sped up at once in time with the cacophony. Daysy knew her mother hadn't answered the question. Perhaps Belén was no longer real, but that did not exclude the reality of her having existed. Had she meant to say, "No, Abuelo isn't crazy," or "No, Belén was not real"?

Daysy knew she should have pressed on, reworked her question to force an answer from her mother. She hadn't been tricky enough in the attempt. Daysy had read once about genies, how wishes asked of those swarthy demons had to be worded just so or risk breath and soul in reckless wishing. Her mother had deceived her like a proper genie, and now she was gone, not in a cloud of smoke and incense, but in a flurry of rubbing and polishing, wiping grime from the walls of the house. She'd lost the moment. If she asked again, her mother would get angry, would warn her that adults weren't to be doubted aloud, and that would be the end of it.

Never had she felt so much physical discomfort. A true fever took hold of her body by that afternoon, and by nightfall, having taken two teaspoons of one of Márquez's potions, Daysy fell into a welcome, dreamless sleep.

≈ ✶ ≈

Daysy felt disconnected in her own home, shapeless like a cloud. Her father's jokes did not seem funny, and even anger, which she tried to conjure in her mother's presence, failed her. Her thoughts

were only on Belén, or what she imagined her to be. Every time her
mother avoided her eyes, or coughed, Daysy considered the possibility of Belén's existence. She saw her sister as if she had been drawn by
hand, the lead strokes smudged around the corners of her mouth,
her hair darkened by a lighter hand on the pencil, so that each line
seemed a strand of gray. If she let herself finish the drawing in her
mind, Belén's form would soon be enclosed in a box, trapping her
forever in a gray, animated space. These were her thoughts, without
much distraction. Her father had called her *un zombi* at dinner, and
made a monster noise deep in the back of his throat to pull her out
of her reverie. "Leave her alone," Magda Elena had said at once, and
then, dropping a few soggy *platanitos* on her plate, said, "Stop day-
dreaming. Eat." But Magda Elena's voice had been strained, lacking
its usual forcefulness. That same night, thoughts of zombies kept
Daysy awake.

Just a few months ago, Daysy knew, she would have asked her
mother again and again about Belén, but she couldn't now. If Abuelo
was right, if she had a sister and had been allowed to forget, Daysy
was afraid she would never forgive her mother or her father, certain if
Magda Elena had lied to her that she wouldn't ever feel the same way
about her again, so she did not take the risk. The weird fog that had
surrounded mother and daughter, not so strangely, given Daysy's age,
had thickened considerably. A part of her wished that things were the
way they used to be, when Magda Elena would come home after work
and Daysy would rush to her, crushing her nose in her mother's shirts
and smelling the oil they used to keep the sewing machines running.
But now such an act seemed impossible. It would embarrass them
both, Daysy thought, and she could feel herself physically recoiling at
the thought.

She tried another tack and asked her father about Belén that weekend while she rode with him out to the west coast of Florida in search
of a part for their van. A brush fire along Alligator Alley reached the

edges of the street and had been licking at cars all day. Angel and
Daysy had missed the news about the fire in their rush out of the
house. They only knew that it was suddenly dark along the highway.
Now, curtains of gray smoke had dropped over the desolate road.
Angel turned a knob and the car's fog lights came on. The Everglades
lay burning along the road, the sawgrass frying and sizzling. Ash
rained onto the car, and the smell of smoke began to come through
the air vents. Still, Angel drove on, racing down the darkening path
toward the junkyard. The man on the phone had said they had what
Angel had been looking for—the joint for a rear window wiper that
cost too much money new.

In the hazy distance, Daysy saw the spinning red-and-blue lights
of the Florida Highway Patrol. The lights multiplied as Angel's car
approached until it was clear that the road had been blocked. Angel
came to a stop and lowered a window. The smoke poured in. A
patrolman approached. "Road's closed, folks," he said, his hand on
the brim of his wide hat. Angel's eyes looked off to the distance.
Daysy leaned out of the window to see what he was looking at. Sitting
in the bed of a pickup truck was a group of people. Two Miccosukee
men and a little boy sat and stared out at the burning glades. They
were wrapped in woolen blankets despite the heat of the fire. Daysy
wondered if they had been caught in the burning grass, wondered if
their home was out there in the flames, or if they hunted alligators
in the swamp.

"I hope no one was hurt," Angel said, shifting the car into reverse.

Daysy got a good look at the boy's face. It was contorted with grief
and fear, which, strangely, made Daysy feel brave. She leaned closer to
her father. "Abuelo told me about Belén," she said quietly, watching
him for some sort of telling sign, one that would indicate that
Abuelo's story was true.

Angel adjusted his grip on the steering wheel. "What did he say
about her?" he said.

Daysy felt suddenly sick at heart. So it was true. She had been deceived. Outside, the wind was stirring the ashes from the fire, and flakes were coming in through the air conditioning. Angel waved his hand through them, and they dissolved in the air. A fleck of charred Everglades landed on Daysy's palm. She observed it for a beat then asked, "So I had a sister?"

"I thought your mother already cleared things up."

"No. No, she didn't really answer anything. I never get the full story about anything from…"

Angel reached out to tap her knee. "There's nothing to worry about," he said, and flipped on the radio to a talk show.

"So there is no Belén," she said, but Angel did not echo her assertion. Instead, he raised the volume of the radio, doing so again a few seconds later, then again, so that the windows shook with the boom of the bass and Daysy felt utterly drowned out. Her father's face was tense, and there was, she thought, dampness in his eyes. Daysy's sense of the general wrongness of things strengthened. She looked out toward the light of fires here and there, formulating her next move.

She had to shout over the sound of the radio. "Papi, I—"

"This discussion is over," Angel said.

"Papi—"

"I'm warning you," Angel added. He lowered the volume at last. Daysy would not fight back. They both knew it.

≈ ⋆ ≈

It was clear now—no one would help Daysy unravel the story of the girl named Belén. So she came up with her own plan. If a baby had been lost at sea in 1980, surely some newspaper reporter, somewhere, would have picked up the story. And that story was hidden in the library across town.

The next morning, Daysy entered Abuelo's room and the smell of

Vick's VapoRub made her eyes water. Abuelo slathered the ointment on his chest and neck every night, and no amount of washing ever took the scent out of his pillowcases.

"Abuelo," Daysy whispered on the side of his bed. Abuelo opened his eyes.

"*¿Qué? ¿Qué?*" he mumbled. Radio Martí, the Miami-based Cuban radio station that attempted broadcasts to the island, played in the background.

"Listen, I'm going out. I'll be okay. Don't worry. And don't get in trouble," Daysy said in Spanish.

Abuelo smiled and patted her cheek. His hands were calloused, rough and warm. "*Bueno, preciosa,*" he said, closing his eyes again.

Daysy left his room feeling a twinge of guilt. That familiar fear, that Abuelo would get himself run over in the street, that he would make good on his promise to swim back to Cuba someday, that he would again sell off a good chunk of Magda Elena's jewelry, as he had a few months ago, trading a diamond anniversary ring for ten dollars and a *cafecito* to a pawnbroker on Okeechobee Avenue, almost made Daysy stay home that day. But her summer vacation was waning, and the chance to use the library just a few blocks away would soon be over.

She couldn't shake the picture of Belén from her thoughts, except now, under the glow of the library's fluorescent light, the baby had taken on the pale blue of death. Daysy shook the thoughts away, thankful that she had never felt an unnaturally cold breeze or the light touch of an invisible hand on her shoulder, or any indication whatsoever that she was trailed by an infant ghost.

The smell of paper, mold, and carpet cleaner energized her. It was a smell Daysy loved, a smell she had explained to her mother as one of her favorites, and Magda Elena had laughed and called her strange. "Better to love the smell of my *frijolitos* cooking, and maybe you'll get some curves on you," she had said. The librarian sat on a high stool behind a wooden counter. She picked at a bowl of stew and was slurping loudly when Daysy asked her about the microfilm machines. "Mm," the librarian said, her mouth glistening, her lips pursed, and pointed her fork toward the stacks.

Daysy looked through the drawer full of film rolls and found the *Miami Herald.* Then she searched for the date—May 13, 1980. That was the day the del Pozos had arrived in Key West, had come off a stranger's yacht and started a new life. At least that was what her mother had always told her. Magda Elena's story was always the same—vague, rosy, short. She'd explain the crowded boat, the sun, the dreams of a house and a job. The details Daysy asked for were always countered with the same phrase—"*Ay, se me olvidó,*" I forgot.

The tiny, brown roll of film with the date on it felt light in Daysy's hand. She balanced it on her palm and watched it shake along with her arm, her body. For a moment, she considered throwing the roll into the trash, extinguishing it, obliterating its potential for truth. But the moment passed quickly enough, and Daysy sat down to work.

First, she selected five more rolls from the drawer, the dates covering the days after she and her family arrived. Then she scrolled through pages upon pages concerning the boatlift—scores of pictures of haggard people, of overfilled boats, of joyful reunions, of young men in handcuffs, lean faces, red-cheeked faces, eyes on one lost in the distance here, another, a young woman with a face so angelic Daysy was instantly reminded of church paintings. Daysy lost ten minutes staring at one picture full of children, searching for herself. A little girl wearing a tank top and short shorts, holding fast to a stuffed dolphin caught Daysy's eyes. Her nails were chewed up. She had two plaits in her hair with lots of curls springing up around her forehead. She had gold earrings. The girl appeared in many photos, and it was clear she was a darling of the media. Daysy felt a ridiculous surge of jealousy, wished the photographers had found her among the thousands of children and selected her as their icon instead.

Next, Daysy read the stories and editorials. Surely there would be a story of a missing baby. There were articles about people who had heart attacks on the boats, or while waiting in the Orange Bowl to be processed. There was the story of one man who called himself Colonel and brought nothing with him but a pair of old castanets that he claimed belonged to the queen of Spain. There was the piece on the lady who swore she challenged Fidel Castro to a game of dominoes and won. There was the man who wrapped himself in a huge American flag, went to sleep on a cot, and didn't wake up ever again. Stories and more stories.

Daysy scanned only the headlines, her eyes starting to tire. Children from one of the local summer camps began to pour into the library, shouting over the librarian's shushing. Daysy put her finger on the off switch to the machine, ready to give up the search. Then her eyes caught sight of a headline on the bottom right corner of the page: SCHOONER CAPSIZES, MARIEL INFANT LOST AT SEA, and Daysy scrolled down to read the rest of it.

Miami— *Richard Thoreau, captain of the sunken schooner,* Big Virginia, *hoped to bring strangers out of Cuba, but not at such a steep price.*

"At least she went down doing good in the world," the 55-year-old Thoreau said.

The replica of the 18th-century schooner sank approximately 50 miles off Cuban shores. There were an estimated 250 people on the ship designed to carry far fewer. All but one, an infant, are believed t o have survived the catastrophe at sea.

Coast Guard representatives have voiced concern regarding over-loaded boats leaving Mariel harbor since the crisis began. Thoreau's story corroborates this.

"We could have safely carried 50 people across the Straits. They [Cuban officials] told us we had to take many, many more.

"It's no wonder the ship broke in half," Thoreau said.

The passengers aboard the Big Virginia *were transferred to a shrimp boat, the* El Ron, *and a private yacht, the* Adalah, *while at sea.*

The Thoreaus claim there was one drowning, though they have no official record of the passengers' names, nor an exact headcount.

"I spoke with the mother when we were nearing Key West. She said the baby fell into the sea when they crossed over. Her name was Belén. A beautiful name, and a real sad thing," Savanna Thoreau said from her hotel room in Miami Beach.

About the parents, Savanna Thoreau added: "A nice-looking couple, with another daughter. But I didn't get any of their names."

So far, none of the refugees have reported the death of an infant.

The Dade County Coroner's office has examined 32 Mariel refugee deaths since April 21st, when the first boat of refugees arrived in Key West. That number is expected to grow as reports of more capsizing boats trickle in and efforts to recover the bodies are made.

On April 11th, President Carter announced that the U.S. would accept up to 3,000 refugees. The number of Cubans having arrived in Key West has already exceeded that number.

"I suppose it was worth it," Thoreau said regarding the loss of his ship. "We got a lot of people out of Cuba."

A dark feeling, heavy and sudden, overwhelmed Daysy. She was convinced of it now—her parents had been lying all these years. And it was a big lie, not a harmless Santa Claus-is-real sort of a lie, but the kind that shatters like glass, injuring people with its sharp edges.

Daysy printed the page off the microfilm and folded it clumsily. A pair of campers walked past her, chattering about the books in their hands. Daysy lowered her face to hide her trembling lip. She shut off the machine and left the library.

STELLA MARIS MORALES-QUINN

PITTSBURGH, PENNSYLVANIA 1990

Stella Maris Morales-Quinn was seven when she found her mother, Anita, dangling from a roof beam. Her father, coming upon the scene moments after Stella did, grabbed his daughter and pulled her away from the sight of her mother's naked feet, toes painted red, flexing and grasping at air. Michael Quinn leapt over his daughter, who had fallen to the floor now, and climbed atop a desk to get to his wife.

Stella balled her hands into fists and pressed them against her eyes. When Stella realized she could still hear the thumping of her father's fist against her mother's chest, she covered her ears and buried her head in her lap, lest the temptation to look overwhelm her. Raising her head after a long time, she saw her mother on the ground, in her father's arms, her limbs as loose as the rope pooled on the floor. Later she'd wonder how her father had not yelled as he worked to save his wife, but had only made a quietly frantic sound, like a whimper, again and again in the back of his throat. The keening would come days afterward.

Whenever Stella remembered that long ago afternoon, it was as if it had just happened, and also, as if it were something about to happen, so that at nearly ten years old, she felt the constant pressure in her chest familiar to the very aged and wise. The feeling was as if she were always on the edge of a precipice, unsure whether she could stop herself from jumping. It was the feeling of standing in line for a horrifyingly tall rollercoaster, or of saying "Bloody Mary" over and over again in a darkened bathroom, casting a schoolyard spell to call forth the image of a bloodied woman in the mirror. It was the feeling of counting heartbeats, and wondering how high the numbers might reach.

Stella and her father did not talk about that morning by unspoken agreement. When strangers asked after his wife, Michael would simply say Anita passed away, as if her death had been quiet and sleepy, a true passing, and not a violent jolting out of life. Those who'd known her weren't surprised at the suicide. After all, she had tried to kill herself twice before—once, by showering in the middle of the night and, wet to the bone, sitting out in a Pittsburgh winter until her skin turned blue.

On another occasion, she crossed the Monongahela River in the early spring, when the ice wasn't thick enough to hold. The *Pittsburgh Gazette* wrote a story about the crossing in dramatic language. Every footfall was described as "desperate" and the act itself deemed "stupidly courageous" by the newpaper columnist who had witnessed the crossing and believed it had been a stunt. He couldn't know that she sought the cracks in the ice and jabbed her heels in deeply with each step, hoping to plunge into the cold water beneath, trapping herself under a casing of frozen glass. Stella knew because her mother had told her later that night, wrapped in two bathrobes to keep from shivering.

An exceptional child, Stella was impatient with others who weren't as intelligent as she was, and she believed her mother had been the smartest person she would ever know. The neat stacks of books at her bedside table, next to the toilet, in the toolshed outside, on the dining room table, and the slender volumes shoved in between the cushions of the sofa spoke of Anita's intellectual avarice. Michael had not put them away, even after so long, and the pages of the books became stiff and musty from disuse, the ones outside swollen like fat hens. Stella's mother had stockpiled books, read them through dinner, and often slept with a few under the sheets, like a dragon warming a hoard of treasure. She told stories straight out of her books, and some came from her own imagination. When she hanged herself, Stella believed that her mother had simply confused reality with the plot of one of her novels. That she'd played out some heroine's desperate last moments and had gone too, too far. Stella returned to that theory often, because it suggested that her mother, in real life, had been happy, and that it had been the stories that had done her in. To think otherwise, for Stella to imagine that her mother had willingly left her and her father, was heartbreaking.

By the time Stella was five, she could read in English and Spanish, could tune a guitar without a pitch pipe, and knew how to convert temperatures from Celsius to Fahrenheit. And, she believed nearly everything her mother told her. Stella loved her mother with such intensity that her hands ached from not touching her while at school, and in the years following her mother's death, Stella's fingers hurt so badly that she'd been to two orthopedic doctors and a rheumatologist, none of whom could diagnose the source of the pain.

Out of options, Michael had arranged for Stella to see a child psychologist twice a week. They'd started out together, meeting Dr. Row, a slender British woman who always had honey candies on her desk, scattered over papers. Stella often took one in her mouth at the start of each session, sucking on the little golden disc for a long time, forcing Dr. Row to speak first and fill in those first few imposing moments of silence with a lovely, accented speech that calmed Stella's nerves.

During those early sessions, Stella would not stay put without her father there, holding her hand. Even so, she would not speak, but would only massage her hands and read the spines of the books on Dr. Row's shelves. So it was Michael who did most of the talking. Dr. Row asked how he and his wife had met.

"I was a student at the University of Miami at the time, three credits shy of graduation," he began. "My last class, International Relations, had us going down to the Orange Bowl where the Mariel refugees were being processed. Anita and Stella were there, alone. She was so beautiful." Michael stopped and squeezed Stella's knee. Stella knew he was steadying himself. He went on to describe how they met on the football field that had become a makeshift dormitory for the refugees. He helped Anita find a job and an apartment, and after graduation, he asked her to marry him during the halftime show of a UM football game. She had picked Pittsburgh out of a map as a place to settle by closing her eyes and pointing to it, saying, "*Sí*, right there. Far from Cuba. She always said she wanted to start over. Be born again."

Dr. Row said, "Don't we all sometimes," laughed a bit, and wrote a few words down on her notepad. Stella wished her father were better at storytelling. She'd heard the story herself many times from her mother, except it was different in key ways. Anita used to say that when she first saw Michael Bernard Quinn, it was as if he had appeared out of nothing, suddenly, and had taken corporeal form right before her eyes. That with his blond hair boyishly parted to the side, and his lanky frame, he looked like the son of a god, just coming into his own, just learning, for the first time, how to string his father's bow and make love to a woman with the same finesse. Anita described him just that way, even though Stella was only a child, a brilliant child, but one who could not understand everything her mother said. She had described, too, what falling in love was like. It was the feeling of being pulled out from deep water, of knowing that there was air in her lungs just when she'd given up on it, when she'd begun to think that she'd only imagined the existence of oxygen in the first place. "Meeting Michael was like that," she'd said.

He'd found the sessions difficult. His Irish mother had taught him to swallow despair and keep it locked away, to cry in private when no one was listening, and to emerge, fresh-faced and as strong and level as a perfectly built house. So, in talking about his wife, Michael chose to praise her endlessly, to describe her beauty ("She was like a small

bird. Delicate. Gorgeous," he'd said) and to enumerate her many gen-
erosities ("I fell asleep each night with her hand rubbing my back")
instead of the frightening times Stella remembered, when her mother
would disappear for days after a trip to the grocery store, or when she
would plant herself in the living room and weep, willowy and
immovable at the same time.

When Stella finally spoke in a session, it was to contradict Michael.
"We never discussed death. She didn't even like horror movies,"
Michael had offered.

"My mother talked about dying at least three times a day. Usually
in between meals," Stella had said, surprising Dr. Row, who startled
at the sound of Stella's small voice.

Michael had patted her knee with more force than necessary and
cut in, saying, "Aw, come on Stella. Don't exaggerate. It wasn't like
that, Doctor."

Her decision to see Dr. Row alone at last had come out of frustration with her father's half-truths. They troubled Stella's memories of
her mother. With Dr. Row all to herself, Stella felt free to recall her
mother with clarity.

Michael had sighed in relief at Stella's pronouncement regarding
her sessions with Dr. Row. He'd asked, "You okay with that, Stel? Just
you and the doc?"

"Yeah, it's okay," Stella had said, sweeping her heavy bangs out of
her eyes. The sessions had felt as if Michael were swirling still waters,
making them unclear. The mud bloomed and thickened in Stella's
memory, and she was forgetting the sound of her mother's voice, and
the smell of her hair, and the way she folded shirts so that the sleeves
made neat triangles. Even that, Stella had tried to replicate and failed.
But now Stella was convinced things would settle down, and her
memories would return intact, like the fish in the Monongahela who
had returned that year at last to clean water, after so many decades of
avoiding the river poisoned by the steel mills.

≈ ⋆ ≈

Once, when Dr. Row asked how Stella felt about being in the sixth grade though she was only nine years old, Stella said, "I'm almost ten. And besides, I belong in high school, really," and pulled at her bangs some more. Michael had suggested she grow them out, but Stella had refused, remembering how her mother had carefully maintained their length, the cold feeling of Anita's scissors against her forehead, the soft touch of Anita's fingers on her face, and the clip-clip of the blades as they sheared off a carefully measured inch. Now her bangs looked a bit sloppy.

"Why do you think you belong in high school?" Dr. Row had asked, and Stella had answered with a question of her own.

"Do you see the color of numbers?"

"Pardon?"

"The color of numbers. Six, for example, is yellow. And two is bright red, like blood. And seven is always blue. If you know the colors, then algebra is easy. They teach advanced algebra in the tenth grade. Another thing," Stella said, on a roll now as she described something only her mother had known about her. "Letters have gender. Did you know? The letter *c* is definitely a girl. The kids at school don't get it." When she'd told her mother, Stella was fearful that she'd say there was something wrong with her head. Instead, Anita patted her cheek and agreed that yes, there was something decidedly male about the letter *f*. Dr. Row had another reaction altogether. She scribbled on her notepad and asked Stella about each letter, whether decimals had colors, too, and what in the world one did with fractions. This eagerness to hear her explanations endeared Dr. Row to Stella. No one but her mother had ever listened to her with such attentiveness, and even then, her mother had taken up much of their time together with stories of her own.

Sometimes during sessions, Stella told stories about Anita, but for the most part she retold her mother's stories for Dr. Row, mimicking Anita's intonations, her hand movements and facial expressions, using Spanish here and there for effect, and translating for Dr. Row. Dr. Row rarely interrupted the stories, and Stella felt that the woman enjoyed them. While Stella talked, Dr. Row would sit forward, elbows resting on her knees, and click her wedding band against her teeth.

One day, in late May, Dr. Row began by saying, "Last Tuesday we talked about how your mother's stories always seemed so sad. Why do you think this was so?"

"The best stories are tragedies," Stella mumbled, her mouth full of candied honey.

"Why do you think so?"

"It's just a fact," Stella said, and swallowed hard. "*Romeo and Juliet, Oedipus, The Great Gatsby*. All tragedies. And they're the best."

"You've read these things?" Dr. Row asked, her eyebrow arched.

"Just about. Actually, mom read them to me. The bigger words are easier to understand that way." Stella worried her hands in her lap, then reached for another candy. Plopping it in her mouth, she unwrapped the candy with her tongue, then drew out the plastic wrapper and set it on the arm of the chair in which she sat.

Dr. Row waited for Stella to finish before beginning again. "Last week you told me about the German gentleman, who…"

"Parisian. *El caballero de París.* He was French."

"Oh yes, the beggar who claimed he was from Paris."

"He roamed the streets of Havana and talked about philosophy and poetry with everyone he met," Stella said.

"And this story is…"

"True. This one is true, I think." Stella tapped her chin with a sticky finger. It was a game she played with Dr. Row, cataloging the stories as true or false.

"Now tell me one that isn't, Stella." There was a story she wished wasn't true, but they'd already gone over the day when Stella and Michael had found her mother hanged. Stella had eaten all of Dr. Row's candy during that session, and at night her stomach ached. She'd also cried a great deal, and Dr. Row had let her blow her nose on as many tissues as she wanted, so that by the end of the session, the floor of Dr. Row's office was littered with fluffy white sheets that hovered over the heating vents like clouds.

"What if I tell you one I'm not sure about?" Dr. Row nodded and settled into her seat. "It's complicated. Like a bad dream," Stella explained. She fidgeted and pulled at a hangnail.

"Go on," Dr. Row urged. Stella wasn't sure how. She did not want Dr. Row to think her mother was crazy. She'd done a crazy thing, of course, killing herself, but that didn't mean that Anita was a bad mother. Stella had already punched a sixth grader in the nose for saying that her mother was in hell. If Dr. Row so much as lifted an eyebrow at what Stella was about to say, she didn't know what she'd do. Stella didn't want to give up Dr. Row, not now that her therapist knew so many things about her, but she couldn't stomach anyone thinking poorly of her mother.

"Here's the thing," Stella said, and took a shaky breath. "My mother told me, the day after she walked across the frozen Mon, that when I was a baby I died once." Stella stopped and looked for a reaction in Dr. Row's face. The therapist had already assumed her usual position, fist against mouth, teeth working the wedding band. Stella saw no response in Dr. Row's face, save for her general interest. "She said I was buried deep in the ground in a cemetery in Havana and that she slept on the dirt above my grave for two nights before the police took her away."

Stella was out of breath when she stopped. She hoped Dr. Row wouldn't ask what she thought of the story, because then Stella would say that she believed it, that logic didn't matter when it came to magic. She would have to admit, too, to having had nightmares of being buried alive, which she did not want to talk about with Dr. Row if she could get away with it. "So," Dr. Row began, and Stella closed her eyes as she waited for the question. "Why do you think your mother did that?"

"You mean sleep on my grave?"

"Yes."

Thrown by the question at first, a little thrill shook her because she knew the answer. "The answer to that is another story."

Dr. Row looked at her wristwatch and tapped its crystal face. "We've got time," she said.

Stella adjusted herself so that she was sitting crosslegged in her chair. She coughed and leaned forward, and began telling the story in the kind of voice Anita used when telling the most haunting tales. Nearly whispering, Stella began: "My mother wished to die, right there over my body. She was hoping they'd bury her with me. She prayed to *La Milagrosa* for it." Stella waited a beat for Dr. Row to ask for more of an explanation, and when she didn't, she plowed ahead anyway, enjoying the sudden widening of Dr. Row's eyes. "According to legend, *La Milagrosa* was a woman in Cuba who died during childbirth long ago. The baby was dead, too, and they buried them together, with the baby at her feet. Years and years and years later, when they reopened the grave, both the bodies were perfect. No rotting at all! And the baby was in her mother's arms. They say she grants miracles. My mother prayed to her." Stella nodded slowly and rubbed her hands.

"Beautiful," Dr. Row said.

"I guess so. It's creepy. And it's a tragedy, which makes it so good."

"And that's what your mother wanted?"

Stella grew serious again. "I don't know. It isn't true anyway," she said as she tucked her hands inside her sleeves and crossed her fingers.

"No, it can't be. You're here, well and alive."

Stella covered her mouth with her hand to keep herself from saying anymore about it. The story could be true, but she wouldn't say
so to Dr. Row. If Dr. Row had pushed Stella further on the story of *La
Milagrosa*, she might have learned that Stella sometimes thought she
remembered being dead. In recalling that state of lifelessness, Stella
felt a void in her chest, as if her heart had stopped beating. But the
feeling scared her, and soon Stella quit thinking about it.

≈ ✶ ≈

On Sunday afternoons when the weather was warm, Michael and
Stella would go to the cemetery. Michael clipped daffodils from the
garden in the spring, coral colored roses in summer, and spider lilies
in the fall to bring to Anita's grave. Stella said that the lilies looked
like "red fireworks, abloom," and Michael had declared that on top of
everything else she was good at, his daughter was a poet. They came
only a few times during the winter, shortly after the suicide. On one
of those visits, on a day that dipped below twenty degrees, they had
arrived to find the small steel vase that held the flowers full of snow.
It formed a white pyramid and painted a picture of such lonesome-
ness that Michael had cried long at the site, sucking in the frigid air
in monstrous gulps while Stella wrapped her arms around his leg and
trembled against him, loving him with such intensity that it made her
cry, too.

After that they avoided the gravesite after snowstorms, but they
were never there long in any weather. Just enough time to remove the
withered flowers and put the new ones, wilting already, in their place.
Around them, other graves sported artificial floral arrangements.
Frayed fabric petals trailed their threads in the wind like kite tails,
and the plastic stems clicked against each other so that Stella always
thought she heard the sound of bones rattling behind her. A year earlier, she would have run between the headstones, tapping each one

with the palm of her hand, playing tag with the dead whom she imagined would rise like a vapor from the ground and chase her. But now, the impulse to run, that thrilling tingle that children feel continually in every muscle, urging them to go, go, go, was gone from her legs. Stella supposed she was growing up, and her sudden disinterest in playing in the cemetery saddened her almost as much as thinking about Anita so far beneath her feet.

One unseasonably warm Sunday two weeks before Christmas, Stella and Michael sat on the moist ground of the grave, instead of standing in silence for a bit and leaving after only a few minutes. Underneath them was a layer of slippery leaves. Stella's hands throbbed, as they usually did at the cemetery, so she hid them in the front pocket of her coat.

When Michael suddenly spoke it was like a great, holy silence was broken. His voice set a trio of nearby Canada geese and one gosling to honking, and they paddled away, leaving a trail of green goop behind them. What he said was as astonishing to Stella as the fact that he had spoken. Michael was a quiet man, before and after his wife's suicide. And when he needed to say something, it was usually a simple thing like "Pass the butter," or "The Steelers are done this season," or "I hate the way that furnace rattles." Rarely did his conversations with Stella rise above practical things. Perhaps it was the fusty smell of old leaves, or the long time spent staring at the words on the headstone, or the warmth of the day so strange when felt in the thin shadow of the bare oak and maple limbs around them. But for the first time in Stella's memory, Michael spoke in the most reflective way.

"She invited this," he said. "She opened her arms to it like she was greeting an old friend. This dying. She loved the idea of it more than anything. More than me, I think." Michael was speaking as if Stella wasn't there. When he noticed her, how still she sat next to him, how scared she seemed, he came back to himself and found a more sensible thing to say. "I should have brought her more flowers when she was alive, Stel. Really, I should have. Because these," he said, and plucked one thin petal off the scarlet lily, "don't count for nothing now."

Michael rose, peeled a few wet leaves from his pants, and walked toward the geese that hissed at him and flapped their wings as they circled the gosling and hid it from view. Stella stayed put, thinking about her father's regret. She regretted some things, too. Anita had once told her about funeral rites around the world. How the Japanese watered the headstones as if they were flowers. How the Maori sat with their dead for days before burying them. How the *santeros* in Cuba sometimes buried their dead with full rum bottles in their stiff grip. Now Stella regretted not having done things like this for her mother, rites she was obviously interested in. Thinking of her in the cramped, dark box below, her hands empty, her headstone dry, her body mourned for only a few hours, filled Stella with remorse.

She was sure now that Michael was right, that Anita had longed for her death, had anticipated it as a woman might her wedding day. Why else would she tell Stella about these things, if not to ensure that they were done? Why explain these practices, and not the things Stella wanted to know? Like why they'd really left Cuba. Or what her birth had been like. Why she had no cousins. From whom did she inherit the upward tilt of her nose or her allergies to cats?

In the dusky sky, the first star of the night blinked awake. Stella watched it for a minute. "I wish you had stayed with me. For *siempre*," Stella whispered, then walked away to join her father.

≈ ✶ ≈

Stella's bedroom had golden stars painted on the walls and the ceiling. At night, they caught the light from the street outside and shimmered. Her mother had called her "*Mi estrellita*," my little star. On clear nights, the two of them would climb the steel fireladder on the side of the house and lie on the roof, pointing out the constellations, making wishes. *Deséos*, her mother called them.

"I wish Daddy won't go bald," Stella would say.

"I wish the wrinkle above my nose would go away," Anita would add.

"I wish you'll always love me."

"That one's already true."

"I wish you'll stay with me. For *siempre*." Always, this was Stella's final wish before the hard shingles on the roof pressing against her spine would be too much and would drive them both back down the fireladder. After Anita died, Stella would drag her father onto the roof, and though they would not play the wishing game, she would press her head against his chest and say, "I love you, Daddy, for ever and ever and ever," extending the "evers" until she was out of breath and Michael was laughing so hard his chest rumbled with joy.

One night, when the faint ghost of the Milky Way was visible overhead, Stella thought to ask her mother about her family. "Tell me about my father."

"*No sé*," Anita said.

"You always say that. How about my grandmother, was she nice?"

"My family never loved me," Anita said without hesitation, but also without anger. She said it the way one might mention that it is raining, or that the mail didn't come today.

"Still," Stella pursued, "I'd like to know about them. The other Moraleses, I mean."

"Just because they share your name, it doesn't mean they were people worth knowing." Again, her mother's bland tone struck Stella, scared her into thinking that here was a person who could not be moved, who would think nothing of stepping off the roof of the house and, on the way down, would feel no fear, no joy.

"I think it's important," Stella said in a whisper.

"You were nameless when you came to me. We all are, at first. But I could have named you Luísa, or Henriqueta..."

Stella wrinkled her nose, and her mother wrapped her arms around her. "Or *caquita frita*," her mother said with a laugh, and Stella, imagining being named Fried Shit for a lifetime couldn't help but laugh, too, up there on the roof with the Milky Way hiding behind a cloud.

"Did you have friends?" Stella tried again.

"I don't remember," Anita said.

The idea of having family tied to her through blood and genetics did not leave Stella's mind. Michael's family was kind, treated her as if she were Michael's through and through. His mother bought all her back-to-school clothes and a new lunchbox every year. She signed birthday cards, "Love, Grandma Quinn," and displayed her school photos on her mantle in her home in Syracuse. But Stella wondered about those other grandmothers, the ones who had seen her when she was just born, and the one who had birthed her mother, fed her, named her.

"Why did we have to leave Cuba?" Stella asked often, and Anita would invariably lift a book off the nearest surface and flip the pages a few times, as if she were doing a card trick.

"For these," she said. "And for this," she'd say, pointing at Stella's forehead. "The most valuable thing you own is yourself, and in Cuba, you can't own that." Anita made Stella memorize the names of Cuba's old provinces, the old names from before the revolution. And she encouraged Stella's little rebellions at school, such as the time she refused to play kickball during phys. ed. Stella brought home an angry letter from her teacher, and her mother had laughed as she read it and served Stella a scoop of vanilla ice cream loaded with chocolate chips as a reward.

When Stella asked about her real father, Anita would shrug her shoulders and answer, "*No sé*," as if she had asked whether ghosts existed or if aliens had assisted the Aztecs. "I don't know." Her mother would leave it at that, resuming her reading with a smile. Stella could force no more of an explanation from Anita than "*No sé,*" and she began to believe that the real reason they'd left Cuba, beyond burnt books and oppressive government, was this mysterious man who'd fathered her.

Sometimes, Stella felt her existence was unreal, as if she were only something her mother had imagined. Everyone else, by contrast, seemed to belong to the world, but she herself often felt removed from the earth. Unanchored. Nothing brought this to mind more than the one picture her mother had managed to take out of Cuba. When Stella saw it, she was disappointed to find that it was not of herself, but of Anita, as a toddler. In the picture, she was sitting on a baby's potty outside, in a backyard in Havana, wearing a ragged shirt, her legs bare and mosquito bitten. In the background was a large white blur. At first, Stella thought it was a ghost. Perhaps a dead great-grandmother? Or an angry poltergeist? But it turned out to be nothing more than a white hen running past. How could her mother ever have been that small, Stella wondered, or that ready to smile, so unabashedly crouching on that potty and peeing warmly in a noon shaft of light? The chicken, the light, the ragged shirt. They smacked of real life. Stella found little that felt real in her own life. Though she'd grown up in Pittsburgh, she wasn't rooted to the place. The sooty walls of the buildings on Forbes spoke of steel mills, the names in the phonebook belonged to people of Irish and Polish descent, to eyes accustomed to the yellowness of western Pennsylvania skies and the muddy brown of its rivers. Stella felt, in her bones, that she preferred blue—blue skies, blue, crystal oceans—and thought that she and her mother were misplaced people, outside of their essential elements. Once, her mother had read her *The Tempest,* and Stella had wondered about that great magician, Prospero, how he'd roiled the seas and then calmed them, how he had monsters and fairies for servants, and she asked whether there was more magic on islands than anywhere else. "Of course," Anita had said, cementing Stella's sense that she belonged elsewhere, in a place where divinities walked the earth.

Logically, Stella knew the feeling had grown out of too many images of idyllic Caribbean scenes in coffee-table books of Cuba, too many of Anita's stories. And yet, seeing her mother's past so vivid and real in that photo, Stella couldn't help but question her own existence. She felt as if she should have found security deep in the South Hills, among the foothills of the Alleghenies, but her past had gone missing somehow.

She often thought about the girl she might have been had Anita decided to stay in Cuba. Stella pulled the light hairs on her arms, imagining her skin a more golden color, exposed to a tropical sun for years. Perhaps she'd be thinner. Her mother had told her about how everything was rationed in Cuba—fruits and vegetables, milk, televisions, even toilet paper and pads. "Dishtowels folded in two," Anita had said once when explaining the menstrual cycle to Stella. "That's all we had." If she'd grown up in Cuba, Stella knew she'd be thinking these thoughts in Spanish, and she wondered if some essential quality of her mind would be different. Would she be more passionate? Words sounded like the crush of water when her mother spoke them. Stella thought that yes, she'd be quite different if her thoughts came in a tongue that evoked other sounds so readily. It was almost as if Anita had spoken three, four languages at once, her intonations imitating birdsong and waves on the shore.

In truth, Stella had lived in Cuba for less than a year. She didn't even have a birth certificate. Her mother told her that it had been left behind. Yet, once in the U.S., new documents were produced, and when asked, Anita said that Stella was born on Christmas. "It's a memorable day," she told Stella, "though I'm not sure it's right."

There were other things Anita had revealed, in bits and pieces. She'd told Stella about their voyage across the sea. Stella did not remember her own experience of the Mariel boatlift, but her mother supplied many of the details about the shrimp boat that had brought her to America, and the owner of the boat, a man so fat that when he crossed the deck from one side to the other, the ship leaned port or starboard. Anita described another boat she saw sinking. "I heard an entire family, including children, went down with that ship," she'd said, wincing.

To have her mother back, to remember what it felt like to ride in a crowded boat, to feel her mother's hands at her waist as she held her high over her head, to peek at a foreign shore once more in life, these things Stella wished for.

≈ ✶ ≈

One weekend, Michael called down from the attic. "It's a mess up here. Help me clean up?" Stella climbed the wooden ladder that led to the upper floor. It was cold. She stepped on a little ball of fur and twine and dry leaves—remnants of a mouse's strange bed. It crunched lightly under her foot. There were upended boxes every-where. Most of them contained baby clothes. "Your mother kept all your things," Michael said.

Stella picked through mostly pink piles. Some of the shirts had orange baby food stains on them. Others were pristine still. Piles of tiny socks pushed out of the way revealed more, toddler-sized ones. There were school uniforms mixed in with broken toys, both expen-sive dolls that Stella had outgrown and twenty-five-cent junk that always broke in Stella's hands. Every item Stella had ever thrown out had ended up here, in the attic.

There were a few stiff dresses with painted skirts, images of car-toon characters drawn onto the fabric with a steady, artful hand. Here, a dress with Pebbles in a sandbox, her hair tied up around a small bone. There, another dress with a fat Winnie-the-Pooh licking honey off a paw. Stella's mother had painted a squiggly *S.M.* right at the hemline of each dress. The tail of the S looped out and swung back to underline both letters. Stella practiced the figure in the air a few times, seeing the letters float for a moment before they vanished, the way sparklers leave a residue of light behind them.

"I'm looking for my old Steelers jersey. Signed by Jack Lambert. I'm wearing it to the game tomorrow," Michael said, frustrated now, tossing handfuls of clothes in the air.

Stella caught a whiff of violets. It came after her father rustled a box to his left. Anita's smell. Lavender colored water in a slender bottle with the tiniest of lids. Stella remembered how her mother tipped the bottle, pouring the perfume into her cupped hand, how the purple liquid puddled on her palm, dime-sized, and how she splashed the nape of her neck with it, rubbing her skin, then drying the excess on her clothes. It was the last, lingering element of Anita's life, a scent so powerful upon her body that when the coffin was closed, a puff of violet-traced air came to Stella's nose. Her eyes watered with it now, and Stella began to dig through the box her father had moved. Her hand landed on a bit of stiff fabric and the smell grew stronger.

"Can I have it?" Stella asked, holding up a denim jacket with a sunset painted on the back. On one of the pockets, in yellow paint, were the letters S and M.

Michael looked up, opened his mouth to say something, but nodded instead.

"Thank you, Daddy! It's Mommy's. It smells like her," Stella said, and put on the jacket. "And it has my initials on it." The hem almost touched her knees, and she had to roll up the sleeves three times in order to get them at her wrist.

They left the attic a few minutes later, Michael's Steelers jersey in his hands, the denim jacket on Stella's body. "She wore that thing the whole time we were in Miami. Painted it herself," Michael said. "Looks good on you, Stel," he added.

Stella wore the jacket day in and out, even when she slept. And in all that time, she didn't feel the urge to cry, not even once, didn't wake up at night scared of strangers lurking in the house, never once heard the bats that had made nests in the walls. Testing herself, she tried to recall the details of the morning her mother died, and found, happily, that she could no longer remember whether Anita's legs were shaved that day. She had known the answer to that once, and now the fact was gone. Hoping that other elements of that foul memory would fade, she wore the jacket as a kind of talisman. Stella knew about things like talismans as Anita had always kept a black stone called an *azabache* on a chain around her neck to ward off danger, and it must have worked, as the only danger that ever touched her was her own doing. The *azabache* now hung around Stella's neck, and it bounced against her chest whenever she walked, knock-knocking to the beat of her steps. Later that evening, when a bee stung the palm of her hand but didn't leave a stinger behind, Stella turned the collar up on the jacket, feeling warm and happy. The bee would live to see another day, and Stella's hand did not swell much at all.

That the jacket was a lucky charm was in no doubt. The faded denim wrapped around her had proven its worth, and Stella was certain that she would never have another unhappy thought again.

≈ ✶ ≈

Stella, like Anita in the past, often latched on to new interests with an intensity that made the world around her go blurry, so that she would stick her nose in a book at noon and look up to find that the sun had set and her stomach was rumbling. Dr. Row called it a sign of her giftedness. Once, she spent a full five months researching ancient Greek pottery. Having convinced Michael to buy her some clay, she had molded a few vases that summer before discovering that she could no more shape a handle or the lip of a vase than she could speak Greek. Stella moved from obsession to obsession, from

Polynesian music to puppet-making to astronomical instruments all
in one summer. Coming home one weekend, she carried two book-
bags full to bursting with the sorts of books Anita had kept from her,
the ones about the revolution in Cuba, the Caribbean, Latino history,
exile politics, and the Mariel boatlift.

Anita had mostly poetry and fiction in the house. The only books
on Cuba were coffee-table picture books, nothing more. On occasion,
she'd bring home reading matter on the Cold War, or a Russian play
here and there, and always, the books would be half-read with Anita
hunched over the tomes and sobbing into the pages. Those books
never lasted long in the house. She gave them away or left them on
bus benches outside, as if they were cursed objects. "They keep track
of these things. Who has them and whatnot," she'd say to Stella and
briskly walk away from the book, the pages often fluttering goodbye.
Even so, Stella thought that some of the events of the years following
Anita's death would have made her quite happy. On television Stella
had watched the young man in China with the small back and thin
shirt that clung to his shoulder blades face down a tank, and had
made popcorn with her father the day the Berlin Wall was taken
down like a gingerbread house. Michael had sighed, said, "Your
mother missed it," in one of the rare moments in which she was
mentioned.

Anita had been a great follower of signs, insisting they be paid
heed, however they arrived. Now, Stella was studying twentieth-
century Latin America in her social studies class, and taking the
reappearance of her mother's jacket as a sign, she began to immerse
herself in research on Cuba. She amassed a collection of history
books and began leaving them in odd places around the house, the
books roosting in the same upholstered nests where Anita's books
had been. Stella learned about the conquistadores, their gold fever,
the delight with which they disemboweled the Taínos, skewering them
with swords like so much pig's meat. She dog-eared the pages on the

Spanish-American War, the ones with the concentration camp pictures from Cuba, of skeletal infants dressed up in baptismal gowns and piles of rib cages, knee knobs, and elbows. On the picture of the Spanish general "Butcher" Weyler, Stella drew horns and sketched the ghosts of dead babies circling his head. It was the first time Stella had ever desecrated a book, and the act filled her with such glee that she made sure to make subversive little marks in every book she got her hands on afterward. Revolutionaries, bearded and otherwise, revealed themselves to her in those books, Trujillo in the Dominican Republic, Papa Doc and Baby Doc in Haiti, Batista and Castro in Cuba, leaning left, right, bloody, thirsty, vain. It was, Stella thought on several occasions, a bit too much. Though she fancied herself an intelligent girl, the variety of opinions on the topic of the Caribbean and Her grisly governments left Stella dizzy. She understood, at last, her mother's distaste for the books. They weighed on her so much that when she realized that the serious young man in the poster in Señora Caballero's room was Che Guevara, alternately known as a hero in one book, a murderous thug in another, Stella lost concentration, unable to make a decision about him, and failed her test on preterits with irregular meanings.

Stella's faith in books wavered as she learned that books were imperfect objects, attempts at answering the unanswerable, all of them coming to different conclusions. Perhaps that is why her mother kept so many books, to balance out the wrong and the right. Pondering all of this during the Spanish exam, she ignored Señora Caballero's perfect handwriting on the page urging students to complete "*Yo* _____ *una carta de amor*" with the right verb, and so failed her first exam.

Later that week, the graded test trembling in her hands, Stella bawled against her father's shoulder. "I bombed tests all the time," Michael tried to console her, but Stella only cried more.

Dr. Row had said that Stella exhibited "perfectionist tendencies," and Stella echoed it now, saying, "I'm a perfectionist," between sobs.

"None of that mumbo jumbo," Michael said. In the end, Stella stopped crying only after Michael, who had been encouraging Stella's interest in her heritage the last few weeks, suggested they go to Miami for Christmas vacation. "It'll be a nice break from this crummy slush everywhere. And we can celebrate your birthday on the beach. Palm trees at Christmas!" he said and tickled her ribs. Stella wiped her nose on his shirtsleeve, laughing as she did so.

Encouraged, Stella convinced her father to take her to the Carnegie Library the Monday after her classes finished. She'd been reading books about Mariel, and in them were glossy pictures of the refugees, and in tiny print underneath each, the words "from United States Coast Guard files." Stella did not tire of them, though the photos were echoes of one another—always the crowds of people on their feet aboard ships, arms up in thanks, in greeting, in prayer. There were never enough pictures for Stella. With Michael's help, she found copies of the Coast Guard archives from the spring of 1980 at the Carnegie. She didn't read them at first but, rather, made photocopies and shoved the papers into her backpack.

"Finished?" he asked, and Stella nodded solemnly, clutching her backback to her chest. The papers inside made a crumpling sound. "How about we go next door for a while?" Michael suggested, leading Stella to the Carnegie's natural history museum. "They've got some stuffed birds in there your mom always liked. Cuban birds. You'll see," he said as they walked past a bronze statue of a seated woman, naked, her knees drawn up, her forehead resting on them. Stella thought of Anita, who she'd seen sitting just that way in bed, more than once. Inside, Stella lingered in the shadow of a dinosaur for a while, reaching up to touch the tips of his claws when the guard wasn't looking.

Michael, who had been scrutinizing a map of the museum, lifted Stella off her feet and adjusted her on his shoulders. The height was such that Stella felt dizzy, and she kept her eyes trained on the shad-

ow she and her father made on the marble walls and floor. The outline of their shadow was soft, as if it were done in charcoals. Michael
put Stella down before a glass case. The sign above it read *Flora and
Fauna of the Isle of Pines*, and inside the display were crisscrossed
branches of small-leafed trees, and perched on one, a woodpecker-
like bird, red-chested and red-eyed, the rest of its body painted in
blue and white. The feathers glistened under the lights, shifting
colors like fish scales do, and Stella moved her head.

"To-toco-tocoro…" Michael stuttered, trying to pronounce the
name of the bird.

"Tocorroro," Stella said, her *r*'s rolling with ease. She put a hand
on her father's forearm.

"Anita's favorite," Michael said.

"I guess."

Stella remembered her mother here, recalled how she shook her
head at the sight of Cuba's iconic bird, dipped in the colors of the
flag. "Migratory," Anita had said, "like all of us."

"What do you mean?" Stella had asked, but Anita did not answer
her. Looking at the small bird now, Stella couldn't help but dislike its
stillness, the dullness of its eyes, how the feathers of its wings didn't
fold over one another comfortably in the way of live birds, but jutted
out in subtle, unnatural angles, the individual barbs of the feathers
oily, separated, the milky, hollow shafts at the base of them visible.

Michael and Stella stood there for a long time, both of them lost
in thought. At last Michael asked, "Does this help? For your Cuban
research?" and Stella saw eagerness in his eyes.

"Yep."

"Good," Michael said, then suggested they see the habitat dioramas
on the upper floors. Stella made a face and shook her head.

"Fine," Michael said, glancing at his watch. "We'll meet back at the
T-Rex in fifteen minutes, got it?"

"Got it," Stella said, bounding away, glad that her father was the sort to let her do things on her own.

Stella sought the polar exhibit deep in the marble-halled museum. This room was always Michael's favorite, with its life-sized igloo in the center of the space. Stepping into the enclosure, bathed in bluish light, Stella sought a space in the corner. She was facing the Inuit family within, who looked at one another with their glassy eyes, handling a fair bit of furry skin.

"Would you like to learn about the Mariel exodus of 1980?" she asked them, and chuckled a bit. The museum was empty, so there was no chance she was humiliating herself by speaking to dummies dressed in fur. It was something her mother often did when at the museum. Anita routinely spoke to the mannequins, these waxy imitations of people in traditional robes, their faces frozen in near smiles. Once, Anita had shouted at the figure of an Andean Indian, poised above the heads of museumgoers, shown in the moment of walking across a wooden plank. "Be careful up there!" Anita shouted when they went through the exhibit, startling visitors and bringing a guard over to reprimand her.

"You've got to have fun sometimes," she would say to Stella. The warmth of the memory passed too quickly from within the confines of the igloo, so Stella left it and walked a bit until she found the Hall of Ancient Egypt. It was the exhibit in which her mother had always lingered longest. Toward the back, encased and yet visible, like Snow White in her glass coffin, was the mummy of someone small and unidentified. The wrappings had browned and thinned, suggesting the shape of the bones underneath. Stella did not visit with the mummy the way Anita had, always leaning over the case and whispering to the dusty body, her breath fogging the glass. Instead, Stella found the small, square doorway that led to a re-created tomb one could reach only by crawling through a tunnel. It was colorful with hieroglyphics, and there was a replicated sarcophagus in the center. In the dim light, Stella spread the photocopies atop the ornate coffin and tried to read them. But it was no use. She couldn't concentrate in this place, so full of her mother.

Touching the colorful walls as if she could read them, Stella recalled her mother's descriptions of Egyptian funeral rites. How in the afterlife, a person's heart was weighed against a feather. If the life had been a good one, then the scales balanced, heart and plume alike, and so the person moved on to paradise. Stella wondered whether her mother's heart weighed the same as a feather. Stella tightened the denim jacket around her body at the thought. Gathering her papers, she took one last look at the mock tomb then crawled out.

"Anything interesting?" Michael asked her a few minutes later from underneath the dinosaur.

"Just the Egyptian tomb. That's always cool," Stella said. Michael raised his arms like a mummy in an old movie, growled deep in his throat, and chased his daughter out of the museum.

≈ ✶ ≈

Stella managed to get through all of the Coast Guard documents in her bedroom that night with the jacket rolled up behind her head as a pillow. She liked the pictures best. Each photograph of a crowded ship took a long time to analyze. Stella moved a magnifying glass over each face, hovering over the babies for a beat longer than the other faces. One ship carried thirty-five infants, and the accompanying headline said that one of them, a boy named Ernesto de la Cova, was born onboard, in the shade of a shrimp net. She lingered over a photo of a Coast Guard officer giving mouth-to-mouth resuscitation to an old man who had suffered a heart attack upon arriving in Key West. The description did not say whether the man survived. Stella searched for any information on the number of baby girls who'd arrived in Mariel, but all accounts agreed that any specific number of anything was too hard to peg. American officials rounded the number of refugees up to one hundred and twenty-five thousand, and left it at that.

One in over a hundred thousand, she thought as she put her research away. That night in bed, she curled into the smallest shape she could, her knees to her nose, and imagined herself on a great, dusty scale, light as a feather.

MAGDA ELENA DEL POZO

MANTUA AND HAVANA, CUBA 1958–1979

Magda Elena Camposanto met Angel del Pozo at a pet shop in Mantua, Cuba. The store was small, no bigger than her bedroom. Crammed in every conceivable space was a cage, and in the cages assorted birds and rabbits, and even a baby java in diapers that howled at Magda Elena all day long, his eyes yolky and sad, his fingers long and thin like a starved child's. Magda Elena had come to work in the store after her grandmother passed away. She was seventeen and enjoyed the job, especially the nursing of just-hatched canaries, feeding them scrambled eggs so that their feathers would come in brightly yellow and so that their voices would soar. She also helped tame the small parakeets, a trick she learned as a child on a visit to El Cotorro with her grandmother to see an aging aunt.

Angel, who'd gone to the countryside to visit a cousin, had wandered in to escape the sun and found Magda Elena with her arm deep in a cage full of parakeets, hanging the small swing the birds had knocked down. "*Coño*," she cursed as she tried to loop the tiny hook around a wire. Meanwhile a parakeet had perched on her forearm and was pecking at her copper bracelets.

Magda Elena had not noticed Angel watching her, and she jumped when she saw his face hovering over the cage, round and moon-like. He adjusted the hook with deft, fat fingers.

"How is it that they don't bite you?" he asked, and Magda Elena loved his voice. Not too deep, not feminine either. He sounded like a man who could sing.

"You break them."

"Like a horse?"

Magda Elena snatched a small turquoise bird off the floor of the cage. It eyed her furiously, black *azabache* eyes latched onto hers, but it did not move to bite. "You choose one with pink feet, skin raw like a burn. That color, you know. At first, it will bite you. It wants to draw blood, wants you to let go. But you've got to be *bien hombre* about it. Don't let the *periquito* know it hurt you. Then, you wrap it in a dish towel."

Angel's eyes widened. He opened the cage and tried to catch one of the parakeets, but it ducked out from under his fingers. Soon, the birds were bouncing off his knuckles, escaping his clutches. All the while, Magda Elena stroked the tiny parakeet's head, and its eyes closed in pleasure.

"Not like that," she said, and Angel withdrew his hand. "Once you've wrapped up the bird so that its little head is uncovered, you'll feel the most amazing thing. Right there, in the palm of your hand, you'll feel the flutter of a heart, a pulse so fast and so soft you cannot tell if it's the beat of your own blood, hidden deep in you." Magda Elena stopped. She'd only ever spoken this way with her grandmother, sharing the odd little things she thought about, but now that the old woman had died, Magda Elena had spent several months in virtual silence, speaking only in meaningless pleasantries. Angel seemed to draw her out, and Magda Elena regained her old voice. She cleared her throat. "It will fight you, the towel, will nip at the loops of cloth, and its pearly beak will sometimes get stuck and it will twist to undo the trap. But you can't let go, even though your own heart is beating pity."

"It sounds cruel," Angel said.

"It is," Magda Elena answered, and released the bird. It flew out of her hands and perched on her shoulder. "You've broken it when the bird is drenched in its own sweat (*sí, sí*, birds sweat, *chico*), when it sits very still in the towel, in your hands. And it will eye you with a thing close to love." Magda Elena said this last in a whisper, and did not look up at Angel again, not even when he purchased the turquoise *periquito* on her shoulder, along with a small, golden cage and some flax seed.

Magda Elena knew that if her eyes met Angel's, he would have seen that they had lost that wild, empty look she'd been wearing when he first walked in, the one she'd adopted in the days following her mother's death in the center of El Santo Rosario church while waiting in line for Communion. Magda Elena remembered pieces of that day, of standing on a wooden pew to see above the heads of the people viewing the commotion. But she remembered no body, no funeral. It was as if her mother had simply ceased to be, not only in body, but in memory. Her mother had left her on the pew with a pat on her small knee, hands folded in prayer. Magda Elena's brother, Eddy, had been there, too, but being older, he remembered more of that day, having pushed his way through the crowds to find their mother, unconscious in the aisle, her hands clutched to her chest. As for the rest of her family, Magda Elena's father had moved to Santo Domingo after she was born, and her grandmother, a tiny, freckled woman with crippling arthritis and a voice like a horn, banned her grandchildren from attending church after her daughter's death, having blamed the heart attack on the shock of seeing the image of Christ crucified above the altar. But she was gone, too, dead in her sleep, an enviable death. Eddy had taken a job in Jibacóa, fishing red snapper. Magda Elena was left behind to fend for herself, an empty shell rolling in the surge, floundering like a scared gull in the open sea.

If Magda Elena allowed Angel to meet her eyes just then, he would see in them a willingness to forget sky, tree, nest, and home, to forsake it all for a perch on his finger.

He visited every day that week and purchased three canaries, a pair of finches, and finally, two lovebirds. So it was that their first home together was more aviary than human abode. The lovebirds cooed to one another all day, picking small bugs out of each other's feathers.

The finches hopped around in their cage, rattling their perches, and the canaries, separated into three cages, with towels hung between them so that they would not see one another, sang long trills and operatic cheeps, calling to one another morning and night.

The birds lived with them, along with Angel's parents, Gregorio and Nieve, in an apartment in Old Havana. Gregorio had picked the place out for its ancient grandeur, belied by the creaking floors and peeling paint. In any case, Magda Elena thought it a step up compared to her life in Pinar del Río's countryside. At night, she and Angel wandered around Habana Vieja, walking along the path of the original city walls and imagining the thunder of cannons in the distance, and the clash of bayonets, and all of the sounds that must have haunted the area in the old days. Vociferous in bed at night, Angel pretended he was a French corsair, and Magda Elena was his captured bride. Then, Nieve would pound on the walls or suddenly feel the urge to make coffee, waking the birds that sang in the dark.

The birds were with them until the following year, when, on a bright January day in 1959, Nieve celebrated the triumph of the revolution by releasing all of the birds as Fidel Castro and his followers paraded past their building. The canaries, unsure of themselves, clung to the balconies, and the lovebirds disappeared into the blue sky, one trailing the other. It was the finches that sensed Nieve's desires and flew down to the passing rebels and flittered among them.

Magda Elena watched the birds go with sadness, as did Angel and Gregorio, but no one moved to stop Nieve from celebrating. Her enthusiasm was catching, as was the hope that rose from the streets that things would be better, that the bloodshed was over. It grew with the sound of the *cornetas* below, bugles mingling with birdcall, human song, and celebratory gunshots. That night, the four of them opened a bottle of champagne Gregorio had been saving for decades, one he'd bought with the paycheck from his first job at the theater, when he still harbored hopes of playing in the pit. As they toasted, a little wren stood watch on the balcony, its voice bubbly and airy. Nieve indicated the bird with her glass and said, "You see, you can still have your birds!"

Magda Elena's grandmother would have said something about birds alighting on windowsills being symbols of infertility and death, and Magda Elena could almost hear her grandmother's complaints. She tried not to think about this moment in the childless years that followed, and found that she, like her mother-in-law, Nieve, was comfortable with a revolution that left no room for blessings or curses, for hauntings or omens.

"A baby will come when the time is right," Nieve would say on occasion, and Magda Elena would try to smile. She often thought of her grandmother, who would have found reasons for her barrenness in scissors left open on a desk, in long walks under a full moon, in evil eyes and curses. The doctors she visited had no reasons at all, but Magda Elena herself suspected the rationed food and the lack of milk to drink.

When Magda Elena finally became pregnant seventeen years after her wedding to Angel, she was plagued by fanciful dreams. In one nightmare, she imagined that she was pregnant with the *yanqui* President Ford's baby, and that she had been thrown into prison for sleeping with an imperialist. She shared her dream over morning *cafecitos*, and her mother-in-law laughed so hard that she dropped her coffee-dunked bread into her lap. In another dream, she found herself in the Plaza de la Revolución during one of *el comandante*'s long speeches, and she could see, through a tear in his camouflaged pants, a glimpse of dark, flaccid skin, but no one was laughing or pointing at him. This dream Magda Elena kept to herself. Decidedly, her imagination had taken a turn both political and ludicrous.

≈ ⋆ ≈

Daysy María del Pozo was born scrawny but healthy. She did not learn to sleep through the night until her second birthday, and as a result, both Magda Elena and Angel moved more slowly than before, crashed into their beds by eight each night, and rarely woke Nieve with their lovemaking anymore. Daysy's birth had softened Nieve's revolutionary zeal only a bit, and the woman spent much of the day cuddling the girl, combing her hair into Shirley Temple–like ringlets, and teaching her songs. Daysy's first word was "No!" shouted repeatedly at such a volume that a neighbor knocked on the door in alarm, imagining that someone was being attacked. Daysy's "no" had come after Magda Elena offered her a slice of guava and cream cheese. The child rejected food often, and Magda Elena thought she was contrary by nature. "No!" she'd shout when presented with a new dress. "No!" again when asked to give her grandfather a kiss. And the shaking of her head (and the subsequent tossing of ringlets) was so violent that it seemed Daysy would hurt herself saying no. The child was such a handful that when Magda Elena learned she was pregnant again, she shut herself inside a closet and cried for an hour, while Daysy tried kicking the door open, yelling "Mami! No!" over and over again.

≈ ✶ ≈

A doctor's appointment months later brought bad news. Magda Elena was sent home from the hospital with a pamphlet about miscarriages and a curt *buena suerte* from the nurses, who eyed her as a lost cause. The cramping, the doctor had said, was not a good sign, nor was the bleeding that still plagued Magda Elena, even though it had slowed now to a sticky trickle. When Magda Elena assured the doctor she could feel the baby moving, he'd eyed her with such pity that Magda Elena felt a surge of anger, similar to the way she felt under Nieve's gaze the night before when they'd argued over naming the baby Damiana, after the saint born on the day she was conceived

(which Nieve thought was a terrible idea), or Yarlenys, one of the
Russian sounding names suddenly fashionable in Cuba.

It was October, and there was a chill to the sea breeze that forced
the sweaters to come out from hiding. They were usually hideous,
dated things, worn only once or twice a year and in very good condition, like preserved relics. Magda Elena, on the other hand, already
swollen and miserable, felt only heat emanating from her stomach to
her breasts, her arms, and flaring up in her face so that her cheeks
were always red and she had no need for old sweaters.

On her way home from the doctor, Magda Elena ran into her
neighbor, Solamaris, who had just given birth to a boy and had
named him Leo after a Russian writer who wrote long, gloomy, brilliant books. Magda Elena knew this because Solamaris, who would
have gone to the university if her father hadn't forbidden it, told
everyone. Solamaris claimed to have taught herself English and
Russian. It was said in the neighborhood that Solamaris would end
up in prison for having too big a brain and too big a mouth.

Leo's father was unknown to the neighbors, and Solamaris refused
to identify him. "That's between him and God now," she'd say when
asked, though her eyes would water prettily when she said it. There
were silvery scars on the white flesh of her wrists, which appeared
around the time Solamaris' pregnancy became obvious. The thin
sickle-shaped scars frightened those who noticed them, and so no
one pushed her to answer the question regarding the baby's father.
The girl's reputation as a slutty know-it-all with dissident tendencies
flourished among the neighbors. Solamaris often walked outside
with Leo in her arms, singing love songs, as if she weren't a disgraced
woman, as if the neighbors weren't all calling her *un desastre*, a curse
on her family, and a *loca pal carajo* to boot. They whispered that if
she were their daughter, they'd beat her with a stick until she learned
to keep her knees together. But Magda Elena admired the slender
brown beauty with eyes that turned up at the corners and hands

forever in motion—despite her recklessness, despite her oddness. In face and body, she reflected neither the sharp features of those descended from Spaniards nor the roundness of those whose roots ran under countless miles to Africa, but rather, Solamaris cut a figure ripped from an old schoolbook, of Cuba's Siboneyes or Taínos, of a people whose line had been extinguished long ago. It was true— sometimes, the things Solamaris said and did made no sense. Once, she bleached her hair and teased it into a fifties-style beehive, wearing it that way for a week before it started looking nest-like. On cool spring mornings, Solamaris could be found outside, conducting birds in their song, her hands twitching along with the chirps and trills of the noisy *sinsontes*. It was almost as if she were a bird herself, a mockingbird in the guise of a Cuban girl, learning the ropes of humanity before soaring off into the sky again to teach its species about people. At least that's how Magda Elena thought of her.

Another time, Magda Elena had accompanied Solamaris in line at the butcher's for the monthly ration. A gossipy neighbor behind them struck up a whispered conversation with another woman about Solamaris' missing lover. Solamaris turned around, stuck out her hand as if offering a handshake, and said, "When you speak to destroy me, please refer to me as *la señorita Karenin*." Magda Elena had been stupefied by Solamaris' statement, as had the women behind them in line. Perhaps Solamaris had meant to say *carita*, or little face, though that made no sense either, Magda Elena thought. Regardless of the confusion, the women were silent during the wait for the pound of beef they were owed each month.

Magda Elena loved, too, the beautiful boy with the Russian writer's name and the way his own little hands moved like a starfish, slow and graceful. Solamaris was nursing Leo on the steps to her building, out in daylight without even a blanket. Magda Elena averted her eyes, and cringed when she heard Solamaris call her name. "*Ven acá*," she called and pulled Leo away from her chest, dabbing the watery milk on his chin with her sleeve. Magda Elena opened the aluminum gate and stepped into a courtyard where tall papayas grew along the fence, tied off with old bits of twine. Up against the wall, tomatos were still growing, and over the back fence, Magda Elena could see the tips of a very tall lime tree. Yams grew in a scraggly patch in one corner, and onions in another. Solamaris had planted all but the tree, despite the laws that forbade such things. What was worse, she sometimes sold some of the small viands to neighbors when rations in the stores were low.

Magda Elena looked longingly at Leo. Despite her earlier misgivings, she wanted the baby within her now so much her throat constricted and her eyes filled with tears. Her grandmother's ancient warnings came back to her often, judging her for wishing the pregnancy away early on. "You've cursed yourself, and that is the worst kind of curse," her grandmother would have said, and Magda Elena believed it. The practicality of the revolution was giving way to the spirituality of her old life in the countryside. Though her dreams were not unusual with this pregnancy, suddenly Magda Elena saw signs everywhere—in the shape of clouds, at the bottom of her coffee cup, in strange looks Daysy often gave her, in the meowing of a feral cat outside her window. Signs, messages, symbols. She'd grown up with them, and now they were returning to her in force, fueled by the fear of losing the baby, by boredom, by empty markets and a ration system that left everyone just a little hungry and prone to hallucination at the end of the day.

"How are you feeling, *mi amiga*?" Solamaris asked, and brushed her hand against Magda Elena's bulging stomach.

"*Bien, bien*," she said, blinking hard and staring past the papaya, past the fence, and down the street where a lone dog was picking through someone's garbage.

Solamaris cradled Leo and whispered, "You can tell me. *Anda.* What's the trouble?"

But Magda Elena could not repeat what the doctors feared, thinking that perhaps saying the words herself would give them credence, would bring them like poltergeists to haunt her neighborhood, her home, her heart. Magda Elena laughed a high, false laugh, and said, "*Ay, mi'ja*, it's just that Angel and I fought over the baby's name last night. And you know, we never fight." Magda Elena blinked again a few times, the tears stinging her eyes.

"You know what they say about unhappy families," Solamaris said.

"No, I don't."

"Ah, well," Solamaris said, holding out Leo for Magda Elena to cradle. She rubbed her cheek against his downy head. The baby slept on, snoring softly against Magda's neck. Solamaris said, "Well, here's my advice then, whether you want to hear it or not. One of my favorite writers once wrote that 'not everything has a name. Some things lead us into a realm beyond words.' Isn't that something? Babies are like that, don't you think? 'A realm beyond words.' "

Magda Elena smiled at Solamaris, who often quoted writers and politicians, though no one ever seemed to understand what she meant. "What's in a name? That's what Shakespeare wrote. Look at my name. Solamaris. Horrible. It means Alone at Sea. And look at me now. Feet stuck firmly on earth, on an island at sea, yes, but alone?" she paused, and patted her son's head. "Alone? *Nunca*."

"Good advice," Magda Elena said, and returned Leo to his mother. Magda Elena kissed Solamaris' cheek and began to turn toward her home.

"*¡Oye!*" Solamaris called when Magda Elena had taken a few steps. "If there's more to your trouble than that, say a little prayer, and if that doesn't work, here," Solamaris drew a small paperback from her back pocket and tossed it at Magda Elena. She caught it by its cover, which tore a little.

"*Ay, perdón*," she said

"*No hay problema*. It's what's inside that counts." Magda Elena watched as Solamaris unbuttoned her shirt once again, repositioning Leo against her bare chest, her breasts full, the skin shiny against Leo's doughy cheek. Up and down the street Magda Elena looked, making sure that no one had seen her friend expose herself. The book, *Martin Luther King Jr. Habla*, was ragged, and several of the pages were folded over. "Read those speeches, mama. You'll see, no one can control you, not really," Solamaris said without whispering. "Not even your husband," she added and smiled up at Magda Elena.

"How did you get this?" Magda Elena asked as she flipped through the book.

"I have plenty. Once you're done with that, I've got some Solzhenitsyn you might learn from."

"*¿Solse-quien?*" Magda Elena asked, the paperback now hidden in her pocket.

Solamaris laughed. "You'll see. It's my own little library. Feel free to come over and borrow whatever you'd like." Magda Elena came toward Solamaris, kissed her cheek, and then made the Sign of the Cross on Leo's head, something her grandmother had always done to her, and which Magda Elena had never done for Daysy. She didn't know why she did it just then, except for the sudden feeling that Leo needed all the blessings he could get with a mother like Solamaris who seemed so intent on landing herself in prison or in a grave.

Later that same night, after reading a letter in Solamaris' book about unjust laws, Magda Elena decided to put together a Christmas tree. It wasn't easy in her condition. She was seven months along and had become clumsy, bumping into furniture and people at the market. And now, she fumbled with the box of Christmas ornaments that had not seen the daylight in nearly twenty years.

Magda Elena remembered the last sanctioned Christmas on the island, how it coincided with her twenty-sixth birthday, and how Angel had bought a pig on the black market and roasted it behind their building. He'd invited his friends from school, and Magda Elena danced a slow waltz with her father-in-law, who knew the proper way to waltz and who sang along with the music in a confident, melodic voice, right in her ear. She wore one of her mother's old dresses, sized to fit and cut shorter to match the current fashion. While she waltzed, one of Angel's friends, drunk on cheap rum, took the silver garlands off the Christmas tree and draped them over Magda Elena's shoulders. That was in 1968. In a year's time, Christmas would be banned, it having been decided in Havana that the celebrations interfered with sugar production and that the veneration of an infant diminished revolutionary zeal. So, the box of Christmas decorations was hidden in the crawl space in the ceiling.

Magda Elena balanced the musty box on her shoulder as she stepped gingerly down from the attic, onto a kitchen chair. She breathed slowly, waiting for the cramping in her stomach to pass. "Take it easy," she reminded herself, and sat down a while. Her daughter, Daysy, was busy in her bedroom, humming a disjointed tune, and Magda Elena found the odd melody soothing. She stared at the box, its lid stained with water, and wondered at the condition of the pieces inside. When she finally opened it, she found that some of the plaster ornaments had melted into hideous blobs, and the tinsel garland that once was draped around her shoulders like a princess' mantle had disintegrated. The box smelled like burnt plastic. But the glass ornaments were preserved, as was the crystal crèche she'd inherited from her grandmother.

Magda Elena balanced the baby Jesús in her hand, then put the glass figure into the glass *pesebre*, completing the picture. She set up the aluminum Christmas tree, another relic from a bygone era, in the corner of their house, away from windows and neighbors who might inform the Party that a Christmas tree had just gone up in the del Pozo home. And just as she had done as a child before her mother died, Magda Elena sat on the floor to arrange the little holy family, thinking of her baby.

That evening, when her mother-in-law, Nieve, arrived from her visit with her sisters in Matanzas, she found Magda Elena still sitting on the floor, admiring the nativity scene with Daysy on her lap. She listened in as Magda Elena pointed the figurines out to her little daughter, who repeated the names in a tone as crystalline as the tiny statues. "*Mira, mi'jita*, this is *la Virgen María. Que linda. Y aquí, Papá José, los Reyes Magos,* and most importantly, *mi amorcito, el niño Jesús.*"

"Trivial and irrelevant," Nieve said, standing behind Magda Elena, who palmed the glass infant in her hand, imagining that her own baby was once just about this size. "Irrelevant," Nieve repeated, and Magda Elena felt the warmth of Daysy's small legs on her own, and a tightening of her muscles. She felt trapped in that moment, too tightly wound and sure to yell at Nieve if she didn't get away. She knew, too, that no matter how anyone argued, the baby would be named Belén, after the city of Bethlehem.

The name came to her from the archives of memory. As a child, Magda Elena had named her dolls Belén, had wrapped old shawls about her head like the Virgin Mary, and had cradled her babies tenderly, inspired by the elaborate nativities of her youth. Her grandmother, Margarita, would build a papier-mâché mountain each year, a fragile, hollow Jerusalem on whose base she would settle the crystal crèche. The building of it started in November, and it was usually February when the scene came down, the mountain peak dusty now, the paper valley nibbled by mice. While she constructed the delicate landscape, Margarita would sing, "*Pastores á Belén,*" a child's carol about shepherds who trek to Bethlehem to see the new king.

"I love it," her husband, Angel, announced when he arrived home, and planted two quick kisses on Magda Elena's neck. From her place in the corner of the living room, Nieve coughed loudly, then bid Daysy alone good night. Later, in the dark of their bedroom, Angel trailed a warm finger from Magda Elena's chin, down between her breasts, and further still, murmuring, "Belén. It's perfect." She could have predicted his reaction to her choice. Shortly after they'd gotten married, Angel's high school alma mater lost its name to the revolution, after the government took possession of all private and religious schools. What was once called Belén School, run by Jesuit brothers in Havana, became the Technical and Military Institute. Magda Elena and Angel had hurried down to the campus to watch the dismantling of the old signs. On that day, late in the currant-skied afternoon, seven dark, quiet men, helped the Jesuit brothers load their things into automobiles lined in front of the school. An eighth man, slight and covered with splotches of paint on his arms and his pants, brought out a brush from his pocket and changed the name of the school forever. The next day, Magda Elena and Angel snuck into the school through a gap in the gate and noted the places where the crucifixes had been removed, the cross-shaped paint clean and white underneath, like ghosts haunting every doorway. "How could he?" Angel had asked then. "It was his school, too," and Magda Elena knew that Angel meant Fidel, one of Belén School's own. She could only shrug her shoulders. Who knew what the answer was to anything anymore.

Nieve had pleaded in the morning, "Why Belén? Why something so obvious? You want it so that the baby can't ever join the Young Pioneers?" But Magda Elena had made up her mind, about the name and about other things. The future was frightening and at once liberating, and she was glad to have her perfectly named daughters with her.

≈ ✳ ≈

Magda Elena had been told that the baby in her belly was dying, but she swallowed back her grief long enough to prepare a New Year's Day dinner to which she'd invite Solamaris. Though women surrounded her at her place of employment, Solamaris was her only friend. Two days a week, Magda Elena worked at a preschool in Havana called The Little Proletariots, helping the three year-olds' class in the afternoons, waking the slumbering bodies from their blankets on the floor, helping them peel sweaty strands of hair from their faces, rocking a few, changing wet uniforms of those who had not yet learned how to use the toilet. The pay was negligible, but so was all pay in Cuba. Even doctors earned little, but those with relatives in Miami and a steady influx of American dollars were the lucky ones.

On Tuesdays and Thursdays, Magda Elena would come to The Little Proletariots, Daysy on her hip. She'd watch as her daughter navigated the world among other toddlers. Daysy was shy, and she'd cling to Magda Elena's legs, nearly toppling her as she tried to walk. How could it be, Magda Elena wondered, that her daughter was so loud, so full and spirited in the confines of their apartment, and only a shadow of herself among other children? The truth was, Magda Elena was the same way. While the teachers at the school had invited her to their homes, to modest birthday parties or walks along the seawall, Magda Elena had always declined. She wasn't herself among them, unsure always of which woman reported to neighborhood watch committees, afraid to complain about the food rations, or hesitant about how to comment on the exiles visiting from Miami, who had begun to flood the country since January, after restrictions were lifted. Magda Elena had seen them on the street with their families, happy, reunited for the moment, jewels at their ears and around their necks, cameras in their hands. She'd longed for some connection in Florida, for someone to arrive bearing gifts for her, too, like Santi Clo at Christmas.

So, Magda Elena counted Solamaris as her only friend, a person with whom she could speak her mind without fear. Solamaris was a strange and out of place woman, and so Magda Elena mothered her a bit. When she invited her to dinner, Solamaris had thrown her arms around Magda Elena, had said, "*Ay, gracias,*" with a voice touched with emotion, as if no one had ever thought to share a meal with her before. Tears had come to Magda Elena's eyes then. She went about making the dinner with great care, cooking two small and expensive black-market hens and glazing them with an orange sauce.

"What a waste," Nieve had said behind her, clucking her tongue.

Magda Elena turned a hen over and rubbed its belly. "We're having guests over," she said.

Using the hem of her shirt, Nieve began to wipe forks and knives clean of spots. She was a large woman, her ankles as thick as a man's. She was freckled all over, and her hair, mostly white, grew in blond patches here and there. Magda Elena had seen a few photographs of Nieve as a girl among school friends, and she had been the most beautiful of the lot. Her eyes were a clear blue, frightening at times in their coldness. Once, after Nieve had said aloud that she hoped the new baby was blond like her, Magda Elena had asked where the law was written that blond was better than brown. She had been thinking of Solamaris in all her bronzed beauty, with eyes that were the color of earth, and of Gregorio, who was brown, too, and who Nieve loved anyway. "There's no law about beauty. Beauty just is," Nieve had said, and Magda Elena had kept her other thoughts to herself.

Nieve often spoke about her Scottish father, a man who had come to Cuba at the turn of the century from the Isle of Skye, in search of warmth and a plot of land, and who had fallen in love with Nieve's mother, a woman named Encantada. Encantada never managed to teach him Spanish, and so he communicated effectively enough via signs and a mixture of Spanish and his own throaty language. Nieve often bemoaned the great loss of not having learned her father's Gaelic. For this reason, she said, she couldn't even pronounce his name, didn't know why he'd come to Cuba from such a distance, said her own father was a mystery to her as long as he lived. As for her own moniker, she'd say, "They'd named me after the snow of the Highlands." On cold days, her frosty eyes looked out the third-story window of their apartment as if she were seeing dark clouds heavy with water and ice on the horizon.

"Those hens would be better off in the stomach of your daughter than in that harlot's from across the street," Nieve announced as she laid down flatware on the table.

"*Ay, por favor,*" Madga Elena told her, exasperated. "She doesn't sleep around, poor girl. You know, she finally told me about the baby's father. He's from Camagüey. In prison for throwing a rock at Fidel during his speech back in February."

"All the more reason not to have such a person in our house," Nieve said. "His was a serious offense. What would the committee think?"

"Leave it alone," Gregorio shouted from his place in the living room. He was helping Daysy spin a top on the floor, and the girl's laughter resonated through the house, mingling with the sound of the wind chime on the balcony.

To Magda Elena's relief, Nieve did leave the subject alone after that, though she wore a scowl on her face all through the dinner preparations and did not rise to greet Solamaris and Leo when they arrived.

They sat down to a table covered with a heavy, white linen cloth, from which wafted that closet smell, of things put away and seldom used. First, Magda Elena brought out a small salad of sliced tomato and avocado. "I left them out a bit too long," she apologized, calling attention to the brown edges of the avocado slices. They glittered with salt and oil. The hens were next, and there was an audible sigh at the sight of them, rare things that they were. Magda Elena had brushed a mixture of orange juice, garlic, and honey over them, and so they seemed to glow on the table.

"They make such good honey in Santiago," Solamaris remarked, her mouth shiny. Leo sat on her lap, and his fine hair was sticking to her face.

"Yes, but I could do without the bees," Magda Elena said, then launched into a story about dipping her hand into a bag of clothes-pins as a child back in Mantua, and disturbing a sleeping bee. Solamaris laughed when Magda Elena described her frantic run through the yard with a bee clamped to her palm. It was only after the laughter died that Magda Elena realized no one else had joined the agreeable conversation. Angel was cutting through his portion of chicken as if it were his last meal, Gregorio was busy cajoling Daysy to eat, making the fork zoom through the air before tapping it against her closed mouth, and Nieve, who had not touched her food, glared across the table at Solamaris.

An awkward quiet descended on the table, interrupted now and again by Leo's high-pitched squeals, which he seemed to let loose at random moments, as if a joyful thought had struck him like light-ning, fading away just as quickly. Solamaris adjusted her son on her lap, clearing her throat as she did so. "Perhaps a toast?" she said, lift-ing a glass of water off the table. "Happy New Year."

"*Sí*," Nieve said, brightening. She, too, raised a glass and said, "To another twenty years."

Magda Elena whispered, "*Ay.*" She knew that Nieve was testing Solamaris, waiting to see whether she would toast the twentieth anniversary of the revolution, celebrated with much fanfare a year ago. Magda Elena's own hand trembled on the glass she held only an inch off the table. She watched as her friend pressed her lips together, put down her glass, and kissed the top of her son's head.

"Your son is *precioso*," Nieve said, pleased now, pausing to take a mouthful of chicken before going on. "He reminds me of Angel when he was a baby." She squeezed her son's shoulder, and Angel smiled at his mother before digging into his food again. "I had a daughter once."

This last Nieve said slowly, and the words seemed to hang about the room, echoing in Magda Elena's ears. They'd not spoken of Eugenia, not since Magda Elena had been told that she might lose the baby she was carrying. It was almost as if they'd decided speaking of the dead infant was bad form and bad luck, without having actually discussed it aloud. Magda Elena felt a weak kick in her belly, and she thanked God for the sign of life in that moment.

"She was beautiful," Gregorio said, stroking Daysy's cheek with his rough fingers. "But so sick."

"How old was she when…" Solamaris began to ask.

"Little. Not quite a year old," Nieve answered. The clinking of cutlery against plates sounded loud in the room. It was a pretty, tinkly noise that jarred with the tone of the conversation. "It starts with a mosquito bite, then a rash, you know. Eugenia looked as if she'd been slapped hard all over her body. It fades. Then the fever comes."

Gregorio put Daysy down to the floor, where the girl scampered away, free from the confines of mealtime. "*Deja eso*," Gregorio said to this wife, taking hold of her hand that still clasped a knife.

For a moment, Nieve's eyes met Gregorio's. Magda Elena watched as Nieve softened a bit, how her back curved into the seat. She imagined the two of them long ago, he in a dapper suit, timid before her foreign father, Nieve beside him, the iciness in her melting alongside the man she loved. Every now and then, Magda Elena understood why Gregorio loved his wife, saw a fragile gentleness in her. For a moment, Magda Elena thought the dinner had been saved from the brink of catastrophe by her father-in-law's intercession. Then, Solamaris spoke.

"What do the Soviets know of mosquito control? They don't care if we all die of dengue," she said, pinching a piece of chicken between her fingers and bringing it to Leo's open mouth.

The knife in Nieve's hand clattered to the floor, having been thrown with great force at her side. "They call it breakbone fever, too, did you know?" she shouted. "*Y mi niñita's* limbs twisted themselves in all directions, until I thought her bones would break. And we couldn't afford a doctor. Not one of those President Machado–loving bastards would help us. Not one." Nieve's voice had risen at each syllable, so that now she was yelling in earnest and Leo, on his mother's lap, was whimpering along with her. It seemed to Magda Elena that there was real grief in his cries, as if he'd known little Eugenia and mourned her.

When Nieve stood, Magda Elena could not look at her. The fury in Nieve's eyes burned like a torch, and her voice cracked with emotion. "Your children get sick now and the doctor sees them for nothing. Free. If Eugenia had been alive today…" Nieve bent down to pick up the knife she'd thrown, then ran her thick thumb along the flat side. "The revolution has given you that gift," she whispered. When she spoke next, after a few long seconds, her voice sounded cavernous, as if it were coming from somewhere deep in her belly. "You're a disgrace. *A gusana desgraciada.* Get out of my house."

Solamaris gathered Leo in her arms and left the apartment without a word. Magda Elena pushed her plate into the center of the table, folded her arms, and laid her head on them. In another room now, Gregorio and Angel were chastising Nieve. For her part, Nieve was silent, having won the battle that evening. Magda Elena listened to the argument, wishing the men had said something while it was happening, wishing they'd stepped in to protect Solamaris, to save the dinner.

The baby inside her turned forcefully, making Magda Elena gasp. She whispered to it, "It's all right. I'm fine," then lifted her head. The dining room was deserted, and the door through which Solamaris had just left stood ajar. Magda Elena rose from her seat, and exited the apartment, closing the door softly behind her.

≈ ✶ ≈

Magda Elena stepped out into the early evening. Outside, the atmosphere was like a steam bath. The breeze was a hot vapor, and it made the moon seem hazy. Magda Elena crossed the street and opened the gate to Solamaris' house. Grass and weeds grew tall, touching the windows. The roof tiles were nearly all gone, some of them still lying where they had fallen into the overgrown vegetation, so that spots of their orange color were visible. Magda Elena had heard that the tiles used to be formed over the thighs of Cuban women, those legs full and curved perfectly, molding the hot clay into the ideal outline. Indeed, the tiles had the profile of a thigh used to hard work, bending and stretching, thighs sometimes pried apart by lovers, or crossed demurely at church. Those tiles were once found on every roof on the island, but as they'd begun to break, the roofs had been repaired with tarpaper or, sometimes, sheets of metal.

Magda Elena knocked softly on the door. Solamaris opened it right away, as if she'd been standing by the door, or spying on Magda Elena through a window as she made her way across the street.

"Come in, come in. Do you want something to drink?" Solamaris asked in a whisper. Magda Elena had never been in Solamaris' house, which was divided into three apartments. Neither had she met any of the other inhabitants, but she had seen them exiting the front door, coming and going. Solamaris' parents had moved out to Oriente, and so the girl was often outside, as if she were escaping the lonely rooms indoors. Always, Magda Elena and Solamaris had chatted on the front porch, or on walks they sometimes took around the city.

"I couldn't rest without telling you how bad I feel about what happened at dinner," Magda Elena said.

Solamaris waved her hand in front of her face. "*No fue nada*," she said, and walked into the house.

"Nieve's behavior tonight was inexcusable," Magda Elena said, following Solamaris inside. The front room was mirrored—all four walls—and was a space shared by the three families that occupied the house. There was nothing in the room but a worn couch and, on the floor, half a coconut used as an ashtray. The two women were reflected over and over again in the mirrors. Though they were alone, Magda Elena felt as if they'd lost a sense of privacy.

"I think I understand where she's coming from," Solamaris said.

"All the same, I'm sorry." Magda Elena's back ached. She sought a seat, and Solamaris led her to the couch up against one of the mirrored walls, holding Magda Elena by the elbow.

"Your mother-in-law is sad, that's all. And too much sadness can make a woman crazy." Solamaris smiled sheepishly, holding up her hand and exposing the scars inside her wrist.

Magda Elena shuddered visibly, and Solamaris lowered her hand.

"When I'd heard he'd been arrested after throwing the stone, well…" Solamaris paused and looked at her reflection behind Magda Elena. "I don't know why I did it."

"You're better now. You won't hurt yourself again," Magda Elena reassured her. "And Leo's father will be out of prison soon."

"Manuel doesn't know about Leo."

Magda Elena considered the young man who had loved Solamaris and had thrown a rock at *el Comandante*. What kind of a person was this, she wondered. Solamaris had said she'd escaped imprisonment by a hair, and that she'd blended into the crowd as soon as the heavy rock left Manuel's hand. She hadn't meant to, she told Magda Elena, but there had been a swarm of bodies over Manuel in an instant, pinning him to the ground. He'd yelled "*¡Corre!*" and so she had, running all the way back home. It was clear that Leo did not resemble his mother, and so Magda Elena imagined Manuel with the qualities of his son—with small, intense eyes close together, a long nose, slender limbs. She wondered how he and Solamaris had spent their time, whether they had talked about books or had planned to leave the island, how they looked together, whether they held hands when they walked.

"I'll show you his room," Solamaris said, as if she'd been overhearing Magda Elena's musings about Manuel. Magda Elena rose and followed Solamaris down a short hall lit only by a dim lamp set on the floor at the end of the hallway. The women cast long shadows on the wall. Solamaris pulled an old-fashioned key from her pocket and slid it into a lock that clicked noisily. She whispered, "The others in the apartment can't know about this room. Imagine if they revealed it to one of the committees? I always keep it locked."

She entered the small, dark space, and Magda Elena followed her in, listening as Solamaris fumbled around for the dangling string to turn on an overhead bulb. Her senses limited in the darkness, Magda Elena was overwhelmed by the smell of damp paper. It clogged her sinuses at once, so that when Solamaris managed to turn on the light, Magda Elena was not surprised to see she was in a room covered wall to wall in books. There were no shelves. Piles of books made up crooked columns stacked haphazardly, so that encyclopedic hardcovers were stacked atop tiny paperbacks. The towering book piles instilled in Magda Elena a certain sense of fear, as if, at any moment, heavy books might smother them. There was something magical about the room as well. The twisted stacks and the colorful book spines gave the space the feel of a fun house.

Solamaris touched the books with one finger at a time, and it looked to Magda Elena that she was stroking the books the way one did the keys of a piano, as if music might be drawn out of the pages and cloth bindings.

"You've got so many," Magda Elena mused, turning now in place to take them all in, which made her dizzy for a moment. "Some of these can get you in trouble," she said, concern in her voice.

"Some can. I feel Manuel's here with me, among the books." Solamaris' face had relaxed as she spoke.

Magda Elena pulled a small book from the center of one of the piles, careful to readjust the others so that the whole heap of them would not come down. "Ah, Hemingway," she said. "This one I know."

"The tourists always have Hemingway with them," Solamaris said. "Sometimes, I'll go down to Varadero Beach. I can get the Europeans to give me the books they brought with them if I let them dance close, like this," she said, and mimed a slow dance, her right leg up in the air, her pelvis rolling forward and back, slowly.

"*Ay*, Solamaris, don't tell me that!" Magda Elena said, feeling her face reddening.

"That's all I do," Solamaris said, still miming the movement. "Dance. Other girls do worse for less important presents."

They were quiet again as each woman browsed the books. Here and there, Magda Elena recognized a title. But many of the books were in German, or Russian, or English, and so she could do little but admire the covers of Victorian women in high collars, or men behind podiums, caught in the moment of shouting, their mouths dark *o*'s. Magda Elena felt as if she were in a small shop, like the ones she remembered from her childhood in Mantua, where one could buy sundry items like soap or birthday candles or juice glasses. She remembered walking around the store with her mother, holding her hand and pressing her cheek against it. Magda Elena remembered her mother's purse lined in white taffeta, how she would pull out coins and count them in her cupped palm, and how a new edition of *Vanidades* magazine smelled—sweet from the perfume samples inside. She hadn't seen such things in a long time.

Leo's strident cries broke Magda Elena's reverie. They left the book room in a hurry and ran into the bedroom Solamaris shared with her son. Once he was lifted out of his cradle, the boy quieted, and at once, Solamaris sat down and began to unbutton her shirt with her free hand.

"I should go," Magda Elena whispered. On impulse, she kissed the top of Solamaris' head, the hair tickling her lips.

"Mmm," Solamaris said without looking up. Magda Elena wasn't sure if she was reacting to the kiss or to the boy who had latched on to her breast with a greedy, slurping sound. Taking her leave of them, Magda Elena made her way down the hall, through the mirrored front room, and out the door.

Later that night, lying in bed and roused by a dream of falling, Magda Elena remembered that Solamaris had not turned out the light in the room of books, and that she had not closed the door, either. She hoped that the mistake was a rare one. What a shame to lose all those words and wonderful pictures, Magda Elena thought to herself before falling back asleep.

≈ ✳ ≈

Nieve did not speak to Magda Elena for months after the dinner fiasco. Angel had tried to reconcile the women, but Nieve had mumbled something about "a country bumpkin ingrate" and Magda Elena, Daysy on her hip and Solamaris' book in her pocket, had said she no longer negotiated with "despots."

A new diagnosis from the doctor had given her courage. The baby would live. The bleeding had been a hematoma, most likely, or some other benign thing. "You're a fighter," the doctor had said, and Magda Elena had taken it to heart. Nieve's icy glares did nothing to move Magda Elena to back down, nor did her moments of softness—making Magda Elena bean soup the way she liked it—incite in Magda Elena a desire for peace.

Angel and Gregorio were quiet men by nature, and so the silence in the house became a living thing the men were afraid to disturb. Suddenly other sounds revealed themselves—a pipe deep in the walls that squealed at noon every day, the faint sound of rock and roll music coming from two floors up, the windows settling in their frames, and Gregorio's long inhalations of air, as if he were taking in his last breath with every breath.

The silence was broken early in February by a new sound, the distinct sound of fire crackling nearby. Magda Elena woke from her nap to smoke in the house. She roused Daysy from her own sleep beside her and hoisted the child onto her hip as she ran for the exit, for surely the fire was inside the apartment. Without thinking, she snatched up the crystal baby Jesus from beneath the Christmas tree she had refused to take down. Then she stopped. From the center of the room Magda Elena pivoted, looking for the fire. The crackling, she soon realized, was coming from outside.

Magda Elena parted the gauzy curtains at the open window and watched as a pile of books as tall as she was burned in the middle of the street. Representatives from the neighborhood's Committee for the Defense of the Revolution stood around the fire, poking the books so that each page was lit. Nieve was there, too, clapping her hands, her cheeks red from the heat. She looked up at the apartment and her eyes connected with Magda Elena's. Nieve smiled wide, her teeth orange in the glow of fire. In her hand was *Dr. Martin Luther King Jr. Habla*, and this she tossed onto the very top of the book pyre. Magda Elena watched as Solamaris' library went up in a conflagration that nearly touched the electric wires above. When she looked at the little house across the street, she saw Solamaris in the window, her palms white against the windowpane, her nose smashed up against the glass. Even from a distance, Magda Elena could see that her friend was crying. Her stomach tightened at the sight of Solamaris and forced her to bend at the waist. Magda Elena cradled her belly but didn't sit down, not even when the fire died down to embers. Her water broke where she stood, and Magda Elena stumbled onto the couch.

Nieve was the first to find Magda Elena, the older woman's skin glistening from the heat of the fire. "¡Ay!" she yelled, and took hold of her daughter-in-law's hand. "Can you walk to the doctor?" Nieve asked.

Magda Elena shook her head. She could feel a crushing pressure between her legs, and with it, a clarity of thought, so that Magda Elena noticed, for the first time, the water stain on the ceiling shaped like a crocodile, and how Nieve's large hands were blackened by soot.

Nieve left her for a moment, and when she returned, a doctor who lived downstairs was with her, the one who had treated Magda Elena's fever reluctantly a few years back. He crouched at Magda Elena's ankles, forced her knees apart with a grunt, and said, "You know what to do, *muchacha*." Moments later, Belén del Pozo was born on the couch in an apartment in Old Havana, her tiny face red, as if lit by a fire from within.

Only after both Magda Elena and the baby had been sponged clean did she notice it, a lingering splotch at the baby's left temple, a bit of redness that did not fade in the minutes after birth.

That night, her core aching, her body feeling as if she'd been run over by a truck, Magda Elena whispered to Angel, "We have to leave this place." The pile of books outside still smoldered, and the smell of burnt paper was thick in the house. "Not just this apartment. All of it, this country."

Angel stroked Belén's temple with his thumb. He sniffed the air. "Name the day," he said, and kissed his wife.

≈ ✶ ≈

Belén was nearing her second month when Magda Elena left her for the first time. She had not been this attached to Daysy, this unwilling to put her down for naps or let others hold her. The child did not cry, which made everyone in the apartment nervous, especially after Belén suffered her first fever and gave no indication of it. Only when Magda Elena pressed her cheek against the baby's forehead did she notice the high temperature. Laying Belén in her crib at night, Magda Elena felt oddly bereft, and night after night, she would sneak the baby back to her bed, careful not to wake Angel.

So it was with great reluctance that she left Belén with Nieve on a warm April day, to accompany Solamaris to the Combinado del Este prison, where her boyfriend was held. "I just want some fresh air," Magda Elena had lied and her mother-in-law nodded, taking the baby from Magda Elena's arms and laying her on a large and flat pillow on the floor. Belén's arms shot straight up into the air when she was released, as if she were falling from a great height, then relaxed and curled close to her small body. In this way, the baby drifted to sleep.

Magda Elena's brother, Eddy, his wife, Catalina, and their son, Amado, were also there that day, and they gathered around to watch the sleeping baby. Eddy called the vibrant birthmark on Belén's temple a sign of her promising intelligence.

"I don't like the look of it," Catalina said. "Maybe a cleansing," she suggested, touching the mark with the pad of her thumb." Magda Elena took the baby in her arms then. God knows what she means by that, Magda Elena thought, fearing Catalina's belief in *Santería*. At once, her imagination conjured animal sacrifices, rings of cigar smoke, and coconuts with cowrie shells for eyes hidden in kitchen cabinets. Once, while visiting Eddy and Catalina, she'd stumbled upon a hairy coconut inside a closet, propped up on a teacup, with slices of cake before it, in offering. Eddy had said, again and again, that such things were Catalina's doing. She wore white all of the time, as long as Magda Elena had known her, and kept a row of red beads firmly around her neck. Sometimes, Magda Elena found dead hens in the alleys between the apartments in her neighborhood, their heads glistening with some kind of oil, and the finds always made her think of her sister-in-law.

"Ah, well. The doctors can get rid of such marks nowadays," Catalina said.

Magda Elena, growing warm with annoyance, said, "I rather like it."

As for her nephew, Amado was a year older than Daysy, but the

two children played well together. Daysy could hardly keep her arms
from around his neck, hugging him and kissing him. Magda Elena
was glad to see that bit of tenderness in her. So often, she'd caught
Daysy smacking the top of Belén's head for no reason at all. Once
even, she'd heard Belén's howl, an uncommon sound that frightened
her so that Magda Elena came running. She found Daysy crouched
low before her sister, her teeth clamped around the baby's thigh.
Magda Elena had spanked Daysy then with the full force of her
hand, leaving a red outline of her fingers on the girl's leg. For her
part, Daysy had cried well into the afternoon, shouting, "No more
babies! This one, and no more!" until she was hoarse.

"Give her time," Gregorio had said as he took Daysy in his arms,
quieting her at last. Now, confident that among so many babysitters
Belén and Daysy would be fine, Magda Elena left the apartment.

She met Solamaris at the bus stop, but did not recognize her at
first. Her friend was much changed since her books had been taken
and burned. Though she carried only baby Leo in a sling across her
chest, Solamaris walked like someone who bore a heavy load. Her hair
fell like a dark curtain on either side of her face. Magda Elena's breath
caught in her throat as she took in Solamaris' arms and legs, which
were now so thin that the veins were visible under her skin, like the
sinister, purple vines that crawled up electric poles on the country
roads.

"What happened to you?" Magda Elena asked as she embraced her
friend.

Solamaris laughed a little. "The doctor said it was too much lying
down, not enough eating. You won't believe this, but he told me, 'You
look like a girl who reads too much. Put down the books and have
fun while you are still young.' What an idiot."

Magda Elena lifted Leo out of the sling and held him.

"Ah, you don't have to do that," Solamaris said. But she did not
move to take Leo back.

"He smells like Belén," Magda Elena mused. "Why do they all smell like this?"

"I haven't seen Belén in a few weeks. She must be getting big," Solamaris said, then craned her neck to watch their bus rumbling into view. Magda Elena tried to read the black lettering on the outside of the yellow bus, mispronouncing the English words. "It says, 'Toronto School District.' Canadian. I read in the *Granma* that we're getting Chinese busses next year," Solamaris said. Once the bus came to a stop, Solamaris banged on the side of it with her knuckles, and the hollow, metallic sound startled the driver, who checked the dials of the foreign bus with a look of confusion.

Both women stepped inside and found their seats. They rolled down the streets at a slow pace, leaving behind a cloud of dark smoke as they went. Sometimes, after a day out in the city, Magda Elena would find that the insides of her mouth and ears and nose were coated in black grime. The prison sat on the outskirts of Havana, and so they drove down an empty highway that traversed the fertile island. The bus passed soft, moist fields, unsown for years. Here and there, woody vines had overtaken palms, and bristly weeds grew as high as a person.

Magda Elena had been intrigued by the scenery at first, as it was a nice change from the buildings in Havana, but now the monotony of green lulled her, reminded her of Mantua, and so she felt both homesick and bored by the kind of view she'd seen all her life. Turning to face Solamaris, Magda Elena was startled by her friend's tilt of the head, an odd sort of position to hold on the bumpy ride, and yet she held it, her eyes turned skyward, her chin lifted to the side. She looked like a blind woman.

"*Oye*," Magda Elena said, and poked Solamaris with her elbow. "Wake up." But Solamaris did not move. Magda Elena was reminded of a horror movie she had seen, one of the few American films shown on the state-owned television channels. In it, a girl had been possessed by a demon, and she'd sit for long hours just as Solamaris sat, until the music crescendoed and the girl, monster now, no longer human, tore at her lover's neck and made him her meal.

"*Oye*," Magda Elena said again. "You are scaring me with your *boberías*. Quit it."

Solamaris smiled then and laughed. "I was just thinking," she said.

"About what?"

"About Manuel. I can't wait for him to see Leo." Then she resumed her previous position. There was no doubt for Magda Elena now— Solamaris was unwell. Perhaps she had been this way when she'd cut her wrists long ago. Solamaris' mother had found her when she'd done it, and let loose a terrible wail that all the neighbors heard. Her parents moved away after Leo was born, and bucking expectations and traditions, Solamaris did not go with them, choosing instead to raise the baby on her own, alone in a big city.

"Why don't you close your eyes? Sleep some," Magda Elena urged her friend. "There are still a few stops to make."

"Sleep makes me weary," Solamaris said and blinked a few times. A growing sense of unease gripped Magda Elena, and she decided there was nothing for it except to hold on tighter to Leo, to check on him more often in the days to come, and to say a prayer over his small head.

The bus broke down about a mile from the prison. The engine choked, made a hacking sound as if it were a man dying of lung disease, and then sighed to a stop. The passengers were made to step out of the bus. Some waited for the driver to finish his repairs, others began to make their way up the road. Magda Elena walked behind Solamaris, carrying Leo in her arms still. They stumbled over vines that had grown out of the fields and onto the street, reaching out with bright, leafy tentacles to the center of the asphalt. A small snake, its center bulging with its last meal, lay dead on the side of the road.

"*¡Ay!*" Magda Elena cried, but Solamaris did not notice it. She stepped on the snake as she went, and Magda Elena's stomach turned at the wet, crunching sound. "Why don't we turn around? The bus is probably working again," Magda Elena suggested, alarmed by her friend's troubling detachment.

"Courage," Solamaris said, pumping her fist in the air. Magda Elena settled Leo more firmly against her body and felt the boy's soft cheek against her shoulder, his warm breath heating her neck. She was about to say that the walk was too much for her when the boxy buildings of the prison rose on the horizon, and so Magda Elena said nothing. They approached with slow steps, and Magda Elena was suddenly reminded of those old stories of knights and dragons, of how intimidating the mouth of the cave must have been to those heroes, of the fearful red marks streaking the ground. Magda Elena tasted iron in the air. The bars of the small windows came into view, sharper now that they were closer. As they approached, other details revealed themselves—the fields of yellowed grass surrounding the complex of gray buildings, an overgrown baseball field for the inmates, yellow-capped watchtowers, like misshapen mushrooms. Sounds, too, began to divulge themselves as the women came near, namely, the discordance of whistles and, following these, incomprehensible shouts of men. Down the long two-way street that led to the prison, black cars with dark windows passed Magda Elena and Solamaris. The cars stirred the air, so that the women felt their hair lifting and whipping around their heads.

"How will we get back?" Magda Elena asked, it having occurred to her that the bus had already traveled forty miles east of Havana.

"A way always reveals itself," Solamaris said, smiling, and walking more swiftly now. She stopped abruptly at the end of the street. Solamaris shielded her eyes from the sun as she scanned the building immediately before them. Only the top two floors were visible over the high concrete fence. "Once," Solamaris said, "I saw a prisoner jump from the rooftop."

"I'm sorry," was all Magda Elena could think to say, but Solamaris ignored her. She seemed to be counting the windows, maybe looking for Manuel's room. Then, she waved, hopping up and down. Magda Elena narrowed her eyes, but she couldn't see what Solamaris saw. Then she heard it, a man's voice, quivering, not quite in tune, singing a song Magda Elena did not recognize. In fact, the words were mumbled things, as if the singer were chewing on them before letting them go.

"Do you hear him?" Solamaris asked.

"Is that Manuel? Does he know you are here?"

"God knows," Solamaris said, and swayed to the music.

"Don't you see him on these visits?"

Solamaris held her hands folded over her heart, her eyes closed. She cut a striking figure in the glare of sunlight, against the chipped prison walls and aqua skies. A whistle cut off the singer's voice, and then there was nothing but the choleric cawing of seagulls.

"Manuel isn't allowed visitors," she said, and pulled Leo from Magda Elena's arms. "Come on. There's a bus stop in Balbuena, a few miles to the north."

Magda Elena was furious. Her arms trembled. Her fingers ached to slap Solamaris, to pound common sense into her, to do what Solamaris' mother should have done. She thought of Daysy and Belén back in the apartment, left motherless for the day, and of her brother and his family, who rarely visited, of her aching, swollen feet. "That's it?" Magda Elena shouted. "We came all this way so you could hear a stranger sing?"

"We shared it, Manuel and I. If I heard the song, he heard it, too. Sometimes, I come out here and we share the sound of a plane overhead, or the rumble of thunder, or the smell from the landfill when the wind is right. Understand, *amiga*," Solamaris implored, her eyes wild as she turned them from Magda Elena to the upper row of prison windows, then back again.

"I don't think I can," Magda Elena said. "It's getting dark. Let's go home." The sun cast its last heavy beams across the road. The sunset was spectacular, but it depressed Magda Elena. "Another day lost," she said, as they began to walk.

Solamaris hugged her friend abruptly, and there was in her face something of the old Solamaris, some leftover joy. "I love the night," she said. "Things are possible in the dark." Then Solamaris lapsed into silence again and did not speak until the two said their good-byes back in Havana.

≈ ✳ ≈

The whispers came at night, like spirits creeping in through the mouse holes in the wall, caressing her ear, telling her about a way off the island. She could hear the neighbors, their voices hushed and hurried, as they discussed the announcement Fidel Castro had made, argued over the possibility that it was true, and made plans to start off for the Peruvian embassy at dawn. It was April in 1980. A bus carrying six would-be refugees had crashed through the Peruvian embassy gates, killing a soldier and demanding sanctuary and passage out of Cuba. In anger, Fidel Castro announced that the gates to the embassy were open to anyone who wanted to leave the island. Suddenly, it seemed the world had cleaved in two—those who wished they'd been on that bus, and those who hated the deserters. The radio address had gone on for hours, but the gist of it was that anyone who wanted to leave Cuba could go with Fidel's good riddance. He called them worms, or *gusanos*, and over the radio, the crowd could be heard cheering. Magda Elena listened to the neighbors make their plans with her sheets clutched around her neck, her toes curled into her feet.

That morning, she'd gone to visit Solamaris and Leo and found they had gone. Her small collection of books had been growing again, and those, too, were no longer at Solamaris' bedside. There was a rectangular mark in the carpet where the books had been, and that small absence left Magda Elena grief-stricken. Solamaris' desertion and the plans of the neighbors overheard outside steeled Magda Elena's own will, so much so that when the neighbors were done talking, Magda Elena rose from her bed as quickly as she could and felt her way to her daughters' room.

Daysy slept loudly, her blankets thrown on the floor, her small mouth open. Magda Elena's older daughter was in constant motion, and the family called her *el grillo eléctrico*, the electric cricket, because her arms were slender like an insect's and she was fast for a three-year-old. At plazas, Magda Elena would turn her head toward a sound, or pause to pick some dirt from under her nail, and Daysy would be gone from her side. Magda Elena would find her in strange places, wading the fountains or cuddled up underneath park benches, toying with scampering lizards until they died in her hands, and then cradling them like baby dolls, kissing the tops of their still, slender heads.

Belén slept in her crib, wrapped in a blanket Magda Elena had sewn from fabric scraps. The blanket was made up of half a yard of Mickey Mouse fabric and another half a yard of pink satin, and a green, felt trim. Magda Elena had stood in line for over an hour for the strange assortment of material. It was the end of the month, and supplies were low. The baby she was still carrying then felt low in her pelvis, and as she stood in the hot sun, wearing a thin cotton t-shirt and her husband's jean shorts, she could make out the baby's hand, then a foot, the knobby limbs pushing the taut skin so that her entire stomach rippled. Though the baby had been so lively inside of her, outside she was quiet as a mouse, and so they called her *la ratoncita*.

Nearing her third month of life, Belén already babbled as if she had something to say, though the babbling only came in whispers. When she cried, she made no sound. She sucked on her blanket at

night, and that was how Magda Elena found her, quiet in the midst
of her sister's snoring.

"*Levántate*," she said to Daysy. "Pack your things, now, now," and
she tugged Daysy's ear and patted her arm. Magda Elena had always
spoken to Daysy as if she were an adult, and the result was a three-
year-old who understood more than other children her age, and who
had grown-up nightmares that left her cold and screaming in the
dead of night.

Daysy woke shouting, "No!" and the rest of the household opened
their eyes to the sound. Angel came rushing into the bedroom in a
pair of boxer shorts and nothing else. He held a socket wrench in the
air, ready to bring it down on an intruder's head, but stopped short
at the sight of his wife.

"What are you doing? It's so late," he asked Magda Elena, rubbing
his eyes. But Magda Elena did not answer because she was busy feeling in the closet for the suitcase, and once finding it, she pulled it
out and let the hill of empty boxes on top of it spill into the room.
Swiftly, Magda Elena stuffed the suitcase with photographs of the
family, then zipped it closed. She ignored both Daysy's continued
shouting and her own hands, which trembled in the air as she tried to
choose what to pack next. In the sliver of moonlight that entered the
room, Angel could see Magda Elena's eyes blinking wildly in the dark.

"Where is the sweater I knitted for Daysy? We can't leave it
behind." She rifled through drawers, her fingertips searching for the
rosette-knit that she was so familiar with.

Angel got a hold of her wrists and asked again, "What are you doing?"

"I've decided. We must go to the embassy. Hurry," and Magda
Elena resumed her search for the rosette-knit sweater.

"You can't just decide something like this on your own," Angel
demanded. "We need to discuss it first, make careful plans, Magda."

"You said, the night Belén was born, that night, you said to name
the day. I'm naming this one."

"Magda, this is…"

"Papo," she said, calling him by the tender nickname she used sometimes, and turned around to touch his cheek. "I want to…want to," Magda Elena struggled for a minute, making sense of things in the dark. "To stand on a street in a big city and feel the vibration of a million cars under my feet. I want to eat beef every day and have milk at every breakfast. I want a library."

Angel shook his head. He remembered, not so long ago, how Magda Elena had balked at the idea of leaving Cuba. She'd said, "Cuba is my north and my south. I didn't lose anything in *el norte* that I have to go looking for it."

"What changed?" he asked softly.

"Nothing. Everything. Solamaris and Leo are gone, too."

Magda Elena scooped Daysy up and pressed her cheek against Daysy's small head. She closed her eyes, feeling Daysy's heartbeat thudding against her own. Magda Elena was afraid. The people at the Peruvian Embassy might all be shot. They might all be imprisoned. And then what? But knowing that just ninety miles away Cubans in America weren't standing in line for food that might not be available, that they spoke their minds without repercussions and named their children what they liked without worrying about being accused of counterrevolutionary behavior was excruciating. And now that Solamaris was gone, Magda Elena knew she would feel a terrible lone-liness, in spite of her friend's strange, disconcerting behavior of late. Perhaps she'd find Solamaris at the embassy, and they could be neighbors once again, far away from Havana.

Daysy was whimpering now, and Magda Elena took her to the bathroom so she could use the toilet.

"Where are we going, Mami?" Daysy asked, still on the toilet.

"On a trip, *mi tesoro.*"

"Far?"

"*Un poco.*"

Daysy jumped off the toilet and pulled down her dress. She held Magda Elena's hand and asked, "Is Belén coming, too?"

"*Sí.*"

All the bustling in the house woke Angel's parents. They shuffled into their son's room in long bathrobes, their eyes fat with sleep.

"*¿M'ijo, que haces?*" Gregorio del Pozo asked, one hand steadying his wife at his side.

"We're going to the embassy. *Nos vamos,*" Angel answered without looking at his father.

A small, choking sound came from Angel's mother. "You," Nieve said then, and pointed at Magda Elena. "This is your doing."

Magda Elena had been dressing Daysy, layering her with as many clothes as she could to make room in the one suitcase. She paused, her fingers holding a button so tightly that it popped off.

"Mamá," Magda Elena began.

"I am not your mother."

Magda Elena took several shallow breaths. "It's for the girls. They deserve more than this," Magda Elena said, indicating the room that badly needed painting, the window with the torn screen, the brown water stain on the ceiling.

Nieve, who liked to remind Magda Elena of her *guajira* roots in Mantua, taking her back to her poor childhood, as if she did not remember that she was once as skinny as the rods people used to knock down mangoes, and that the concrete building they shared now was a fair sacrifice for the revolution, lost all the color in her face. "*¡Ingrata!*" she shrieked, and lunged at her daughter-in-law. Her husband took hold of her shoulders, and her son pleaded, "*Mami, ya, ya,*" until she went limp in Gregorio's arms. By then, Magda Elena had dragged both her daughters out of the tight bedroom, shushing Daysy's tears as she went.

Later, Angel's mother tried to stop them at the door. The woman stood there, her arms outstretched. "You'll have to kill me first before

you take my granddaughters!" Daysy played her part, trying to jump
out of her father's arms toward her grandmother. Nieve stepped out
of the doorway to take hold of her. It was then that Angel pulled his
family out of the house, and when he tried to kiss his mother goodbye, tried explaining that he'd send for her so that they could be
together again, she slapped his face and turned, sobbing.

Outside, Magda Elena held Daysy by the waist, her body parallel to
the floor. "¡Ta!" she yelled for her grandmother. "¡Ta!" Daysy, who
once could not pronounce *abuelita* settled on Ta as a name. The child
wriggled so violently that she slipped out of her mother's arms and
scurried back to the house, clawing at the door and screaming "¡Ta!"
Magda Elena could hear Nieve crying just on the other side of the
door. Daysy cried along with her, as if she understood that this was
the last she'd see of her grandmother, the woman who didn't drink
any milk, saving her ration so that Daysy could have more, who
hoarded guava paste and white cheese because they were Daysy's
favorites, who rocked Belén during those hard newborn days when
Magda Elena and Angel had reached the breaking point of exhaustion. Magda Elena's eyes watered, too, and she stood there, letting
her daughter scratch long strips of paint off the door until she heard
Gregorio take Nieve away. Through the ordeal, Angel held Belén
inside the car, his head resting on the steering wheel. When Magda
Elena entered the car, she kissed one of his cheeks and rubbed the
other until he sniffed loudly and said, "*Ya, basta.* Let's go."

They rode to the embassy in a 1955 Ford Fairlane. The car was still
its original aqua blue, and chips of the paint flaked off as it moved.
Everything, Magda Elena thought as she brushed old paint off of her
pants, is flaking away here. *This is a faded world*, she decided. She put
all her hopes into this trip to the embassy. It had been Gregorio's car,
and Angel promised he would leave it for him two blocks from the
embassy, with the key under the seat. Gregorio, Angel's father, had
embraced his son and daughter-in-law in the darkness of his bed-

room in the back of the house. "Give the girls a kiss from their *abuelo*. Don't pay attention to your mother. We'll join you as soon as we can. Be safe, *m'ijo, m'ija*," Gregorio had said, and he and Angel cried onto each other's shoulders, forgetting the old *los hombres no lloran* line.

The road stretched out before them. Daysy sat between her parents in the front seat, whining every so often. Belén slept on in Magda Elena's arms.

"So," Angel said to Magda at last, smiling now for the first time that night, but he didn't finish his thought. For her part, she wanted to explain that Solamaris' empty room had finally done it, had driven the impulse to pack up at last and leave Cuba, that tiny growls in Daysy's stomach had a hand in the decision, too, that she couldn't stand another day of Nieve giving her sharp looks, that she wanted a house full of birds again. But there was no way to explain it all.

"Same reason you want to leave, too," she answered, and Angel nodded, as if he had read her mind.

≈ ✶ ≈

They'd been driving for a while when Magda Elena suddenly jumped in her seat. "Stop the car." Angel drove on. "Stop it," she said again, more forcefully, and Belén stirred in her arms.

"We're losing the night. It's best if we get to the embassy under cover of darkness," Angel said. Nevertheless, he pulled over to the side of the road. The street was empty, save for a small cat crossing the road slowly, its tail twitching. "What is it?" Angel asked.

"Eddy." Magda Elena had not thought of her older brother and his family until now. "We can't leave without Eddy."

Angel shifted the car to reverse. He drove fast, turning into side streets, hitting potholes so deep that Daysy woke up and began calling for Ta again. Magda Elena stroked her daughter's cheek until she fell asleep. Angel drove onto a long street curved like the moon. On the left were rows of palms, and beyond them was Havana's hazy skyline. The shapes were dark in the moonlight, but flickering lights could be seen here and there. On the right were large houses that had been converted into apartments. Terracotta tiles gleamed red atop the homes. The street was empty except for a lone man carrying a book bag, walking in the middle of the road. They stopped at the end of the street, at a house with an arched doorway and exposed cinderblock walls.

Magda Elena wrapped the blanket more tightly around Belén. "Stay here," she told Angel, and stepped out onto the driveway. She knocked on the door and waited. No one came to answer. Magda Elena turned and made a sign to Angel, then walked around toward the back of the house. She tapped again, this time on her brother's bedroom window. "*Soy yo,*" she said quietly, and heard her brother get up out of the creaky bed.

The front door opened, and Eddy, his wife, Catalina, and their son, Amado, stood there, surprised and worried. Magda Elena's nephew peered out from behind his mother.

Catalina took a step backward and bumped into her son. "Is everything okay?" she asked, and kissed Magda Elena on the cheek.

"*Sí, sí, todo bien.*" And then, "*Nos vamos, Eddy.*" Catalina's face became stone, and Magda Elena, who had been gauging her sister-in-law's reaction, looked away.

Without having to ask, Eddy knew why his sister had come. "We can't come with you, *mi hermana.*"

"But Eddy," she pleaded, and her breath caught in her throat. *I can't do this without you,* she thought to herself. And suddenly, Magda Elena was imagining a future in which her nephew would not know her. She would miss his birthday parties, his school graduations, and his sweet embraces. Magda Elena knelt, balancing Belén in her arm, and drew Amado into her chest, pressing her chin to the top of his head.

"What if Amado…," Magda Elena began.

"Amado stays here. His place is with me," Eddy said.

"Eddy," Magda Elena said, "be reasonable. What will he become here? You can…"

"You want to take all that I have," Catalina said suddenly and stared at her feet. She dug her right toe deep into the grass, lifting up the sod and revealing an earthworm that hopped about in the newly revealed light. The little *gusanito* twitched for a while, then burrowed its head into the soil, convulsing as it fought for darkness again. "Fidel is right, you know," she said when she looked up again, anger suddenly in her eyes. "Those of you who leave are no better than this *gusano*." Magda Elena fought the urge to cry.

"It isn't like that," Magda Elena tried to explain. "Both of you should come, too! The family being together is worth more than this…this…" she looked around as if the words would come to her, thinking of the streets with potholes, the long food lines and the closed libraries. "This experiment!" she shouted at last, and took hold of her brother's hand.

"Experiment?" Catalina shook her head and tried to leave the room, but Magda Elena took hold of her hand, too. Now Magda Elena was pleading with both of them. She knew that the suggestion was out of the question, but she couldn't help herself. If she could take Amado with her, then she'd have a piece of Eddy, too. Catalina lifted Amado back onto her hip. His long legs dangled, his left sandal barely hung onto his foot.

"Is it really so bad here?" Catalina asked, and Magda Elena paused. She remembered her childhood as a barefoot *campesina*, was grateful for her schooling, and, for a while, had been thankful for the simplicity of life in Cuba. But that hadn't been enough for her in a long time. The caution with which she found herself speaking with neighbors, afraid of saying something that might be misconstrued as counterrevolutionary, had worn on her. It didn't even seem safe to say that the weather was lousy anymore without someone scowling, as if the laws being made in Havana determined the behavior of the skies. Magda Elena's answer to her sister-in-law's question would have been "yes," but she said nothing. Instead, she watched Catalina climb the porch steps with her son, disappearing into the house, her white nightgown there and gone like a flash of light that leaves behind a lingering image.

"*Adiós, Tía*," she heard Amado call out. Magda Elena buried her face in Belén's blanket and could feel the warmth of her little daughter, her deep breathing. Eddy kissed the mark on the side of Belén's head, then Magda's cheek.

"*Cuídate, hermana*, and take care of the girls, too," he said, and watched her leave.

≈ ✷ ≈

They left Gregorio's car several blocks away from the Peruvian embassy. Once outside, they could hear faint shouting coming from the embassy's direction. Angel and Magda Elena had only talked about what to say and do once they were already within the gates. They hadn't worried about actually getting in. As they approached the black gates, they saw a crowd milling about outside, stalking to and fro, some throwing rotten food at the people inside the embassy, others searching the street, looking for would-be deserters of the revolution.

The acts of repudiation had begun. The Committees for the Defense of the Revolution had been quick to organize once the gates to the embassy were opened. Counterrevolutionary activity was squelched in neighborhoods and workplaces all over the island. Controlled mobs called themselves the Rapid Response Brigrade, and these were gathered in great numbers outside the embassy, punishing those who so publically sought escape, despite Fidel's permission.

Angel, Magda Elena, and their children hid behind a parked Chevy that was sticky with broken eggs, its windows smashed, the carefully preserved paint job ruined by deep scratches. The owners seemed to be nowhere in sight, and Magda Elena figured they had gotten into the embassy. From her position behind the car, she watched as a young man ran to the gate and scrambled up and over before anyone could get his hands on him. He was agile, and was wearing a school uniform. Magda Elena felt a pinch in her throat. His parents, she thought, will go crazy missing him. She was reminded of Eddy, then, of his own school days when he played baseball on the school team. He had been fast, too, and could probably still climb a fence like a schoolboy.

Within half an hour, she watched an old woman pelted with so many rotten eggs that she fell to the ground. It was like an image out of the Bible of a martyr being stoned to death. She watched a young couple caught in the midst of the crowd, watched as the husband took a swing at one of his attackers and was punched in the jaw for it. The chanting of "*Que se vayan*" over and over again, shouted so rhythmically that Daysy started clapping her little hands to the beat, ate away at Magda Elena's nerves. She didn't have to say, "Angel, let's go home," because she could see him considering that very decision.

They could turn around and return to Gregorio's car and pretend they'd never been to the embassy. But some neighbors had already seen them with their bags, and certainly the acts of repudiation would swell beyond this street. They wouldn't be safe at home now, either.

"I have an idea," Angel said at last. "You and the girls run for the gate. I'll be right behind you if the crowd gets bad. But don't turn around." Angel's eyes were red-rimmed. She knew what he was planning. To protect them from the rocks that were being thrown, from the hands that reached out to scratch and pull, he'd shield them with his body. He pulled Magda Elena tightly to him, crushing a squealing Belén between them. Then he held Daysy for a long time. "Don't pay attention to me, *chiquitica*. Okay? Whatever I say, it's just a game, understand?" Daysy did not understand and clapped once and twice to the chanting, before losing interest. Magda Elena would not remember her husband's terrified look later except in dreams.

Angel pushed them away from the Chevy and followed a few paces after them. The crowd's attention was now on another schoolboy, one who wasn't as fast as his classmate. They'd caught him by the pant's leg and dragged him down from the gate, calling him a *gusanito* as they tore his uniform to shreds. So it was that only a few of the protestors noticed Magda Elena and her daughters.

"*¡Miren!*" the shout was then coming in her direction, as nearly forty heads turned to look at Magda Elena. In an instant, she felt surrounded by angry faces. She held Belén in one arm and Daysy supported on her hip. Both girls were crying, Belén's a silent wail, Daysy's face dug deep into her mother's neck. Around her the voices shouted "*¡Gusana!*" and "Go to hell" and hurled at her all manner of insults. The closest voice, and the loudest, was Angel's, screaming "*Váyanse*," urging them to get out in a tone that was furious in its double-meaning. Every time Angel yelled at them, pretending he was one of the angry mob, he got closer, and his large body shielded them from much of the abuse aimed at them. With every shout from Angel, Daysy screamed.

In truth, the entire ordeal could not have lasted more than a few seconds, but Magda Elena felt she had lived an entire lifetime in those moments. Angel shoved her into the gateway that one of the Cubans inside held open for her, but when he tried to sneak in behind her, he was pulled back. The embassy crashers wrapped sympathetic arms around Magda Elena and urged her not to look behind her. It wasn't until much later, when she had settled herself and the girls beneath the shade of a massive sea grape, that she did look back upon the crowd and found Angel sitting on the corner, crying into his hands, like a man praying.

≈ ✶ ≈

Magda Elena had been separated from Angel for two days, and his absence at her side made her skin erupt in goose bumps every so often, as if an essential piece of clothing were gone, or the circulation of blood in her body had been cut off. He'd gotten them all inside, had used his own body as a shield, and at the last moment, right at the gate, he'd managed only to get one arm into the embassy before he was yanked back, lost in the crowd of protestors. Magda Elena heard his last words in her ear, "*Váyanse*," when the embassy quieted for moments at a time. Her grandmother had told her when she was a girl that the synchronous moment of muteness in a crowd, when everybody held their tongues for a second or two, marked the passing of an angel overhead. Magda Elena heard her husband's voice in that sacred space, and sent a prayer to that hovering spirit that her husband might join them soon.

Magda Elena wasn't sure they'd survive this adventure, didn't know if she'd end up in prison, or Peru, her children taken away from her. *El Comandante* had promised that anyone who wanted to leave Cuba could, but over the years, there had been many promises made, and few kept. At times, Magda Elena thought of the island as a naive girl, dressed in green and blue, a made-up coquette for a rough man with a beard who promised her the world. Again and again, she had fallen for the positive assurances, the candy-sweet guarantees of plenty, only to be let down after a heady speech. Already, the black cars of Cuban government officials were circling the compound. It would be easy to aim a few rifles out of those dark windows and pick off the embassy crashers, trapped in a pen as they were. Those at the embassy hoped the Peruvians would grant them asylum. Magda Elena wondered what life in Peru would be like. It was cold in the mountains, she knew, and she hoped there would be enough coats to go around. Perhaps we can

own a pet llama, she thought and laughed at herself, then cried when
the laughter filled her with guilt and hopelessness. Her cries interrupted one of Daysy's songs, and the girl said, "No, Mami. My song,"
and resumed a slow, mournful melody.

Magda Elena found a new spot in the shade, underneath an arbor
on the side of the embassy. The arbor held the twisted, slender trunks
of a bougainvillea tree upright. The papery flowers had finished
blooming, and they fell onto Magda Elena and Belén with every slight
breeze. Daysy had decided to climb the sturdy arbor, despite the
prickly leaves, and Magda Elena had let her do it. In another time,
another place, she would have reprimanded Daysy, would have
spanked her if she'd persisted in her climb, but now there seemed to
be no use for that. The other refugees in the embassy yard didn't
seem to care that they were trampling the beautiful lawn, stripping
the *flamboyán* of its flowers by sitting on its branches, or that everyone was beginning to smell. Besides, Daysy was better off atop the
arbor than on the ground. They hadn't eaten since they'd entered the
embassy, and Magda Elena had caught Daysy scooping up dirt with
her fingers and putting it in her mouth. As for Belén, Magda Elena
nursed her three times a day, ashamed to have to do so in public,
and planted her finger in the baby's mouth to satisfy her the hours
in between. If food doesn't arrive by tonight, she told herself, I'll be
nursing Daysy, too.

Life in the embassy began to take on its own rhythm and pattern.
No food arrived the second night, but in the morning, embassy workers distributed water and crackers. In the afternoon, the foreign press
would gather to ask questions of those standing at the fence. Some of
the refugees had taken off their shirts and printed messages on them
using bits of charcoal they'd found on the ground. They'd written,
"We don't need water. We need to leave!" The reporters had no
answers for them. No one knew what was taking so long. The
Peruvian officials hid inside the embassy and peered at the Cubans

on the lawn through parted drapes. Always, always, the shouting from the crowds outside, shouts of *escoria,* a word that Magda Elena used once in her life when she was eight and had pointed at a homeless woman by the side of the road, calling her "scum." Magda Elena's grandmother stopped her in the street and slapped her in front of the homeless woman. Then she took off Magda Elena's gold bracelet, her only piece of jewelry sent by her father from Santo Domingo, and handed it to the beggar. The lesson took hold and Magda Elena had come to hate the word *escoria.* They shouted "*¡Paredón! ¡Paredón!*" too, calling for the death sentence for all those inside the embassy, resurrecting the shouts of "To the wall!" used when the revolution first triumphed and the executions of men and women lined up against a bloodied wall had been televised. With each shout, Magda Elena held Daysy and Belén closer, singing them lullabies.

By the third morning, Daysy had begun to look pale, and her hands were cold and limp. Weak herself, Magda Elena lifted her shirt and pulled her older daughter to her. Daysy struggled at first, said "*Ya, ya, Mami*" so loudly that others looked, then turned quickly away in embarrassment. It was during this struggle, while Daysy squirmed against her mother's hot skin and Magda Elena sobbed into her daughter's hair, that a familiar hand touched her cheek. Magda Elena looked up to see Angel, his left eye closed shut and his face swollen.

"Papi!" Daysy shouted and pushed off of Magda Elena. She leapt into his arms with renewed energy and cried into his neck.

"*¿Cómo?*" Magda Elena asked, and Angel shook his head. From underneath his shirt he drew two small oranges and gave one to Daysy. He'd hidden, too, half a loaf of bread down his pants leg and a mushy tomato in his pocket. The family ate their odd breakfast in the shade of the bougainvillea, sweeping petals off their food every so often.

"I couldn't get in," Angel said, and motioned to the world outside the gates, where a few black cars with dark windows were parked. Magda Elena had noticed them the day before, cruising up and down the boulevard, the windows cracked open only an inch, thick enough for the barrel of a rifle to slide through. "There was talk outside," Angel said, "that they were going to shoot anyone else who tried getting into the embassy. This morning, I told myself, *'Pal carajo,'* and went for it, bullets or no."

"*Ay,*" was all Magda Elena could say, in the softest of whispers. Then she said, "Your eye," and her hand fluttered up to touch it.

Angel pushed her hand away, explaining how in the rush to get into the embassy, one of the protestors had thrown a handful of pebbles at his face. A tiny stone scratched his eye, and it became swollen immediately. Now, the entire left side of Angel's face had ballooned and turned red. A woman near them, claiming she was a nurse from Matanzas, peered into Angel's eye, then suggested Angel leave the embassy and go to a Cuban hospital, but he refused. "I'd rather go blind," he said, than risk leaving the embassy and his family again.

By the end of their first week at the embassy, Angel's face ached so badly that he huddled on the ground underneath the arbor and moaned. People gathered around him, so many people now that there was standing room only at the embassy, and suggested he leave, prayed over him, told him stories of their own eye infections. Magda Elena no longer knew what to do. If Angel died here of an infection, or lost his sight, what good would life in Peru be? She left Daysy with her father and told her, "Do not move an inch away from him, *entiendes?*" and the girl had cried after her mother, watching her and Belén being swallowed immediately by the swaying crowd.

Magda Elena, holding Belén close, called out in the midst of people, "*¡Médico! ¡Médico!* We need a doctor! Surely there's a doctor here." She had looked for a doctor twice already, and found no one who could help. Trying again now, she yelled until she felt her throat constrict, yelled at the men standing atop the embassy portico, crushed roof tiles under their feet. She yelled at the foreign press for help, blond men and women who shook their heads in sadness. She called out until she thought she was hearing an echo of herself. "*¡Médico!*" she called, and heard another voice, younger, feminine, call out "*¡Médico!*" too. She listened for the voice, the fellow sufferer. Through the stinking bodies that pushed and stewed in place, Magda listened and called out "*¡Médico!*" It was then that she recognized Solamaris and her eight-month-old baby, Leo.

"Solamaris!" Magda Elena said, and embraced her old neighbor. Solamaris was tense, her face sunburnt.

"*Mi hijito,*" she whispered, and Magda Elena pulled back the blue sheet wrapped around Leo. The boy's face was white, his lips purple, his eyes half open. Magda Elena held her breath. She put her hand on the boy's stomach, the same way she did when checking on her girls at night, in those dark moments when they'd been feverish as babies and she wasn't sure enough of her own mothering yet to know if they were alive. Leo did not move.

"*Ay,*" Magda Elena said. "*Ay,* Solamaris," and she cried as she watched her friend tuck Leo closer to her, wrapping him tightly.

"No," Solamaris whispered. "There's still a chance!" Her eyes were hard and round like coins.

"I don't think…"

"What can I do, Magdita? What can I do? If he's gone, then I follow him. There's hope in that, too." Solamaris nuzzled Leo's hair and then called out "*¡Médico!*" again as she pushed through the crowd.

≈ ✳ ≈

The weeks went by like an endless sleep while they waited for Fidel Castro to make a decision concerning everyone at the embassy. A part of Magda Elena understood why he was taking so long to make another announcement. Around her were faces that were young, black, white. There were people from the countryside, and even some still wearing their government uniforms. All were seeking escape. These were the very people the revolution had aided, and now they were turning their backs on it. For a moment, Magda Elena felt a touch of sympathy for Fidel, as if she were witnessing a man abandoned by his children and left with a crumbling house he could not maintain on his own. But Magda Elena placed a cool hand on Angel's injured eye, and anger took the place of compassion. Once the swelling went down in Angel's face, he found that the vision in his left eye had gone dark, and Magda Elena had cried so loudly everyone on the embassy grounds could hear.

The four of them huddled under the arbor, arms around one another for hours. Sometimes, it was Daysy who would begin to cry and call for her grandmother, her favorite doll, the old pacifier she'd abandoned long ago. Other times, it was Angel crying, pounding his fist against the wooden structure and showering them with dried flower petals. In those moments, Magda Elena began to feel a jitteriness in her legs, a never-ending twitching of muscles, willing her to move, to pick everyone up and go, back home, back to Eddy and Amado, to Nieve and Gregorio and their apartment in Old Havana.

She nearly did leave the embassy once early on, two days after Angel had come back to them. It was a cloudy dawn of threatening thunderstorms that never came. The sun had not yet begun to peek over the buildings in Havana when a shrill cry disturbed the morning quiet at the embassy. Magda Elena stood to watch as three Peruvian embassy workers struggled to take Leo's body from Solamaris.

"No!" she cried, choking and coughing into the baby's hair. The body had begun to smell, and wherever Solamaris and Leo went, a path opened before her. When Magda Elena had tried talking to her, Solamaris had screamed, "You have your babies! *¡Déjame sola!*" and she'd kicked at Magda Elena, falling down in a heap.

Two older Cuban women joined the Peruvians and got close enough to stroke Solamaris' hair. "*Niña,*" one of them begged her, "give him up. He doesn't need you anymore."

"*Muchacha*," was all the other could bring herself to say before she managed to uncurl Solamaris' fingers from the blanket so that the Peruvians were able to pull the tiny corpse away. Then, Solamaris fell at the feet of the women and would not move. Neither did she cry, but her face was frozen in grief, her eyes squeezed shut, her mouth open, soundless, a dry void as if her breath were being pulled from her. She sat that way for hours, and no one could budge her, even when the noon sun struck her shoulders and began burning her skin. Men who tried to lift her couldn't, and exclaimed she weighed more than a boulder. They said she was rooted to the ground—a dry, stubborn weed. They said she'd been cursed.

Shortly afterward, Magda Elena whispered to Angel, "*Vámonos.* This is a foolish desperation. Things were not so bad, after all," but Angel glared at her with his one good eye, an eye that became both more tender and more terrifying now that it worked alone. Magda Elena did not ask again.

That night, Magda Elena had a dream, spooky in its grayness, its slowness. She dreamt of a grown-up Leo, who spoke of lighthouses and hurricanes that rip the beach right off the coast. In her dream, Magda Elena saw lighthouse upon lighthouse, with blinding beams of light, in all shapes and sizes. Leo, wrapped in his blue blanket, a small trickle of blood running out of the corner of his mouth, pointed at each tower perched on the coast, and Magda Elena felt herself become warm and clammy in the dream. Suddenly, Leo and the light were gone. It was terrifying to walk in darkness, to imagine, for the moment, the grains of sand underneath her feet, sharp like cut glass, to tune her ears to the distinct possibility that she might hear a voice leading her astray.

The cresting surf was a guide through the blackness, and the glare of the setting sun illuminating the skin of her eyelids, like the red yolk of an egg seen through its shell, lit up a red world. The dream then gave way to thoughts about Angel's blindness, and Daysy and

Belén. Magda Elena woke up.

That night, she prayed three rosaries and threw up twice in the corner by one of the makeshift toilets. And when she finally slept, leaning on her husband, the coral brick walls of the embassy dappled with moonlight, Magda Elena dreamt of more lighthouses, and of Leo, standing at a ship's prow, his hand shading eyes that scanned the sea for ships in distress.

≈ ✳ ≈

April was a month without days. Each morning dissolved into a blistering afternoon, which gave way to the restless night. Magda Elena no longer knew if they'd been sitting under the arbor for one week or three, or if the last few days had happened at all. "Five weeks," Angel said, when she asked. He'd been pressing his nail into the wood of the arbor, and there where thirty-five half-moon dents in the wood. Monotony had settled uncomfortably in the embassy, broken apart by the arrival of Cuban government workers distributing a few boxes with cooked rice and water every so often. The embassy grounds were ruined. Trees had been stripped of leaves used in place of toilet paper, in tasteless teas, as playthings for bored children. Magda Elena was sorry for the once fragrant mango in the far corner of the embassy grounds. Its branches were cracked, its fruit eaten. Only the oblong leaves at the top of the tree remained, and these were limp, crushed by the circumstances of its existence.

Daysy and Belén still nursed from their mother, and all the food Angel could barter for within the compound went right to Magda Elena, so that Angel had lost not only his watch, his undershirt, and a sock, but at least ten pounds that April. His left eye became infected again. Angel only abandoned his seat to find food, then settled in the shade again to sleep.

Magda Elena thought that they would die here. It was possible.

Daysy was too thin, and dark circles under her eyes resembled smudges of grime. Magda Elena often licked her fingers and wiped at the grayness of her daughter's skin. Though she hadn't seen a mirror in nearly a month, she knew she probably looked the same. Her mouth felt dry all of the time. There was never enough water to go around. Already, several children, suffering from dehydration, had been taken away to the hospital, and Magda Elena had not seen them return. Only Belén looked healthy. The creases at her wrists, her knees and neck were still deep and sweet smelling. Her blue eyes were as clear and long-lashed as ever.

And yet, Magda Elena thought even Belén's health couldn't last. It was rumored that ten thousand people awaited exit papers at the embassy. The crush of human bodies had encroached upon their space under the arbor, and they shared the shade now with a young man named Rolando, who had wrapped a t-shirt around his head and slept for much of the time. He was so quiet that the del Pozos often forgot he was there, and accidentally bumped into him sometimes. Magda Elena had tried to save the space for Solamaris, but a few days after Leo was taken away, the woman had disappeared, too. Rumors flew about the embassy and transformed Solamaris into legend, so that by the time Magda Elena heard her name again from one of the refugees, it was to describe a middle-aged woman who had lost her grown son to dehydration and had hanged herself shortly thereafter. In truth, Magda Elena guessed that Solamaris had returned home to her parents, ashamed that she'd risked and lost her son in this venture.

It wasn't quite May yet when the Peruvian and Cuban officials began offering passes to the embassy crashers. The passes, they promised, were tickets to the marina at Mariel, where American ships would transport them to Florida. People were initially suspicious of the passes. Some thought that they were merely distractions, a way to clear out the embassy and leave them with no asylum at all. Others felt the passes were tickets to prison, and to take them would be reckless. Then there were those who thought that people staying at the embassy would be rounded up and made to disappear. Magda Elena and Angel talked over the meaning of such an offer the length of a night.

"And if it's a trap? What if we take the passes and are arrested?" Angel asked, his hand pressed over his eye.

"Could be." Magda Elena had both girls on her lap, and Daysy had one hand deep in her mother's hair, tugging it sleepily.

They were quiet for a while. The embassy sounded like a great cathedral right before mass. Ten thousand people were murmuring in hushed tones, and many of them were praying. "We can't go home to your mother," Magda Elena said at last.

Angel shook his head. "Eddy's place, then. If it doesn't work out, if there is no ship, *bueno, por lo menos...*"

"*Por lo menos* we tried. We tried." Angel leaned forward to kiss Magda Elena. She pressed her mouth against his and was very still, afraid of hurting his eye. Her breath tasted sour from lack of food and she knew it, but his lips yielded to the kiss anyway.

"If there weren't so many people here..." Angel murmured as he bent to kiss Magda Elena's collarbone. Daysy reached up and pushed her father's chin away.

In the morning, Angel took the passes from the gruff Cuban official who was handing them out.

DAYSY DEL POZO

HIALEAH, FLORIDA 1990

Daysy left the library in a daze. A peanut vendor on 49th Street, moved by the sadness she wore on her face, gave her a little cone filled with nuts. "*Para tí*," he said, and smiled toothlessly. Daysy muttered *gracias*, and walked on until she reached her house at last. She took a long look at the iron door then kicked it, savagely.

"Abuelo!" Daysy called, throwing open the door and making a dent in the wall behind it. "Abuelo!" she shouted, her voice breaking as she searched the bedrooms, the kitchen, the bathrooms. Panicked, Daysy pictured all the things that could have gone wrong with her grandfather. She saw him run over in the street, torn in half, his shoes filled with gore. She imagined him drowned in a canal. His bed was rumpled. His toothbrush still wet. A lemon rind was placed carefully on the edge of the sink. All of it was evidence of Abuelo, but where was he? Dead; lost; confused; swindled; kidnapped, Daysy told herself over and over, counting the ways in which her desertion had hurt her grandfather. *I've killed him*, Daysy thought, and sat down to cry. But there were no tears. She wished for them—big, sloppy, snot-infused tears instead of this bitter aridity.

Daysy heard the squeal of the iron door as it opened. She turned to watch Abuelo coming in, tucking keys into his pocket, a steaming *cafecito* in his hand from the bakery a mile down the road. He came to Daysy, stopping to kiss the top of her head. Daysy could feel the heat from the coffee near her face as he bent down. Daysy breathed deeply to take him in—coffee and Grecian Formula. He patted her cheek. His palm was cold.

"Abuelo," Daysy asked, "it's so hot outside. How do you manage to keep cool?" She smiled at him and held his hand. Abuelo was having a good day, and for the moment, thoughts of Belén had dissipated.

"*Bueno*, the air conditioner in the Buick works really well."

"What?"

"*El aire, muchacha.* You need to use the air conditioner or you die out there. But in Cuba? No, in Cuba we had the sea breezes. In Cuba, we…"

"You drove?" Daysy asked again, her hand firm around his.

"*Claro.* Do you think an old man like me can walk to the bakery? Once perhaps, but not now."

Daysy pressed his open palm against her cheek and closed her eyes. He could have killed himself, but he didn't. He managed to turn the car on, point it in the right direction, park it. It was a wonder considering the many times Abuelo would wake up frightened in the night, unsure of everything, thinking he was still in Havana, or how often he'd confused Magda Elena for Nieve, how he'd pinch her thighs from behind, how Magda Elena would scream at him, confusing him further. It was as if time had melted for Abuelo, and he was swimming in it, going in any direction he pleased—back thirty years one moment, in the present the next. Daysy thought that perhaps Abuelo hadn't forgotten anything after all, only that he was in a different space in time at any given instant.

Daysy said, "Abuelo, tell me about Belén," hoping that perhaps he was there with her in his mind, but he looked at Daysy with knitted brows, they way he did on days when he struggled with names, and Daysy knew the clouded look, knew the moment of clarity had gone.

"Is this her?" Daysy tried again, putting the photograph she'd found in her mother's drawer back in his hands. She carried it with her all the time now, and the photo was softening from wear.

Abuelo stared at it for a long time. He swayed a little where he stood, and Daysy took hold of his forearm. "She was the most delicate *bebita*, white like sand, blond. Blond like her grandmother. The only real *rubia* in the building. You should have heard the old women in the park. 'That baby can't possibly be your *nieta*,' they'd say to me. Ha!"

Daysy felt a click in her chest then thought that perhaps she'd imagined it. "Tell me more about her."

Abuelo closed his eyes and began to hum. The skin on his eyelids was heavy and shiny.

"Belén, Abuelo. Focus, just this once!" Daysy had lost control of her voice then, and it echoed in the house. If her Spanish were better, she thought she might be able to explain to him how much she needed to know about her sister, about the lie she'd been told, but the moment was one of those that reminded her how very slow the brain can be, as the words in Spanish failed her, one by one. "*Dime. De mi* sister. Come on. *Hablame.*" She knew she could do better, but the language wouldn't shape itself in her mouth. "Tell me something about her," she pleaded at last. "Anything."

"My grandmother once loved a pirate," Abuelo said, and Daysy moaned. Stories that began this way were often long and pointless, and she knew that he wasn't going to answer her question.

"Abuelo, *por favor.*"

"The man she loved was named Don Virgilio de las Cruzes, and he sailed a brigantine. He was hanged in Camagüey, you know."

"No, I don't know anything. That's the problem! Please, Abuelo!"

"But before he died he told my grandmother about his hidden gold, and when the authorities tried to get the location of the galleons from her, she refused to speak. Or maybe, she just forgot."

"Abuelo!" Daysy was standing now, yelling, shaking her grandfather. He was hard as a statue underneath her grip, though warm. The doctors had described the damage in his brain as a sort of ossification of the tissues, of the memories, and Daysy wondered now whether his body was not becoming stone with each passing day.

"*Bueno,*" Abuelo said, and stood. He smiled and nodded his head. Daysy's hands fell off his shoulders. She watched Abuelo walk toward his bedroom, and his shaky steps suggested some sort of illness in him, something beyond the deterioration of his brain. Daysy's throat ached, and she swallowed again and again, as if trying to wash down something very bitter.

"She never told anyone," Daysy heard Abuelo say to himself from within his room. "*Imagínate*, we could have been rich."

Later that afternoon, when the hottest part of the day was over, Abuelo stepped into Daysy's room. She'd been studying the photograph, the one with the baby in Magda Elena's arms. Try as she might, she could discern no information from it. Abuelo sat on the edge of her bed, twirling in his hands a top he'd carved. It was smooth and painted with red nail polish, so that it gave off a potent, acrid scent. She watched as Abuelo twirled the thing in his hand, deftly, the way he handled his flute. As a little girl, Daysy had loved watching him play, imagining his fingers were spiders' legs, so delicately did they press upon the finger holes.

"Do you have any string?" he asked as if he were a child.

"No, Abuelo," Daysy said, wanting only to sleep and forget. Later, well rested, she planned on talking to her parents about Belén, on showing them the article she'd found. The prospect frightened her.

"But I need some," Abuelo insisted.

"Sorry."

Abuelo patted her head, then scratched softly at her back, the way he did when she was little. "Would you like to see Belén?"

Daysy sighed. "She's dead," she said, folding the article and the photograph together and slipping them into the back pocket of her jeans.

"She isn't!" Abuelo shouted, standing and yanking Daysy along with him. "We'll go in the Buick," he announced, as if they owned a fleet of cars and not just two.

At first, Daysy tried to restrain her grandfather, but he was still strong, and though she pulled at his shirt, tearing the pocket off the

guayabera he always wore, he got past her, sprinting down the driveway and getting into the driver's seat of the Buick before Daysy could
stop him. Part of her wanted to believe him. He insisted again and
again, "I'll take you right to your sister. You should see how big she is
now," and Daysy let herself imagine that it was true.

The "Buick" was actually a colossal Ford van, painted blue, with
curtains in the windows. The back of the van had plush seating and
a Formica-topped table anchored to the floor. Abuelo called all cars
Buicks, especially those vehicles he most admired. "*El Buick*," he'd say
often, "is stronger than a tank." Angel had purchased the van a few
months ago at a bargain price, with the idea that sooner rather than
later, his father would be wheelchair bound, and a van that size could
hold him, his wheelchair, and any other medical equipment necessary.
Magda Elena hated the van, had whispered "*solavaya*" at it, fearing the
van itself would hasten Abuelo's illness.

Outside, Daysy held onto Abuelo in the front seat, gripping his
shoulder and tugging, saying, "Abuelo, *anda*, let's go inside. I'll make
coffee." But Abuelo turned the ignition, the van thundered to life,
and so Daysy had no choice but to get in. She didn't trust Abuelo's
driving on the highway, so she suggested he drive side roads instead.
Obeying, he avoided the crowded expressway and drove down 16th
Avenue with one hand on the center of the steering wheel, ready to
pound the horn at every poor driver, which he did with frequency.

"Where are we going?" Daysy asked.

"Eh?"

"You said you knew where Belén is."

"Of course I know!" he shouted again, and banged the steering
wheel with his fist closed. "*Caramba*, you ought to trust me more."

He said it so convincingly that Daysy leaned over and kissed his
stubbly cheek. Abuelo chortled and then, his face changing in an
instant from gladness to something more melancholy, heaved a broken sigh. As for Daysy, she was happy for the distraction, if not a little

nervous at having her very unstable grandfather driving an enormous van.

They drove through Miami Springs, down Le Jeune, and across South Miami, until they found themselves in the elegant, oak-lined streets of Coral Gables. Abuelo drove past rows of wedding dress boutiques that prompted him to declare how odd it was that Nieve, his dead wife and Daysy's grandmother, weighed only one hundred pounds with her wedding dress on. "She was a very fat woman by the time she died *del corazón*," he said.

"Heart attack?" Daysy asked.

"Broken heart," he said, and he flicked the headlights rhythmically. Oncoming drivers flicked them back at him. "She was so sad when all of you left us. You don't remember her, do you?"

Daysy shook her head. How odd, she thought, that her Alzheimer's-stricken grandfather was quizzing her memory.

"Your grandmother was a hard woman, but your absence softened her like a piece of bread. '*Daysy, mi Daysy*,' she would mumble to herself. *Por Dios*, how she missed you."

"Then Belén died," Daysy said, helping him tell the story.

"Died? Who died?" Abuelo asked, stopping at a green light for a second before reconsidering and pressing the accelerator again.

"Belén," Daysy said.

"Such a name! It caused all sorts of trouble," Abuelo said. Before Daysy could ask him what he meant, Abuelo had rolled down his window as he drove and pointed at a garish car dealership on the corner. Then Abuelo told of the time he worked at a car lot in Hialeah painting trucks, how he'd tripped on a discarded battery and hit his head, and the owner, "*ese desgraciado*," had tricked him into signing papers so that he couldn't get his workman's compensation. "So long ago," he said and whistled when the light turned green.

"Abuelo, it was last year."

"*No, m'ija*, it was ages ago." Daysy said nothing. At another large intersection, the road they were on ended and ran smack into a six-lane mega-street. Daysy's sense of direction failed her.

"*¿Ahora que?*" Abuelo asked, and Daysy faltered.

"How am I supposed to know?" she shouted over the din of people behind them pressing their horns. "Just turn! Right!" Daysy pointed at last, and Abuelo took a sharp left then hit the brakes.

Around them, drivers swerved into other lanes to avoid the stopped van, honked their horns, and waved middle fingers at Abuelo. He tightened his seatbelt once again and shifted the van back into drive. "Trust me," he said to Daysy.

Daysy undid her seatbelt with a vicious swipe, stumbled to the back of the van as they lurched forward in traffic. Rush hour was just beginning, and the van moved and stopped, moved and stopped. Daysy felt her stomach twisting with the motion. But Abuelo didn't seem to mind. He hummed a few bars of "*Por un Beso*," and his voice was especially deep and resonant, as if the feeling of driving again after so long, of being out in the thick of Miami, surrounded by reckless drivers and colorful billboards, had refined his talent.

Daysy said, "I think we're lost. I think this was a big mistake."

Abuelo took another sharp left at that moment, and Daysy strapped the seatbelt on. They were in the heart of downtown Miami now. Buildings wrapped in glass towered into the blue sky, and between them, Daysy could see glimpses of a gray sea in motion. So much water, she thought. Abuelo began humming to himself again, and the hum took the form of words, and his voice grew until he was belting "Guantanamera" so loudly that the van's windows shivered. He revved the engine at the height of the song, just as he drew out the *guantanameeeeeeeera* melismatically, and the force of it threw Daysy back into her seat. The engine bellowed its accompaniment as they drove through Miami, out of downtown and back into the neighborhood grids.

When they got to Calle Ocho, they found it gridlocked. Street vendors, mostly men Abuelo's age, darted in between cars, handing out white paper bags with sweet churros to paying customers, while clear plastic bags filled with small, green *mamoncillos* hung from their belts. On the corner, El Cristo restaurant was so full that people were standing outside to wait for seats. The men and women were dressed in dark suits. Some had white flowers pinned to their lapels, their dresses.

Watching the milling crowd, Daysy remembered the newscast from earlier that week, the one about the Cuban crooner, Cruz García, who had died from a heart attack. This was the day of the funeral mass, held at the Miami Cathedral, and naturally, the fans and distant relatives had gathered in Little Havana for dinner before heading back downtown to stand in line at the Freedom Tower to view the body of the famous Cruz García one more time. Daysy noticed, then, the music blaring from all of the storefronts, songs like "Regreso" and "Mi Perla Preciosa," songs by various artists about Cuba and exile that played at every wedding, every New Year's party, and every time the news gossips predicted Castro's death. The songs, sung by high-voiced men and deep-voiced women, were nearly always flute-heavy, and trumpet blasts started off the choruses rousingly, and always, at the weddings and parties, the handkerchiefs would come out and the toasting would begin, the calls for "Next year in Cuba" accompanied by the dull clicking of plastic glasses filled with *sidra*. Daysy rolled her eyes and tapped her grandfather's shoulder.

"We're stuck. It's that stupid Cruz García funeral. Try a back road," Daysy said, interrupting his singing.

Abuelo's face went blotchy at once, his eyes liquid. It looked as if he were suffering a sudden allergic reaction. "*¿Estúpido?*" Abuelo asked. "*¿Estúpido? Mira muchacha*, I watched that '*estúpido*' perform back in La Hábana for six months from backstage, and he was a real artist. *¿Me oyes?* A real artist." As he spoke, he waved an open palm in the air as if he would slap her. Then, Abuelo opened the car door and stepped out. He pulled his flute out from an inner pocket of his light jacket and held it high in the air. He had left the transmission in drive, and Daysy tumbled into the front seat as the van rolled forward. She threw on the emergency brake, turned off the ignition, and pulled out the key.

Since he'd become ill, Abuelo had also become easier to anger. With the onset of dementia, he sometimes exploded into violence. On one occasion, after Angel had refused to give him his car keys, Abuelo began to pound his son with his fists, bruising Angel's shoulder and cheek. The doctor had said it was normal. He said confusion would give way to sporadic violence, which would give way to mute submissiveness. Daysy was glad her grandfather had not chosen to hit her with those coiled fists, those hands laced with veins that could pull out stubborn banana trees by the roots with one tug. Instead, he disappeared into the crowd on the sidewalk. From inside the van, Daysy could hear him singing, "*Ay mi Cuba, mi perla del mar...*" in his beautiful, broken voice, and she heard cheers from the crowd.

"Oh, my God," Daysy yelled, and jumped out of the van. She crossed the intersection, nearly stepping on the dry carcass of a runover cat. Soon, she was stuck behind a wall of dark suits, all transfixed by Abuelo, who had begun playing an old Cruz García favorite on his flute. She whimpered, "Excuse me," a few times, but no one moved from his or her spot. Rather, the wall of mourners was swaying back and forth, like snakes charmed by Abuelo's music. A Channel 23 camera crew made its way toward the sound, too. A stout reporter, also in a dark suit with a white carnation in his lapel, broke through the crowd with his microphone held like a sword. Daysy swept in behind the man with the camera.

Abuelo was just finishing his tribute with a long, trilling note, only one hand on the flute, his chin vibrating with the crescendo, his left hand a fist over his heart. Around him, the mourners wiped tears from their eyes and then exploded in applause. Abuelo kept his hand on his chest and bowed slowly.

The reporter, whom Daysy recognized as Albert Arroyo, a small-time celebrity in Miami, pushed away Abuelo's admirers and held the microphone two inches from his mouth.

"Tell us," he asked in Spanish, "what is it about Cruz García's music that so moves you?" The cloudy look had come over Abuelo's face again.

"Eh, Cruz García? García?" Abuelo rubbed his forehead. "Eh, García is playing at the Teátro tonight, I think. *Sí, el Teátro Martí.*"

Daysy heard the crowd sigh, heard the words she'd heard before in public places, "*Ay, pobrecito,*" again and again, a phrase that revealed both genuine pity and relief that the crazy old man was in someone else's family.

Albert Arroyo signaled for the camera to be shut off. "*Muchaaaa-cho,*" Abuelo said to Arroyo, and clapped his hand on the reporter's shoulder. "You're the one we can depend on. Help us find a little girl," Abuelo said, looking right into Albert Arroyo's eyes.

Arroyo laughed then. "You remind me of my grandfather," he said, and shook Abuelo's hand. "*¿Y tu familia?*"

"*No sé,*" Abuelo said, looking around.

Arroyo frowned, glanced at his watch, and said, "I'll treat you to dinner."

Daysy moved quickly and held Abuelo by the wrist. "He's with me," she said. "He's my grandfather."

"Well, it's dinner for you, too," said Arroyo.

"We shouldn't. We have to get home. It's late, and..."

Arroyo smiled at her, and Daysy understood what was meant when someone was said to have star power. "You won't get anywhere in this traffic. Neither will I. I'll spring for dinner. It's the least I can do to pay your grandfather for the great show he gave us." Arroyo patted the camera held by his assistant, and he smiled again. Daysy nodded and followed him into the restaurant.

Inside El Cristo's, the hostess seated the group that included the cameraman and his equipment in a room in the back of the restaurant. Before anyone could say a word, plates of *congrís* and *lechón asado* were on the table, as was a pitcher of *sangría*. The waiter whispered something into Arroyo's ear, and Arroyo patted the man on the shoulder.

Arroyo loosened the carnation from his lapel and placed it on Daysy's placemat. Nodding off in his seat was Abuelo, exhausted from the day's excitement. The flute was back in the interior pocket of his jacket.

"What brings you out to the funeral festivities?" Arroyo asked.

Daysy didn't answer right away. She'd been tracing the outline of the Isle of Pines on the paper placemat before her and thinking of a good answer.

Arroyo ate a bit of his rice and pork then tapped Daysy's placemat with the back of his knife. "It isn't called the Isle of Pines anymore. Did you know? It's the Isle of Youth. Funny how they won't use the new names here. Were you born in Cuba?"

Daysy did not take the bait. But the question bothered her, reminded her of Belén, of the past she'd imagined, the one she couldn't really remember.

"I was born in Cienfuegos," Arroyo offered. "But I don't remember much." Daysy noticed then that Arroyo was quite young. There were no lines anywhere on his face. His hair was full, dark, and defined by a perfect part and a subtle wave at his forehead. Being a bit on the heavy side suited him. "So what's your story?"

"My grandmother knew a pirate…," Abuelo said suddenly, his fork pointed at Arroyo.

"I have to pee," Daysy interrupted, and pushed her chair away from the table. "Can you, you know, watch him?" she asked Arroyo and motioned to her grandfather. Daysy sprinted down the corridor that led to the restaurant proper, into a bathroom, and locked herself in a stall to think. There was always escape. The bathroom had big enough windows and the jump down to the street wasn't far at all. Daysy looked at her watch. Her parents would be home by now, angry and worried, too, she was sure, but that didn't bother her. She still felt a crushing anger whenever she thought of them, one that made her both miserable and determined.

Daysy opened the stall, looked upon a wall of urinals, and screamed. At one of them stood someone, his pants hanging precariously from his hips. Startled, he turned and saw Daysy. "Holy shit," he said, "what are you doing in the boy's bathroom?" Iggy Placetas zipped up his pants and pushed his long hair from his face. Daysy felt weak and stumbled back into the restaurant.

By the time she reached the back table, she was crying in jags and thought she might stop breathing altogether. Arroyo snapped his fingers, and suddenly, a glass of cold ginger ale appeared. Daysy watched as the world changed colors. Everything looked like a photonegative. Arroyo's face became a dark hole, his hair bright white. Her stomach threatened to empty itself right there, and she felt a cold drop of water run down her chest and settle on her belly button. Then everything faded to black.

≈ ✳ ≈

When Daysy woke up, she was lying on the floor of the Channel 23 van, and Abuelo was fanning her with a paper fan that had "El Cristo, the Best Seafood in Miami" printed on it. Albert Arroyo was looking at the picture of Belén as well as the article Daysy had found. She could also see Iggy Placetas peering at her from outside the van, taunting, "I won't tell nobody you use the boy's bathroom." Behind him, a woman with eyes that resembled his hit him on the head with a rolled up placemat, and yelled, "¡Pero niño!" He winked at Daysy before disappearing, his mother's hand gripping his collar and pulling him away.

Daysy sat up and the glass of ginger ale appeared in her hands again. Abuelo and Arroyo stepped out of the truck, their faces wrinkled in concern, and behind them, that same crowd dressed in black, though the numbers had lessened by then. Daysy closed her eyes again as she clutched the cold glass. She didn't know how long she sat that way, but when she opened her eyes, she saw Albert Arroyo in the front seat talking on a phone. "*Sí*," she heard him say, "your daughter is right here."

"Give me the phone," Daysy said quietly, and Arroyo put it in her outstretched hand. Amplified through the speaker came the sound of her mother breathing on the other end. "Mami, *soy yo*," Daysy said, breaking the silence.

"*Ay*, Daysy, we've been dying of fear. I swear, when you see me in that coffin, don't cry, because you..."

Her hand weakened and she nearly dropped the phone before saying, "Mami. I know about Belén. I know the truth." There was no sound save for the breathing on the other end.

On the other end of the line, Daysy heard, for the first time in her life, her mother cry. "*Ay*," Magda Elena said, her voice cracking, overtaken. Then, Magda Elena hung up the phone. For a moment, Daysy pretended that she was still connected to her mother. She doubted what she'd heard. Her mother's sob had chilled her, injured her in some way so that Daysy wanted nothing more than to sink to the ground and crush her face against the gravel there, to cancel out the hurt she was feeling in her jaw again. She tried not to think of her mother crying, her head down on the dining room table, or locked in the bathroom as she cried on the toilet, but the images came to her anyway. *You have five seconds to get it together,* she told herself, and when she opened her eyes, Daysy found strength in her limbs again and the sick feeling in her stomach and her jaw and throat almost gone.

"How did you get those?" Daysy asked Arroyo, snatching the photograph of the del Pozos in Cuba and the article she'd found in the library from his hands.

"They fell out of your pocket," he said. "So what's the story here? And why does your grandfather keep asking me if I know a little girl named Belén?"

Refusing to answer him, Daysy pulled the keys to the van out of her other pocket and handed them to her grandfather.

"I don't think your grandfather should be driving," Arroyo said as he eyed the keys.

"What is he saying about me?" Abuelo asked in Spanish, and Daysy translated.

"*Muchaaaacho,*" Abuelo said again, his mood jovial, no longer sleepy. "I've been driving since before your parents imagined you could exist," he said to Arroyo in Spanish, then smacked the back of Arroyo's head with a quick swipe. Arroyo looked at his cameraman, who averted his eyes, busying himself with a few turns of the complex dials on the camera.

"I think I'll follow you home anyway," Arroyo said. Daysy shrugged, hopped out of the Channel 23 van, and headed toward their own van. She was done. The afternoon had been a waste of time. Night had come on quickly, and Abuelo would have to drive in the dark. And now a reporter, who had looked at the picture of Belén a beat too long, who had, it seemed to Daysy, begun taking mental notes, was following her home. She'd watched Albert Arroyo every night last fall, when her Social Studies teacher began giving current events quizzes. Arroyo was famous for his investigative stories. "Go, Arroyo, Go" was a nightly segment in which the popular reporter uncovered the many ways in which unsuspecting South Floridians stood in peril. Daysy remembered the story of the supermarket that dunked fillets of mahi mahi in vats of bleach in order to sell them past their expiration date and, once, how Albert Arroyo had gone undercover as a substitute teacher in a Dade County School, to expose the revolting condition of the bathrooms. He'd stepped in puddles of urine, had his camera zoom in on the sad, empty rolls of toilet paper, and rubbed his finger on the inside of a leaking faucet, drawing crumbling rust from within. Then he'd shoved a microphone into the beard of the principal, demanding answers. Daysy continued watching the news, even after the current events quizzes ended. Arroyo had never come up empty-handed in any of the segments.

The Cruz García funeral crowds had dispersed by now, and Calle Ocho was finally navigable. Whatever weakness had caused Daysy to faint was now gone. When she'd heard her mother cry she'd felt a little wobble in her legs, but that soon passed. It was the sting of pity she felt for her mother that now threatened. If she'd seen her, seen the tears, the contorted face, Daysy was sure she would have cried, too. Cried and forgiven her mother for lying to her about Belén. But distance made Daysy feel strong and cruel, and so she shook off thoughts of sympathy.

Albert Arroyo's van followed them closely. He was in the passenger seat, writing notes with one hand and holding a car phone with the other. The shops along Calle Ocho were closing for the night. Big, iron gates rattled as they were pulled in front of shop windows that advertised "*Envios a Cuba*," and "*Guayaberas*, 15 Dollars." Electronics stores left the televisions running to scenes from the evening news, where every day it seemed hundreds of rafters were washing up on the shores of the Keys or gathered in the middle of the sea, lost and disoriented. The churro vendors were still out. Business having slowed down, many of them leaned on telephone poles, counting their money.

Daysy watched her grandfather driving, how well he looked behind the wheel, as if there were nothing wrong with him. What a sham his composure in the driver's seat! People looking at him as he drove could never imagine how ill Abuelo was, how easily he could disguise it at times. Disguises, deception, lies, Belén. Daysy wondered what

else her parents had hidden from her. Her mind reeled now with the
possibilities of it, and she began to plan accordingly, thinking of ways
to punish her parents in some way for their dishonesty and betrayal.
Perhaps she would run away, pack up and go. She thought about taking a boat to Cuba, how out at sea she could think of her sister's
bones fathoms beneath her and feel her spirit. She might find her
cousin, Amado, the only family she had on the island, and move in
with him and his mother. Perhaps they could tell her the whole story
of Belén's life. But Daysy was aware that her fantasies were impossible. That the truth of it was, she had nowhere to go. And though she
tried to feel angry and pitiless, she was hurt more than anything else.

Abuelo began to sing as he drove, low at first, then louder and
louder, an old *bolero* Daysy knew bits of. She sang along with him,
"*Solamente una vez*," and plunged her sadness into it, so that Abuelo
exclaimed, "*Caramba, que lindo*," midsong. Embarrassed, Daysy
stopped and fixed a severe look on her face. Her house had come
into view at last, and the lights were all on inside.

≈ ✳ ≈

When Abuelo pulled the van up into the del Pozos' driveway, the
first thing Daysy saw was her mother sitting on the front lawn, tearing grass out in big fistfuls. A porch light cast a yellow glow on
Magda Elena. In the garish light, Daysy saw that her mother had
ripped out a good portion of the lawn before her, revealing jittery
beetles and thin, pulsing worms that tried to hide from the light.
Arroyo's vehicle paused for a moment on the street, honked its
horn lightly as if saying goodbye, and continued on its way.

To her surprise, Daysy began to cry, the tears coming so suddenly
that she first noticed she was crying only when she felt the tickle of a
droplet on her lip. Daysy cried in the darkened van, partly because
she'd never done anything so wrong as letting Abuelo drive her all

over Miami, leaving no note behind, no message, lying and sneaking and endangering herself. She felt a bit as she imagined a runaway might, both defeated at the sight of home and reluctant to admit that it was a place she longed for. She cried, too, because the sight of her mother satisfied her like pouring water into an empty cup, filling the empty space the way it should be filled, and that realization made her angry. She wanted to renounce her parents, her mother in particular, the way they had renounced Belén's existence. Daysy felt, for the first time, a deep allegiance to someone aside from her parents. She couldn't stop the weeping now, even when she tried. It came on her like a hiccup, or a fever. The crying was inevitable at the moment, and mindless, too, despite her will to stop.

Abuelo, exhausted now, didn't notice Daysy's crying. He opened the door and stumbled out of the van. "*Ay, m'ija,*" he said to Magda Elena. "*Mira muchacha, dame una mano,*" he said, and extended his arm for her to take. Magda Elena stood and shook torn blades of grass from her lap. They fell like green confetti to the ground and onto her feet. Magda Elena held out her arms for her father-in-law.

"*Viejo,* you gave us such a scare. You know you shouldn't drive. Come inside and I'll cut you a slice of guava and cheese, the way you like it." Magda Elena pulled Abuelo into the house, but not before turning to glare at Daysy. Daysy looked up in time to see her mother's face contort for a moment before scowling in her direction. She led Abuelo inside and closed the door.

Daysy approached the iron door slowly, couldn't seem to catch her breath, and she whimpered every so often without wanting to. When she turned the handle, she found her mother had locked it. "Shit," she said, and rang the doorbell.

It was Angel who opened the door and immediately pulled Daysy into his chest. "You are in so much trouble," he said, trying to sound stern, but his eyes were full of water.

For a while, Daysy stood at the doorway and watched her mother.

Magda Elena looked tense and startled, her hand resting on Abuelo's shoulder as she watched him smear the cheese on the sticky slice of guava. Under the brightly lit chandelier over the dining table, Magda Elena's face looked too sharply drawn, as if all her wrinkles were being highlighted, so that she seemed far older than her fifty years.

That morning had been so full of promise. Daysy thought it would be easy to find information in the library, to track down a missing girl, like characters in a movie who uncover mysteries and redirect their lives in two short hours. But in the course of one day she'd only complicated matters. The small house in Hialeah felt as if it had shrunk considerably, made her feel phobic and overwrought. Magda Elena's drawn face was suffocating her, filling up the dining room, *la sala*, the kitchen, and the Florida room. Daysy felt her heart beating fast now and found it hard to breath. She could actually hear her breaths in the quiet house, and knew her mother could hear them, too. Wishing she were more poised, more controlled, she thought that if anyone should be falling apart, it should be her mother. But Magda Elena was as stiff and mournful looking as a totem pole. The unasked questions became so distracting that everyone else stopped moving, except for Abuelo, his mouth slick with cheese, his dentures coming loose as he ate.

Suddenly, Magda Elena's hand came down on the dining room table, palm flat on the mirrored surface. The slap startled Daysy. Magda Elena turned so quickly toward her that Daysy cringed, expecting that same heavy hand to make contact with her face. But Magda Elena trembled before her daughter for a long time, her face reddening with each second.

"Mami, I..."

"Not a word! *¡Baja la vista!*" she said, and Daysy obeyed, lowering her eyes and staring at her mother's bare feet. "You're lucky to be alive," she yelled. "Your grandfather could have driven you all into a wall! Or a canal! You would have drowned! And your father and I?

What would have become of us then? Eh? *¿Entonces que?*"

Daysy could no longer make out her mother's feet through the tears. She knew her tears must be falling to the floor, knew that her mother's toes were getting wet, but she couldn't force her hands to her face to wipe it. Instead, her arms, wrapped around her body, pinning herself down, as she if she might flee without meaning to.

"*Ya, mi vida, ya,*" Angel urged, as he rose and took hold of Magda Elena's hand. She pushed him away and he stumbled.

"No! Always, always, I'm *la mala* who punishes her, and you are *el santo!* What if they'd been killed, Angel? What if we lost her the way we lost Belén?" Magda Elena's voice broke on the name, as if it were a scratched record, an old thing long unused, so that it became three syllables instead of two. Silence took hold of the house again, and Daysy was afraid to look up at her parents, afraid that they might be watching her now for a reaction. Daysy feared most of all to see them and find that the secret they'd held had diminished her love for them. So she ran for her bedroom, instead.

≈ ✶ ≈

The door to Daysy's bedroom always stuck a bit. She forced it closed by slamming it shut with her hips. In the corner was a Barbie dollhouse she no longer played with, built wrong from the start by Abuelo one Christmas morning. The roof angles did not meet in the center to form a pretty peak. Rather, they jutted out, left and right, like some modern interpretation of a dollhouse. The fuschia carpeting in the room was matted, and every so often, a stray flea, leftover from the day earlier in the summer when she'd brought home a sad-looking dog hoping she could keep him, would jump out from between the fibers and bite Daysy. Turning off the light, she fought the urge to use the bathroom or venture out into the hallway for any reason, and waited for her mother to come open the door.

She pretended to be asleep for a long time. She heard Magda Elena weeping, a noise so foreign to Daysy that it wracked her nerves and made her arms shake. Daysy thought that perhaps she should cry alongside her mother, but she couldn't will herself to do it. Sometime around two o'clock, a crack of light slashed before Daysy's eyes. She turned to see Magda Elena in the doorway and watched her mother for a long time. Her mother's eyes were still full of light from the hall, so she was squinting hard to make out Daysy's form. Daysy couldn't guess what her mother had come to say. That she was sorry to have lied? Daysy didn't think she was. If she were sorry, she would step into the room, fling herself on Daysy's bed and ask forgiveness. Magda Elena did nothing but stand in the doorway, and then, after a long time, she stepped out into the hall and closed the door.

Daysy had watched her mother the entire time, had looked her in the eye without blinking, but her mother left anyway. Daysy turned onto her side and pressed her back against the cool, stucco wall. Once, she had thought her mother anchor-like, mooring her and fixing her to life, and also holding her in place. Now, Daysy felt as if that anchor had dislodged itself from a muddy bottom, and she was untethered in a wide sea. In the dark again, she rubbed her eyes and felt her hands shaking, her muscles twitching. A sort of tremor within her grew, so strong that the headboard knocked every so often against the wall. It unnerved her, made her want to cry again. All the while, sleep tugged at her eyes, and despite the shaking, she fell asleep.

≈ ✳ ≈

Magda Elena knocked on Daysy's bedroom door in the morning, opening it herself after a moment.

"Leave me alone," Daysy muttered from underneath her pillow.

"I have some things to show you," Magda Elena said, and Daysy could hear her mother unzipping something, heard the creak of a hinge. A damp smell filled the room. Daysy lifted her head.

"Your Papi and I, we should have told you a long time ago," Magda Elena said. She was sitting cross-legged on the floor of Daysy's room, like a child. She ran her fingers over the contents of a yellow, fabric-covered suitcase, touching the stiff photographs inside, delicately.

Daysy slipped out of bed and sat next to her mother. "What are these?" she whispered.

"*Fotos de Cuba*."

Daysy lifted one of the rigid little pictures and held it close to her face. "Me?" she asked.

"*Sí*. And this one," Magda Elena said, pulling out another picture. "That's your sister."

"Belén."

"*Sí*."

Still, Magda Elena would not say the name, and Daysy felt a rush of annoyance that washed away the moment she took in the photograph. There was the baby, on a blanket that was laid out on a terrazzo floor. She had placed one chubby finger on her cheek, as if in deep thought, and the space atop her nose was wrinkled. There was a red blotch on her temple, the kind Daysy had seen on other babies in less fortunate places. "We didn't look alike," Daysy said.

"*En nada*," Magda Elena answered, letting loose a weak laugh that faded quickly.

"How did she...?"

Magda Elena answered fast, as if she had rehearsed it. "It was after we'd left Mariel Bay and were in open waters. Our boat was sinking. She drowned before we escaped on another ship." She did not meet Daysy's eyes as she spoke, but stared at her hands instead.

Perhaps there was some trace of Belén's death on her mother's skin? Did her conscience prick her at night and keep her awake? Could she even sleep after such a thing? Daysy was sure that in her mother's place she would have jumped into the sea after the baby.

Maybe her mother did jump. Maybe her fingers grazed the baby in the water but couldn't hold on.

"You never told me. You let me forget her," Daysy said, and felt her throat tightening. The photograph in her hand dropped back into the suitcase without Daysy's noticing.

"We didn't want you to know grief at such a young age. The morning after she died, you asked, 'What happened to Belén?' and it stopped my heart. Your Papi was quick. He told you she turned into a fish, a beautiful goldfish, and I, I..." Magda Elena could go on no longer. She sobbed without sound, covering her face. A little pile of pictures fell out of her hands, slapping her lap quietly, making a sound like rain.

"It's okay, Mami," Daysy said, unsure of whether to hug her mother, or even touch her, so distressing was the sight of Magda Elena falling apart.

"Then you stopped asking about her. Pretending to forget seemed easier. *Fue por tu bien*," Magda Elena said thickly. "It wasn't your fault your sister died. Help me with these? I want to put them up now."

"*Por tu bien*" was a phrase Daysy had heard many times, usually after she was made to do something disagreeable that her mother claimed was for her own good. Every vitamin she was forced to eat, every coat she had to wear in seventy-degree weather, every sleepover she wasn't allowed to attend was for Daysy's benefit. "*Por tu bien*," she was told time and again, though it never felt true.

"Why would I think it's my fault?" Daysy asked, and her mother gripped her hard.

"I said it wasn't your fault," Magda Elena repeated, staring into Daysy's eyes intently. Daysy felt a long tremor in all of her mother's being.

A sudden epiphany came to Daysy, that her mother caged her because she feared, at any moment, that Daysy might drop into a midnight sea and never return. It was fear that impelled Magda Elena

to put up the chain-link fence in the backyard, a barrier between
Daysy and the cloudy waters of the canal. Fear, too, was why Daysy
had not yet been to a party where her mother had not sat in the living room, steel-eyed, the whole time. At last Daysy understood why,
the day she learned to float on her back at the beach, her mother had
come splashing into the water, jumping mild waves, and slid her
hands behind Daysy's back. "Just in case," she'd said, her eyes wild
with worry.

Magda Elena released her. "You mean the world to us, Daysy. Do
you hear that? Do you?"

Daysy did hear it. Stunned, she followed her mother out into the
dining room, where there were, laid out on the table, frames of different sizes and colors. One by one, Magda Elena sorted the pictures in
the suitcase into piles, coughing every so often. Then, Magda Elena
put photograph after photograph into frames, and when she was finished, she hung them from nails on the wall in an artful semicircle.

Angel watched them from the kitchen where he'd been having
breakfast. Before he left for work, he sought Daysy and hugged her a
long time, his black lunchbox banging against her back. Then he left.

"Poor Papi," Daysy said. Magda Elena huffed, hanging the last
picture, one of Daysy's third birthday party. In the forefront of the
photo was a long table with a flat, white cake in the center. A toy
clown holding plastic balloons sat on a little pile of frosting, and at
his feet were the words, "*Feliz Cumpleaños Daysy.*" Behind the cake,
Daysy stood on a chair, and at either side of her were her parents,
smiling broadly, her mother's stomach revealing the smallest of
bulges. Daysy touched the picture and left a foggy fingerprint there
on her mother's belly.

Her uncle's wife, Catalina, and their son, Amado, were in the picture, too. Amado was standing on the table, leaning back against his
mother. He had knobby knees and wore red sneakers. Daysy guessed
that her uncle Eddy was behind the camera. Daysy's grandparents

stood far in the back, behind the others. Abuelo had been caught midlaugh, Nieve with her mouth pursed tightly.

There was another child in the photograph, held by a woman of striking beauty. Her hair was long and curled at the ends, so that the dark locks made figure *s*'s against her breasts. The baby boy in her arms had a happy look on his face, his mouth open in a big, gummy smile.

"Who are these two people?" Daysy asked her mother, trying to sound casual. The morning had been difficult for Daysy. Here she was on the brink of learning about her life in Cuba, and yet she was afraid of asking too much, of frightening her mother back into silence and secrecy, of making her relive the horror of Belén's loss. Every once in a while, Magda Elena's eyes would fill with tears, the coughing would start up again, and she would have to get a drink of water to make it stop.

"That was my dearest friend, Solamaris, and her little boy, Leo." Magda Elena lifted the frame off the nail.

"Why are you taking it down?" Daysy asked.

"My friend, she lost her mind. I'll find another picture to replace it."

Later that night Daysy would wonder at herself, at how quickly she snatched the frame from her mother's hands, at the unnamed impulse that drove her to save the photograph from the confines of the suitcase. "No, Mami," she'd said, clutching the frame against her chest. "I really like this one. Leave it up."

"*Ay*, Daysy, I…"

"You owe me one. Or a million," Daysy said, trying to joke, unsure of how this might end.

"*Bueno*," Magda Elena said, shaking her head. Daysy hung up the picture and again put her finger on the image of her mother's stomach, imagining her sister there, tiny, warm, yet invisible. Daysy took another look at herself at age three, in awe of this new likeness, how it was possible that the little girl she had been had no knowledge of a sister then either, and how pleased she looked surrounded by family and friends.

Daysy found herself staring at the wall of pictures for long stretches of time. In the background of the birthday photograph was an open window, through which could be seen the top of a house with half of its terracotta tiles gone, and beyond that, like a silver tray, the ocean. She noticed that a fresh-cut gardenia stuck out of her Abuelo's pocket in the picture, and that her grandmother, Nieve, rested her hand on Abuelo's chest. The window had no curtains. The tablecloth had four-leaf clovers printed on it. The wall had a zigzag crack in it, just near the ceiling. Daysy's tiny fingernails had been painted pink. Her cousin, Amado, had a small scrape on his left knee. Catalina held him too tightly, so that his flesh underneath her fingertips was white from the pressure. And the woman, Solamaris, was the only person not looking into the camera. Her eyes were off to the right, gazing out the window, as if she were contemplating a walk outside.

≈ ✳ ≈

The revelation of Belén's existence did not alter the family in any significant way, except for the wall of photographs in the dining room and Magda Elena's reluctance to eat there now, taking her meals at the counter in the kitchen, her plate crowded by cereal boxes and appliances. Angel had been angered by this, had yelled at her, "Take the damn pictures down, then!" and Magda Elena and Daysy had both answered, "No!" simultaneously, from different parts of the house, so that the word surrounded Angel like an ambush, and he, taken by surprise, left the matter alone.

The photographs served the good purpose of jogging Abuelo's memory, so that at dinner, he often stared at them as he ate, then told stories of meeting Nieve on a dirt road in Matanzas, where she was selling dried palm fronds shaped into crosses for Palm Sunday. He seemed to remember Eddy and Catalina well, and talked about how handy Eddy had been with the interior workings of the old Fairlane, the perfect lentil soup Catalina made every New Year, even without the ham. Abuelo spoke of them with such clarity that when a letter arrived at the end of the summer announcing Amado's arrival in late August, the family attached a kind of mysticism to Abuelo's memories, as if he had called Amado out of Cuba with his stories.

The news had been delivered in a red, white, and blue airmail envelope. A photograph of Amado was enclosed, taped to a note that said, "Amadito will be with you on August 23rd. Wait for him," in the elegant writing of Amado's mother, Catalina. The arrival of the letter, just three weeks before the stated date, set off a scalding argument once Angel came home from work.

"What kind of stupidity is this?" Angel demanded. "'Wait for him.' Where? Did they secure an American visa for him? And if they did, how did they get the money for it? Those things take time. Why didn't she write sooner?"

"*Mi amor*, calm down," Magda Elena pleaded.

Daysy, who'd been listening to the argument from her bedroom, crept into the hallway for a closer listen.

"Especially someone like Catalina," Angel said, her name a low hiss. "A *Santera* like that. A Fidelista like that..."

"*Ya*, Angel. *Ya*," Magda Elena warned, and Daysy knew the argument would soon be over. The word "Fidelista" wasn't bandied about lightly. Her father's cheeks colored at the mention of a Fidelista, and he'd launch into a rage. Once, her normally gentle father became so angry with a neighbor three doors down over the matter of visiting Cuba and staying at a tourist-only hotel that he'd gone for a long drive well into the night, and when he called, sounding himself again, he announced that he'd made it to Key West and would be home in the morning, promising a key lime pie and a bucket of conch soup for Magda Elena. When Daysy asked what the neighbor had said, her mother responded, "It doesn't interest you."

"You mean concern. It doesn't concern me, but it *does* interest me," Daysy corrected her mother.

"I know what I mean!" Magda Elena had shouted, and left Daysy alone to ponder her neighbor's sin.

"Catalina has changed," Magda Elena said after a while. Daysy heard her father's derisive snort. Magda Elena pressed on. "We'll just have to wait at the airport on the 23rd."

"*Oye*, you don't think they're taking to the sea?" Angel said.

"On a raft? No."

Magda Elena sounded sure, and Daysy agreed with her. The images of those Cubans floating on inner tubes and old tires didn't seem to match pictures of Amado she'd seen. The camera crews were always there to catch the *balseros'* first, feeble steps on land after days at sea. The people always looked the same—hollow cheeked, sunburned, eyes swollen, clothes rigid from salt spray. One group of *balseros* rigged a 1952 Dodge to sail on a bed of tires. Sometimes, they wore homemade lifesavers, which were only two sheets of Styrofoam strung together with shoelaces, hung against their chests. Once, when she still played with such things, Daysy tried floating a wide-eyed, stiff-haired baby doll she didn't like much anyway on some leftover Styrofoam in the canal behind their house. The sheet had cracked, and the doll had floated away, disappearing finally in green canal gunk.

In the picture Catalina sent along with her cryptic note, Amado was sitting in someone's living room, a shelf full of knickknacks behind him, a coffee table with plastic daffodils in front of him. He wore a wrinkled t-shirt and acid-washed jeans, and smiled so that only one of his front teeth showed. Daysy thought he was handsome, if a little out of style in those jeans. He was two years older than Daysy, sixteen, but looked younger. He seemed healthy, and certainly not the kind of boy who would wash ashore like a clump of seaweed, Daysy thought.

Daysy and Amado had kept up a short correspondence when they were younger. But the mail from the U.S. to Cuba was unreliable, and slow. Letters that had only a short swath of sea and land to travel took six months en route. As soon as Catalina's letter arrived, Magda Elena had dashed off a letter of her own, as well as a telegram, asking for more information about Amado's arrival. "Waste of time and money," Angel had said about the letter-sending frenzy. The letter would arrive in half a year, there would be no way for Catalina to answer the telegram, and there were no working telephones within six blocks of Catalina's house.

Daysy spent the rest of that muggy summer watching Abuelo during the day and helping her mother prepare for her cousin's arrival in the afternoons. The heat made everything sticky, as if furniture knew how to sweat, and while Daysy had wanted to swim at the Milander pool with friends, Magda Elena made her stay indoors in their oven of a house and clean. They cleaned the base moldings, scrubbed the grout between the Italian tiles on the floor, added a fold-away bed in the hallway outside of Daysy's room, a contraption her mother called a *pin-pan-pun* for the three steps it took to open it up and for the sounds it made, steel against steel, creaking springs.

They worked hard every day so that the house was presentable, and in the end, it was better than that. The place had never been so clean, so free of clutter. Magda Elena took down the plastic beaded curtain that divided the Florida room from the dining room, then put it up again the next hour when she thought the space looked too empty without it. She bought blue cotton sheets for the *pin-pan-pun*. Even the garage, with its labyrinthine maze of boxes and old bicycles, its carpet of rusted screws and hinges, was clean, the tools and other oily accoutrements hung on big rusted hooks or put in labeled boxes.

≈ ✶ ≈

The baggage carousel clanked into motion at the precise moment that Magda Elena, Angel, and Daysy entered the airport. "*Coño*, he's already here," Magda Elena said when she eyed the lonesome parcels as they went round. The sign above the carousel announced Continental Flight 629 had arrived from Havana. And it was the only plane coming in from the island that day.

The trio rushed past travelers, bumping into luggage and pushing aside empty strollers, up escalators encased in mirrored walls, past rows and rows of sticky vinyl chairs filled with sleepy passengers, running on the moving walkway that led to international Gate D outside of U.S. Customs and Immigration and the crowd that waited there.

Daysy counted forty, maybe fifty people standing around them behind a torn velvet rope. The plane sat outside, still filled with people, as airport security and a host of flight attendants came in and out of the tunnel that led to the airplane. The people around them pushed and called out names. Some were crying.

"*Mi hijo, mi hijo*," one woman said, "I haven't seen him in twenty-three years." She held a bouquet of white roses to her chest. And there were others. A pair of women on the outer edge of the group held hands and trembled. A young man in a mechanic's uniform strummed a guitar he rested on his hip. His companion, similarly dressed, craned his neck to look into the tunnel. Beside Daysy, a toddler set free from his stroller tried pushing his way between her ankles to retrieve a pacifier. Most of the people were waiting for relatives who had won the visa lottery in Cuba, six-week passes to visit abroad. Many of the visitors would stay forever, leaving behind spouses and mothers and children, biding their time until they were made residents, and hoping that the families left behind would win the visa lottery, too. Others were returning to Miami, having traveled to Cuba to visit relatives on allotted U.S.-approved, once-a-year visits. The room was hot from too many bodies, and Daysy feared being swallowed by the pushing, pulsing group.

"Who are you waiting for?" a young woman who'd been fanning herself with a gossip magazine asked Magda Elena. She wore large hoop earrings that swung back and forth in time with the makeshift fan.

"My nephew. *¿Y tu?*"

"*Mi papi,*" she said, and stopped fanning for a moment to wipe sweat out of her eyes. "I came in 1980. Mariel, you know. Haven't seen him in nine years." The woman undid her ponytail, raked her nails through stiff knots in her hair, and gathered it all up again. "So," she said after checking her eyeliner in a compact mirror, "how long did it take your nephew's visa to come through? We waited years on this end."

Angel leaned in and whispered, "What did I tell you?" in Magda Elena's ear, crushing Daysy between them.

"Years," Magda Elena answered, but Daysy could see her mother had become suddenly pale.

At last, a single traveler emerged from the tunnel that was as dark and endless as a wolf's mouth. A cheer rose from the crowd, and soon people broke out of the pack to watch the tunnel. A man, leaving his place behind the velvet rope and dashing through the crowds, collided with an old woman whose hair was wrapped in a colorful sheet, like a Yoruban queen. The man crushed his face into the neck and bosom of the woman. The woman, for her part, hugged him a long while, and a small circle of people stood around them, sighing at the reunion. Daysy watched, enchanted, as the strange woman, undoubtedly saddened by the loss of time, sang softly to the man, "*Ay, Mama Inés, todo los negros tomamos café,*" over and over, an old child's song about coffee, and comfort, and memory.

The cries of recognition surged and quieted, the "*Ay*, how you've changed," and the "How I missed you, *mi vida*," and all the other sweet words of reunion after a long separation faded down the passageways of the airport. The last passenger came and went, the cleaning crew dragged their vacuums behind them into the tunnel, and Magda Elena had someone check the plane to make sure that the boy Amado had not trapped himself in the bathroom.

"Are you sure," Angel asked, "that the letter said today was the day?"

"Yes, yes, today. How could I forget?" Magda Elena's hand went through her hair. Daysy knew her mother was thinking about the solution to the problem. Magda Elena began to babble to herself: "Did Amado miss his flight? Should we return tomorrow? What if they take him to Krome Detention Center when no one comes to claim him? He's only sixteen, *por Dios*, what could have happened?"

"Call Cuba. Call Catalina," Daysy said, trying to help.

"*No tiene teléfono.*"

"Oh."

They stood there quietly as Angel asked the lady at the gate desk for some information. He wrote down a long list of flights, all incoming from Havana for the next week, folded the paper and shoved it into his shirt pocket.

They drove home in silence. Angel punched the radio button and a blare of salsa music rushed in. Magda Elena shut it off with a quick swipe of her hand. It wasn't until they were turning the corner of their street, when the iron door came into view, that Angel said, "It's not my fault Amado is not here yet. Catalina should have given you more information."

They were inside the house again, a house that still smelled like Pine Sol from all the cleaning. The beaded curtain trembled in the wake of a fan set on "High." The *pin-pan-pun* still stood, open and welcoming, dressed in powder blue sheets, waiting for Amado. It was quiet in the house.

"Nelba," Magda Elena called. Nelba Alonso lived next door, and she often watched Abuelo a few hours a day. There was little to do, really. Nelba's real job was to call 911 in case of an emergency and to stand at the door whenever Abuelo threatened to walk to Havana.

"Nelba," Magda Elena called again, and the neighbor came rushing out of the living room. She smelled like the coconut cream Magda Elena always spread over her legs. She had been dipping into Magda Elena's lotion. The smell was all over Nelba's hands and neck.

"Magda Elena, quick. Look at the television," Nelba said, after she kissed Daysy hello, their cheeks sticking together for a moment because of the lotion. "There's a kid on the beach the coast guard have their hands on. I think it's your nephew." The family did not stir.

"The kid keeps saying he needs to see his Tía Magda. Go look, Magda Elena, Angel, somebody! I think he just washed ashore." Nelba pushed through the small knot of people before her, and turned up the volume on the TV. Abuelo, who was snoring in his recliner, was startled awake for a moment, then sank back into sleep. Magda Elena sighed and turned to watch. Daysy watched, too, her breath caught in her throat. There Amado was on the screen, shielding his eyes from the sun, being led away by the Coast Guard.

≈ ✶ ≈

Daysy had fallen asleep in the car as her father drove south to the Krome Detention Center, where Amado was in custody. She had been dreaming of being on a boat, a large schooner, the sails raised and puffy in the wind. Belén was in the dream, small as she was, crawling up and down the deck of the boat. Magda Elena had been yelling all along, "Catch her! She'll drown!" over and over again, until Daysy's legs became leaden and she slowed and watched as Belén jumped over the side of the boat. She howled twice, then her little head went under. It was the kind of dream that stuck. Later in the week, Daysy would feel suddenly sad, and she would trace the events of the day, her breakfast, the news of more rafters on TV, and follow the root of her sadness to that dream of her sister.

But she was able to forget it in that moment when they pulled into Krome Detention Center. They parked with relative ease and entered the front door. A receptionist ignored them and tapped a manicured nail against a clipboard on her desk. Daysy approached the visitor's roster and wrote first her father's name, then her mother's, and finally her own.

Daysy waited. The receptionist answered a phone call. Daysy sighed. The receptionist began to rifle through her purse. "Excuse me," Daysy said, and the woman finally looked up. "We are here to pick up Amado Camposanto."

"Sure," the receptionist said, and immediately got to work on the keyboard, her nails clicking prettily on the keys. She pursed her lips. "They're being processed," she said. "What about his mother? Are you claiming her, too?"

"She's here?" Daysy asked, her mind going at once to the *pin-pan-pun* made for one, not two.

"*¿Qué pasó?*" Magda Elena insisted behind Daysy.

"Catalina is here, too," Daysy said. Magda Elena frowned and looked at her husband at once. Angel's face stiffened, and the tips of his ears began to turn red.

"Can we see them?" Daysy asked and the receptionist nodded and pointed to the seats in the waiting room. They sat together on the vinyl chairs, and Daysy tucked her hands under her thighs to keep them warm in the frigid, air-conditioned room. She thought what a relief this air conditioning must be to her cousin and aunt who had spent so much time in the blazing sun. There were no magazines and no small television anchored on the wall like in a doctor's office, but it felt just as tense. Every so often, Magda Elena forced Daysy to ask the receptionist, "How long?" The woman always shrugged her shoulders and shook her head.

They had been sitting for nearly two hours before a phone rang at
the desk. The receptionist answered, then stood up and stretched. She
sighed and said, "Follow me," and the del Pozos stood up, backs and
necks aching from the hard chairs. They went through a set of double
doors and down a long, white corridor. The receptionist unlocked a
room with a key from her pocket and motioned for them to enter. A
brown vinyl-covered couch and a coffee table that leaned to the left
were inside. She closed the door after her and left Magda Elena,
Angel, and Daysy alone in the small room. They sat in silence for
a long time, until Angel said, "I don't want her in my home."

"We can't leave her here. She'll need us to sponsor her."

"She can go to hell for all I care," Angel said a bit more loudly
now, and both Daysy and Magda Elena jumped a bit in their seats.

"She let us stay in her house when we needed…"

"Your brother let us stay. Not her."

"Papi, what did Catalina do?" Daysy asked.

"*Comunista*, through and through," Angel said without looking at
Daysy, and his voice trembled a bit as he said it.

"People change. Situations change," Magda Elena said, reaching
again for Angel's hand.

Just then, the door swung open. A heavy-set woman with peroxide
blond hair in a bun walked in. Behind her, Daysy could see the dark
head of a boy.

"Catalina," Magda Elena said, low and soft.

"*Hermana*," Catalina answered and opened her arms. She was
dressed all in white, down to her shoes. Her eyes were dark, dark like
the roots of her hair, and her nails were painted red. Magda Elena
stood and embraced her sister-in-law. Tears streaked Catalina's sunburned face. Magda Elena did not cry, though she looked as if she
might.

When they let go of each other, Catalina stepped aside. "My son," she said, and Amado came into the room. Magda Elena took hold of him immediately. Now Amado cried, saying, "*Tía, Tía,*" over and over again.

Angel stayed on the couch with Daysy, his arm now wrapped around her tightly. Daysy could feel her father tense. He'd never known what to do when women cried around him, so he said, "Don't cry, please," and reached out to pat Catalina's hand. Catalina smiled then, revealing the smallest, whitest teeth Daysy had ever seen. Then Catalina hugged Magda Elena again and laughed so hard that she opened her mouth wide, and Daysy saw the unreal redness of her tongue and knew that Catalina had just eaten a lollipop.

Amado stood behind his mother, his hand on her shoulder, but his gaze on Daysy. Afraid to meet his eyes, Daysy studied his feet. White sneakers, white jeans. Up her eyes went to his hands. Long fingers, trim nails. His skin was dark from the sun, but the palms of his hands were pale. His hair was black, nearly blue, and it curled at his ears. Brown eyes, small mouth, his back had the slightest bend to it.

"*¡Prima!*" he said at last, and came out from behind his mother. He hugged Daysy where she sat, but she, startled, did not return the embrace.

They talked in the tight room for over an hour before someone came and took Catalina and Amado away. They would be free to come home in the morning, after mounds of paper had been moved. Angel had not said a thing though, and no one in the room tried to get him to speak, afraid whatever peace he'd made with Catalina would shatter with one wrong word. Neither did anyone mention the raft, the harrowing trip. No need to talk about it. It was on Catalina's red face, on the blisters on Amado's lips, the stains on their clothes, their breath, the smell of McDonald's hamburgers—their first meal in the States, bought for them by someone from the Coast Guard. It was there in the way they swayed side to side as they sat, as they talked, to keep with the timing of the waves trapped in their ears. There would be time to talk about the pitching waves, the circling sharks, and about the other people who came on the raft with them, the ones who did not survive the trip.

For now, Catalina continued to embrace Magda Elena every few minutes, and the two women held each other for a long time before parting. Magda Elena promised to come back in the morning and told them a bed was waiting just for them.

≈ ✳ ≈

Daysy sat on the wicker chair in the Florida room and watched as Amado pulled items out of a cardboard box they had given him at Krome. The box was big, and Daysy thought it must have originally held an appliance, a microwave or something. He was sitting on the edge of the *pin-pan-pun*, which had been moved into the room along with a brand-new second one for his mother. His arms were buried inside the box. In the kitchen, Daysy could hear Catalina talking with her parents, her mother's voice easy now, picking up the rhythms of Catalina's Spanish, a Cuban cadence that Magda Elena had somehow misplaced in nine years of American living. Coffee was brewing on the stove, the steam rising from within the espresso maker, pushing the aluminum lid up and down. Soon, Magda Elena appeared with tiny cups of coffee, complete with handles too small to put a finger through, and little saucers. "*¿Niños, café?*" she said to them, and Daysy's mouth watered at the sight of that dark liquid, creamy foam on top, a hidden layer of sugar at the bottom. She swallowed it all in one gulp and stuck the tip of her tongue into the cup to lick up the sugar.

She watched as Amado sipped his coffee slowly, savoring it. When he was done, he began to unpack, working methodically, arranging his few possessions in a straight line beneath the *pin-pan-pun*. Every so often, he'd look up and smile crookedly at Daysy, then return to the line. As the conversation in the kitchen turned toward Catalina and Amado's voyage, Amado stopped unpacking altogether, and he twirled a cassette tape in his hands. Daysy listened to the voices in the kitchen, too.

"We thought you'd gotten visas," Magda Elena said.

"Those are impossible to get. Expensive, too. *Y, bueno,* I wasn't sure you'd claim us."

There was silence again, except for the tinkling of cups being arranged on the counter, in a line like Amado's things.

Then, "How long were you at sea?"

Quiet consumed the house again. Daysy thought the ticking of the grandfather clock had never sounded so loud.

"Four days rowing. By the fifth night we were too tired. On the sixth night, the raft overturned and we lost Guillermo and Sarita. I heard their heads knock together, and they disappeared, like that." Catalina snapped her fingers and it sounded like a gunshot in the house. "Amado helped me right the raft. We ran into a sand bank near the shore on the seventh day."

"Who were they?" Angel's voice broke in. "Guillermo and…"

"Sarita. My neighbor and his daughter. It was his idea." There was the sound of crying now, and then, between sluggish breaths, Daysy heard Catalina say, "Eddy would have liked him." A sigh escaped Amado then, and Daysy looked up in time to catch him rubbing his eyes with the inside of his shirt.

"So you and he?" Magda Elena asked, caution in her voice.

"A widow twice over, you might say," Catalina answered.

"You were married?"

"Not legally. But in my heart…" Catalina trailed off, and suddenly, the sound of glass against glass, and the soft gurgling of coffee brewing filled the house. Amado returned to his box.

"*Prima,*" Amado called, breaking Daysy's concentration on the goings-on in the kitchen. Sitting in the Florida room with only

Amado was awkward. Daysy could not help but think that this room would never be the same. Now, the wicker couch had been pushed off to the side to make room for Amado's bed. His white sneakers had already taken residence by the sliding glass door. And the smell of him, of sweat mingled with a sweet, banana-ish scent, filled the room. The longer she sat in the Florida room with Amado, the stranger the room felt, as if she did not belong in it anymore.

Amado, though, seemed at ease now that the conversation in the kitchen had ended. "*Ven*," he said, and patted the bed beside him. Daysy sat on the bed, far from the place he had pointed to. She teetered on the edge of the mattress, and the bed's steel mechanisms creaked. Amado had pulled out the Walkman that the social worker at Krome gave him. He put the headphones on Daysy's head and pressed play. The music came through at top volume and Daysy jumped.

"What does that mean?" Amado asked in Spanish. Then, in English: "I wanna dan wis ju, go."

Daysy laughed and pulled the headphones off. "It's, 'I wanna dance with you, girl,'" she translated for him. Amado would sing that song, that one line, over and over again for a week. Sometimes, he'd grab Magda Elena around the waist while singing it, twirling his aunt around and laying a kiss on her cheek. Or he'd come up behind Daysy and pull her hair in tune with the words. He sang with Abuelo, and Abuelo would raise his arm as if to dance with Amado, blinking hard as he did so, then grinding his teeth to the music.

Daysy inched closer to him on the bed. "What else is in the box?" she asked in Spanish. Amado looked at her then, his eyes narrowing, his lips pursed.

"Your Spanish is terrible," he said. Daysy felt a weight in her throat. Then Amado ruffled her hair and said, "*Mira, prima*, my English is worse." The two of them in the Florida room reminded Daysy of all the times she went *de visita* with her parents, visiting old friends from Cuba, distant relatives. There was always some other young person there with whom she was expected to become fast friends. And there was that awkwardness of being left alone with that person, the expectancy in the eyes of the adults, the hope that the friendships they had sustained from Cuba would live on in the new generations. It felt that way with Amado in the beginning, and so Daysy perched on the edge of the bed again.

"*Mira, prima*," Amado began again in what Daysy quickly noticed was his pattern—look cousin, look, here, *mira, mira,* even when there was nothing to look at in particular. In the days following his arrival, Daysy heard so many *miras* that she no longer noticed them. *Mira*, he would say then go on to describe a television show he had watched the night before. *Mira*, he would whisper to her, then ask her to keep quiet about the slice of cake he took from the refrigerator.

But this time, there was something to look at. Daysy caught the smell of seawater, the damp scent in his few possessions that had not yet dried. Inside were some cassette tapes, a book that had swollen like an accordion, two pair of ratty underwear, a Yankees baseball cap, and a waterlogged watch with a scratched face. His thin fingers pushed aside the items, and from within the book, he removed a photograph. It, too, was warped and swollen. A bubble had formed on the top right corner and a chunk of the bottom was missing, but the image was visible. Amado glanced over Daysy's head toward the kitchen. The adults were still inside.

The picture was of a slender girl, her hair in two long plaits. She held a jar of honey in her hands.

"Who is it?" Daysy asked.

"Sarita. My girlfriend," Amado said, and slipped the photograph underneath the pillow of the *pin-pan-pun.*

Then there was a loud clap from the kitchen. Angel emerged with blankets for Amado, and a kiss for his daughter. "*A dormir, mi amor,*" he said, as he pulled her up and turned her in the direction of her bedroom. Daysy wanted to stay up, to get to know her cousin, to ask him to fill in the details of the life she might have lived had there been no Mariel.

≈ ✳ ≈

Later, deep into the night, Daysy heard her bedroom door click open. "*Oye*," she heard Amado whisper, and Daysy felt her stomach twist.

"What are you doing here?" Daysy said and sat up in bed. She covered her pajamas with a blanket.

Amado sat on the carpet and crossed his legs. "I can't sleep," he said. "There's too much noise." Daysy stopped to listen. The rush of cars did not slow down at night, and often, the sirens of ambulances and police cars sounded in the distance. The grandfather clock in the living room struck a sharp note every fifteen minutes, and the air conditioner turned on and off with a heavy clank.

"What noise?" Daysy said. Those were the sounds of night as she knew it.

"In my old house, the only sound was the flapping of clothes left on the line," Amado said as he sat on the floor and crossed his legs. "Except, right before we left, a new hotel being built on the east side of the village kept me awake." Amado stretched out on the carpet and folded his arms beneath his head. He was quiet for a long time. "You remind me of Sarita," he said at last. Daysy heard him sniff, once, twice.

"The one who drowned," Daysy said.

"I was asleep when it happened," he said. "Only my mother was awake. She says the sea was flat as a plate. Out of nowhere, a wave knocked the raft over. I woke up under water. When we flipped the raft back, it was as if Guillermo and Sarita were never with us at all. Like we'd had ghosts for companions."

Daysy's flesh turned goose-pimply. "I'm sorry," she whispered.

"Me, too," Amado answered. He was on his side now, his legs curled up to his chest. Daysy thought he was asleep after a while and settled herself down on the bed. But Amado spoke up again. "Maybe Sarita could be alive. She was a good swimmer." Daysy did not know what to say. Amado seemed at a loss as well. "I think," he started up again, "I think it could be my fault that Sarita died. She'd wanted to hold my hand at night, and I didn't want to. Her hands were sweaty and it was just so hot."

Daysy didn't know what to say to the boy who was crying now. She'd never seen a boy cry, and as she listened to him struggling to catch his breath, she heard herself saying, "Soon you'll forget." She knew, as she was saying it, that this was the wrong thing to say. Why would he want to forget Sarita?

"Oh, I won't forget, Daysy," he said, recovering a bit. "I remember things from long ago. I remember being a baby. I remember my father crying when you left us for Mariel. People don't believe me, but sometimes, I think I remember being born. You can't imagine what that's like, to have your mother's screams in your head, *prima*."

Daysy shuddered again. She gripped her pillow more tightly and wondered if, after all, Amado wasn't just a very good actor. This boy she hardly knew was saying creepy things in the middle of her room at night. Daysy wanted to kick him out, but part of her also wanted very much to hear his stories. Her left foot had fallen asleep, and the million needles she now felt distracted her, but she wanted to listen so badly that she stayed put, despite the numbness in her foot.

"So you remember Belén?" she asked.

"Of course. Don't you?" Daysy shook her head. "Maybe it's best not to remember such a tragedy," Amado said. "Sarita is dead and it's my fault. I'd like to forget. Lucky you. Guilt is hard enough without the memory to go with it." Amado looked up at his cousin for the first time in a long while. His eyes were watery, and Daysy was suddenly afraid. Amado said nothing for a long time, then started to rise.

"You can't go! Not now!" Daysy whispered fiercely.

Amado sat down again. "*Bueno*, I remember, too, my parents talking about your family at night. I could hear everything through the vents in my doorway. And one night, I heard my parents talking about what happened to Belén. How she died like Sarita."

Daysy's toes began to curl involuntarily. She rubbed her foot and tried not to cry out. Amado heard her whimpering.

"It's okay, *prima*," he said, misunderstanding. "It was a long time ago."

"It's not that," Daysy said, regaining her composure and the feeling in her foot. "Did they tell you the whole story?"

"No. My mother says, 'There are things children are not ready to know yet.'"

"God, I don't remember anything at all about it," Daysy said. There was a tightening in her chest, like the pins and needles in her feet but stronger. Daysy looked at Amado's profile. She tried to imagine him out in the middle of the ocean, alone, sunburned, watching the shadows of sharks beneath him making little whirlpools with their fins just under the surface. Amado's hair was damp from sweat. She wanted him to keep talking. "What was it like? Out there?" she asked.

"*Fue así*," he began to explain in Spanish, surprising Daysy with the rapidity with which he answered, as if he'd only been biding his time until she'd ask. "Mamá woke me up in the middle of the night. I got so excited. I thought we were going to the beach in Varadero, because we often left in the middle of the night to get there in the morning." Amado was talking fast. As he spoke, he rubbed his thumb and middle finger together over the callous formed by years of schoolwork.

"You know the feeling. Your eyes want to close and you want to keep dreaming about fishing or flying, but you also want to go on this great trip, so you sit up in bed, swaying, thinking *fish, trip, fish, trip.* I'll tell you, *prima*, I never want to dream about fish again. Mamá kept giving me kisses on the cheek, and I thought, *coño*, she's really lost her mind. And I kept wiping the kisses off my cheek and she would kiss me again and cry a little. That's how I knew this wasn't a vacation.

"When my father died, she cleaned out the house, so that all we had left was a mattress. She said she needed more space in her life. You know, she even threw out our television and the pictures of Fidel and Che. All of it, in the trash, and it was soon picked up by neighbors. By that night, every single item was gone, in someone else's house. Sometimes, I'd visit friends and see our chairs in their house, or our couch." Amado laughed a bit then and rolled his eyes. "It was like she went crazy when he died. When Guillermo and Sarita moved in next door, things got better. I knew another boy in my class who had been a *balsero*, too. His name was Vincente Piedra and he was no Pioneer. He wouldn't say that he wanted to be like *el Che* or anything like that. So the teachers always made him stand at the fence in the sun and hold up history books. He stopped coming to class, and later the teachers told us he had turned *gusano* and had left with his father on a raft. His girlfriend, Leticia Gonzalez, burst into tears in class after the announcement, and the teachers made the whole class stand at the fence all day because Leticia loved a *gusano* like Vincente. She was out for a whole week after that, which was probably a good idea since my classmates and I were ready to grind chalk into her hair, or hide dead spiders in her purse, or something, anything, for having us all stand at the fence. Later, I heard they'd found Vincente's head, just his head and a little bit of his spine, ashore off of the Bahamas. That's what the principal announced, anyway."

"Do you think it was true?" Daysy asked in a whisper.

"Who knows? Vincente's bones were all I could think about as Mamá packed a plastic bag with some of my clothes."

"How long were you out there?"

"A few days," Amado said, and lay down.

They were quiet, and for the first time, Daysy noticed how loud the streets were outside. The zooming of the cars sounded like rockets in the dark, and in the distance, she could hear salsa music.

"About Belén," Daysy whispered.

"Forget about it. It's a blessing you don't remember. Trust me."

"Get out," Daysy whispered in English.

"¿Qué?" Amado asked.

She wanted him to leave. He didn't understand how scared she felt all the time since learning about Belén, how out of control of things. "You should probably go," she said again.

"Go where?" he asked. "My mother and I have nowhere else to stay." Amado had misunderstood her. Daysy sighed. Everyone seemed to misunderstand her. It was as if she had become a stranger to her family, and they to her.

"Forget I said anything," Daysy said. Amado turned on his side, and soon, his breathing became deep and steady.

Daysy turned her body toward the wall and eventually joined her cousin in sleep.

≈ ✳ ≈

Magda Elena cooked a celebratory dinner the next night in honor of Catalina and Amado and invited friends, coworkers, neighbors, and distant cousins to a feast in their backyard. Amid streamers, balloons, and pounding salsa music, people surrounded Catalina and Amado, asking them questions like, "What is Cuba like these days?" and "I have a cousin who's a foreman in a factory in Opa-Locka. Can you sew?" Out of Catalina and Amado's earshot they whispered, "The Cubans who arrive nowadays aren't like the ones who came before," and "She's a *Santera*, dressed all in white like that." Daysy wandered the backyard hearing it all, stopping now and again when someone said hello, offered a "Look how you've grown!" and a kiss on the cheek.

Giant platters full of *congris, platanitos,* and *yuca frita* were arranged on a picnic table, and in a wooden box to the side of the house, a pig was roasting. From the narrow canal behind the house, on the other side of a chain-link fence that demarcated the end of the del Pozo property, came a sour smell, like that of a tree rotting in water, and indeed, up the canal, were the remains of a *flamboyán,* half-submerged. Daysy clicked open the fence's gate and sat for a while at the water's edge. The canal was useless for swimming, gunked up as it was, and mosquitoes hatched in the shallows, so that the del Pozos did not come out at night for fear of them.

Amado joined her on the bank. "So you got away?" she asked him in Spanish, and he laughed.

"They're terrible. All of them," he said, grinning from ear to ear. "But it's the kind of terrible I think I like, you know, like the way…" He stopped, his face frozen and his eyes wide. "*Mira, prima,*" he said.

Daysy looked where he had indicated. Across the canal, an alligator had just slipped into the water. She'd seen its thick tail disappear first. Then, his snout broke the surface, not two yards from where they sat. Daysy and Amado jumped up, yelling through the crowd of guests, "*¡Caimán!*" Magda Elena ushered the women inside the house while the men leaned against the fence, throwing rocks at the creature until it dove beneath the muck, disappearing for good. Even so, the house remained full and warm, and once the pig was finished roasting, it was brought into the kitchen and carved up on the counter, the back-yard abandoned except for a few men, who hovered by the canal in hopes of seeing the alligator again.

As the evening wore on, people gathered in the dining room, many of them examining the wall of photographs. Daysy and Amado situated themselves at the large table with their paper plates of food and listened to the commentary as it went—how Daysy, rightly named, resembled her great-grandmother on her mother's side, or how so-and-so went back to Cuba yearly, staying at Varadero resorts like a tourist, *el descarado*. One woman, a second cousin of Magda Elena, who went by the disagreeable nickname of Monga—a joke of a name, an insult lobbed at the slow or ungainly—spoke during one of those odd silences that often descend upon groups, and the sound carried through the house and caused such a commotion that the party broke up soon afterward.

Monga said, "*My tía*, Nieve, God bless her, she warned them about leaving through Mariel. That baby would be alive now if they'd listened."

"*Ay*, Monga, please," the voices went up trying to quiet her, but the woman went on, louder now, the glass of rum in her hand wobbling to and fro. "It's not secret anymore," she said, and pointed her glass at the pictures on the wall. "You know, I'm the one who claimed them *en el Mariel*. If not for me, they'd have gotten relocated to some god-forsaken place up north. You'd think they'd visit an old woman like me, who Angel owes so much to, more often." The woman dipped her finger in her glass and sucked on it. The people around her no longer met her eyes, and a few tried to change the subject, weakly, to talk of the weather. But Monga spoke up again, her voice thicker now, as if those last few drops on her fingers had tipped her over the edge. "And that daughter of theirs. So skinny! It's her conscience eating her alive!"

Magda Elena, who had not heard the comment over the sound of the electric carving knife, and Angel, who had been outside, were surprised when the party broke up so quickly. There were mounds of leftover food, and some of the guests had not even said goodbye. They had ushered themselves out, the first of the group taking Monga with them.

Daysy watched the parade of friends and distant relatives disappear. It was true, Monga had claimed her family when they arrived. Magda Elena and Angel had other friends who'd come through Mariel with no one at all in the States, who'd been sent to places like Fort

Chafee in Arkansas for a while and then, later, to Milwaukee. That they owed Monga something was true. Every Christmas, Magda Elena made sure to buy Monga a silk shirt from Burdines, the kind she liked to wear, as well as a bottle of Bacardí. But Monga was not invited to intimate family dinners. When Magda Elena emerged from the kitchen to find her living room empty, the party ruined, Daysy told her why.

"*¡Ay, pero esa Monga!*" she said, exasperated, and tore her apron off her body savagely. When Daysy mentioned what Monga had said about her conscience and her body, Magda Elena reddened further, saying, "Don't pay any attention to that, Daysy. She's a jealous, old woman."

"*Sí,*" Angel added. "She's only angry because that daughter of hers, Maylín, is as big as a cow, and you," he said, kissing the back of Daysy's hand, "are *una belleza.*"

Catalina, who had been in the dining room, too, disappeared now, and returned with a silver chalice in her hands. From the rim of the cup dangled silver bells, and a silver lid set atop the cup was adorned with a tiny silver rooster, its left foot raised.

"You need this, *hermana,*" Catalina said, climbed one of the dining room chairs, and set the chalice on top of the china cabinet. The little bells jingled happily, but Daysy felt cold. She knew the cup had something to do with *Santería,* knew the red and white beads that circled Catalina's neck did, too, and she was reminded of the bananas and their bright ribbons, the ones her mother blamed for Abuelo's illness. *Solavaya,* Daysy thought and rubbed the goose bumps on her arms.

"That's Osún's cup," Catalina said. "He has to be put in a high place. If he falls over, we'll know trouble is on its way. The little *santo* will let us know." Catalina's announcement was met with silence, and she, pushing the dining room chair back to its place, did not acknowledge the awkward moment. "With people like Monga in your lives, you need Osún," Catalina said.

The del Pozos weren't churchgoers, really, though their house was decorated in the old Catholic way, with iconic images everywhere and the waxy smell of tall votive candles with pictures of *la Virgen* printed on them in every room. The paintings and idols around the house, of Christ at Gethsemane sweating blood over the lintel of the front door, or the bust of *la Virgen* atop the television, were like good luck charms, not at all for contemplation. This was different. The little rooster cup made Daysy uneasy, as did Monga's declaration that Daysy suffered from a guilty conscience. Had the cup been put in its place before the party, Daysy wondered, would the rooster have toppled before Monga spoke? Would the cup have warned them of Abuelo's oncoming dementia? Could it have prophesized the death of Belén long ago? The air conditioning turned on with a whoosh that set the bells on the cup clinking tinnily.

"Where did you get it?" Magda Elena asked wearily.

"There's a *botánica* on 8th Avenue," Catalina said, waving her hand over her head, signifying both the location of the store, of which there were a few in Hialeah, selling folk medicines, statuary, herbs, and other tools of the *santero*'s trade, and Catalina's wish to skip over the uninteresting origin of the cup.

"*¿Botánica?*" Angel asked. "Those places are, are…," and he sputtered a bit. Daysy knew what he meant. There was a smell about them, of blood and incense, and the patrons coming in and out of the *botánicas* had a kind of stealth about them, as if their visit were prohibited and they had to sneak to get there, as if their faith were shameful. For the most part, if a shopping center had a *botánica* in it, Magda Elena and Angel shopped elsewhere.

Yet, here was Catalina, her cheeks glowing as she looked up at the silver chalice. Angel cleared his throat with a growl, looking as if he were about to say something, but didn't, ultimately, and Magda Elena stared at the cup with her arms crossed, rubbing her skin.

"You'll see," Catalina said, grinning.

≈ ✶ ≈

When Amado snuck into her room again that night, Daysy tossed him a pillow. He settled onto the floor without a word. Daysy turned over Monga's words as she listened to Amado's breathing, and there stirred in her, not so much the sense of betrayal she'd felt when she'd first learned that a secret was being kept from her, but a feeling of guilt, unspecified, yet having to do with Belén's death.

"Do you think I killed her? Pushed her overboard or something?" Daysy asked in the darkness.

"You couldn't have," Amado said, lifting himself up on an elbow.

"What if I did?"

"Come on, Daysy. You're being ridiculous," Amado said, lying down again as if he were too tired to go on talking. "*Buenas noches, prima.*"

Thinking that things wouldn't seem so dire in the morning, Daysy tried to sleep, but sleep evaded her. Instead, her mind turned to varying scenarios of herself on a boat out at sea. Perhaps that dream where she'd chased Belén on a deck was not a dream but a memory. Perhaps she'd failed to stop the child from slipping to her death. Maybe, when her mother wasn't looking, Daysy had pushed Belén into the ocean, just to see what would happen. As she grew sleepier, each scene that played itself out in Daysy's head was more ridiculous than the one before, culminating in a fantasy in which Daysy had sold Belén to one of the lunatics onboard for a piece of chocolate. It occurred to her, just before drifting to unconsciousness, that her mother had gone to a lot of trouble keeping secrets, and though the feeling surprised her, Daysy felt deeply, deeply loved.

≈ ✶ ≈

Knowing that Abuelo's affliction worsened by the day, the family took care to please him, to give in to his demands of ice cream for dinner and not complain about the radio in his room that blared politics all day at full volume. That fall, he began wetting himself, and Magda Elena took on the chore of helping him change out of the damp and sour clothing.

"What's happened to me?" he would sometimes ask several times a day to anyone who would listen.

Only Daysy would answer him, squeezing his hand and saying, honestly, "I don't know, Abuelo."

He no longer recognized Catalina or Amado, whom he'd remembered so well at first. When they walked by him, Abuelo would sometimes startle, or he would eye them distrustfully, as if they were strangers. As for Magda Elena and Angel, Abuelo occasionally forgot them, too, and once called Angel "*un maldito hijo de puta*," out of nowhere, the old man's face red and scrunched up, his mind lost in a long-ago fight. Angel locked himself in the bathroom afterward. Daysy lingered by the doorway until she heard a choked sort of sob from inside. Then she stepped away, embarrassed. When Angel emerged at sunset, his eyes were wide and raw. He had never looked so young to Daysy, or so afraid.

It was Daysy whom Abuelo remembered best. Though she was too big for it now, Daysy would sit on her grandfather's lap for long stretches of time, and the two of them would whisper to one another, growing quiet whenever Magda Elena came near. Daysy was a head taller than Abuelo when they sat this way, and she would lean her cheek against his rough, iron-colored hair. He would put his big paw of a hand on her knee, tapping it to some secret music he was hearing.

"What are you talking about?" Magda Elena would ask.

"Nothing," Daysy would say.

One time, Daysy had asked, "How exactly did Belén fall into the ocean?" and Abuelo had answered, "Nieve and I, we always thought

you were a little jealous of Belén." Magda Elena must have overheard
the conversation, because she barreled into the room, clapping her
hands to get Daysy and Abuelo's attention.

"Daysy, that room of yours needs a good vacuum. Gregorio, how
does a snack sound?" Daysy rolled her eyes, stood, and started to drag
her feet to her bedroom. Magda Elena put her hand in Abuelo's in
order to help him stand, smiling at him as she did so. But then a
strange thing happened. Rising, Abuelo jerked his hand out of Magda
Elena's grip, swung it back, the fingers curling as they went, and
punched her in the neck. He stumbled as his body followed the arc
of the swing and fell on his knees. Magda Elena clutched at her
throat, coughed painfully, said, "No," a few times, as if scolding a
child, and fled the living room, leaving Abuelo on the floor muttering. Horrified, Daysy stepped away from her grandfather until her
back hit the wall. He looked at her and cocked his head, the way a
stray dog might. Daysy screamed and ran, afraid of Abuelo suddenly,
and did not stop screaming or running until she was in Magda
Elena's arms.

≈ ✳ ≈

In a week's time, Daysy's parents found an empty spot for Abuelo
at Fair Havens Nursing Home in Miami Springs. Angel and Magda
Elena went to see him settled, pillows and blankets in their arms since
they were planning on staying with Gregorio the first few nights. Just
before they'd closed the door behind them on their way to the home,
Daysy caught sight of herself in the big mirror hung on the wall
above the couch. She was standing in the middle of the room, her
hand up to her side, as if she'd begun to wave goodbye but then
frozen. It was as if Daysy were seeing herself for the first time, or,
rather, had caught herself not looking. This was the way others
viewed her, she thought. There were the spindly legs, the soft mounds

of her breasts underneath a t-shirt, parted lips revealing large, not-quite-white teeth, and a certain something in her moist eyes that was similar to Abuelo's now that he was ill, an artless glance that suggested neither one of them had a comprehension of the affairs that had governed their lives, Abuelo having forgotten them on his own and Daysy having been allowed to forget.

≈ ✳ ≈

Abuelo stopped talking by the end of his first month at Fair Havens. The nurses there said that loss of speech was a common thing, that dementia can be slow at first, then progress all at once, that the del Pozos should expect him to forget how to chew and swallow eventually. Even without speaking, Abuelo seemed to enjoy time in the common room, where he played his flute over the sound of the large-screen television in the corner. One woman, who sat in a wheelchair, her white hair tied in ribbons, her mouth a slash of red lipstick, sat with him, humming along to the music. She told the del Pozos that her name was Pearl Gentry, that Abuelo, who put his hand in a fist and pressed it to his heart as she spoke, was her boyfriend.

So it was that Magda Elena and Angel began to depend on Pearl to watch over Abuelo while they were away. "He ate all his dinner last night," she would say, or "He's fixin' to talk again real soon, you'll see," patting the back of Abuelo's hand all the while. Magda Elena would bring hair clips for Pearl, little butterflies with rhinestones on the wings or barrettes with tiny beads on them. Pearl would put them in her hair deftly, crooked fingers working the clasps and hinges.

During those visits, Abuelo would sometimes play music for them all, but the songs now sounded strange, disjointed, Abuelo forgetting the notes one by one. Angel would cringe at the mistakes, as if the off notes were a diagnosis, a symptom of his father's worsening condition. "*Que lindo, Papá,*" Angel kindly told his father one morning after Abuelo had played an especially disordered song.

"My, when he plays," Pearl said, her hands folded on her enormous chest, "I see spirits over his head, like blue lights. This is a haunted man."

Confused by Pearl's drawl, Magda Elena asked Daysy to translate, which she did all through Pearl's long, rambling story about how she had never seen a spirit the whole time she lived in Loachapoka, Alabama, how at the moment she crossed the Miami city limits, she started to see and hear things that would send her Baptist pastor back home down on his knees, how she never told anyone about it, and how her family would just say it was her own fault, after all, for leaving Alabama and going to work in a city full of so many Catholics.

Angel asked Abuelo to play "Silent Night," which he did, slow and clear this time. Nurses and patients drew near as he played. Applause erupted on the last note, and some of the patients went on singing the song, in English and Spanish, in thin, quivering voices.

When the clapping died down, Daysy heard a man say, "It's the flute player of Little Havana!" then watched as Albert Arroyo embraced Abuelo, who patted the young man on the shoulder a few times. "I'm Albert," he said, and shook hands all around. Even here, in a nursing home, Albert Arroyo maintained the appearance of a celebrity. His dark hair was thick and shiny, the part in it ruler straight. His teeth were overly white, and the crease in his pants was sharp. Everything about him described order and care and the money it took to keep things looking so nice.

"*Mucho gusto,*" Magda Elena said, crossing her legs at the ankles.

"You again," Daysy said, and her father smacked the back of her head.

Arroyo turned to face Abuelo again. "What happened, Abuelo?" he asked, and shook Abuelo's knee. "My great-aunt is here, too. Upstairs," he said.

"*Ay, la pobre,*" Magda Elena commiserated.

Arroyo drew a chair into their circle, put it next to Daysy, and sat down. "What a coincidence," he said, smiling. No one smiled this much at Fair Havens, even the activities nurse, who Daysy supposed was paid to smile. Daysy found she could not smile at all while in the nursing home, not even to pretend.

There was silence then, the del Pozos waiting for the celebrity in their midst to speak again. He leaned forward, his elbows resting on his knees. He licked his lips. "So there's a feature we're doing for the show," Arroyo began. "It's the ten-year anniversary of Mariel. You and Abuelo here would be great in it."

"No way," Daysy said. Arroyo raised an eyebrow at her.

"I don't know, *m'ijo*. Our story is a tragedy," Magda Elena said.

"The exile community ought to remember Belén," Arroyo said, as naturally as if he'd been saying her name all his life.

"You remembered her name," Daysy said.

"I'm good with names," Arroyo said, smiling still. Daysy looked at Arroyo for a long moment, thinking how his smooth face would sink into wrinkles one day. Perhaps Arroyo would have to come here to live, when even he didn't remember the life he once led, and when he could no longer conjure up his own name.

Arroyo clapped his hands loudly, breaking Daysy's reverie and startling a nurse who'd been walking by, so that she dropped a tray full of medicines. Arroyo did not notice her. "I'll have someone call you to set up the interview," he said, not waiting for the del Pozos to agree. He handed his business card to Angel, dropped a kiss on top of Abuelo's head, and left, as quickly as he'd come.

"What a handsome young man," Pearl cooed as she fiddled with a bow in her hair.

STELLA MARIS MORALES-QUINN

MIAMI BEACH, FLORIDA 1990

Classes broke for the winter holidays on the twenty-first, a day that brought a fresh snowfall. It was a pretty snow, the kind Stella most liked. Clumps of white fell in zigzags, crashing into other clumps then dropping like stones. She spent the afternoon with Dr. Row, with whom she spoke at length about everything she had learned so far concerning the island she came from, about a story she'd just imagined and written down, wherein the bats in the walls of her house had turned to parrots and cockatoos, been poisoned by the exterminator, and formed mounds of feathery green and yellow hills in the attic, just above her bed.

"Here," Stella said, handing the pages over to Dr. Row. They were written on pink paper in purple ink. "I thought you might want to read it."

"That's so sweet," Dr. Row said, turning the pages over one at a time. She narrowed her eyes for a moment, then asked, "What's this? A different story?"

Stella leaned over, peering at the pages in Dr. Row's hands. Then, she snatched them away. "You weren't supposed to see this story. Just the one about the birds."

"What's it about?" Dr. Row asked. "The other story, I mean."

"Do we have to talk about this now?" Stella asked. She folded the papers into thirds and shoved them into her pocket.

Dr. Row pressed her lips together, waited a beat, then asked evenly, "When would you like to talk about it?"

Stella took a deep and shaky breath and said, "My mother said I came back to her at sea. She said I appeared out of nowhere, like a falling star, and that I had changed from what I once was, and that I saved her. That's why she called me Stella Maris. Star of the Sea.

That's what the story is about."

"And you...?"

"I think I believe it. I mean, I want to believe it. I don't want to talk about it," Stella said in a rush.

"Okay," Dr. Row said, but Stella told her anyway about the kind of magic her mother attracted on so many occasions. Once, she and her mother had been driving down Forbes when a sheet of newspaper fluttered over the windshield. The headline, cut off by the wipers, read DEATH COMES TO, and Anita had pressed the brakes hard, the cars behind them squealing in their haste to stop. "*Ay*," she'd said, tears already in her eyes. "Michael's father!" Indeed, that night Michael's father suffered a heart attack that left him dead on the sidewalk, the dog's leash still in his grip, and Argo, the mastiff they'd given him as a Christmas gift, curled up against his stomach. Other signs came in the form of dreams. Anita would dream that her teeth had fallen out and clattered to the floor like a broken string of pearls. "I've dreamt I was all gums again," she'd announce over breakfast. "I am so sorry," she'd say, too, apologizing for what she knew was to come, for weeks of her turbulent moods and nightwalking that the dream portended. Another time, Stella and Anita came home to find a dead bluejay on their front porch. The little body was whole. No cat had gotten to it, but rather, it seemed as if it had merely grown tired of flying and had dropped from the sky. Stella watched as her mother lifted the body, so light it seemed hollow, a papier-mâché bird, a tiny piñata, which opened might reveal miniscule candies. Anita kissed it lightly on its feathered head, then took the bird through the house and out through a back door. Outside, she dug a hole in the dirt with a spade and laid the blue creature in the damp earth. From that space the next spring erupted a hyacinth as blue as the jay had been. Who was to say the bird had not become a bulb, had not returned to life in the darkness of earth and winter? Stella could not bring herself to dismiss the miraculous in her mother. Stella, who prized her intelligence as if it were a thing she could lay a finger on, something she could keep in a box and wait for it to gather worth, could find no argument against her mother's magic.

When she was done relating all that, Stella reached for a handful of honey candies. She stuffed her mouth so full of them that there was no longer anything else to say or do, except watch the snow.

≈ ✶ ≈

In the morning, she and Michael left for Miami on an airplane that wobbled in the sky, buffeted by a winter storm that threatened to ground them. In a few hours time they had arrived. As Stella and Michael waited for their luggage, an elderly woman, also waiting, dropped a coin purse full of pennies, and the coins bounced off her black shoes. Stella was on the ground instantly, gathering the money, when she felt a thwack on her shoulders and head. "*¡Mi dinero!*" the old woman yelled, and tried stomping on Stella's fingers.

"I don't want your money! I was just helping," she tried to explain before Michael pulled her away.

Michael rented a car, and they headed south. They would spend Christmas in Miami Beach and then a few days visiting museums and local cultural sites. "Whatever you want to do," he'd said, "Just don't hide behind a book all day, okay?"

The car wove through rows of one-story houses, painted in pinks and bright oranges, windows barred in ornate ironwork, past tile warehouses and airplane hangars, past flea markets, *supermercados*, *botánicas*, and all manner of businesses with Spanish signs lit neon in the middle of the day. Michael got lost, taking three wrong exits off the expressway. It had been years since he'd driven around South Florida, and the new construction on the highway confused him.

Michael drove down side roads in search of I-95 while Stella took a few pictures with a disposable camera, leaning out of the window.

She snapped photos of a boy at the edge of a canal with a tiny, wiggling fish in his hands, of a bakery window with enormous, fluffy white cakes and colorful piñatas dangling from fishing line, of a truck on the side of the road with clear plastic bags of tomatoes, onions, and garlic hanging from its side, of a house shaped like a conch shell, of a billboard for a lumber yard with a cartoon man made of two-by-fours, of her reflection in standing water when they stopped at a red light, of a palm tree shaped like an *r*, a dragonfly perched on the side-view mirror, its wings a blur in the wind, of Michael's hands on the steering wheel.

It was clear to her that the Miami featured on travel programs and in travel books was only a little strip of land on the shore, that the real heart of the city did not beat in time to the waves lapping the sand, but to the irregular honking of horns on the highway, the rapid jackhammer sounds of construction downtown, and the occasional ambulance siren. Somewhere, in all of this, she and her mother had once lived, Stella thought.

Things improved a good deal once they reached their hotel on the beach. While Michael checked in, Stella removed her shoes and stepped onto the cold terrazzo floor, her skin pale against the cool, speckled surface. Their room faced the ocean and smelled fishy and salty, as if the sea had seeped into the wallpaper and bedspread. They left the musty room for the seaside within minutes.

Stella and Michael had the beach to themselves. Even the lifeguard stands were deserted, reflecting the local disbelief that two people would actually *want* to go swimming when the temperature was peaking at seventy-five degrees. Stella had laughed that morning at the Miamians in wooly sweaters and shiny New York Yankee jackets. On the way to the beach, they passed a girl about Stella's age, accompanied by a grandmother-type, who struggled to cover the girl's nose and mouth with a handkerchief, urging her to hold her breath, saying, "Don't let the cold air into your lungs, *niña*. That's how the bronchitis starts!" The girl's eyes met Stella's, and Stella saw embarrassment in them, and some longing, too. For her part, Stella was wearing a tank top and shorts, and around her neck, the straps of her new bathing suit were visible. Stella and the passing girl were a study in contrasts—she in a blue cardigan and jeans, the grandmother's gnarled hand smothering her, and Stella, walking three feet behind her father, her sandals flapping on the sidewalk. Stella carried her mother's jacket with her, though, and planned to lay it out on the sand and lie on it.

The morning sun bided its time to bake the world. For now it was cool, and Stella imagined the beach covered in snow, how the piles of white would sit on the letters of the hotel signs and bend the awnings with their weight. Anita had loved the snow, too, a surprising proclivity given her tropical past life. On the first snowfall of each year, Anita would stand in the front yard, wearing only a housedress, and say, "*¡Soy una americana de verdád!*" and eat the snow as it came down, in communion with winter.

The sea was not quite warm when Stella first stepped in, but felt better the longer she waded. She doggie-paddled for a bit, going out as far as a sandbank that reduced the water to two feet deep. The shore seemed tiny from so far out. She sat on the sandbank for a while, wishing the beach were full of people who might see her and imagine she was sitting on the surface, like a miracle. When she felt the bottom shift under her feet, she let herself float and watched the plumes of sand as they sank to further depths. Examining a clump of seaweed, Stella pulled its fruit, tiny jade beads, and threw them toward the horizon. Slimy stones on the seafloor met her toes, and she expected a crab to take a chunk of her foot at any moment. She took a second to pee, guilty about doing so, feeling her own heat swirling around her legs and disappearing, leaving her colder than she was before. The water was dark and sand-churned. A foot down underwater was like diving blind, reminding Stella of the muddy Mon back home. Michael swam a few yards away, pulled south by the current. He'd come back, long arms slapping the water, and soon be drawn away again, as if some immense drain had been unplugged somewhere.

Stella discovered that afternoon that an empty beach with innumerable gallons of water all to oneself, to either swim in or swallow and drown, was conducive to the most crystalline of thoughts. Perhaps the salt in the air helped cure the brain, slowing down the process of cell decay, or maybe it purified the air in her lungs like a filter. Whatever the reason, Stella thought long and hard about her mother while waist deep in the water, wondering how much she didn't know about her.

She felt none of the usual pressure, no panic in her chest save for the brunt of the ocean against her body. Her hands, too, felt fine. Stella pivoted, faced south, looked past her father, who was floating on his back, his chest reddening. Everything moved in that direction—the seaweed, the schools of silver fish that swam by, fresh urine, Michael, an abandoned, inflatable raft that dipped below the surface and bobbed up again several feet away, Stella's own body, which leaned southerly, toward that open drain. Stella focused on the furthest point she could make out. It was only a suggestion of a building, most likely another hotel. Beyond that, Stella's imagination burst out to open sea, skipped along a string of islands, then slid, snake-like on the wavy surface of the Atlantic, Cuba-bound. In this daydream, she reached the shore in seconds, cartwheeled on a white beach and dug her hands so deep in the sand that when they emerged, they were clean of skin and tissue—white, white bone that felt no pain. Stella wanted to bury her whole self and materialize again a new, glowing being. She'd rename herself—maybe something ancient, like Diana, like Cleopatra, or just a sound, a long, quiet *s* sound, like a whisper or a sigh. She'd trade in her Stellaness for something of her own making.

Michael interrupted her reverie, splashing her with a violent, spastic kick as he swam by. The thunking sound of his legs in the water worked like the snapping of a hypnotist's fingers, and Stella was suddenly cold.

"I was thinking," Michael called from a distance then stopped to spit out some seawater. "I was thinking that we might get some Cuban food tonight. The good stuff, like your mom used to make."

Stella treaded water until she was face-to-face with her father. The swim had cheered him so much that he seemed far younger than before. Unable to help herself, Stella took her father's face in her hands and smoothed back the skin, erasing wrinkles. She thought she could see the face of the boy Anita had fallen in love with.

"Hey, quit it," Michael said, and splashed her with water. "You used to do that all the time as a baby. You've gotten stronger." He rubbed his cheeks and winced dramatically. "So what do you say? Dinner?"

"I miss her," Stella answered. She hadn't meant to, but it was what she'd been thinking, and the words found a way out. The light mood darkened. As if on cue, the sun hid behind a cloud, and Stella was sad to have ruined things so quickly.

The swim was over then, and Michael trudged up to the shore, kicking clods of sand behind him. Stella followed him out, and the breeze chilled her so that she trembled everywhere, from the inside out it seemed, and she couldn't speak. Wrapped in a scratchy hotel towel, Stella plopped down beside her father and waited. His glance was up and away, toward the horizon.

"What are you thinking?" Stella asked.

Michael shook his head and dug his toes into the sand. One of his feet had splotches of tar on it, and Stella checked her own to find similar stains. Rubbing her feet in the sand took off the tar, and she and Michael chafed their skin cleaning it.

Stella did not ask her father again. She knew what he was thinking, because she was thinking it, too. He missed Anita also, so much that he couldn't speak. And there was this thought as well: Anita had always been mad. Stella was just now believing it. The wind had deposited little hills of sand on the denim jacket. Stella shook it hard to clean it off and draped the jacket over her head like a hood. Covered this way, Stella could no longer see her father from the corner of her eye.

"Do you remember the time the ceiling came down in the living room?" Michael asked.

Stella nodded, recalling the crack in the ceiling over the sofa that once sat in their house, the one left to soak up rainwater one afternoon with such rapidity that it was as if it had been rained on for a month without ceasing. Stella had watched the sofa thicken and gain weight, puffing at the seams. Underneath, the rug too began to dampen, and the moisture grew in a wide circle around the couch. Stella thought of that sofa often, how once she had found Anita curled on it, sobbing into the cushiony arm. When her mother lifted her face at last, Stella saw how tears, snot, and spittle had soaked the fabric. The wetness left a ring that disappeared when the ceiling opened up, the surrounding fabric darkening to match the evidence of her mother's anguish.

And all the while, Anita had merely watched the destruction, hypnotized by the dripping that became a gush, ripping an even larger hole in the ceiling overhead. Chunks of white plaster crumbled into milky puddles. She and Stella watched as the roof opened more. Dark rain clouds appeared so close over the hole that Stella thought they might sneak in, dim the house in their smokiness. She wished they would, wished they'd obscure her vision so that she didn't have to witness her mother's dumb staring at the sofa. If she'd been older, stronger, Stella would have moved it herself. Instead, she could only stand hand in hand with her mother, the water sloshing around their feet. Later, Michael moved the enormous wet thing outside, where it continued to swallow the brunt of that storm, drinking every drop until each spring rusted, until the fabric fell away like rotted skin, leaving only a mechanical skeleton to dry in the sun.

"I remember," Stella said.

Michael took in a deep breath. "She just watched it happen. Just watched. That's when I knew." He picked up a bit of sand then and rubbed it against his elbow on another tar spot.

"Knew what?"

Michael looked at Stella for a long time, his eyes hard on hers. "Nothing," he said at last.

Stella wondered whether he was looking for bits of her mother in her, a residue of lunacy perhaps. It wasn't as if she hadn't tried, too— long minutes before a mirror, pulling down her bottom eyelid in search of hints of hysteria, of morbidity in herself, hunting for even some kind of physical likeness of which she never found any. Stella couldn't blame Michael for seeking out potential madness in her.

"Let's get back inside," he said at last.

≈ ✴ ≈

That afternoon, while Michael showered, Stella flipped through the local phone directory, killing time, wondering where Michael would take her for dinner. She came across the *M* names by chance. She estimated there were at least a thousand Moraleses listed, maybe more. Stella sighed. She lifted the phone and called the first, Abelardo Morales.

"Are you related to someone named Anita?" she asked, and noticed that her hand shook, the receiving end of the phone tapping her chin.

"¿Que? No hablo inglés, hija," the man answered, and Stella hung up, then tried one more number. She closed her eyes and pointed to a name on the page, a Timotéo Morales, who said hello in perfect English.

"Do you know Anita Morales?"

"Nope," the voice said.

After three more failed attempts, Stella quit trying. So many Cubans, she thought. What a wonder to turn left, right, to spin in circles and see others who'd come from the same place she had, whose molecules had formed in the same briny air, fed by the same earth. Back at school, Stella's Cubanness had gone mostly unnoticed. Her dirty blond hair and blue eyes belied the deeper, earthier colors dormant in her genes. She was an ace in Spanish class, but then again, Stella earned A's in every class. Stella never reached for the salsa bottle during lunch, showed no aptitude for dancing, and was as outwardly equanimical as a saint (she never called to mind Ricky Ricardo's flaring temper). Classmates dismissed the Morales in Morales-Quinn, and more often than not, pronounced it as "More Rails," a mistake that Stella did not ever correct. But she noticed the differences, knew they ran deep, and once made a long list of the many ways she was dissimilar to the girls around her.

Dr. Row had suggested the list in an effort to show Stella just the opposite—that she wasn't alone in the universe. However, the list she put together silenced Dr. Row on the subject. Stella titled it "The Things I Know." It included no less than sixteen Cuban superstitions that Stella and Anita adhered to; an extensive medical definition of a "hangman's fracture," the name given to the fracture of the neck vertebra; a recipe for *picadillo*; and the atomic number for neon, among many other sundry things. The last item on the list read: "I am decidedly different." Dr. Row left it at that.

She ran her finger across the tiny names in the phone book, concentrating hard on her fingertip, sure that if she connected for just a moment with a relative, she'd feel a tingle, a volt of kinship race through her. Like having a metal detector in her blood. It seemed like the kind of thing Anita, who had claimed to feel snowstorms beginning in her knees before they started in the skies, might do. But there was no prickle, no fateful zap. Stella closed the book in wonder, nevertheless. So many Moraleses. And to think that her mother had chosen Pittsburgh over Miami.

The shower shut off and made a deep-throated sound in the walls, rattling the pipes as it traveled the length of the room. Michael emerged in a cloud of steam and dropped down next to Stella, who still sat with the phone book on her lap.

"What were you looking for?" he asked.

"The other Moraleses. Mom's family. You think they're here?"

"Oh, Stella, I don't know," Michael said, and gave her a hug, engulfing her in his arms so that she felt as if she were such a tiny thing, so very young. "I wish I'd been better at getting her to talk, to tell me things. Maybe then..." He did not finish, and it was as if he couldn't think of anything else to say. He held on to her.

"There was a lot we didn't know." Stella spoke against his chest, and her words sounded muffled. "Daddy," she said after a long while, "can I tell you something she told me once?"

"Sure."

"She said I died and was buried and came back to her at sea. She said that."

"My God, Stella," was all Michael could manage, but it wasn't what Stella wanted to hear. What she wanted was a clear explanation that would do away once and for all with opaque memories and impenetrable stories, for Michael to say, "No darling, this is the truth, plain as it is, you were a baby like any other, and your mother was not well, not well at all."

Michael tried to stand, to get away, and Stella could see that he was trying hard not to cry. Stella's feet unrooted themselves then, and she launched herself at Michael, who caught her, midair, and held her. Stella's legs dangled a few feet off the floor, and for the first time in months she felt her age, wanted to cry like a baby, wanted to howl and bray and bleat like an animal, then lose her breath and hyperventilate the way toddlers did when they cried too long. And so she did, and Michael rocked her, and to Stella, the movement felt like floating down the Mon, and like jumping waves at the beach, both things at once.

DAYSY DEL POZO

HIALEAH, FLORIDA 1990

The camera crews arrived at the del Pozo house the week before Christmas. Albert Arroyo was not among them, and it became clear that he would not come. A young woman in jeans and a Metallica t-shirt, with a walkie-talkie in one hand and a ragged index card in the other, was directing the action. Dressed in their best clothes, Magda Elena, Angel, and Daysy stood to the side and watched as crew members picked up the dining room table and carted it away, lined up stools in front of Magda Elena's wall of photographs, and began setting up enormous lights. The house was brighter than it had ever been, and Magda Elena fretted, whispering to Daysy that the baseboards in the dining room weren't white after all, but a dingy shade of gray, and pointing out the dead spiders curled in the corners.

"*¡Ay, no!*" she said at last, unable to restrain herself, and grabbed a broom. Crewmen gave her plenty of space as she swept, as if they were intimidated by the ferocity with which she managed the broom. In truth, Daysy's mother was anxious to the point of illness. Márquez, the pharmacist, had given her a pill for her nerves in the morning, but the effects were wearing off. "How did we let Arroyo convince us so easily?" she'd asked Daysy earlier that day as she scrubbed the kitchen cabinets down. "We've always been so private. Now everyone will know that the del Pozos were *Marielitos*, that we lost a child, that a cloud of misfortune hovers over us still, and that we live in a dirty house."

The del Pozos were seated before the photographs. Using a hand-held camera, one of the crew filmed the pictures, lingering over each one before moving on. The woman in the t-shirt had explained that the photos would serve as context and asked if there were any recordings of Abuelo playing the flute for the background music. Angel had handed her a cassette tape covered in dust.

Another camera, this one set on a tripod, was put before the del Pozos. "Tell the story whenever you are ready," the young woman said, and the room fell quiet.

Daysy's leg bounced up and down like a jackhammer until the woman in the t-shirt reached out and stilled it for her. She couldn't help it. The cameras would demand the story in its fullness, and Daysy wasn't sure she was ready for it. It felt as if bees were trapped in her body, buzzing noisily, searching for a way out of the darkness.

"It was the four of us," Magda Elena began. "*Sí. Bueno.* The four of us. Angel, Daysy, me and, and..." Daysy felt herself tensing, anticipating what would come next. "And the baby," Magda Elena said at last, looking suddenly old, fragile, shrunken. She'd crumpled a bit then straightened, as if deciding she wouldn't make it harder for everyone by being weak. "*Bueno,*" she hesitated again. "They put us on a big boat named *la Big Virginia.* We'd only been on the ship a few hours when it began to take on water. *¿Verdád, Angel?* Only an hour or so?" Angel didn't answer. Daysy thought he couldn't speak.

"*Pánico* then. The captain got on his radio calling for help. 'Mayday!' he kept shouting, and I remember thinking, *ridícula que soy*, that 'Mayday' would be a beautiful name for a girl, and *me acuerdo*, holding onto the two that I had, that if *Dios y la Virgen* ever sent me another daughter, Mayday would be her name. *Ay,*" she said again, and stopped speaking.

Angel's voice broke in. "It was dark. We couldn't see anything. Then the ship made a noise and lurched. A pair of boats came to the rescue. One was the *Adalah*, the other..."

"*El Ron*," Magda Elena choked out.

"That's right. And they put a metal ramp between the boats for us to cross from one to the other. Lots of people were crossing at once. *Pero coño*, it was so dark. *Y bueno*, Magda Elena went across with

Belén, and this is when she, she, when, *bueno*, she lost hold of Belén," Angel said.

Daysy released a long breath. The room felt as if it were moving, like she'd taken one of Márquez's medicines.

"*Ay*, tears," Magda Elena said when she looked at Daysy. Daysy wiped the wetness off her cheeks. The room steadied.

"You told no one," the woman said, but she wasn't looking at the del Pozos anymore. Rather, she fiddled with a beeper in her hand.

"We were afraid someone would accuse us of losing her on purpose. In Cuba, you hear so many terrible things about the American government, and you know, you don't want to believe it, but still…," Magda Elena said.

The room fell quiet, and a few of the men holding equipment shifted their feet back and forth. Next, the young woman in the t-shirt asked a few questions from the index card. "Standard fare," she'd called it, asking what conditions had been like at the Orange Bowl upon their arrival, how long it had taken them to adjust to life in the U.S., and what they thought of the growing numbers of rafters at sea. Angel spoke most of the time. Magda Elena cleared her throat, and Daysy knew that her mother had been suppressing that nagging cough of hers all along, not wanting to ruin the interview. Daysy reached over for a glass of water just off camera and handed it to her mother.

"Cut," the girl running the show said. "Angel, please answer that last one again. And Daysy, don't move."

Daysy rolled her eyes and said, "Really?" She couldn't help herself. The word had become part of her vocabulary, popping into her mouth on an hourly basis, as if some sarcastic demon had taken possession of her vocal chords.

"Really," the girl said.

"Don't embarrass us," Magda Elena whispered, and Daysy hoped her mother would choke on the water.

"One last," the girl said, holding up a finger. "It's been a decade since Mariel. Looking back, what has the experience taught you?" She read from the index card with disinterest, her voice unmodulated, lifeless.

"Sadness, *nada mas*," Magda Elena said, then rose from her seat, giving in to the cough that had been tickling her throat all along. Doctors had diagnosed her with everything from bronchitis to post nasal drip, but the cough persisted.

Daysy watched as the men dismantled the cameras and lighting and put back the dining room table, one of them bumping into Daysy, who stumbled back against the china cabinet.

Catalina's silver cup fell then, rattling loudly. One of the bells came loose and rolled into the kitchen. Magda Elena did not pick it up, afraid to touch it. Nor did Angel or Daysy now that it had fallen, portending God-knows-what. Even when one of the cameramen accidentally kicked it, and the cup rattled underneath the china cabinet, no one touched it. It was Catalina who lifted the cup from the floor, reattached the bell, and set it up on the china cabinet again.

"What does it mean, *Tía*?" Daysy asked her after the television crew had gone.

"I don't know, but whatever is coming," Catalina said, "we can make it right." She gave Daysy a hug, then disappeared into the back room. Thinking of those colorful ribbons tied around bananas, Daysy shuddered, crossed herself, and whispered "*Solavaya*" at the cup, before turning her back on it.

≈ ✶ ≈

It was Sunday, and Catalina had been in the backyard since dawn, a shoebox in her hands, as she gathered the various weeds and herbs she needed to stave off Osún's warning. Daysy watched her from the patio. Catalina was bending at the canal's edge to pick some water lettuce, unraveling the tender vines of the *cundiamor* off the fence, and sniffing a bouquet of porterweed before pulling it out by the roots.

"*Oye*, Daysy, does your father fumigate back here?"

"No," Daysy answered.

"Good," Catalina said, and filled the shoebox to the top. Watching Catalina made Daysy feel like rolling up her sleeves and joining her. She hadn't played in the backyard since Abuelo had gone to live at the home. It felt like his space, sacred and full of her grandfather. It wasn't the same being out there without hearing his humming, low and melodious. So far, Catalina had identified nearly every weed in the backyard, attributing to each little plant one power or another. In her eyes was a glimmer of excitement as she gathered them, like a child on the brink of learning some new skill. The moment the silver cup had fallen, Catalina had sprung into action, planning the *despojo* that would abate the coming danger, a cleansing of sorts that required a spiritual bath made of herbs. That the herbs grew in Daysy's backyard was no surprise according to Catalina. "The little gods provide what we need," she'd said, and set to work.

"Mami says she doesn't believe in that stuff," Daysy said as she approached her aunt. "But she respects it."

Catalina looked at Daysy with narrowed eyes, her jaw working on a piece of minty gum. "Respect is a start," she said at last, and brushed past Daysy as she headed inside the house where Catalina set to work on the *despojo*, boiling the weeds until they disappeared into green water, creaming and foaming on the surface. A bitter smell that made Daysy's eyes water filled the house. As she stirred, Catalina told the story of a woman she'd known in Cuba long ago, who'd miscarried seven times. A meticulous *despojo* had cured her, so that her eighth pregnancy produced a beautiful baby girl. "The spirit is eternal," Catalina said. "One way or another, that baby would find life. And believe me, Daysy, we endure, are born again and again. Belén lives, though you may not know her anymore."

Daysy said nothing. Only Catalina ever said Belén's name with such ease. It struck Daysy that perhaps her parents avoided it out of dread, the name marked by despair, and Catalina, who did not fear death, gave the baby's name no more weight than it had had when she lived.

Carefully, so as not to spill a drop, Catalina carried the heavy pot of boiled plants to the bathroom. She pushed the stopper in the tub, and poured in the liquid. Daysy watched over her shoulder. "Step in," Catalina told her.

"*Que va.* I don't believe in these things either."

"It's just a little bath. What can it hurt?" Catalina asked.

Daysy touched the surface of the hot water. Green drops fell from her finger. Behind her, Catalina had begun to murmur in another language, her voice a low growl. Daysy closed her eyes, felt a violent shudder in her chest, and goose bumps erupted on her arms, though the day was warm and the air conditioning was not on.

Daysy began to unbutton her shirt, and had managed most of the buttons when Magda Elena barged into the bathroom.

"What is this?" she asked, crinkling her nose.

"*Un despojo,*" Catalina announced, as if it were the most normal thing in the world to cook up weeds and talk about curses the way one boils rice and discusses the weather.

For a moment, Daysy thought her mother would begin to yell, but Magda Elena only sighed, saying, "It's not for me. Not for us," and led Daysy out of the bathroom.

"Something is coming. Mark it down, Osún has warned you," Catalina called after them.

In the living room, Magda Elena took a long time buttoning Daysy's shirt. Daysy let her do it, and tried to remember the last time her mother had dressed her. It had been a long time, and yet, how deftly her mother's fingers worked the buttons and the dressing of another. Daysy thought about all the things her mother knew how to do, knew infinitely well—how to rinse rice, how to sweep a room so that not a speck of dust remained, how to braid a fishbone braid into Daysy's hair when she was little. And there were other things she must have known, thought Daysy, like how to leave the country you were born in, how to carry it around in your heart like a piece of shrapnel that throbs in constant reminder, or how to grieve a child. Daysy felt small in her mother's grip at that moment, and when Magda Elena pulled the last button through the eye in the fabric, letting her go, Daysy felt even smaller.

"Tía Catalina knows a lot about her religion," Daysy said. "She's an expert or something."

"But she doesn't know the will of God," Magda Elena whispered. "No one does."

The statement surprised Daysy, who was unused to talk of faith. "I guess not," Daysy said, thinking that if she did know the will of God, could ask Him why her sister had to drown, she might never recover from His answer.

Magda Elena looked at Daysy brightly, suddenly, as if her eyes were lamps that had just been turned on, gleaming with an idea. "The last time I saw my mother, your abuela," she began, "was at a church. Her hands were folded in prayer beneath her chin, a lace veil over her head, her eyes, the scalloped edges grazing her shell-shaped ears. How beautiful she was. Very earnest in prayer. Very different from Catalina's weeds and curses."

"We never go to church," Daysy said.

Magda Elena nodded and ran her hands down Daysy's shoulders, as if flattening the wrinkles in her shirt. She cleared her throat and smiled, satisfied with something. Then, she looked at her watch. "Perhaps we should," Magda Elena said, and Daysy found herself nodding yes. Living in rituals, of the kind that had nothing to do with secrets or guilt, might offer solace, might replace what had become a dark storm cloud in Daysy's imagination, the thunder booming Belén's name over and over.

"*Sí*, Mami," Daysy said.

At that moment Catalina emerged from the bathroom. Her hands and feet were wrinkled, and her skin smelled like a freshly mown lawn.

≈ ⋆ ≈

The five o'clock mass had just begun, and so the small church was filled to the brim. Magda Elena and Daysy watched from the vestibule. Even so, they had a clear view of the altar, flanked by massive, potted poinsettias. Incense burned on brass dishes that dangled from brass poles on either side of the altar, and the smoke spiraled up into the ceiling, curling like ribbon. The church lights were filtered through the smoke and created a downy kind of halo around the priest's head. Daysy could just make out the tops of the nativity scene at the foot of the altar. There was Mary's shawled head, smooth and blue, and a patch of brown that must have been Joseph's hair. Little else was visible from Daysy's vantage point. The service went on in song and Bible readings, and they stayed until the end, standing still as the congregants walked past them, flowing rapidly out of the church, chattering as they went. Daysy felt like a stone in a river.

By the time the final notes of the recessional died away, the church was empty save for Daysy and her mother. No one ever stayed for the recessional song. They sat in the closest pew, and though she tried to restrain it, Daysy felt her face crinkling like wrapping paper, felt the burning in her throat. Catalina's *despojo* had been too much. There was so much hope in Catalina's eyes, so sure was she that bad fortune could be averted, that death was temporary, that souls returned in other guises, that Daysy felt that the ground was shifting under her. *There will never be more than this*, Daysy heard a voice in her head. This sisterless life. This mysterious existence. This aching guilt. *I think I killed her. I think I pushed my baby sister into the sea*, Daysy thought, not for the first time, but forcefully for once, as if she were done keeping that secret from herself.

The organist took up a new song, practicing, it was clear, since he stopped here and there to examine the sheet music. Daysy recognized the carol, *"Los peces en el río,"* and as the song progressed, one about Mary, who untangled her hair with combs of fine silver by a river brimming with fish, Daysy cried, her tears bursting all at once like a star appearing in the dark sky.

Magda Elena, noticing, slipped her arm around Daysy's shoulders and said, *"Ya, ya, está bien,"* though her own voice was choked.

These were not the first tears that had sprung into Daysy's eyes like a leak that afternoon. The mass had been too much. When the priest processed in, a plaster infant Christ in his arms, the tears had come, quiet at first. And when he asked them all to bow their heads and ask for God's blessing, she cried some more, and when the first communicants of that year sang "Joy to the World" in voices accented, sweet and off-pitch, their small mouths round and moving like parakeet beaks, Daysy began to tremble and couldn't stop. Had she always been this way? This fragile? Daysy felt like a pan of shallow water most days—there was very little substance to her and any bump, any disturbance, would spill her. This was real grief, she supposed, this sense of depthlessness.

After a while, Daysy's mother let her go. She watched as Magda Elena genuflected on the cushioned kneeler, placing her knee just above a crack in the blue vinyl where a fluff of old foam poked out. She prayed in silence, moving her lips every so often. Above her nose a deep crease formed, and she wove her fingers so tightly around one another the skin purpled. A loud click echoed in the high ceiling. The lights above began to fade. Daysy closed her eyes, too, and tried to pray, but the words wouldn't come. When she opened her eyes again, they were sitting in the darkened church, illuminated only by the glow of the noon sun coming in through the stained glass, casting patches of colorful light like diaphanous jewels.

"*Mis hijas,*" a deep voice announced its presence. Daysy looked up to see the priest taking a seat beside them. He was a delicate sort. Every bone in his body broadcast itself through his skin. He took a long drag of water from a bottle, screwing the cap off and on with fine, thin fingers that seemed to dance around the plastic thing. Daysy had never seen a man so graceful. He cleared his throat, and that, too, was refined, a quiet sort of *hm-hm* that triggered deeper stillness in her. The kind of man who said great things, or simple things that reminded one of greatness, is what he seemed to Daysy, and without realizing it, she reached out and touched the priest's arm. Unsure of herself suddenly, whether to yank her hand back and apologize or thank the Father for his presence, Daysy could only stare down at her feet.

"You are troubled," he said, and held her hand. His palm was cold and smooth like buttery leather. He said, "God squeezes but doesn't suffocate." Daysy heard it as a way of saying that the trouble would pass. He looked at them both with hard eyes the color of hazelnuts. "It is the season of Christ's birth. *La virgen* sought Bethlehem through hard desert for many nights. We are more fortunate. Every year, Bethlehem comes to us. We don't have to seek it. Keep that comfort in your hearts as you pray, *mis hijas.*" The priest pumped Daysy's hand a few times, as if resuscitating the limb. Then he made the sign of the cross over their heads and left, tucking himself into the shadows of the church until he was swallowed.

Magda Elena had said nothing, but now she was the one in tears. Daysy tried to comfort her mother. "What he said feels right, Mami. We aren't suffocating. We're breathing, see?" she said, and took a deep, dramatic breath for her mother's sake, so deep it left her dizzy.

"Squeezing, suffocating. *Ay,* what does he know of it?" Magda Elena said. She was staring straight ahead, her gaze steady and her body still as if she were wearing armor instead of a flower-print dress.

"I already suffered the ultimate torment when Belén slipped into the water, Daysy. So quiet, such a hushed death." Now, Magda Elena grabbed hold of Daysy's hands, squeezing them together as if she were fighting the memory itself, winching it up from the past and holding it fixedly, as if to keep it from doing more harm. "I would have traded anything to hold Belén's hand as she drowned, like I'm holding yours now." Magda Elena gulped for air and went on. "To say to her, I'm sorry *mi chiquitica, mi amorcito*, so sorry, but I'm here, it will be over soon, *mi vida*. This passing into the dark has an end, it has to, just hold on a little while longer…"

"Mami, stop," Daysy said. "I'm scared."

"*Ay. Ay*," Magda Elena said, as if coming to herself again. "You're right. I've lost my mind. I'm sorry."

They were both quiet for a long time. A door squealed somewhere inside the church and clicked closed. The silence broken, Daysy thought to ask, "Wasn't that funny, Mami, how the priest said that 'Bethlehem will come again'? I wish it were true."

Magda Elena took a deep breath. Her hand fluttered to her cheek. "He was right, and your *tía* was right. Belén is not gone from the universe. I feel her still, here," she said, and placed the palm of her hand over her heart.

"Home, please," Daysy said. Her tongue felt thick in her throat.

"Of course," her mother said, and they left the dark church.

≈ ✳ ≈

What she'd experienced at the church seemed to have so muddled Magda Elena's thinking that she made two wrong turns in the thick of Hialeah, onto streets without lights, confusing her further. Her leg bounced even as she pressed on the accelerator, and Daysy felt the car thrust forward and slow in time with it, making her a little carsick. It was as if the turbulence in her mother's soul was leaching into her muscles. Once home, Magda Elena ignored Angel's request for dinner as she entered the house and didn't appear to notice the mess Amado had made in the living room, his filthy socks atop the television set, cassette tapes scattered on the floor.

Quietly, Magda Elena went to the kitchen where she fished out a bottle of Bacardí and filled a juice glass to the top. She drank the rum in a few gulps, then filled another. Daysy watched in silence. The bottle was dusty, and Daysy ran her fingers over the glass, rubbing the dust between her fingers. Did rum go bad? She didn't know, and it didn't seem as if Magda Elena noticed any difference.

Angel came into the kitchen, took one surprised look at his wife and daughter, and asked, "What are we celebrating?"

"*Nada*," Magda Elena said, and tightened the cap back onto the bottle. "I've decided. Daysy and I have some work to do." Magda Elena rose and took Daysy by the wrist, dragging her into Abuelo's room, where she immediately began to clean out the sick man's closet.

Curious, Angel had followed them and watched from the doorway, arms crossed tightly against his chest, his head shaking no every so often. When Daysy dropped a stiff folder from which hundreds of yellowed sheets of music dropped, unbending like dead things, Angel muttered, "*Coño*," and walked away.

"Maybe Papi is right. Let's leave Abuelo's things alone. Let's just…"

"Don't worry about him," Magda Elena said, laying an arm on Daysy's shoulder and stopping her from following her father out.

Daysy stopped, cut off by the sound of her mother drawing the deepest of breaths. "You smell that? Like old wax," Magda Elena said, closing her eyes and inhaling again. "Your father smells like this sometimes." Magda Elena stood on tiptoe, swayed a little as she lost her balance then regained it, and tapped the bare lightbulb dangling from a cord over her head. Once, twice, she flicked it hard with her nail, but the light would not come on. "No matter," she announced, and stepped into the dusty depths of Gregorio's closet. Well inside it now, Magda Elena called Daysy to join her, and didn't notice when Daysy did not come.

Something had happened to her mother in that church. Magda Elena's grief had frightened Daysy. It had pitched toward her all of a sudden, like a bat escaping a narrow tunnel at dusk. Magda Elena had given into her sorrow and then, quick as anything, had turned from it, the way a ship turns to catch the wind, half in flight, vibrating with some new idea that frightened Daysy.

"When I was little," Magda Elena began from inside the closet, seemingly lost in memories sparked by Abuelo's things, by the smell of wax that could mean anything—old birthday candles, the glue in photo albums, the loose soles of old shoes—"back in Mantua where I lived, we had a deep closet like this one in the back of the house. My *abuelita* kept it full of bolts of cloth that stood up nice and tall like knights. There was an ancient icebox, too, the kind you don't see anymore, with space for a block of ice. I used to hide back there and write on the walls with bits of chalk I'd steal from school. Daysy? Where are you? Come and help me," Magda Elena called. Her speech was a little slurred. Daysy realized that she'd never seen her mother drunk. It was like watching her move at half speed.

Daysy stepped into the dark closet. "*Aquí*," she said. It was a walk-in closet, the biggest in the house. Without the light overhead, the darkness made all of Abuelo's things look slightly animated, as if they moved in the periphery of Daysy's vision and, like in a horror movie, stopped the moment she looked at them head on. "I can get a new lightbulb," Daysy said.

"All out of lightbulbs," Magda Elena said as she rolled up a polyester tie and set it aside with three others. It flopped like a snake when she set it down, unrolling itself. Magda Elena hissed at it, then chuckled.

"Then, let's wait until tomorrow, when it's bright out," Daysy suggested, but her mother did not answer her. Frustrated, Daysy fetched a small flashlight, which she held steady under her arm as they worked.

Daysy explored Abuelo's closet with her hands, touching the many plastic bags he had knotted into tiny balls, opening more boxes full of junk, mainly things like keychains and spare keys to who-knew-where, unraveled cassette tapes, unopened packages of soap, a hundred tiny packets of ketchup from fast-food places, plastic chess pieces—mostly queens without their mates—and here and there, wads of cash, ones and fives folded up into triangles like flags.

Telling stories as she worked, the rum in her veins loosening her tongue, Magda Elena went on about the time after her abuela had died, how she'd emptied that closet, too, and painted it a blinding white, covering up her chalk drawings, the lyrics to *boleros* she had written on the walls, the spider web she'd traced in all its tiny detail. She talked at length about the time her brother Eddy had fixed her rollerskate wheels to swivel, so that Magda Elena rolled in all directions at once and, in a moment of glorious speed, careened down a hill and landed in a gutter, breaking her shoulder. There was the time Eddy mouthed off to their grandmother and the little old woman had asked him to bring her a step stool so that she might stand on it and slap him hard across the cheek, and he did so, obediently, taking that stinging cuff like a man.

On and on she went, lost in remembrance. Then, suddenly, Magda Elena asked, "Do you think she'd like a yellow room?" and went on cleaning and talking, using one of Abuelo's socks to wipe a pile of dessicated pill bugs out of the corner.

"What?" Daysy asked, her arms encumbered with three pairs of pleated pants Magda Elena had given her to put aside for charity.

"What?" Magda Elena returned in a disinterested sort of way. She'd just found a stack of dimes wrapped in Christmas paper.

"You plan on painting this room yellow? For who?"

"It's just an idea," Magda Elena said, sniffing the dimes that were all stuck together. "Daysy, did I ever tell you about being seven years old and sleeping through the hurricane of '44 as it ripped through Mantua? We woke up in the morning to find that most of the homes in our neighborhood still had roofs, but that the Mantua river had heaved its bed onto the banks. Everything was flooded with mud."

"Mami, for who? Who would stay in this room?" Daysy interrupted.

"The floor of our house was wet, brown, and shiny after the storm," Magda Elena went on. "I made shapes in the mud with my toes. I remember how Eddy cried in our abuela's arms, and how she said, 'Ay mi niño, no llores,' again and again. And you know what? I was surprised by all that sadness, because the mud had made me happy. It was like the molding clay my abuela had never let me have, saying it would make too much of a mess, and just like that, there was a houseful of the stuff."

"Why won't you listen to me?" Daysy yelled, breaking Magda Elena's reverie.

Pocketing the dimes first, Magda Elena stepped out of the closet and squinted in the light. Despite the brightness, she managed a fierce expression, but it softened at once. "One time, I yelled at my abuela the way that you just yelled at me, niña, and do you know what the old woman did? She walked away without saying anything, and so I relaxed. Then, just a few moments later, my abuela came charging into my bedroom with a broom, hitting me on the head with the straw end of it. If I had a broom now, Daysy..." Magda Elena's raised her finger and pointed it like a pistol at Daysy, who was holding a flashlight at such an angle that the light shone in Magda Elena's face, illuminating her nostrils that flared and glowed red.

"No Mami. Stop it," Daysy said. The flashlight shook in her hands.

"I have more stories. So many. Do you ever feel like this? Like you are no longer here, but that your mind is somewhere far away. Somewhere long ago?"

"No. Never. Why are we doing this?"

"You were there. You heard him," Magda Elena said, tapping the lightbulb overhead again. The filament was loose inside, and it tinkled faintly.

"Where? Who? Mami, I don't understand," Daysy said. The flashlight shook in her hands, and the effect was cinematic, reminding Daysy of dream sequences in movies, or the ways cameras replicated the sensation of fainting. Perhaps she actually was on the verge of fainting. Daysy couldn't be sure. Either way, she felt off-balance, as if standing in place for any length of time her legs would betray her and send her to the floor.

"The priest. Saying that Bethlehem comes to us, remember? Belén comes to us. To us, she comes. She comes…"

"I know what he said. He didn't mean her."

"And I overheard what Catalina told you, about Belén living, though we might not recognize her. What if, Daysy? What if…" Magda Elena cupped her hands around her daughter's cheeks and stared into her eyes. Her mother's pupils were large, quivering black discs. Daysy thought of black holes. She thought of the sea at night and grew dizzy from the smell of rum on her mother's breath. "We could adopt. We could," Magda Elena said.

Daysy pressed her face against her mother's hands and then, in a choked voice, asked, "Aren't I enough?"

"*Ay, mi niña*," Magda Elena said, and held onto Daysy, who was crying now and sniffing into Magda Elena's shoulder. Daysy hadn't been held in months. She'd shied away from embraces, questioned everything these days, felt such passion about the smallest things and had so little power to do anything about any of it. A chorus of angry roars sounded in her pulse all the time, except only she could hear it. Even so, she made herself small against her mother, and Daysy had the impression that the years had rolled back, that she was a little girl once more.

"Aren't I?" she asked again, and Magda Elena kissed the white line on Daysy's scalp where the girl had parted her hair so severely. Daysy wished she hadn't asked. An honest answer might undo them both.

"*Sí, mi amor. Sí, sí,*" Magda Elena mumbled between kisses. "I'll be better," she said, her lips moving against Daysy's hair. "I can be better at this." And Daysy nodded in agreement, her tears gone now.

That's how it was with Daysy, sad one moment, angry the next. She could go from blubbering to stony in an instant. As her mother held her, she tried to put herself in Magda Elena's place. She imagined that her mother's heart had been halved when Belén was born. And now that half was gone. There was no mending it. Not Angel's tenderness, not Daysy's stubborn insistence. Yet, like a ghost limb, the other half of Magda Elena's heart, the part that belonged to Belén, throbbed and ached.

Then, muted through the house, came the sound of a used and battered flute Angel had bought for himself at the thrift shop. Both Magda Elena and Daysy lifted their heads to hear it, little noting the places where Angel took time to breathe, or the notes that were stridently off, but feeling, rather, as if they were listening to Gregorio playing again.

"*Qué lindo*, Angel," they heard Catalina say as she clapped her hands.

"*Toma,*" Magda Elena said, handing Daysy the triangles of folded bills along with the sticky dimes. "Abuelo would have given these to you. We'll clean out his room some other time." They left the piles of Gregorio's confused years on the floor and followed the broken music out into the lighted hall.

STELLA MARIS MORALES-QUINN

MIAMI BEACH, FLORIDA 1990

Michael and Stella ordered room service for breakfast the next morning and sat on the bed to eat and watch television. Michael took in a Dolphins and Steelers replay for a good while before he clicked away, pausing at a local station. "Wait," Stella said, and yanked the remote control from her father's hand. Stella leaned forward and raised the volume. There had been a black-and-white picture of an overloaded boat on the screen, the photo just like the ones Stella had found in her research. The picture faded and was replaced by the image of a small family sitting uncomfortably on wooden stools. Script at the bottom of the screen identified them as the "Del Pozo Family," then faded away. They were talking about Mariel.

"Listen, Daddy," Stella said, and got very close to the television, her nose a few inches from the screen, her little body tense and quivering.

The woman's accent was thick, and her English was peppered with Spanish, words that Stella knew for the most part. The man's accent was worse. As for the girl beside them, her eyes were cast downward, toward her lap, as if she did not want to be recognized. A fluttering began in Stella's stomach, and she felt the way she had when she'd gone through the phone book. Here were people who shared her origin, who traversed the sea the way she and her mother had. Again, Stella wished they'd stayed in Miami, among such people, and she put both hands on the screen.

"Stel, move those hands," Michael said, scooting toward the television. Stella did not step away from the screen, but rather, inched even closer. The family onscreen told how they'd lost their daughter. The father said the baby's name, "Belén," as if it were an invocation, a spell to summon the child out of the mists. Stella's eyes watered.

The interview was brief, and the segment ended with a montage of family photographs, a lonesome-sounding flute playing in the background. The music bothered Stella, made her feel as if she didn't have a friend in the world. The pictures blurred into one another, of the family, young, at the beach, of the older daughter with her sister on her lap. They were yellow, fuzzy images, and Stella thought they weren't anything like the coffee-table books about Cuba she'd seen. Where were the bright Caribbean colors? The polished vintage cars? The sun setting on a crystal sea?

As they watched, Stella felt a brush of cold air on her bare leg. The lights flickered just a touch, almost unnoticeably, but Stella was hyper aware of everything now. She heard a rumbling overhead, as if someone in the room above were doing cartwheels. The smell of violets came and went. Three times Stella almost told her father about the noises and the smells, but he was engrossed now, watching the television. As for Stella, she was all eyes and ears to the ticks and creaks of the room, the waves of scent, the changes of light—signs, in Stella's mind, of her mother's presence. Perhaps Anita's spirit had entered the room. When a commercial for an accident lawyer came on, Stella closed her eyes, praying that her mother's spirit refrain from materializing. The trouble was that now she'd thought up an imaginary phantom, its luminous and terrible head cocked at a broken angle. Stella was afraid to open her eyes again, certain that the pale thing would be standing before her. She dug her hands into the pockets of the denim jacket. The sounds died away when she did so, her breathing slowed, and Stella opened her eyes and saw no ghost, saw nothing but the television program that was back on. They'd moved on to another family, this one an elderly couple and their three grown children, who had their own story about Mariel. Michael and Stella watched to the end, through the stories of five different Mariel families—the del Pozos, the Martinezes, Garcías, Robainas, and Casanovas.

"That was neat," Michael said, shoving a last bit of scrambled egg into his mouth.

Stella nodded, but she had been shaken. She didn't want to voice it to her father, though. She felt stupid, emotional. Why would such an interview affect her so strongly? There had been something about the way the people onscreen spoke, a familiarity to the way they moved their hands, emphasizing this word or that, the way they wore too much jewelry, the thickness of their eyebrows. It was, for Stella, as if she were watching Anita again, but costumed in new flesh. How had Daddy not noticed it? she wondered.

Michael stood and shook crumbs off his shirt. "Ready?" he asked, clapped his hands once, twice, then opened his arms as if waiting for Stella to applaud in return.

"Ready," Stella said, and the two of them headed out into the bright sunlight of a Miami morning. The itinerary Michael had set for them was busy. While the morning was fresh, they spent time at the Venetian pool, a limestone grotto fed by natural springs, the water emerald colored, the stones at the lip of the pool jagged and beautiful.

Their bodies warm and loose from the swim, they headed toward Little Havana, where Michael parked the car on 8th Street and the pair began to walk the cracked sidewalks. They went into *La Casa de los Trucos*, a magic shop bursting with costumes and plastic wands and rubber masks, to escape the heat that had descended rapidly on the city, as if the sun were falling slowly toward the earth. Inside, the salesman made a red rubber ball disappear from Stella's pocket, but Stella did not laugh, worried for a moment that the ball would reappear in her stomach, or some other place inside of her where it could not be reached.

They wandered in and out of little shops, walking past the famous Domino Park, which was abandoned that morning, the rickety wooden tables lonesome-looking without their elderly attendants. "You should hear the noise of the tiles when it's in full swing," Michael said, reminding Stella that he, too, had a past here, a life once in Miami.

Famished, Michael led Stella to Versailles Restaurant. "It's famous in town," he said. "But you'll have to order for me." The restaurant was full and busy. Waitresses in green-and-white uniforms brushed past Michael, bumping him with the trays on their shoulders without a word. Michael held Stella close to his body, and when they were seated, Stella saw her father relax. The place was mirrored on every wall, and Stella wondered at the way she and her father were replicated, again and again into infinity. She thought of all the people who had eaten in this place, Cubans nearly all of them, how they, too, had appeared in these mirrors repeatedly, and her head began to ache with the impossibility of counting all of those reflections.

"What does this mean?" Michael asked, pointing at the menu.

"That's a steak sandwich," Stella said after a bit. Her Spanish had gotten rusty after Anita's death, but she felt it returning to her now, like a familiar song. She ordered for her father, and the waitress winked at her in approval.

"*Perdón*," another aproned waitress said, pushing the back of Stella's chair with her hip so that the chair slid forward, opening a path for herself and the family she was seating. Stella looked up at them and startled. It was one of the families from the television program. There was the melancholy daughter and the father with the injured eye. The mother was the next to sit down, and she sighed as she did so. Another woman, blond and wearing a flowing white dress, joined them. With her was a boy who was busy winding the glossy brown tape of a cassette back into its plastic case.

"It's them, Daddy. From TV," Stella whispered.

"Wouldn't you know it," Michael wondered, and watched the family for a bit. "They look like nice folks."

"Daddy, let's talk to them. I have loads of questions about Mariel. Like, were things all that bad in Cuba? And how scary was it, really?

Maybe they knew Mommy."

"That island isn't as small as you think it is."

"Come *on*, Dad."

"They're eating, Stel. Like us," he said at the moment that two plates of steaming food were set before them. "Dig in."

But Stella could not eat. She was busy watching the del Pozos, comforted by their gestures that reminded her so powerfully of Anita. Her body leaned toward them, as if it wanted to join them, mindlessly, instinctively.

"Oh, for Crissakes!" Michael said at last, putting his knife and fork down on the table with a clatter when Stella's chair tipped dangerously backward. She righted it noisily, her half-empty glass of water tumbling to the floor. "Fine, Stella. If I do this, can we eat in peace?" he asked, and Stella bopped up and down in her chair.

"Excuse me," Michael called. "Excuse me, folks, sorry to interrupt. You're the del, del…"

"Pozos," Stella whispered fiercely.

"Sorry. Del Pozos. Right."

"How can we help you?" Angel asked, turning his chair completely in their direction. The entire family was looking over at Michael and Stella now, forks paused midair.

Michael shifted his chair closer to the del Pozos, too, so as not to have to shout. "My name is Michael Quinn, and this is my daughter, Stella. We saw you on television."

"Ah, *bueno*, that's good," Angel said, his cheeks reddening.

"You see, my daughter here, she's a bright girl. Inquisitive. She and her mother came here through Mariel, and she, Stella, she…"

"Want to know what it was like. I was a baby then," Stella said. While she spoke, she wrapped a linen napkin around her left hand, so tightly that her fingers were turning purple.

"Mariel, you say?" Magda Elena asked, putting her hand to her cheek.

The food on all their plates was no longer steaming. In fact, the rice was beginning to clump distastefully together, and the buttered toast was wilting. Michael said, "Perhaps now's not the time," as he looked down at his food.

"Maybe we could come to your house," Stella said, and Angel laughed. It was such a soft, tender laugh that Stella took note of it.

"*Porqué no?* Day after tomorrow then," Angel said, still smiling despite the strange looks his family was giving him. He removed a pen from his shirt pocket, clicked it, and wrote the address on a paper coaster.

"I don't know," Michael said as he took the coaster. "Such an intrusion on a holiday."

"*Olvídense de'so,*" Angel said, waving away Michael's concern. Michael's eyes widened.

"He says, 'Forget about it,' " Stella translated.

"Okay," Michael said to Stella, then, "Okay," again, more loudly, to the del Pozos. Each family returned to their cold dishes, speaking now in whispers. Stella tried hard to listen to what the del Pozos were saying, but it was all muttering now, a buzz, like standing near a beehive.

"I can't believe we just did that," Michael whispered, but there was laughter in his voice, the way he sounded when he used to play tricks on Anita, pulling her pants down while she did the dishes, and she would scold him like a boy.

≈ ✳ ≈

Back in their hotel room that night, Stella listened to what she thought was a mouse scurrying in the wall behind her. The cold draft was back, and the curtains were twitching, as if dancing. It was Anita again, making herself known, a sign, Stella was sure of it, that she and her father were meant to meet the del Pozos, to learn more about the world Stella had come from. What Anita couldn't explain in life, she had partly revealed to them through the television, through circuits, pixels, and glowing filaments, like a burning, untouchable trail to Cuba.

"Christmas Eve's tomorrow," Michael said. "What do you think about a visit to the Seaquarium? The brochure says they'll be open. We'll have some fun, go see Flipper?"

"Sure," Stella answered, distracted.

"And the next day, we'll visit those folks from TV. Get some answers for you, you know?" Michael said, and wrapped his arms around Stella. She curled her legs around his waist, and he lifted her, rocked her a bit then put her back in bed. "You don't mind going on Christmas, do you?" he asked, his face hovering over hers, covering the ceiling light. "It's your birthday, after all." Stella shook her head. It would be fine, she told him, certain that her life was a coiled spring on the verge of revealing its fullness. She felt such anticipation she was sure she didn't need to sleep that night, or, perhaps, ever again.

Michael finally shut off the television near midnight. By the time his lawnmower snore started up a few minutes later, Stella had turned in bed a dozen times, feeling very much like a dry leaf in the wind, unable to keep still. A few hours into the night, Stella thought her protesting body, so averse to tranquility, would drive her mad, and she considered for a moment her mother's body before she killed herself, how Anita must have felt this way, too—jittery, frightened, but most of all, eager for the moment of release. It was that thought that stilled Stella, wrapped her in sorrowful bindings she couldn't struggle against, reminded her that the visit to see the del Pozos might not reveal anything, but rather, bring more heartache.

In his sleep, Michael laughed, a thing he did often, as if his dreams were all comedies. He produced that cozy rumble of a sound that Stella so loved, and one that had once been accompanied so beautifully by Anita's own musical laugh, with its own kind of drumming sound. When they laughed together, it was like a percussive treat. The

sound of her father's laughter now reawakened in Stella memories of
Anita as a beautiful woman with rounded cheeks, like a baby's, with
dark brown eyes that always glimmered, even when she was ill, even
in death, just before the paramedics had closed them for her. She'd
worn pearl clips to hold back her hair. Stella remembered now how
she'd held her through nightmares; that she'd loved her husband, and
at night, Stella had heard her moan, "*Mi vida, mi vida,*" to him,
assigning him her very life. She thought of her capturing daddy-long-
legs in the basement, ones with broken limbs, and cradling them in
her hand before setting them along the edge of the woods outside. All
of this Stella remembered with clarity, and she told herself she would
share it with the del Pozos.

Under her head lay the denim jacket, softer now as it had been
washed several times. She rubbed it for a while, and her mind eased
up, allowing her to imagine a mermaid in the ocean, singing to Stella,
the mermaid's face that of her mother. She hoped it would become a
dream instead of a willful imagining, but the stories Stella conceived
never turned into dreams. Her subconscious would not take hold of
them, or relieve her of the burden of having to supply an ending to
the stories she told herself.

DAYSY MARIA DEL POZO

HIALEAH, FLORIDA 1990

On Christmas Eve, Daysy found she had little appetite for the *lechón* her mother had prepared that morning, cooked not in the ground and roasted whole, but in a slow cooker instead. She thought bitterly of Abuelo's absence. They'd all been to Fair Havens that morning to visit with him, including Catalina and Amado, who often stayed back in the house, declining other visits to the nursing home, Catalina saying, time and again, that she did not like the way the patients stared at her. Pearl, at Abuelo's side, was holding a hand towel speckled with blood, wadded up in her hands. "For when he coughs," she said, holding it up. Then, on cue, Abuelo cleared his throat violently. There had been a flurry of movement then, Angel racing out into the hall to find a nurse, Magda Elena listening to him shouting, "What do you mean the doctor isn't here?" and the nurse answering, "Christmas Eve," like an apology, fear in her voice. The rest of the morning was spent at Abuelo's side, Angel having taken the bloodied towel from Pearl's hands, wiping his father's chin with it again and again. As for Abuelo, his eyes were unusually wide now, and Daysy thought she saw in them a sudden understanding that this was the end. Daysy felt as if somebody ought to comfort him. It was a crushing kind of helplessness that drove her to plant her cheek against her grandfather's and stay that way, very still, until she felt him lean against her. "Be strong, *Abuelo*," she whispered to him, and he had sighed.

They left once his eyes closed and the snoring began. Pearl took hold of his limp hand, said, "Y'all enjoy your holiday. I'll be here," and settled into her chair.

Back home, Angel missed his father to the point of distraction. Outside, he'd tried to busy himself by chopping down the low-hanging branches of the avocado tree with a machete, but he sliced his finger in the process. The digit had gushed blood, and Magda Elena was certain it needed stitches, but Angel had staunched the flow with a clean rag and some duct tape, refusing to see a doctor. Daysy and her cousin, Amado, spent long hours in her bedroom playing Monopoly, though the games did not go smoothly. Twice, Daysy had flipped the board in anger at her near-bankruptcy, and Amado, mild as he was, waited out her temper in the living room.

It took a while to gather the family to the table. Daysy had dragged her feet, the shadows on her face had deepened, and her eyes lingered on the seat where her grandfather once sat. Catalina was late, having spent too long in the bathroom setting her hair in curls. Only Angel had taken his seat early and pressed one hand over his wounded finger, as if it were still bleeding. His anger at the meal was hardly suppressed. Earlier that day, he'd stood in the kitchen watching Magda Elena handle the pork, and he'd said, "We aren't still doing *Noche Buena*, are we?"

"It's tonight," she'd said.

"It isn't right. My father's dying."

"We have to eat, don't we?"

Angel had left the kitchen in silence, a deep quiet that signified his anger, the way scowls, or wrathful looks, or foul exclamations marked ire in other men. At the dinner table, he hovered over the meager pot of slow-cooked meat, a spread markedly different from other years when he and his father had prepared a whole pig in the backyard and Magda Elena would cook enough rice to feed a multitude. Angel cleared his throat, raised his glass of water, and said, "*El año que viene...*" but stopped before finishing. Daysy heard his voice catch, watched his jaw working hard. So she ended it for him, whispering, "*en Cuba,*" before taking a big drink. Her father looked at her then, and smiled.

They finished their meal in silence, the forks and knives clinking solemnly on the china. The quiet was so profound among them that

when the phone rang, Daysy jumped in her seat a little. Angel rose
to answer it, moving rapidly to stand, as if he were glad to get away
from the table. Daysy stopped eating to listen. She heard her father
say, "You take the Palmetto north. No, north. Get off at 122nd. *Sí.
Claro*," then listened as he described the house.

"It was *el americano* from Versailles."

Magda Elena sighed deeply. "I wish you hadn't invited them. They
are strangers."

"We've been over it. They're good people, I can tell."

"Oh, *sí*, Angel the mind reader. I forgot," Magda Elena said and
began clearing plates still full of food off the table. "The house is a
disaster. We aren't ready for visitors," she added.

Angel shrugged his shoulders and took his plate out of Magda
Elena's hands.

There was nothing for it now, Daysy thought, looking around the
house. Outside, the back porch lights illuminated apricot-colored
pavers that had been hosed down that morning and a sparkling tile-
topped table. Daysy helped her mother clear the dining room table
when they were done eating, wrapped the tablecloth into a bundle,
and carefully shook it over the sink. As a little girl, when she'd first
learned about the rules that governed a Cuban household, Daysy had
taken a crumb-filled tablecloth outside to shake it out. Her mother
had heard the snap of the fabric and come running. It was bad luck
to do such a thing after dark as it augured death, and indeed, their
neighbor, Pura, had died the next week. That the woman was ninety-
nine years old was of no consequence. It was the dirty tablecloth
whipped about in the night that had done it.

≈ ✳ ≈

They opened Christmas presents early the next morning. Daysy
and Amado's gifts, unwrapped, had been put out on the sofa for them

to find, as if they still believed in Santi Clo. Daysy walked slowly toward her gifts—a yellow-and-gray-striped sweater rested alongside a new stereo and a pair of silver heels. She could feel her parents watching her, the way they did when she was little, encouraging her to open her gifts faster, to try things on, to tear through cardboard and plastic wrapping in a frenzy, and then, afterward, to sling her arms around her parents in joy and gratitude. She considered how, not long ago, it had been dolls and stuffed animals perched on the furniture. This year, Amado's presents had encroached upon the sofa; his new skateboard was propped up against a cushion as if on display at a store.

Daysy found she couldn't stay in the moment, or recall the buzz of happiness she'd felt on every other Christmas morning. She'd been wondering all night about the people who were coming to visit, about the strange forthrightness of these *americanos*. It was all so different from the way she'd been raised, surrounded by people with a different brand of confidence, one reticent among the unfamiliar and unbridled in the company of friends. To say that a person was too easygoing or too forceful among strangers, to describe them as having *mucha confianza*, was a grave sin among Cubans. The American and his daughter certainly had *mucha confianza*.

After the gifts were opened, Magda Elena clapped her hands and started picking up balled wrapping paper. Daysy knew what she was thinking. Soon, the strangers would be here. The house was a mess, and this was unacceptable. Feeling helpful, as well as grateful for the Christmas presents, Daysy stepped out, broom in hand, to sweep the front porch. She banged the broom against the decorative iron rail around the elevated porch, and it clanged like a church bell. When the sound died down, Daysy heard a voice say, "Hi!" It was a sweet, musical voice.

Daysy turned and watched the girl from the restaurant, and her father, come forward. The girl's eyes were framed by heavy bangs. Her hair was a bit too long over her eyebrows, and she blinked longer strands away. She wore a summery dress, printed with sunflowers.

The man approached, took a deep breath, and Daysy saw a faint trembling at the corners of his mouth. "Hi there," he said. "The name's Michael." Daysy nodded, but said nothing and felt herself stiffen awkwardly, the way she always did around strangers. How Daysy wished she were a little more at ease in the world. This girl before her was a different sort. Vigorous. Sprightly. It was clear her father didn't concern himself with her hair, which showed knots here and there, or her nails, which were chewed into jagged shapes. And her ears were bare and unornamented. The girl had none of the somber look Daysy saw in the mirror and had come to recognize as singularly hers. She could already predict where her frown lines would come in and had pressed the skin on her face forward to see if they would appear, giving her a glimpse of herself years from now.

"Merry Christmas," the girl, Stella, said leaning heavily over the iron railing. Her eyes were large, and in the glare of the morning sun, the pupils were tiny and black, the blue of her irises glistening, as if tear-filled, though it was clear the girl was in a state of panicky joy.

"You should come in," Daysy said, and moved aside as the pair stepped into the house. Magda Elena saw them at once and invited them to sit. A dusting rag was still in her hand as she spoke, and when she realized it, she thrust the dusty cloth at Daysy, who fumbled with it. Michael and Stella sat in the living room, the girl choosing a seat next to the Christmas tree. Immediately, she began to examine it, brushing an ornament of a wooden train with the tips of her fingers.

"Angel. *Están aquí*," Magda Elena called, announcing the visitors' arrival.

Angel strode in, followed by Catalina and Amado. "*Mucho gusto*," Catalina said, extending her hand for Michael to take. The others took their seats, the furniture squeaking under them.

"So," Michael began, and it was clear he didn't quite know what to say.

"Would you like something to drink? Water? Soda?" Magda Elena offered.

"Water's fine," Michael said quickly, and Magda Elena left for the kitchen, eager to escape the uncomfortable situation in the living room. Daysy followed her. Inside the kitchen, Magda Elena and Daysy looked at each other with odd expressions on their faces.

"They're weird. Why are they here?" Daysy asked.

"One of your father's whims. You know how he is," Magda Elena answered as she selected a pair of water glasses etched with vines and leaves on the outside and painted delicately in gold. She filled the glasses with water from the tap then picked out a few well-shaped ice cubes to plop in. Then, she took two sheets of paper towel and wrapped one around the base of each glass, so that her guests' hands would not feel the cold and damp of the ice water.

She and Daysy returned to the living room, each with a glass in hand. They'd interrupted a bit of conversation, and Angel looked up at them, his eyes lively, the way they looked whenever he talked about Cuba with someone outside the family.

"Magdita," he said, "Did we know anyone named Anita Morales?"

"No, we didn't know anyone named Anita," Magda Elena answered.

Daysy caught sight of Stella then, who was crumpled forward in her seat, resting her chin on her hand dramatically, her eyes growing wet. There was something odd about Michael's face, too, as if he were straining to keep his features relaxed, neutral.

"Anita was…"

"My wife," Michael said. "Stella's mother. She passed."

The man, Michael, had taken on that look of the bereaved—eyes sunk into his cheeks, his lips pressed together. The girl mimicked him, showing her sorrow just as plainly.

"*Ay*, no," Magda Elena managed to say, at which Michael nodded. "Was she sick?"

"In a way," Stella said before Michael had a chance.

Daysy thought she saw shame in their eyes. Whether the woman had been ill for a long time or poisoned herself, it was best not to know. "I'm sorry," Daysy said quietly, and her family nodded around her.

"Look, here," Michael offered, and drew his wallet from his pocket. The leather was bent from sitting on it, as were the cards and pictures inside. He fiddled with it a bit and pulled out a picture of Anita posing before a turn-of-the-century steam engine at Station Square in Pittsburgh.

Magda Elena put the glass of water in Michael's free hand and took the photograph from him. Her eyes widened. "*Mira*, Angel! It's Solamaris!" Daysy rose at once, eager to see the picture of this woman she'd heard about. She felt her heart in her throat. How strange Solamaris looked in a thick coat, a red wooly scarf around her neck, hiding the beautiful length of it. She was paler in this picture than in the one her mother had hung on the wall, as if the brown of her skin had washed out.

"You're from up north?" Daysy asked.

"Pittsburgh," Stella said.

"*Imagínate eso*, Angel," Magda Elena said, addressing her husband.

Daysy could not seem to locate Pittsburgh, as if the North American map in her head had suddenly gone blurry north of Georgia.

Taking a look at the photo in Magda Elena's hand, Angel nodded, his mouth pressed into a thin line. "And she's..."

"Yeah. She passed a few years ago," Michael said.

"*Ay*, Solamaris," Magda Elena said, her voice tight.

"Her name was Anita," Stella said.

"No, no. Solamaris. Solamaris Morales," Magda Elena said. "She was my friend, my dear, dear friend. Look," she said, and pointed at the wall of photographs. "Solamaris is there. The one on the right."

Daysy watched as Michael hoisted Stella up on his hip with one hand, his other still gripping the glass of water, how he walked slowly toward the wall, how both of them stared at the photograph of Daysy's third birthday, where the family had gathered whole for a moment long ago, he putting his fingers to his mouth, and she lifting her hand to touch the glass.

"Don't touch," Michael whispered.

"No, she can have it." Magda Elena put the frame in the girl's hand.

"Thank you."

After her father had put her back down, Stella said, "But that's not me," and pointed at the baby in Solamaris' arms.

"No, it's Leo," Magda Elena said. The girl and her father looked puzzled. "*Ay, mi Dios*, didn't Solamaris tell you about Leo, about her firstborn?" Magda Elena asked.

Michael swayed a little, and Angel rushed to put a chair behind him. He sat there in silence for a long time. "Anita," he murmured at last, and covered his face with his hands. "She told me she wanted a fresh start in this country," Michael said, then he cleaned his face with the inside of his shirt, like a boy. "I didn't think she meant it so, so..." Michael waved his hands in the air, as if shooing away the words he couldn't remember. "Her name? Sola-what?" he said, and his hands were up again, as if imploring a higher power.

The gesture struck Daysy as particularly Cuban, and she thought that some of Solamaris lingered in this man.

"I'm sorry about all this. We just, my daughter just would like to know more about her mother. Now we learn she had a son. Where is he?" Michael asked.

"His name was Leo. He died quite young," Magda Elena whispered. Catalina and Amado had joined them in the dining room, exchanging eloquent glances with one another every so often. The air conditioning kicked on with a clank and whir, and Osún began his tinkling. Catalina pointed at it and mouthed the words, "I told you" to Daysy.

Michael made as if to stand, but Angel patted his shoulder a few times, said, "*No hombre*, take it easy," and Michael slumped into the seat again.

Something shifted inside of Daysy, as if her heart's capacity had grown in that moment. All of her own grief—whether Iggy Placetas liked her enough to make her his girlfriend, whether Abuelo would remember her the next time she visited him at the home, the secrets her parents had kept from her—felt small and insignificant in the face of death. The day would come, thought Daysy, when her own light would be extinguished, and her mother's and father's, and that of her cousin and aunt, and one day, Michael and Stella would be gone, too. Who knew the day? Perhaps today was the day, the anniversary of a dark day in the future. A shiver overtook Daysy, and she found that she could not shake the cold that remained in its wake.

"Stella?" she called to the girl, feeling sudden, warm feelings for her. "Want to come to my room? I have some old dolls I don't play with anymore. You can have them, if you'd like. You can—"

But Stella took no notice of Daysy. Instead, she took hold of Magda Elena's hand. "Tell me about her," Stella said, gripping Magda Elena's hand in appeal.

"We lived on the corner of Soledad and Desague in Havana," Magda Elena began. "Your mami was in a house across the street from our building. *Bueno*, those old buildings, *imagínate*, are in terrible disrepair. They are old things, from the colonial days, the pirate days, and they haven't been fixed in thirty years. Sometimes, the balconies fall right off of them."

"Magda Elena, no, not this story," Angel interrupted, glancing sideways at Stella and back to his wife.

Magda Elena inhaled deeply. "It's the best thing Solamaris ever did," Magda Elena argued. "The most important thing a person can do."

"*Bueno*," Angel said, throwing his hands up, as if to say, "*Allá tú*," that's your business.

"One day, as we were walking down Peñalver Street, I think it was, we watched as one of those balconies broke away from the wall, all in one piece. It made such a rumbling sound, a sound you could feel deep in your chest, and it fell right on a young man, maybe twenty, twenty-one, who had been on the sidewalk. I couldn't move. I was frozen to the ground. But not Solamaris. She ran across the street and knelt right by the man, stepping in growing puddles of dark blood as if it were only water. She said to him, '*Dame tu mano,*' and took his hand. She handed Leo over to me so that both her hands were free, and she swept the hair from the man's face. He said, 'I'm dying,' and she said, 'Maybe. God knows. But you can, you know. You can go if you want to.'"

Magda Elena stopped and covered her mouth, as if overcome with the memory. Stella was nodding, encouraging Magda Elena to go on. "Your mami said this and you could see the man relaxing, getting comfortable with the idea of dying. Then Solamaris said, 'I'll hold your hand. I'll hold it and hold it, okay.' And he said something like, 'Don't let go, *mamita linda,*' something like that, *imagínate*, a man flirting at that moment. But slowly, his eyes lost a bit of light, the puddle of blood had grown so that it dripped down the sidewalk and into the sewer, mingling with everyone else's refuse, as if it were trash and not a man's life. I couldn't watch it all, to tell the truth. I held onto that baby and sang into his hair because I didn't think he should be paying attention either. But your mami held on and on until the man died, and I think that's the very best thing a human being can do, to have the courage to stay to the end that way. If nothing else, you should be proud of your mother, no matter what else she did in life."

Stella nodded, said, "That was a good story," then squeezed Magda Elena's hands again. "Mommy and I came over on a boat, during Mariel," Stella said, and there was a ghost of a smile on her face now. "Like you."

"*Bueno*, your mami and I..." Magda Elena stopped cold.

Daysy, who had been listening to the story in a trance, lost in it as if she could smell the concrete rubble and the iron sting of the dying man's blood in her nostrils, snapped to. Something didn't fit. "How old are you?" Daysy asked.

"Ten. Today's my birthday."

"That doesn't make sense," Angel said, catching on.

"You were born in Pittsburgh? Yes?" Magda Elena pressed on.

"No, Cuba," Michael answered for his daughter. "I met them both down at the Orange Bowl during Mariel.

There was quiet for a moment. Daysy found herself counting backward on her hands, trying to reason out the puzzle. A terrible trembling took over her fingers.

Then came Stella's voice, like a wild note: "I was born in Cuba. Mommy said I was buried in Havana and was born again. That's why you don't remember me."

"Stel," Michael said, his voice a warning. Daysy watched as he went to grab his daughter, to take her arm and pull her, maybe quiet her, but Stella moved like a slippery thing.

"That's what some folks believe, yes," Magda Elena tried to explain. "That the souls of dead infants are reborn again. I'm sure it's what she meant."

Daysy looked at Catalina, whose eyes had gone wide and unblinking.

"But you aren't Leo," Magda Elena said. The air conditioning turned on with a roar, and Osún's cup tipped over, jingling for a moment.

There was a murmuring then. Catalina was chanting, so softly it was barely a sound, "*Ago, ago, ile, ago.*" She had righted the cup atop the cabinet. "*Ago, ago, ile, ago,*" she sang.

Stella began walking crablike, sideways and away from the dining room. Daysy glanced at Michael, who looked stricken and did not move. He said, "Oh, God, she's just like her mother. Just like," and sat back into the chair with such finality that his head struck the wall behind him and made a rapping sound, like someone knocking at a door. The glass of water in his hands fell, splashing Daysy's feet. Only a bit of the rim chipped off the sturdy glass. The sound drew their attention, and Catalina began singing "*Ago, ago*" more loudly.

There was a tight circle around Michael, who'd gone ashen, each of them encouraging him in their own way. Magda Elena said, "Solamaris loved you, no matter what," while Catalina fanned him vigorously with a catalog. Even Amado jumped in, saying, "*Consooorte*," and patting Michael's back, as if he were a man, too, buoying up an old friend. All the while, Michael rubbed his face with his hands, apologizing every so often.

Then Daysy announced, "The kid went outside. She's outside," and all eyes looked toward the back patio.

Daysy was the first to move. She was thinking of the canal as she went, always the canal, that slow-moving stretch of water that smelled of fish and rotting vegetables. Her mother had been the one to insist on the chain-link fence when they bought the house and had instilled in Daysy a healthy fear of the stinky canal, its loping alligators and its sluggish current.

Daysy scanned the backyard, but Stella was nowhere to be found.

Magda Elena shouted, "*Angel! ¡La niña!*" and he came running, followed by Michael, Catalina, and Amado.

"Stella!" Michael called, his voice thin, as if it might break. The others joined in, and a chorus of "Stellas," alternating and blending like a song, echoed in the yard. They searched inside the hot shed, underneath the workbenches Abuelo had lined up against the side of the house, between rows of banana trees, in the small alcove where the garbage can stood, ranks of empty beer bottles at its base. It was Michael who jumped the fence in one leap to search for her in the water, and it was Angel who saw her clinging to the *flamboyán* tree trapped sidewise between banks.

The men waded in together. Daysy watched as they struggled to release the girl's denim jacket from where it had been caught on a gnarled tree branch. As they tugged at it, Stella heard the fabric rip and she began to howl. Stella's voice as she cried was an injured creature's screech, an ibis with a broken wing, a heron caught by a snake.

"My jacket," she wailed, then, "Mommy! Mommy!" between sobs. Michael pulled her away from the jacket, kicking as she went, splashing mucky water in their faces. Michael pinned Stella to the ground. She went on flailing, intent on retrieving the jacket.

"What were you thinking?" Michael yelled, his face an inch away from Stella's.

Stella cried on, "I fell in, Daddy. Th-there was a b-beetle drowning. I wanted to h-hold it while it died, like Mommy did for the m-man. Please, Daddy, my jacket! Mommy!"

Daysy looked at Stella, her features twisted in anguish, and that look impelled her to move, to wade into the canal. She reached the *flamboyán* in a few strokes, her nose already filling with the sour smell of the water. Nimbly, Daysy ran her fingers between the denim and the wet bark, loosening the threads from the splinters one by one until the jacket was free. She could hear her mother screaming her name, but the sound came and went like a siren in her ears, growing louder then quieting, then louder again. Small creatures brushed against her bare legs underwater, and Daysy sent up a small prayer concerning water mocassins. Daysy kicked hard, the jacket in her hands ballooning behind her, slowing her down. It bore a small gash now, easily mendable.

Daysy emerged from the water and knelt by Stella, who had been watching all along. "Look, your jacket. Don't cry anymore," Daysy said, and swept the hair out of Stella's eyes with her wet hand, drawing the strands of blond hair up and back. There was canal muck on the girl's face, and Daysy wiped it clean, first a great chunk of it off Stella's cheek, then a bit on the side of her head. Here, Daysy stopped, ran her fingers against a birthmark visible now with Stella's heavy bangs swept back. It was a faded pink, as if Stella had been playing with makeup and gone too far with the rouge.

"Mami," Daysy whispered at the sight of the mark. She remembered her mother's description of another birthmark. Daysy had seen it in photographs, and, later, had searched her own body for a similar mark in places she never looked—behind her knees, between her toes, on the back of her neck using a pair of mirrors—but she found nothing on the smooth expanse of her brown skin, except for a fresh crop of acne beginning on her forehead.

The breeze grew rougher and whipped Stella's hair about, so that Daysy had to uncover the mark again. Seeing it was like plunging into the canal—there was no way for it but to jump in all at once, to dive for the truth now that it was in sight.

Magda Elena pushed forward and traced the shape of the birthmark with a wet finger. She whispered, "Stella, *niña*."

Daysy's own mouth started to form another name, but she repressed the urge to give in to what had begun to take form in her brain—that this was Belén. It had come to her as a shimmering, incandescent possibility that this girl was her sister, returned whole and lovely. There, yes, was Magda Elena's mouth, the plump bottom lip. And her grandmother's eyes. Those were Nieve's, too, as far as Daysy could tell from pictures. The upturned nose, like Daysy's own.

Magda Elena took her hands from Stella's face, from the stain on her temple. She sought Michael and lunged at him, clutching his shirt. She pulled him around to face her and Michael, staggered, stared at Magda Elena's face. "What boat?" she asked, close to him, looking from a distance as if she were about to kiss him. "What boat? Do you remember the name of the boat Solamaris was on?"

"No," Michael said.

"*El Ron*," Stella whispered to him, and he nodded, remembering.

"And she disembarked with Stella?"

"My daughter, yes."

Magda Elena laughed, and Michael seemed injured by the sound. "What are you getting at?" he asked, his eyes moist.

"Wait here," Magda Elena said, crying now. She ran into the house and Daysy followed. Together, they tumbled toward Magda Elena's bedroom and the closet where she kept the yellow suitcase, lighter now that many of the photographs had been framed.

"Do you think, Mami?" Daysy began to ask.

"*Sí, sí,*" Magda Elena answered, breathless.

Clutching the suitcase to her chest, Magda Elena ran back outside. She laid it on the grass at Michael's feet, unzipped it with such force that the jagged teeth of the zipper cut her knuckles.

"*Mira, mira.* Look! My baby, look at her," and she held up pictures of Belén for Michael to see. Here she was propped up on a sofa, too young to smile. And there, another photograph of Belén in Daysy's lap, her chubby round belly in contrast with her sister's slender body. In all the photographs, the birthmark was visible. Michael gaped at the photographs, and Daysy saw recognition and fear in his eyes.

"Solamaris had no child with her when she boarded that boat," Magda Elena said. "Leo was only a few months in the grave. We were trying to cross over to the *El Ron* when I lost Belén. Somehow, Solamaris saved her. My Belén! She saved her and stole her. *Dios mío.*"

"No way," Michael said, and broke away from Magda Elena.

For his part, Angel had fallen onto the grass, and his eyes were on Stella, too, his lips moving in silence.

Looking at Stella now, Daysy thought that her birthmark was her most prominent feature with her hair out of the way. She thought, wildly, of Hansel and Gretel and the part in the story where the children leave a path of crumbs in their wake. What if the birthmark was a breadcrumb trail, a part of herself Daysy had left behind in her mother's womb, a sign for her sister to absorb and take up as her own.

How often had Daysy wondered what it would have been like to have an accomplice in life, a partner so that her parents would not outnumber her? What would it feel like to know she was not alone in the world? Or that she could face her troubles with a small ally not unlike herself? Daysy remembered that she used to wish for a little sister at every fountain when she was little. She would toss in a penny (the shinier, the more likely the wish would come true was her thinking) and wish herself a sibling. When she first learned to pray, it had been her first prayer. *Papá Dios, send me a sister.* And now, now...

Magda Elena was grabbing at the photographs in the suitcase, not caring if they bent or tore, and filling Michael's arms with them. "Is this not the Stella you remember?" Magda Elena shouted at Michael, and he shook his head forcefully, eyes closed.

Above, foamy clouds floated by in peaceful indifference. Magda Elena knelt where she had been standing, her knees coming down on Michael's toes. He stepped away with a hop, gathered Stella in his arms, and made to leave.

"No!" Angel shouted, and stood before Michael.

"This was a mistake," Michael muttered, ramming his shoulder against Angel's chest.

"*Hombre*, wait! That could be our daughter," Angel said, and Michael stopped. When he turned, his face was contorted. Stella's own face was hidden in her father's neck, and her little body shook from the cold water.

Daysy was bothered by her father's "could be." She was certain, as certain as she was of her breath that came and went.

Magda Elena got to her feet. "Belén," she said and took two floundering steps toward Michael and Stella. She seemed to be uttering a syllable that dimmed and died on her tongue. Where to begin? It seemed that they had reached the decisive and dangerous point. Stella shivered against her.

"Belén," Magda Elena said again.

"I'm Stella," the girl said, lifting her head a little. "I want to go back to the hotel."

"Okay," Michael said, fear on the edge of his voice so that it vibrated a bit in his throat. "I think it's okay, Stel. We'll go in a minute." Michael did not take a step toward the door, though he looked at it longingly.

His hesitation was all that Magda Elena needed. "*Mi alma, alma mía*," she began, and Daysy thought her mother was calling out to her soul and not knowing whether she meant some smoky spirit within herself or the girl before her, her soul outside her body. Later, Magda Elena would voice her anger at Solamaris that rippled and flared beneath her joy. Daysy suspected that the feeling would never go away, would live side by side with her mother's love for her old friend.

For now, Magda Elena said to Michael, "Your wife was a good friend to me. The most wonderful woman. She was loved. I loved her. We have that in common, don't we? Maybe we can remember her together. Both of us can forgive her." Michael tightened his grip on Stella. His mouth was set in a line. "Please," Magda Elena said. "Please."

Stella wriggled, loosened herself from her father, and peeked up at Magda Elena, who, seeing her chance, gathered Stella up like a baby and hid her face in the crook of Stella's neck. Magda Elena rocked the girl, and it was as if Stella had just fallen out of her arms into the sea and the horror of the last ten years had only lasted a half second, reduced to *un gran susto*, a big scare, a momentary stopping of the heart.

The sun was midway across the sky. It bathed the backyard in a haze of yellow and made the shadows disappear directly beneath everyone's feet. Daysy felt a strange pull beneath her navel as she watched her mother and Stella. What a wonder it was, how well they fit together, Daysy thought, like spoons nestled in a drawer. Daysy wondered if her mother could feel Stella's pulse in various spots—

where the girl's wrist pressed into her back, where the bend of her arm cradled her waist. A Morse code, somewhere deep in Stella's neck, perhaps, tapped its rhythm on Magda Elena's skin. But what it was saying was a secret to Daysy, one she wished she knew.

At some point, Magda Elena transferred Stella into Angel's arms, and he held her without moving. When Angel had put her back on her feet, they examined Stella in silence, Angel and Magda Elena each holding one of Stella's hands. Then, at once, as if a spell had broken, they launched into speech.

"You haven't changed, *tan linda como siempre.*"

"*Mi niña, mi niña, mi niña...*"

"I just might die of joy now, I just might..."

They couldn't help but touch her, stroke her cheek or rub her arm, as if the loss of contact would make her vanish again.

"Let her go," Michael said after a moment, and Magda Elena and Angel released Stella's hands. They stared at each other then, tensely, the way armies faced one another in wars of old.

Stella was the only one who moved, crushing a patch of crabgrass with her foot. It crunched lightly, making the only sound among them. "You said you loved my mommy," Stella said softly.

"I did," Magda Elena said.

"Good," Stella said, crunching the crabgrass again. Her chin was up, though, and she was flexing the fingers in her hands, as if getting ready to fight.

Yes, thought Daysy. I'm glad you're strong. You'll have to be in a family like this. For a moment, Daysy forgot that Stella was a new creature to her. It was as if she could remember the child she had been, and somewhere in those flexing hands and face tilted to the sun, Daysy thought she could imagine the grown-up Stella would be.

≈ ⋆ ≈

They went inside to talk, seated at the dining table, the wall of photographs behind them a reminder of what they were preserving now. Catalina and Amado bid their goodbyes, and Catalina even kissed Michael on the cheek, as if anointing him into the family. Amado hugged Stella, who did not lift her arms or hug him back, and he told her, "*Mira, primita*, for you," and handed her a chocolate bar he had in his pocket. Daysy could tell it was half-melted, but Stella thanked him anyway.

"Didn't I tell you?" Catalina whispered into Daysy's ear.

After they left, the adults made plans. There would be blood tests and lawyers. There would be holiday trips up north. Every so often, Daysy heard Stella sigh so deeply that another noise from within her followed the sigh, like an echo.

At one point, Magda Elena warmed up leftovers from the night before. Michael took two bites of *pan con lechón* then started to sniff, crying before long. "Take Belén to your room to play," Daysy's father suggested.

"Stella," Stella corrected him, before following Daysy down the hall to her bedroom.

≈ ⋆ ≈

"So," Daysy said.

"So," Stella repeated, then walked over to the short bookcase full of comics. "I like to read, too," Stella said, "but not stuff like this."

Daysy sat cross-legged on the floor before the bookcase and began pulling down issue after issue. "This one?" she'd ask, presenting Stella with a Catwoman book or a recent Fantastic Four, but each time, Stella would shake her head no.

"I have a coloring book somewhere. Maybe some old crayons…"

"Coloring is for babies."

"Right," Daysy said. Then, "Listen. I can't imagine how weird this must be for you."

"You can't."

Daysy was quiet for a minute. One thing was clear. Stella belonged to herself. She wasn't Daysy's, or Magda Elena's, or Michael's. She was her own creature, an unattainable presence, the physical embodiment of an answer that Daysy needed to the question, "Who am I?" and "Where do I belong?" But the reach of Daysy's longing and soul-searching ended here with this flesh and blood girl, who was neither meaning nor symbol in the end.

"Right again," Daysy said.

"Do you think the number thirty-two has a color?" Stella asked without looking at Daysy.

"No," Daysy said, regretting it at once. Perhaps it was a game. "Purple?"

"Are you just guessing?" Stella asked, her voice small.

Daysy nodded, then tried something else. "I have makeup. You can give me a makeover," Daysy suggested, to which Stella chewed her bottom lip and agreed.

For a while they played, with Stella's hands on Daysy's cheeks, steadying her face as she applied eyeliner and mascara and shadow in pinks and purple. The makeup was new—a gift for Christmas and a sign that Daysy's parents were letting her grow up. Daysy tried not to wince as Stella poked her in the eye and gouged out the creamy lip-gloss from its tin, ruining the smooth surface forever. When she was done, Daysy and Stella looked into a mirror together. They stared in silence. Even the adults in the other room had quit talking for a moment.

Then, they laughed. They laughed until the black mascara that Stella had applied in hideous clumps began to run down Daysy's cheeks. They laughed when Daysy pointed at her front teeth, covered in red lipstick as if she'd bitten someone and drawn blood. They laughed when Stella started speaking with a Transylvanian accent, and they laughed even as the room darkened and stars began to pop into the sky.

"Next time," Daysy said, "I'll teach you how not to make me look like an insane clown."

"Yes, of course," Stella said, and together, they wiped Daysy's face with a wet hand towel until her skin was raw.

≈ ⋆ ≈

Michael and Stella left early in the evening, Stella's arms full of presents Daysy had picked out from her room and wrapped. Michael promised to return, though Daysy wasn't sure of him.

Daysy felt panic rise in her throat as Michael and Stella walked down the porch steps. Her words came out muddled, as if her lips weren't working right. "Please," she told him, "don't take her away from me." Not again, she thought desperately. It felt as if a sob was forming in her throat, or deeper maybe, climbing her spine like a cat, wanting to claw its way out. "I want to know my sister," Daysy managed to say, then cleared her throat to keep the cat inside of her from howling. Michael squeezed her shoulder with a firm hand, nodding, and the hard knot in Daysy's throat dissolved.

The del Pozos took turns hugging Stella with quick embraces and kisses to her round cheek. Magda Elena clasped Stella hard, and the girl smiled up at her. Daysy was amused to see that Stella had left purple fingerprints from the eyeshadow she'd played with on the back of Magda Elena's dress. "I've missed you," Daysy heard her mother say, and a sweetly sad feeling settled in Daysy's heart. Stella wrapped thin arms around Magda Elena's neck. She whispered something into Magda Elena's ear, which made her laugh. Magda Elena shook with the force of it, lifting Stella up and down with her. Daysy had never seen her mother laugh this way. Perhaps she had never found a thing so wonderful as this in all her life. It was the first of many sudden attacks of wild joy that would assault Magda Elena daily, replacing the quiet cough she'd nursed for a decade.

When it was Daysy's turn to say goodbye, Stella spoke first. "It's like a dream how all of this happened. So suddenly, like a dream." She spoke in whispers, as if conspiring, and Daysy returned the favor.

Daysy remembered her dream journal then, so thick now that the binding had cracked in half and was held together by duct tape. "I'd like to hear about your dreams. It's a hobby of mine. I collect them," Daysy said. She wondered if she could draw lines connecting Stella's dreams to her own. Perhaps they'd even had the same dream at one point, the way it was said that twins did.

"I never dream," Stella said, barely above a whisper.

Daysy considered this and thought it strange. Some nights, she wished she could shut the dreams off like a faucet. Some nights, she thought she would drown in dreams upon dreams. "Well," Daysy said, hugging Stella so hard she thought she might hurt the girl, "I've been dreaming for both of us."

≈ ⋆ ≈

Even after her mother and father had gone inside, Daysy stayed on the porch, leaning against the door, the lion's sharp iron fangs digging into her back. She didn't want to join her parents, or interrupt their joy at finding Belén, or their heartache at having to say goodbye to her again, even if only temporarily. She had no words for them or for herself at the moment. She closed her eyes against the pale pinpricks of light in the sky. The world felt steady under her, though she knew it was rocketing around the sun at unimaginable speed. No, she'd never felt this sure on her feet. Perhaps it was the fact that she was tired and leaning against the door felt good, like a weight had been taken off. She thought of what Stella had said about not dreaming, and Daysy thought that perhaps tonight her own dreams would stay away for once, leaving only a blank, restful darkness, like the sky on a cloudy night, or like the sea in deep water.

MAGDA ELENA DEL POZO

MARIEL, CUBA 1980

The del Pozos were back at Eddy and Catalina's house by midmorning on the 30th of April, 1980. It was Eddy who opened the door and, without saying a word, lifted Magda Elena off her feet in an embrace. They cried together in that way for a long time, and Catalina and Angel stepped away from the front porch, both embarrassed by the emotion. The first thing Eddy said was, "Look at you," and Magda Elena cried some more, not knowing if and when the officials would come to take them to Mariel.

"Angel, your eye," Catalina said, her hand rising to touch his face.

"It's nothing," he muttered.

"Reconsider this foolishness," Catalina said softly. When Magda Elena shook her head, Catalina sighed, said, "*Bueno, entra*," and led them into the house.

That first dinner at Eddy's house was silent. Magda Elena, Angel, and Daysy gulped down their food, not bothering with napkins or sips of water, while Catalina fed Belén mashed *malanga*. "We tried to visit the embassy," Eddy said, "but couldn't get near it." Magda Elena smiled and patted her brother's hand. She hadn't expected him that whole time, and the fact that Eddy risked coming to see her choked her up. No one at the embassy had any visitors. Cuban tanks had begun to line the streets leading up to the compound to prevent any more citizens from becoming refugees. The announcement that anyone who wanted to leave was free to do so was really only a short-lived promise. Those with relatives in Miami wealthy or desperate enough to charter boats to Cuba were already waiting at Mariel to be picked up. Those without, embassy crashers like the del Pozos, would have to wait.

"You'll need someone to claim you in the U.S.," Eddy said, and Magda Elena heard a note of hope in his voice, as if he were counting on this fact to deter their leaving.

"I know," Angel said. "There's always my mother's niece."

"Not Modesta!" Magda Elena said, thinking of the woman she'd met only once at her wedding, who had criticized everything from Magda Elena's dress to the *puerco asado*. A month later, Modesta was in Miami with her husband, where they opened a florist's shop. They regularly sent pictures of their store, of their new car, of the additions to their house, of their ugly daughter, and Magda Elena thought the woman was a horror and a braggart.

"Who else?" Angel asked, then, turning to Eddy, said in a low voice, "They call her 'Monga.' Can you imagine anything worse?" They all laughed, including the children, who reacted to the sound of happiness, which they'd not heard in a long time.

"She'll hold it over our heads for a lifetime," Magda Elena said, laughing still.

Amado climbed into Magda Elena's lap as she ate. He was a lanky five-year-old, and the bones in his bottom dug into Magda Elena's thighs. "Amadito, no," Catalina said, "your *tía* is tired. Let her eat in peace." But Magda Elena protested with a mouth full of rice and held onto her nephew with one arm, kissing his cheek and leaving it sticky.

"Are you kidding?" she said after swallowing. "I thought I wouldn't see him again until he'd grown a beard." Amado leaned back onto his aunt and watched her finish her dinner. Later, Magda Elena would arrange Daysy and Amado in the same bed, kissing them both and saying a quick prayer to *la Virgencita* over them, asking her to keep the children safe through the night, to make them bold, to make them happy. Eddy put Amado's old crib back together and laid Belén in it. She fussed until she turned over onto her stomach, then gurgled a bit and went to sleep.

In the living room, the adults sat around Eddy's tiny, new color television, a prize from his boss at work for exemplary service, and watched the state news drone on about the crisis at the Peruvian embassy. Images showed only a few hundred people left on the ruined lawns, the ones who did not trust the Cuban offer to get them on boats, and who were now bound for Peru. They watched the grainy image until the electricity went out, as it did for several hours every evening. Catalina lit kerosene lamps and sat down on a wicker sofa to fan herself with yesterday's edition of the *Granma*. Angel fell asleep halfway through the newscast, his arm bent over his face, covering his bad eye, as was his new custom.

In the darkness, Magda Elena commented on her brother's house. "It's a great house, Eddy. Big." Her brother's place was not only close to the ocean, but large and airy. The telephone in the kitchen and color television in the living room were the perks of working for the Ministry of the Fishing Industry. Government jobs required a certain degree of loyalty to the state. For Eddy and Catalina, housing Magda Elena and her family until they left for Mariel was a risky move. Still, Eddy was certain that his position at the ministry was such that he was immune to acts of repudiation. Besides, everyone in his office seemed to be related to someone either at the embassy or on the way to Mariel.

The kerosene lamp placed on the television illuminated the framed photographs of Fidel Castro and Che Guevara atop the TV. Eddy caught his sister staring at them. "You know," he said, interrupting the silence, "you think I only have two choices. I can suffer indignities here or leave for *el norte* and work my ass off in a low-wage job. Then, I'll spend my life looking back here, longing every night for family, for sea breezes. But there's another way. Maybe I become the man who accepts things as they are. What does a framed picture or two mean in the end, *hermanita*? Nothing. It's nothing. I have a job, food on the table, safety, an education. A man can't survive on idealism."

Magda Elena watched her brother in the darkness. Her eyes had adjusted to it by now, and she could see his face clearly, pleading with her to stay, to make life in Cuba work for her. She thought of Daysy and Belén and imagined her two girls dressed well, going to American schools, where the lights didn't shut off at any given moment. Magda Elena loved her brother too much to fight with him about politics. And she had the sensation that there would not be many more nights with him like this, dinners shared, children tucked into bed together. She went over to Eddy and hugged him, hard. "*Ay, mi hermano,*" she said, remembering him as a little boy whom she followed around with a wooden spoon, poking his back with it. "*Buenas noches,*" Magda Elena said, and went to sleep on the floor of Amado's room, where Catalina had laid out a pillow and blanket for her.

≈ ⋆ ≈

They'd come in the middle of the night two weeks later, banging on Eddy's front door, waking the adults in the house. Magda Elena knew now was the moment of departure. They wouldn't have a chance to gather many things, to say a long goodbye. Outside, a windowless bus waited, full of refugees.

"*Ya voy,*" she heard Eddy say loudly as he ran to the door. If she knew her brother, he'd be stuffing the soldier's pockets with money to protect her. Magda Elena and Angel gathered the girls. Daysy had been sleeping in Amado's bed, and their small arms were thrown over each other's faces. Magda Elena did not want to wake Amado, though she longed to see his brown eyes for the last time. She kissed his forehead, felt his small breaths on her cheek for a moment, and lifted Daysy from his side. Angel cradled Belén in one arm and held their travel bag in the other.

The soldier stood in the living room, holding a cup of coffee that Catalina had made him. He drank down the last of the cup and handed it back to Catalina, who still held a small tray in her hands.

"Hurry up," the soldier bellowed and glanced at the bus outside. "I said hurry!" he yelled again, as Magda Elena and Angel appeared in the living room.

"*Hermano,*" Magda Elena said weakly and held open her arms to Eddy.

"Courage," he whispered in her ear, and Magda Elena held him more tightly with her free arm, Daysy crushed between them. Magda Elena and Angel took turns hugging Catalina. Angel and Eddy shook hands, and Catalina kissed Belén's forehead, then Daysy's.

"Are you certain you won't come to the U.S. someday?" Magda Elena asked, holding Catalina's hands.

The women had made peace in the last days, moving past political alliances and finding some common ground as they watched Daysy and Amado playing together. A few times, Catalina would point at the children as they ran about, saying, "They will be strangers to one another if you go," and tears would always spring to Magda Elena's eyes.

A deep crease formed in the center of Catalina's forehead. Magda Elena gave her one last kiss before leaving the house.

The night was muggy and the air thick. Magda Elena and Angel boarded the bus and found there were no seats together for them. Each family group had taken up its own row, leaving an empty space here and there. Angel sat with Belén in an open seat near the back, and Magda Elena and Daysy sat near the soldier who had come to get them. She watched, surprised, as he settled into the driver's seat. She looked around for more soldiers. They'd sent only the young man, and Magda Elena watched as his hands trembled on the ignition key. With the windows gone, Magda Elena could make out Eddy's house for a long time as the bus swerved down the street, starting its long drive east from Havana to the bay at Mariel.

The roof above Magda's head had a sticky, brown glaze on it and smelled distinctly of sulfur. At her feet, crushed eggshells made strange, floral patterns. The bus was purposely windowless in order to assure that the passengers inside were easy targets for protestors who knew the bus carried *gusano* deserters. Magda Elena thanked *la Virgen* that it was night and the streets were empty. Nevertheless, she wrapped Daysy's head in her arms and turned to see that Angel held Belén in a similar way, his back to the window opening. She kept thinking of bullets, rocks, glass bottles, hard objects that could do real damage when sent flying. She ducked her head and tightened her arms around Daysy.

The drive was long, but no one on the bus chanced sleep. Instead, they kept their eyes prized on the bus driver, whose head nodded now and again, as he fought sleep himself. Once, the bus lurched to the right as the driver awoke suddenly, and one of the passengers had the temerity to yell, "*Oye*, wake up. You'll kill us all." Magda Elena turned to glare at the yelling man, wishing he hadn't thought to give the driver any ideas, but the young man at the wheel pretended not to hear. Magda Elena watched as the tips of his ears reddened, how his knuckles whitened on the steering wheel. He didn't fall asleep again.

The wind had turned cold by the time they reached the town of Mariel. The driver sped through town, and Magda Elena strained her eyes as she watched the low houses rush by, hoping to keep them in her memory somehow. She hadn't seen much of Cuba—just the countryside in Pinar del Río where she grew up in the shadows of the Sierras with their limestone walls in the distance, the streets of Havana, and her brother's small fishing town. She had never seen Columbus' cross in Baracóa, or walked the cobbled streets of Santiago, or visited the Isle of Youth to see the giant sea turtles lay their eggs in the sand. Magda Elena knew she was leaving an unexplored Cuba behind and felt a little like the pirates of the past, who had plundered and used the land but hadn't stopped to love it. Daysy struggled to shake off her blanket, but Magda Elena held the cloth tightly, irritated by the child's fussing.

"Mamá," Daysy whined. "Where's Papi? Where's Belén?"

"Shh," Magda Elena said through her teeth, feeling herself wound too tightly, wishing to take it out on someone, no matter how small. Her neck ached from holding Daysy, and every time she heard Belén's cries in the back of the bus, Magda Elena stiffened more, afraid to stand and stretch without permission from the driver. She fought the urge to shoosh the crying that filled the bus.

"Mamá," Daysy whined again, and placed a small, cold hand on Magda Elena's cheek. Just then, with a screech of brakes, the bus stopped. Magda Elena and Daysy crashed into the seat in front of them, Daysy's mouth closing on the sticky surface, her lip torn open. Beneath her feet, Magda Elena felt the wild thumping of whatever it was the driver had hit. The thumping seemed to move down the aisle between the seats, and emerged at the back of the bus in the shape of a tall goose, faltering on its feet, its long neck bent at an odd angle. The sound of the goose against the bus resounded in Magda Elena's chest with a light knocking, and she would feel that knock for days afterward, faintly.

There were cries of "*¡Ay!*" and "*¡Mi madre!*" as the passengers stood to watch the goose stagger to the side of the road and sit, then glance up at the sky and stay that way, as if in supplication. Daysy's cries were muffled by the sudden chatter, which followed the release of tension. Angel took the opportunity to push his way to the front of the bus. He passed Belén to Magda Elena and gathered Daysy in his arms, and she quieted at once when it became clear that her lip was not badly injured. Magda Elena marveled at the way Angel calmed Daysy as she adjusted Belén in her arms. Yes, she thought, Daysy is her father's, and Belén, all mine. People had rearranged themselves in the commotion, and a seat had become available in front of Magda Elena. Together, they watched as the soldier tried to regain control of the passengers. He was smaller than most of the men onboard. His uniform was loose on him, the seat of his pants baggy and wrinkled.

His hands, Magda Elena noticed, were shaking as he pointed to the seats, and he, too, seemed distracted by the goose, dying now, it was clear, on the side of the road.

"Stay inside," he growled at last, and stepped through the door of the bus. They watched in silence as the young soldier approached the goose.

"What's he going to do?" a woman asked.

"Put it out of its misery," said another.

"Eat it," someone else offered, attempting humor. No one laughed.

"Not him," Angel said. "He's harmless." They watched as the driver neared the goose. Almost there, Magda Elena thought, cheering him on in her head. She realized suddenly that she'd grown fond of the thin, nervous boy. But just as he reached the goose, the animal fell over, still, its feathers rustling in the cool wind. They watched as the soldier covered his face with his hands, his shoulders shaking.

It was Angel who was the first to move. He left Daysy on the seat and made his way out of the bus toward the soldier. He put a hand on the young man's shoulder, and the passengers heard Angel say, "*Hombre*," loudly, and then, "Come on, you've got a job to do."

Magda Elena trembled with anger. How could he? Angel exhausted her. His kindnesses left her feeling small and afraid. When he reentered the bus, Magda Elena did not meet her husband's eyes. It was only when the bus rattled past a tall chain-link fence and the horizon became a field of masts bobbing up and down that Magda Elena sought Angel again in the seat before her, taking hold of his hand over his left shoulder.

≈ ✳ ≈

The port of Mariel hummed with movement and sound. The driver parked the bus and waved at an older officer outside, who guided him in. He turned off the ignition and pocketed the key. Then he faced the passengers. He seemed to want to say something to them. Perhaps something about the goose, about whatever it was that drove him to tears on the side of the road. But the moment passed and Magda Elena watched his face harden. She winced as he barked, "Get out of here. All of you!" For a moment, Magda Elena imagined a grown-up Amado in a similar uniform, his eyes red-rimmed and fearful.

Another soldier waited for them outside and helped the older passengers manage the steps off the bus. Magda Elena, Angel, and the girls were soon sorted into groups and made to wait with the others bound to board a boat named *Big Virginia.*

"Virginia," Angel repeated when the name was announced, and he looked to Magda Elena.

"That's right," she said and felt, for the first time in over a month, that things would turn out well. Nothing will go wrong, she thought, if the Virgin herself is the boat's namesake.

The *Big Virginia* was the only tall rig in the harbor. The other ships dotting the sea were mostly fishing vessels with names like *El Dorado* and *Tiki Tiki.* The passengers of the *Big Virginia* were called aboard, and Magda Elena and her family lined up as instructed and began to walk toward the ship. Once the two naked masts came into view, Magda Elena stood still, afraid. It was a beautiful schooner, Magda Elena thought. The white paint gleamed so brightly it was hard to look at, and the woodwork was so polished that the ship looked wet. Even the tires, hung on the side of the ship to keep the hull safe when docking, were shiny and new. Still, the other ships seemed so much sturdier. The *Big Virginia* swayed in the water like a toy, and the line of passengers seemed much too long to fit onto that ship. The other boats were crowded, too, and here and there, ship captains had come ashore to complain that their vessels could not carry so many bodies. Magda Elena listened as the captains, mostly Cuban exiles from Miami, complained loudly to authorities, and always, the same response was given: "If you want to take your family home, you take everyone else onboard your ship, too."

Other lines were forming across the various docks, heading to other ships. Magda Elena hoped that this would be the last line she would ever have to stand in again. The scene reminded her of shopping in Havana, with processions extending from storefronts, at the end of which was a single loaf of bread, or a meager bag of chicken. The difference here was that no one was talking. Rather, each person seemed to shrink away from the one nearest him, unsure if that person was good, or well, or in his right mind. Magda Elena had never seen so many crossed arms.

In the distance, lining up to board a rusted shrimp boat, was yet another line, with a singular figure at the end. A small woman, on her knees, was writing something onto the wooden boards of the dock with a bit of charcoal. She seemed familiar to Magda Elena, who stared at her so long that she didn't notice her own line had begun to board the *Big Virginia*. The woman's long hair shielded her face as she worked, and Magda Elena looked on. When the woman flipped her hair back, Magda Elena recognized her at once.

"Solamaris! Solamaris!" Magda Elena called, and Angel stopped, too. Solamaris looked up at her old friend and cocked her head to the side, as if she didn't recognize Magda Elena. Solamaris had become thinner, but somehow more angelic since the days Magda Elena had seen her at the embassy. Looking at her face, even from a distance, seemed like admiring a seraph from a picture book. Her skin was pale and her mouth red. Her eyes, framed by heavy eyebrows, had the quality of angels in Renaissance paintings—liquid now, no longer hard coins, but remote, and terribly sad. Magda Elena squinted, imagining that the sun was playing tricks with her vision.

"Solamaris!" Magda Elena called again, bouncing now in agitation. Her line had moved further, and she was nearly onboard the ship. She didn't want to board without saying goodbye, without arranging a meeting place in Miami, or telling her that she would light a candle for Leo.

A soldier walked past Solamaris' line and pointed at the message she'd scribbled on the dock.

Solamaris looked up at the soldier and cocked her head to the side, scrutinizing him the way dogs do their masters before obeying a command. Then, Solamaris yelled, "*Vengo!*" her voice rising above the din of the crowd, her arms straight at her sides. It seemed, on the surface, an obvious thing to say. "I'm coming," she was telling the ship, Miami, the future. But the word chilled Magda Elena, who imagined a different meaning, who saw her friend jumping off the ship midvoyage, or worse, prodding the soldier before her until he drew his weapon and she joined Leo in the grave. The soldier tapped his foot against the word written on the boards, and Solamaris crushed the charcoal in her hands until her palms were black. Then she rubbed her arms until those, too, were blackened. She blurred out the word she had written on the dock and her shoulders shook. Magda Elena could see tears making clean tracks on her dirty face.

"Not that, too," Magda Elena whispered as she watched Solamaris erase what she'd written, reminded now of Solamaris' books, more words lost to flames. Magda Elena's line moved once again, and now, Solamaris was no longer in view. She'd forgotten to check the name of the ship Solamaris was boarding, and she realized she might have lost Solamaris forever.

They loaded the *Big Virginia* without speaking, and the boat, weighed down now, stopped swaying. The captain, a bare-chested, slender man in jean shorts and a baseball cap, handed out small bags of dry cereal to the passengers, patting some on the shoulder and calling out "*¡Aventuras, amigos!*" in accented Spanish. Magda Elena thought they'd had adventures enough without the captain calling for more. Even so, she thanked him for the cereal when he came by and felt she might throw her arms around him and cry in gratitude. "*Aventura,*" he whispered to Magda Elena, and she nodded in agreement, feeling more courageous then.

Magda Elena and Angel settled their daughters between them on the deck, their backs to the side of the ship. Magda Elena sat Daysy on a high pile of coiled rope. She watched her oldest daughter playing with the intricate knot at the end of the line for a long time, and when she looked up again, the ship was full. Magda Elena and Angel had to sit with their knees against their chests to make room for everyone else. Still, more refugees were climbing aboard.

"There's too many of them!" the captain had shouted at the soldiers onshore at last, his gentle face now twisted in anger. The leading officer stroked the barrel of his rifle and glared at the captain, who turned back into the ship without another word. "Hurry up, then," the captain said to passengers boarding. He helped carry a toddler onto the ship second to last and patted the final man to come aboard so hard that the man stumbled. "Let's go!" he shouted into the air, and a gray-haired woman, lithe and young despite her hair, appeared from below deck. She sprinted to the wheel, and the moment her hands gripped it, an engine beneath Magda Elena came to life. The sails were still tied down, and Magda Elena longed to see them unfurl and get fat with wind. She was so busy watching the gray-haired woman working the wheel that she didn't realize how far out into the harbor they'd gone.

"One last look," Angel whispered in her ear, and Magda Elena turned to see the diminishing Cuban coast. A gray haze blurred the shore now, and Magda Elena could no longer make out people or individual ships. Now and again, a seagull broke through the filtered sunlight like a white flare, cutting through the vapor in a speedy dive, then flying back to the island, a bit of silver wriggling in its mouth. Soon, even the gulls were hard to see, until there was nothing but ocean in the direction of Cuba. "And so it goes," Angel said, and bent down to kiss the top of Daysy's head.

The ship's passengers had been silent until then. One, a woman with hair in long curls down her back, let out a whoop the moment the island disappeared, but only two other people answered her with weak clapping that died in the wind. Daysy clapped, too, once, twice, then returned to the knot she was now trying to undo. The quiet was broken once more by the gray-haired woman, who Magda Elena guessed was the captain's wife only because they resembled each another in the way of old couples, each one mimicking the other's movements as they worked. When the captain cupped his mouth and yelled, "Sails!" his wife echoed him, calling "Sails! Sails!" to no one in particular. The two grappled with the mainsail, the woman clambering over the boom as if there weren't a thousand feet of ocean beneath her. The captain began unspooling the line from around the tightly bound sail, handing the rope to men seated nearby who held it limply in their hands.

"You're island people, aren't you?" the captain yelled again and again in Spanish, forcing a few men onto their feet, showing them how to pull and tighten, pull and tighten until the sails were all up, outshining the dim sun with their whiteness.

"*Hombre*, if we owned sailboats, we wouldn't need you," one of the men answered once the sails were finally full. The captain laughed. Magda Elena laughed, too, and the sound felt strange in her mouth, partly because the wood oil smell was affecting her throat, partly because she hadn't laughed in so long that she'd forgotten how pleasant a sensation it was and what a release came with it, and partly because the joke held a touch of sadness in it, too.

Once the wind picked up, the sails stretched to their fullest and the waters beneath them darkened until the bottom disappeared. Magda Elena watched the shadows of large creatures gliding by for a while. She sang songs to occupy Daysy. "There was once a little ship that couldn't, couldn't, couldn't sail," she sang, and Daysy moved her head side to side, a living metronome for her mother. "*¡Más!*" Daysy demanded, and Magda Elena would take up the melody again. They played this way for what seemed like hours, though only a little time had passed. She stopped when Angel patted her thigh and pointed to the horizon, where a purplish cloud had billowed and grown like an enormous flower, darkening the sky. People stood as they watched the cloud approach.

The captain and his wife began to trim the sails in silence, and a few of the men stood to help, but the sudden gale came upon them before they were done. The topsail pulled at the line and slapped against the wind. Magda Elena and Angel held the girls against their chests, and Daysy covered her ears against the sound of the clapping sail. That, and the barking of the *Big Virginia*'s mascot, a chihuahua as white as the sails, made up the only noises at sea.

"It's not too bad," Angel said as the storm dumped water on them. Magda Elena agreed. They'd seen enough hurricanes to know when a squall held danger, and this, thought Magda Elena, was a weak one. Still, the boat, burdened with too many passengers, creaked underneath their feet, and though Magda Elena could not be sure, the *Big Virginia* seemed to be sagging in the middle, as if the ship were folding itself in half.

High-pitched screams came from beneath the deck. The dog answered the screams with more frantic yelping, and the captain began tapping men on the shoulder and motioning for them to follow him below. Angel did not wait to be asked, but kissed Magda Elena and the girls, disappearing below deck with the other men who were able. There were shouts coming from underneath, and through square, one-inch holes in the deck Magda Elena could see moving shadows. Soon, the *Big Virginia* was leaning starboard, despite the wind that came portside. Around them, the sea rippled as if set to boiling, and the sun was dropping between the schooner's two masts.

Now, with Angel apart from her, Magda Elena really looked at her fellow passengers for the first time. Nearest to her were a woman and her teenage daughter, holding onto one another. The girl was digging her nails into her mother's neck. To their right, an old man with milky eyes clutched a worn, canvas bag to his chest. There was panic now and people began tossing bags overboard to lighten the ship. The old man's bag was taken from him, crumpled up newspaper and a few brown bananas spilling at his feet, and he cried as if it had been a child. He searched the deck for his things with hands that moved like spiders, and began tucking them into his pants as he found them. Magda Elena wanted to comfort him as he sobbed, but she feared the old man. Rumors had run wild at the embassy that Castro had emptied the jails and asylums and sent the worst of the criminals— pedophiles and murderers—to Mariel. But for the life of her, Magda couldn't guess which of the passengers might be criminal, insane, or simply escaping just like her. All she knew was that the real men were below deck trying to save the ship, and the cowards were tearing bags full of photographs and smuggled mementos out of the hands of old women and flinging them to the sea. Magda Elena, imagining suddenly that Belén and Daysy might be seen as excess weight too, clung to her girls and prayed the best *Ave Maria* of her life, even if she did muddle the words.

There were all kinds of items flying from the ship now, and Magda Elena imagined that, from a distance, the ship must have looked like a fountain, spitting its contents in wide arcs away from the center. One of the passengers, a pot-bellied man with muscular arms, removed the compass from its base and held it high over his head, ready to pitch it into the darkening waves. The captain's wife, her long gray hair plaited so that the braid resembled one of the many lines that held up the sails, came up on deck, pointing a flare gun at the man with the compass. "Stop!" she screamed in accented Spanish. "Help is coming!" For his part, the pot-bellied man halted, spoke to another man to his left, as if confirming what he'd just heard, and put the brass compass back. Sure enough, two ships could be seen in the distance. One was a shrimp boat bathed in the light coming from the other, a white yacht. The captain's wife sighed then and leaned on the side of the boat, her arms stretched out before her, her head hung low, sobbing.

Angel emerged from below, soaking wet, and rejoined Magda Elena. The ship was still listing to the right, and the sun had gone down.

"*¿Las niñas?*" he asked, and patted both daughter's cheeks.

"*Bien. ¿Tú?*"

"I've been better," Angel said. He shivered a little when the wind stirred, and Magda Elena leaned into his shoulder.

"Help is here," Magda Elena said, pointing at the ships in the distance. Angel held up a shaky finger, signaling for her to be quiet for a moment. Magda Elena could see he was trying to catch his breath. Salt water ran off the tip of his nose and joined the puddles beneath him. Angel drew a long breath, picked up Daysy, and groaned before standing to see the shrimp boat with the name *El Ron* painted with an unsteady hand on its side, and the yacht, the *Adalah*, its name stenciled in gold. Magda Elena held Belén close to her chest and stood beside him. She could feel Angel with Daysy pressed up against her back. Daysy's hands fiddled with the hair on the back of Magda Elena's neck, and she reached around to touch the little fingers. The captain's wife now balanced on the stem of the schooner with the captain. He had his left arm slung around her shoulders and was wiping his eyes with his free hand. Neither one of them seemed worried about their safety, standing there on the stem, just a few feet from the inky depths. Rather, they both seemed to be taking in their ship, memorizing the billowing topsail, the dangling lines and the intricate brasswork.

El Ron and the *Adalah* had both killed their motors as they stopped near the sinking ship. The captain and his wife clambered down from the stem and began conversing with the captains of the two other ships across the water. They spoke in rapid English, and though Magda Elena had studied a bit of English when she'd been in

school, she understood nothing. A ramp, broad enough for two
or three people to cross together, was soon set up between the *Big
Virginia* and the shrimp boat, because it was nearest, and the Cubans
slowly made their way across it, abandoning the tall ship and over-
loading *El Ron* with more refugees. Magda noticed that only standing
room was left on the boat and hoped the spacious *Adalah* would sidle
up and load passengers soon. The one-hundred-foot yacht glowed in
the dark. The passengers already onboard watched from the deck,
crowding and pushing to shout encouragment to those aboard the *Big
Virginia*. But Magda Elena could see that inside there was still plenty
of room. She saw cushioned sofas, a well-appointed kitchen, and
nearly all of the passengers aboard carried cans of soda. She figured
that the owners of the *Adalah* had bribed enough people at Mariel to
keep their yacht from being overloaded.

The *Big Virginia* groaned underneath Magda Elena's feet and the
pushing began. Magda Elena could hear Angel grunting against the
sudden weight at his back, straining to keep from pinning Magda
Elena and Daysy with his body. There were shouts and insults hurled
at the people crossing the ramp between boats. "*¡Apúrate, comemierda!*" came one shout, which was soon echoed by others, encouraging
those making the crossing to hurry up, to make room, to think of
those behind them. The schooner rocked a bit then and caught a sudden wave, sending the tall ship into the *Adalah* with a crack. The
Adalah's lights flickered for a moment and went out. A scream sounded in the blackness, and then was multiplied. More pushing. The dark
seemed to penetrate Magda Elena's skin, her eyes, her lungs, so that
she couldn't tell anymore if she still breathed, or if her eyes were
open or closed.

She could feel Belén sweating in her arms and Daysy pressed close
behind her. Angel had wrapped an arm around Magda Elena's waist,
had whispered, "Stay close," in her ear, and clung so tightly that
Magda Elena's ribs ached. A few globes of light appeared in the night

as flashlights and lanterns came on in all three ships, casting ghostly circles. The pushing continued in the semidarkness and Magda Elena could feel herself getting moved along, her feet sometimes lifted off the ground. The flashlights and lanterns seemed to turn off and on as their owners ducked behind others or lowered their arms. The sudden flashes made Magda Elena dizzy, and she closed her eyes again to fight sudden nausea.

Aside from the movement—of the water, of the passengers—there was the deafening sound of it all. Paired with the blackness, the effect was disorienting. The little dog was barking incessantly somewhere on the ship, in a pitch so precise and insistent that Magda Elena's ears throbbed. Shouts mingled with the occasional yelp of someone stepped on, pushed too hard, made to move. Daysy was howling right at Magda Elena's ear, and the sails cracked like whips, like thunderclaps overhead. Magda Elena stood behind an old man who was on all fours, feeling the ramp with his hands. For the moment, a flashlight was trained on them, and she saw his hands crawling like spiders over the lip of the boat, scratching at splinters with his tough nails. He was the one from whom they'd taken the carpetbag, and now he was moaning, calling for it, "*Mis cosas, mis cositas,*" my things, my little things.

"That's not important," Magda Elena yelled. The old man's hands froze on the ramp. "Go on," she called again.

"I'm blind. I'll fall," he moaned.

"No, the ramp is wide enough," she said. The old man sat, his legs in a V before him, as he scooted across the ramp. Just then, the flashlight that had been on them flickered out, and everything was dark again. For a moment, Magda Elena imagined that the old man had toppled into the ocean, then thought better of it when she heard him whimpering, "*Mis cosas, mis cositas.*"

"Up," she heard Angel roaring behind her, but Magda Elena could not move. "Up," he bellowed again over the din. She lifted her left leg high, her toes searching for the rim of the ramp. Her foot brushed the

old man. "*Perdón, perdón,*" she said, excusing herself, and the shaki-
ness of her voice surprised her.

"You can do it," Angel called. "I'm right behind you."

Magda Elena held onto Belén with one arm, and steadied herself
with the other. She tried hard not to think of bull sharks and miles of
deep black beneath her. Please be still, she thought, hoping neither
ship would lurch, praying that the wind would not blow her away,
begging that the world would just stop turning for the moment it
took her to cross from one ship to the next. In truth, the ramp was
quite short. Some people were leaping from one boat to the other
in desperation, but in the darkness, the path seemed infinitely long.
Magda Elena, her toes again brushing the back of the old man seated
on the ramp before her, shifted her weight onto her raised leg when
Big Virginia groaned again, and Daysy screamed "*¡Mamá!*"

Magda Elena felt her daughter's arms circle her throat. Daysy
clambered onto her back, out of Angel's reach. "Wait!" Magda Elena
yelled, trying now to hold onto Belén, Daysy, and the ship's railing at
once. "*¡Mamá!*" Daysy screamed, and Magda Elena could hear her trying to catch her breath in preparation for another howl. "*¡Mamá!*" she
wailed again, drawing out the syllables. Then, wrapping her fingers
around Magda Elena's neck for balance, Daysy swung her small body
around to face her mother, and pushed hard against her sister with
her little feet, loosening Belén from Magda Elena's grip.

Magda Elena screamed. The pandemonium of sound engulfed her
so that she felt off-balance. Magda Elena felt her arms full now with
another sobbing child as Angel reached out and pulled her off the
ramp and back aboard the *Big Virginia*.

"*¿Que pasó?*" Angel yelled.

"No!" she screamed and fought against her husband. If Belén had
fallen into the ocean, she would follow, either fish her out or swallow
the sea. But Angel had pulled her back, and when his hands searched
for Belén on the ramp and came up empty, he, too, began to scream,

begging those with flashlights to point the thin beams at the ocean. The *Big Virginia* was creaking and moaning in earnest, and so Angel's cries were swallowed in other noises, other varieties of anguish. The short ramp had been removed, and *El Ron* was backing away, making room for the *Adalah* to load her passengers.

When Angel slipped into the water, only a few people noticed. Those at *El Ron's* railing shouted at him and some cast their lights downward. Angel, a poor swimmer, splashed about between the ships, and twice sank under the waves. He saw no sign of Belén, and when the captain of the *Big Virginia* finally threw down a life preserver, Angel took it and climbed the side of the sinking schooner, his sobs piercing the night.

The crowd behind the del Pozos pushed past them, even gave them room, not wanting to be caught in the grief they didn't understand. Magda Elena had fallen to the deck, Daysy still clinging to her neck. Her eyes closed, Magda Elena could see an echo of the world, a photo-negative imprint of lights, of an illuminated ship, of Belén's face.

Angel was crying into her hair one moment, then standing once more to look down into the dark water. When the last of the passengers had loaded the *Adalah*, the del Pozos allowed themselves to be lifted by the *Big Virginia*'s captain and his gray-haired wife, walked across the ramp, and settled onto the white vinyl cushions on deck. The *Adalah* remained on-site, and the passengers, more shaken than before, watched the tall ship sink, its topsail the last to surrender, floating on the surface like a white island. Even the little white dog had gone quiet in the captain's arms and had watched with limpid eyes and slow, deep breaths as the ship sank. Of course, Magda Elena could not stop thinking of her daughter, tiny limbs flailing underwater, little lungs filling, bow tie lips going slack, baby tears mixed with the sea. In the distance, *El Ron* rumbled until it was a speck against the rising sun. When the *Adalah* turned on its motor at last, Magda Elena gave a little scream and then lost consciousness.

≈ ⋆ ≈

That night aboard the *Adalah*, Magda Elena wished more than once for another capsizing. When she allowed herself the thought, closing her eyes and seeing her body, Angel's, and Daysy's floating in a vast, dark blue, caught forever in the act of mourning, Magda Elena's chest loosened, and she found she could breathe again. Dead together was better than alive and fragmented. But such escapes were momentary. A creak of the yacht, a cry from somewhere aboard would bring her back to her grief, to Daysy, alive and sleepy against her chest, and Angel, hoarse now and silent. Magda Elena thought, too, of Solamaris and Leo, wishing she could apologize to her friend for not understanding her loss, for thinking that Solamaris had been unreasonable, deranged even, holding onto Leo so long after he'd died. If given the chance now, Magda thought, she would hold Belén and Daysy until they were all dust.

When Daysy stirred for a moment, and asked, "Where's Belén?" Magda Elena stood and leaned deeply over the side of the boat, retching and coming up empty, hoping the weight of her upper body would send her plummeting to the sea. It was Angel who held her waist, who rested his cheek against her back and shook in silence, soaking her shirt with tears and pinning her to the railing.

"Where's Belén?" Daysy asked again, and Angel, gravel-voiced, told her that Belén had turned into a beautiful goldfish, with a long white tail, like a bride's veil. Daysy sat pensive for a moment, then she cupped her hands just under her chin and whispered, "When she comes out of the faucet, I'll catch her, like this." The three of them listened to the sound of the waves slapping the side of the boat for a long time.

Key West appeared like a knife on the water just about the time the sun rose. Angel and Daysy, finally sleeping, missed the dramatic display of sun striking water and shore. Magda Elena watched, alert. She felt as if she'd never sleep again. The couple that owned the *Big Virginia* had not slept either. The captain sat near the bow of the *Adalah*, leaning forward every once in a while to try and touch the surface of the water with one of his long fingers. Every time he did so, his wife, sitting near the del Pozos jumped, half rising, as if to stop her husband from doing something stupid. She'd been the first to spot tiny Key West and announce its appearance, and she stood and stretched her muscular arms, her elbows creaking loudly. She undid her gray braid and plaited it again, never taking her eyes off the sea.

Magda Elena watched her for a long time, thinking no clear thoughts in particular. When the captain's wife finally looked away from the ocean, her eyes found Magda Elena's. Before Magda Elena could turn away, signaling her desire for solitude, the captain's wife was seated next to her and had covered Magda Elena's left hand with her right one.

"*Cayo hueso.* Bone Key," she said, looking out once again toward Florida, her hand resting heavy on Magda Elena's. "That's what its real name is." Her Spanish was accented, but good.

"Frightening and appropriate," Magda Elena answered, and the captain's wife squeezed her hand.

"Names are funny things," the captain's wife said. "I sometimes think that the quality of a name can shape one's destiny." She was switching between English and Spanish. Her hand was steady and warm over Magda Elena's. The *Adalah* had slowed on its approach to Key West, and most of the refugees onboard were on their feet now, willing the yacht to get on with it.

"What was your baby's name?" the captain's wife asked suddenly.

"Belén," Magda Elena whispered. She couldn't bear to hear the name out loud, rattling around in her head, mingling with other, everyday words.

"That's a powerful name. With a name like that she would have seen the world." The woman squeezed Magda Elena's hand again. "I think the soul is an invincible thing. A real thing. You named that baby well." Magda Elena understood some of what the captain's wife had said, and wished she had enough English at her command to ask for her name and to thank her for bringing them out of Mariel.

Angel carried Daysy out of the ship because Magda Elena could not hold her now, not even to hug her or clean her nose. It was Daysy who'd dislodged Belén from her arms, her small, suffocating love that had cost her a daughter. Besides, Magda Elena's arms felt like dead things. They had failed her, and now she distrusted her strength. There were American soldiers onshore, and Magda Elena was so sick of looking at men in uniforms that she stared at her feet the whole time. That night, on a cot in the center of the Orange Bowl, among thousands of other Cubans who snored and argued and laughed and sobbed, Angel spoke in a voice so different from his own that Magda Elena was startled at the sound, as if a stranger had suddenly addressed her in the dark. "I've never hated anyone or anything in my life," he said.

"Who do you hate now?"

"All of them. The owners of that *mierdero* ship, the soldiers. *Comunistas.*" Magda felt too tired to respond. Besides, she didn't know what to say. In the middle of the night, Angel woke again and said something about a dream in which he heard Belén crying and couldn't reach her.

"Belén cried without making a sound," Magda Elena said, and that was the last time her mouth shaped her daughter's name for a long time, her silence a tribute, a castigation, as exactingly adhered to as any ascetic's regimen. Sometimes, she would see a shadow of Belén's face in Daysy's, and the name would erupt in her throat, her mouth, and she would choke on it. So often it happened, and so violently did she suppress the sound that a persistent cough plagued Magda Elena night and day, and no amount of *jarabe de tos*, sickly sweet and concocted by old Cuban women in Miami for Magda Elena's condition, ever relieved it.

SOLAMARIS MORALES

AT SEA, 1980

Solamaris could still feel the weight of her dead son in her arms. There, on the shrimp boat *El Ron*, she'd held onto him, though he wasn't really there, gripped his phantom torso and steadied herself against the waves that rocked the ship. She sang him lullabies, like "*Duérmete mi niño*," and hymns, like "*Pescador de hombres*," to hush the crying only she could hear. Others onboard the ship gave her a wide berth and crowded against one another to avoid touching her or breathing the same air as her, disturbing the woman who cradled her arms around nothing.

Solamaris had told no one that she still saw Leo. When he died at the Peruvian embassy Solamaris only thought he'd gone to sleep. When he was buried and the first pile of dirt landed on his tiny coffin with a thud, Solamaris felt something crack inside her chest, like the binding of a book breaking open, and had the sudden sensation of a small, hot mouth suckling her. By the time Leo's grave was filled, Solamaris' shirt was soaked with the milk that had failed her at the embassy, and her wrists ached from holding up her baby's invisible body.

"What's wrong?" her mother had asked soon afterward, forcing Solamaris to straighten her arms by rubbing them with alcohol.

"*Nada*," Solamaris had replied, thinking that if she told her parents that she could still feel Leo's presence, that she smelled his sweetness like a new rose, that she fed him night and day, ruining all her bras, they'd find a way to take him, to bury his spirit, too.

Mothering Leo's ghost reminded Solamaris of the early days after his birth, when she found it hard to concentrate on anything but him. The deep ache in her core intensified when he nursed, and now, so many months after his delivery, she felt the cramping anew when she imagined him. His pale fingers, sheathed in new skin and resembling a translucent, undersea anemone, once wrapped themselves around Solamaris' own coarse fingers. His gentle touch had made her milk flow faster, so that Leo would often choke and gag as he drank. Solamaris used to say to him, "If the house burned down around us, I wouldn't notice, *mi amorcito*," and she would coo into his fragrant neck. She repeated it now, bending low into the nothing in her arms.

A part of Solamaris remained quite sane. She recognized that portion of her soul, could inhabit it at times. When the Cuban officer brought her pass to Mariel, Solamaris felt entirely her old self, pocketing the ticket, offering the soldier some coffee, and even feeling a kind of attraction to the young man, which made her stomach fluttery and heated her thighs. But it was so much easier to be this other Solamaris, the one who wanted to replace all that she'd lost no matter the price. It was so easy to believe that Leo still lived, that his father had not been imprisoned, condemned to an unspecified number of years for throwing a rock at Fidel, to imagine that her library of books had not been burned. Picturing the many ways she might kill herself was satisfying, too, and by the time she scrawled Leo's name on the dock, mumbling "You will repent of this" to the soldier who had made her erase it just before boarding the *El Ron* headed to Key West, she'd envisioned her death a thousand ways.

When all the lights went out onboard the *El Ron*, Solamaris was reminded of the dark stain her burning books had left on the road, and her arms cramped at the thought of it. They'd come upon another ship, which tilted at an angle to the water and rocked back and forth. The passengers from the sinking ship clambered aboard the *El Ron* via a wide board. Solamaris watched from a distance, could make out the shadowy heads and limbs of the new travelers. The space around her tightened, and suddenly there was no room, no distance at all between her body and the others. She smelled rancid

onions, the stink of unwashed skin, and sought to cover Leo's nose.
But the illusion failed her just then, and Solamaris' arms felt light and
useless, as if they might float away from her body and glide back to
Cuba without her, fingers clenching at the wind, returning to Leo's
grave. That image, too, soon faded, and Solamaris took deep breaths
as the clarity of her current situation sharpened. She heard a woman's
screaming, then her bitter howls, accompanied by a man's deep cries,
a subterranean sound that rumbled in Solamaris' chest. The voices
came from the sinking boat, and Solamaris thought that they'd been
denied passage, that they'd been condemned to descend with the ship.
The woman's cries sounded familiar, and she imagined that it was her
own anguish, disembodied, calling out to the wide bowl of night sky
overhead.

Leo's ghost did not weigh down her arms again. The lucidity continued through the night, and Solamaris understood, for the first
time since her son's death, the situation in which she found herself.
There would be books in this new place, of all kinds, and no flames.
There would be snow, and English, and perhaps even a university
to attend. But there would be no Leo, and Solamaris cried into her
hands at the thought of his little body, dessicating, motherless,
surrounded by strangers.

It was through teary eyes the next morning that she saw a blind
man struggling with a baby. He'd stuffed it under his shirt, and
Solamaris could see the pudgy legs sticking out at his waist, and
heard the muffled wailing. The man was pounding on the wiggling
form with an open hand, and each dull whack brought about longer
and more piercing cries from the child. Solamaris looked up in the
dawning sky. A single star was visible, and then it blinked out, out-
shone by the sun. A cry went up from the front of the ship, "Key
West!" and then another echoed the first, until the words were being
repeated like a prayer from mouth to mouth. The baby inside the
blind man's shirt cried along with the shouting, and the sound was

similar to Leo's hunger cries, so pitiful, that Solamaris began to cry, too. She crawled on her hands and knees around and between the legs of passengers who were jumping up and down with joy now. The deck was already warm under her fingers, and she felt the piercing jabs of long splinters in her knees. By the time she reached the blind man, they two were the only ones not standing, and the people on their feet shaded them entirely.

"*Mi bebé*," Solamaris said, and put one hand on the baby's head, hidden underneath the man's torn, cotton shirt, and another on his jowly cheek.

The man, whose limbs had been trembling all this time as he smothered the baby against him, relaxed, and lifted his shirt. "*Mi cosita*," he said as he drew the small child out from under his shirt. It was sodden in the man's sweat and its own, a sour smell coming from its mouth, evidence of its hunger. Solamaris felt her breasts go leaden, hanging heavy on her chest. When she took the baby in her arms, the child turned toward Solamaris' skin, mouth wide open. Solamaris fed it in the shade cast by the people who were dancing now, and jumping to see the coast.

"How did you find him?" Solamaris asked.

"A boy? I'd thought it was a girl," he said. Troubled, Solamaris dug her fingers into the child's wet diaper.

"I meant 'her,' of course. My daughter."

"Of course," the man said, continuing. "As I was crossing over to this ship. I felt the board with my hands and sat down on it, my legs across the ramp. You know, they took everything I owned and threw it overboard, those bastards. I scooted, feeling where I was going with my hands, throwing my weight back in case I moved into nothingness. There was pushing behind me, in front of me, pushing, pushing, screaming, everyone in the dark like me. How the dark unhinged them all. They were like souls gone to Hell, clawing at each other to get a foot onto the other boat. It takes patience to live in a blackened world." The man rubbed his hands together as he spoke, and the sound of skin against skin was like the soft rush of wind through palm trees.

"The world spun, my ears throbbed, and I sent up a prayer to *La Virgen*, and for good measure, to Zeus, to Yemayá, and Shiva," he went on. "All the gods I read about when I had sight. And then, like that, I felt something heavy against my head, dropping into my arms. She fell from the sky and I caught her, covered her head with my shirt until I felt her press against my ribs, muffled her crying because I couldn't bear to hear it, held her tight and scoot, scoot, scooted down the ramp into the next boat. *Mi angelita*, who saved me, anchored me, just when I was about to drown."

Solamaris had a sudden vision of the old man in a white tunic, weaving tales for a crowd of men and women hungry for images, for guidance, for evidence that others had suffered, too.

"That's when I dropped her. Crossing over," Solamaris said, and felt it was true. "You saved her for me."

The blind man reached out to touch the place where the baby had latched onto Solamaris. He rubbed his fingers and tasted the milk. "*¿Cómo se llama?*" he asked.

Solamaris did not answer right away. When the baby looked at her, she turned away, so powerfully was the sunlight reflected in her small, blue eyes. The child looked so familiar, as if she'd known her in a dream. Already, her life in Cuba was being reduced to still images, like patches in a quilt. She remembered Leo, but not her own mother. In the shadows made by the standing crowd, the baby's eyes were nearly violet colored, and Solamaris thought of Leo's air-starved lips. On the side of the baby's head was a mark like an angry wound. It was Leo, returned in a new form, and the purple in the baby's eyes and the splotch on her temple were the signs of it. Hadn't they hurt Leo at the embassy, just there, just on the side of the head, when they'd torn him away from Solamaris? "Stella Maris," she answered at last, and then clarified, "Star of the Sea," thinking of Cuba's patroness, the Virgin at El Cobre, who appeared in the form of a small statue that floated toward three boys out in a terrible storm at sea, calming the roiling waters for them. How peaceful Solamaris felt now, with this baby in her arms. She understood what relief the three boys named Juan, the ones from the Virgin's apparition story, must have felt.

"Of course. After *la Virgen*. It's better than calling her María, like so many others do with their daughters. And your name?" the man asked and his cheeks quivered.

"Alone at Sea," she said, and smelled the top of the baby's head.

"That's terrible," the old man said.

"It is. Lonely names suit me, I think."

"Change it then. It's a new life we're all headed to. You can be anything you want."

"What about Ana? There's a book I love with a very sad woman…"

"Anita. *Me gusta*," he said, interrupting her. His smile revealed bumpy, grayish gums.

"The sun is out now," the man said later, and turned his face up to the sky. "I see red shapes I didn't before now. Stay with me, Anita?" he asked, and Solamaris took his hand.

"For a while. Yes," she said. "It's probably best not to be alone when we disembark."

"I can be her grandfather," he said, and smiled.

Solamaris did not answer him, but watched as he peeled open a banana and ate it slowly, his mouth open and slick. Later, onshore, she'd let him hold the baby. He said he'd never held a child, and that he thought her touch was bringing back his sight. Solamaris had relented, reluctant to rob a man of his miracle in case it was true, but he always gave her back, and the baby would quiet in her arms as if she knew she was home in them. Once, the child had been startled by a series of flashes, the blinding light from a photographer's camera.

She'd howled at the sudden radiance, and Solamaris understood because she was seeing them, too—tiny suns etched onto her retina. Solamaris took the baby back into her arms then and pushed her hot palm against her eyes, soothing her right away.

All that day and the next, while the Mariel volunteers organized papers, sorted people into groups, or called out for their lost relatives, Solamaris cared for the baby. When one of the volunteers asked her name, Solamaris had answered, "Ana Morales." When she was asked her date of birth, she made up the date and year, doing the same for the baby.

"City of birth?" the volunteer asked, but Solamaris looked at her blankly. "Havana?" the volunteer suggested, and Solamaris nodded. She answered all the questions this way, remaking herself as she went, out of utter necessity. The past had blurred for her irrevocably, and now, staring at the baby in her arms, she had a hard time remembering Leo's features.

"It is the heat here," she told herself, feeling as if the Florida sun were more scorching, more powerful than the one she'd left behind in Cuba, "It has made me forgetful."

At night, Solamaris would lean back against a wall, prop Stella Maris up on her lap, and whisper a long story into her ear. Rocking the baby, Solamaris would describe the life she wanted for them, somewhere cold, not as brightly lit as Cuba, with marbled libraries in every neighborhood. In the diminished heat of the night, Solamaris kept Stella awake as she told her about the origin of stars, how the Milky Way is a long boat full of all the people ever meant to be, flickering far away like a great swarm of fireflies, waiting to be born; how sometimes, stars fall out of the sky and become people, and how on earth the luckiest of these are loved beyond measure.

ACKNOWLEDGMENTS

I am grateful to the wonderful people at Carolina Wren Press for giving this story a home. To my editor, Robin Miura, thank you for your time, expertise, good humor, and encouraging messages. To Andrea Selch and everyone, past and present, who continue to make sure that Carolina Wren Press meets its mission and delivers beautiful books, thank you. My gratitude goes to Moira Crone, who selected this novel for the Doris Bakwin Award.

I owe the early stirrings for this book to my dear friend, Arlenys Casanova, who shared her own Mariel story with me long, long ago, when we were just kids sitting on a sidewalk in front of Diane Berkley's house in Hialeah, Florida. I carried her story with me all these years. Didi and Arlen, I love you both. Thank you, sweet friends.

There have been many wonderful readers who helped nurture this book (and this author!) by offering feedback. My heartfelt gratitude to Rachel Basch, Emma Bolden, Andrea Cabrera, Hallie Johnston, Mary Donnarumma Sharnick, Nat Sobel, and Judith Weber.

To Hilary Wyss, thank you for excellent lunches and even better advice. For their friendship, good cheer, helpful plot-busting, and useful hand gestures, I'd like to thank Rachel Hawkins and Ashley Parsons.

Importantly, this book could not have been written without time spent in the research trenches. Most helpful was Mirta Ojito's excellent book on the Mariel exodus, *Finding Mañana*.

I am grateful to Auburn University, the College of Liberal Arts, and the Department of English, for the time and support given to me so that I could work on this book. My colleagues and students challenge and inspire me every day. Thank you.

A small scene in this book originally appears as a poem, "Taming Parakeets," in the *North American Review*. Another originally appeared as a poem titled "Fracture" in *American Poetry Review*. I am thankful for their support.

Without my family, I would not have the heart or courage to put pen to paper. To my grandmother, Maria Asela, for having the valor to leave Cuba long ago and creating a future for us here, and to my parents, Marta and Jim, for their limitless love, thank you.

To my husband and best friend, Orlando Acevedo, who is my inspiration always, I love you.

Finally, this book is dedicated to my daughters, Penelope and Mary-Blair, who remind me every day of the importance of wonder, imagination, and the beautiful bond of sisterhood. My girls, my everything, I love you.

GLOSSARY

Terms explained explicitly in context are not listed here.

"a las buenas o a las malas"—"the easy way, or the hard way"; literally, "the good way, or the bad way"

ago, ago, ile, ago—Santería chanting; meaning "open up, open up"

"Ah, sí, la universidad"—"Oh, yes, the university."

anda—to go; often meaning, "come on"

arrepentida—(slang) one who is ashamed of her heritage; literally means remorseful

"¡Atrevida!"—literally "daring," meaning, "How dare you?"

azabache—a small, black stone, usually hung from a necklace, and meant to ward off the evil eye or other maledictions

balseros—name given to those who left Cuba via raft; rafters

bebita—baby

"bien hombre"—a real man; macho

bien—good

boberías—silliness

buena suerte—good luck

bueno—commonly used, meaning something like, "Well," at the start of a sentence; literally means good

cafecito—little coffee, usually espresso with milk and sugar

caramba—(slang) mild curse, like "damn"

chiquitica—affectionate term, meaning "little one"

"¡Claro que no es Eugenia!"—"Of course it's not Eugenia!"

compañero—like comrade, borrowed from Soviet usage of the word

consorte—(slang) meaning friend, or pal

coño—(slang) vulgar, though commonly used; similar to "damn"

"Coño, me queme la lengua"—"Damn, I burned my tongue!"

congrís—black beans and rice

cornetas—bugles

chico—(slang) meaning "boy" or "man"

claro—of course

el Comandante—a name for Fidel Castro; literally "the Commander"

comemierda—(slang) vulgar term for someone foolish or wasting time; literally means "shit eater"

comunistas—communists

cuéntame—"Tell me"

"en este país"—in this country

de visita—visiting

"Deja eso"—"Leave it alone"

"Déjame decirte algo, niña"—"Let me tell you something, girl"

"¡Déjame sola!"—"Leave me alone!"

descarado—fresh; shameless

Duérmete mi niño—lullaby; "Go to sleep, my baby"

"El año que viene... en Cuba"—"Next year... in Cuba"; an exile toast that has become traditional in Miami

el norte—the north

"¿Entonces que?"—"And then what?"

Envios a Cuba—Shipments to Cuba; these businesses facilitate the delivery of goods to Cuba

fuacatá—a sound word, similar to "whack"

"Fue así"—"It happened like this"

desgraciado—disgraceful

galante—gallant

guajira—a country person; unsophisticated

"gusana desgraciada"—disgraceful worm

"¡Ingrata!"—"Ingrate!"

fiebre del caballo—horse fever

frijolitos—beans

hermana/o—sibling; also used between people who are close, in the figurative sense

imagínate—imagine

"*la mala… el santo*"—the bad one, the saint

"*la señorita Karenin*"—the lady Karenin

la Virgen—the Virgin Mary; for Cubans, specifically, it is often a reference to Our Lady of Charity, Cuba's patron saint

la moda—fashionable

"*la muy hija de puta*"—like "son of a bitch"

la sala—a formal living room

lechón asado—roast pork; also called *puerco asado*

"*Levántate*"—"Get up"

"*Lo que tú quieras*"—"Whatever you want"

loca pal carajo—crazy as hell

los hombres no lloran—men don't cry

"*Los peces en el río*"—"The Fish in the River"; song title

malanga—yam

"*Ay, Mama Inés, todo los negros tomamos café*"—lyrics to traditional Cuban folkloric song; literally, "Ay, Mama Ines, all the black people drink coffee."

me acuerdo—I remember

"*¡Mi madre!*"—literally, "My mother!"; an exclamation similar to "Oh my God!"

"*Mi amor, ya.*"—"My love, that's enough."

"*Mi Eugenia, mi tesorito*"—"My Eugenia, my little treasure."

mi tesoro—my treasure

"*Mi Perla Preciosa*"—My Precious Pearl

mi'jita, m'ija—shortened versions of *mi hija*, or "my daughter"

"*¿M'ijo, que haces?*"—"Son, what are you doing?"

mira—look

"*Mira, m'ijita, this is la Virgen María. Que linda. Y aquí, Papá José, los Reyes Magos, and most importantly, mi amorcito, el niño Jesús*"—Look, my daughter, this is the Virgin Mary. So pretty. And here,

Joseph, the Three Kings, and most importantly, my love, baby
Jesus.

"Mira pa' eso"—"Look at that"

muchachita, muchacha—a young girl

"¡Muchacha, ten cuidado!"—"Girl, be careful!"

"Mucho gusto"—"My pleasure"

muñequitos—cartoons, comics

nada—nothing

nadie—No one

nieta—granddaughter

"No fue nada"—"It was nothing"

"No hay problema"—"No problem"

"No, no me la lleves"—"No, don't take her from me!"

"No, qué va"—sarcastic, meaning, "No, of course not."

"No sé," "No sabes"—"I don't know"; "You don't know"

"Nos vamos"—"We're leaving"

noviecito—boyfriend

nunca—never

oye—listen; a common expression

pal carajo—(slang) to hell with it

para siempre—forever

para tí—for you

pasando hambre—going hungry

"Pastores á Belén"—carol; "Shepherds to Bethlehem"

perdón—pardon

"Pescador de hombres"—hymn; "Fisher of Men"

pesebre—stable

periquito—parakeet

platanitos—plantains

pobrecito—poor thing

por lo menos—at least

precioso—precious

prima/o—cousin

pudín de pan—bread pudding

"*Regreso*"— song; "Return"

"*ridícula que soy*"—"ridiculous as I am"

rubia—blonde

que lindo—how pretty

"*Que se vayan*"—"Let them go"

que sufrimiento—what suffering

"*¿Quien es ella?*"—"Who is she?"

Santería—an Afro-Cuban religion, with roots in West Africa, that merges the reverence of a pantheon of gods with Catholic saints

"*Sí, mi vida*"—literally, "Yes, my life"; closer to "Yes, dear," in sentiment

sidra—sparkling cider

sinsontes—mockingbirds

sobrino—nephew

sola—alone

solavaya—of Afro-Cuban origin; used to ward off bad luck, like knocking on wood

"*¡Soy una americana de verdád!*"—"I'm a real American!"

un desastre—a disaster

vámonos—let's go

"*Ven acá*"—"come here"

viejo—old man; commonly used as a term of endearment

"*Y ahora*"—"and now"

ya—enough

yanqui—Cuban expression meaning "American"; reference to the word "yankee"; preferred over gringo

1. Does the inspiration for the Del Pozo family come from a particular family or several families, or is the family completely fictitious?

The del Pozos are an amalgam of many families, I suppose, though if pressed, I couldn't tell you who came from where. I can say that the kernel of inspiration for the novel came from a story an old friend told me when we were teenagers, of how she came over on the Mariel Boatlift when she was only five years old, how she was lost for a brief time, and found in the arms of a blind man. That part is a true and beautiful story I heard, and it has been percolating in my brain for years.

2. How does the focus on the 1980 Mariel Boatlift connect the distinct narratives of the novel?

The story of Cuban-Americans in the United States came into sharp focus during 1980. Sure, Ricky Ricardo had been on television since the 1950s, and José Martí in the late 1800s had made a name for himself in New York City as a poet and orator. And, of course, the Cuban Missile Crisis put the island front and center in the imagination of Americans. But it wasn't until the Mariel Crisis that Cubans and Cuban-Americans themselves were seen as a complex, forceful community in this country. The characters in the novel circle around that event. Like a vortex, it pulls them in, shapes them, and spits them out as different after all is said and done. In much the same way, Mariel changed everything about the way Cubans and Cuban-Americans are viewed in this country. Some of that change was good. Not all of it was. *Scarface*, for example, is a terrible example of the kind of stereotyping the Mariel Boatlift inspired.

3. In creating the novel, what led you to sequence the sections in a way that is not chronological?

I am very interested in time as a fluid notion, instead of a fixed and steady line. Humans are who they are because of their pasts. We have no recourse but to look to it, and acknowledge its role in our lives. As of this writing, I am thirty-eight years old. But I am also thirty-seven, and twenty-five, and fifteen, and two. This idea first became clear to me after reading Sandra Cisneros' delightful short story, "Eleven." Later, reading Jorge Luis Borges, I learned of his notion of "circular time." In that way of thinking, and in trying to define myself, I am also partly my mother, and my mother's past, and I am partly a consequence of the Cuban Revolution, and of the Spanish-American War, and so on and so forth. So, these characters embody one another and what came before them.

4. How does the term *gusano* help to explain familial conflicts?

Gusano was a derogatory term for Cubans who left the island and abandoned the Cuban Revolution, which is considered to be ongoing. It means "worms," of course, and was used broadly on the island. The term itself represents one kind of familial conflict particular to Cubans, and that is the division of families over ideology. As an American, the stories of brothers during the Civil War, one fighting for the North, the other for the South, comes close to what I'm talking about regarding Cuba. Some of these political differences run so deep that families have been forever severed.

5. How do some of the religious beliefs (*Santería*, for example), magical beliefs, superstitions, or supernatural beliefs of some Cubans function in the novel?

For some of the characters, belief in the supernatural or the divine represents a kind of hope. Catalina is one of these characters. Her life's path is different from what she has imagined, and so, she relies on her faith to see her through. For others, like Stella and Daysy, who are modern children and filled with doubt, faith is less palliative. There's something, too, about the way magical beliefs and faith in the divine set a particular tone and mood. Cuba and Miami, in part, are really magical places. Miami's nickname is "The Magic City," and one can see why this is so. Statues of the *Virgen* Mary dot front lawns, children wear *azabaches*, or pieces of jet set in gold to ward off the evil eye. The weather is sultry, and in the summer, mirages appear on the highways, like slicks of oil, and you can't trust your eyes. Magic and mystery are part of the fabric of the tropics.

6. How is this a coming-of-age story for Daysy? For Stella?

They are smart girls, torn by their loyalty to their families and their crushing need to know the truth. They are both at the "age of not-believing" to quote Walt Disney's *Bedknobs and Broomsticks*, and their self-doubt is especially acute. As adolescents, Daysy and Stella have this notion of solitude that affects everything they do. And that's a common feeling for adolescents everywhere. That their search leads them to an end to that solitude felt like a kind of growing up for them both.

About the Doris Bakwin Award

The Doris Bakwin Award for Writing by a Woman was established by Michael Bakwin in honor of his late wife, Doris Winchester Bakwin. Doris was a warm-hearted and engaged listener and storyteller. As her daughter Lisa Lindgren wrote: "My mom loved thunderstorms like most people love a beautiful sunset. She would sit by an open window and breathe it in. My earliest memory is sitting with her in a rocking chair by the screen door enjoying a storm together. I still have a strange fondness for the scent of rain on a screen. We talked of dancing in the rain. I guess that's my image of my mom—dancing in a storm— strong and happy. Her life was like that. No storm she couldn't handle." Doris always wanted to write down her own life story, but did not get to it before her death in 2004.

Carolina Wren Press gratefully acknowledges the generous contributions made by members of the Bakwin extended family. The gifts have enabled us to make the Doris Bakwin Award an on-going competition:
  ~ *Submission deadline is March 15th, in even-numbered years.*
  ~ *Full guidelines are available at www.carolinawrenpress.org*

—Andrea Selch, President, Carolina Wren Press

The text of the book is typeset in 10-point Minion.
The book was designed by Lesley Landis Designs
and printed by BookMobile

CWP